Praise for *Save the Date*

"Delicious . . . Laugh-out-loud humor, overwrought bridezillas, and a runaway puppy . . . an absolute delight!"   —*AARP*

"Andrews's latest and possibly greatest book yet."   —bookreporter.com

"Funny, witty, tender, and compelling."   —*RT Book Reviews*

"Storytelling at its best."   —*Delta Magazine*

"Charming."   —*Booklist*

"Andrews's latest will have readers entranced, waiting to see if Cara will triumph over her many obstacles before the last petal drops. *Save the Date* definitely deserves a spot on your calendar."   —*Shelf Awareness*

"*Save the Date* is a vintage Andrews rom-com, a colorful bouquet of a book that's filled with her trademark wry wit, good humor."   —examiner.com

"Andrews is a writer who knows just the right amount of humor, romance, sex, and charm to introduce as ingredients in her story. . . . She always delivers a bright summer read that is impossible to resist. She has certainly done that once more with *Save the Date*."   —*The Huffington Post*

"This solid beach read gives hope that love is out there."   —*USA Today*

"A deft mixture of romance and humor in a story featuring a likable protagonist and cute critters: It's a date Andrews fans won't want to miss."

—*Kirkus Reviews*

Praise for *Ladies' Night*

"Andrews presents a delightful novel. . . . A wonderful blend of action, repartee, and offbeat characters in a just-plain-fun story. Humorous and witty, and as entertaining as a good night out."
　　　　　　　　　　　　　　　　　　　　—Kirkus Reviews

"Her newest novel offers another engaging and satisfying tale of life, loss, and love."
　　　　　　　　　　　　　　　　　　　　—Booklist

"Mary Kay Andrews's novels have become a summer staple like a new pair of sandals. The *New York Times* bestselling author returns with the perfectly mixed cocktail of romance, mystery, and comedy."
　　　　　　　　　　　　　　　　　　—The News & Observer

"This is her best book yet, and it combines all of the strengths we have come to expect from this audacious and beguiling author."
　　　　　　　　　　　　　　　　　　　—The Huffington Post

"A court-ordered therapy session is the site of the action in Andrews's zesty, amusing latest."
　　　　　　　　　　　　　　　　　　　　—People

"Mary Kay Andrews blends heartache and hilarity in a story line filled with surprises."
　　　　　　　　　　　　　　　　　　　—Southern Living

"If there were a literary genre dedicated to great beach books, the novels of Mary Kay Andrews would set its standard for excellence." *—Cape Gazette*

Praise for *Spring Fever*

"Andrews deftly combines a winsome love story and compelling family drama, and the idyllic small-town setting and surprising twists and turns are tailormade for laid-back summer pleasure reading."
　　　　　　　　　　　　　　　　　　　　—Booklist

Save the Date

ALSO BY MARY KAY ANDREWS

Christmas Bliss

Ladies' Night

Spring Fever

Summer Rental

The Fixer Upper

Deep Dish

Savannah Breeze

Blue Christmas

Hissy Fit

Little Bitty Lies

Savannah Blues

Save the Date

Mary Kay Andrews

St. Martin's Griffin
New York

SAVE THE DATE. Copyright © 2014 by Whodunnit, Inc. All rights reserved. Printed in the United States of America. For information, address St. Martin's Press, 175 Fifth Avenue, New York, N.Y. 10010.

www.stmartins.com

The Library of Congress has cataloged the hardcover edition as follows:

Andrews, Mary Kay, 1954–
    Save the date / Mary Kay Andrews.—First edition.
        p. cm.
    ISBN 978-1-250-01969-1 (hardcover)
    ISBN 978-1-250-01968-4 (e-book)
    1. Florists—Fiction. 2. Weddings—Fiction. I. Title.
    PS3570.R587S29 2014
    813'.54—dc23   2014009454

ISBN 978-1-250-01970-7 (trade paperback)

St. Martin's Griffin books may be purchased for educational, business, or promotional use. For information on bulk purchases, please contact the Macmillan Corporate and Premium Sales Department at 1-800-221-7945, extension 5442, or write to specialmarkets@macmillan.com.

First St. Martin's Griffin Edition: May 2015

10   9   8   7   6   5   4   3   2   1

This book is dedicated with love
to Tom, my starter husband, lover, partner,
and best friend, who truly did save the date this time around.

Acknowledgments

The author wishes to thank the fabulous Meg Reggie of Meg Reggie PR in Atlanta for accidentally giving me the idea for *Save the Date,* as well as for throwing a damn good launch party. Also thanks to Julie Driscoll of Garden on The Square in Savannah, for allowing me to hang out and ask dumb questions. Genius wedding stylist Elizabeth Demos of Savannah answered every question I threw at her, and offered amazingly good plot twists. Tybee Island and Savannah friends Susan Kelleher, Diane Kaufman, Carolyn Stillwell, and Polly Powers Stramm made great sounding boards.

The members of the Weymouth Seven writers group: Alex Sokoloff, Brenda Witchger, Diane Chamberlain, Margaret Maron, Katy Munger, and Sarah Shaber were, as always, invaluable midwives who helped me deliver this baby.

The professionalism, encouragement, and tender loving care given to me and my work by my agent, Stuart Krichevsky, and the team at SKLA, Shana Cohen and Ross Harris, mean more to me than I can say. I am so very blessed to have them along for the ride! And speaking of teams, Meghan Walker of Tandem Literary and Jennifer Romanello are the world's best and most talented at marketing and public relations.

Huge thanks, as always, go to the entire St. Martin's Press gang, but especially to wonder-editor-adviser-lifesaver Jennifer Enderlin, whose patience and wise counsel helped shape and complete this book. Thanks, too, to publisher Sally Richardson and the rest of the Flatiron Building team, including but not limited to John Karle, Matt Baldacci, Jeanne-Marie Hudson, AnneMarie Tallberg, Jeff Dodes, Stephanie Davis, and Michael Storrings, who gave me another great cover.

My family keeps me grounded and sane—and feeling loved. Thanks and love to the home team, Tom, Katie, Mark, and Andy—and my precious babies Molly and Griffin.

Last but certainly not least, thanks to you, dear readers—wherever you are—for allowing my childhood dream of becoming a writer to come true.

1

Something was off. Cara Kryzik was no psychic, but the minute her bare feet hit the floor that morning, she sensed it.

She sniffed the air apprehensively and was met with the sweet perfume from the tiny nosegay of gardenias—her favorites—that she'd placed in a sterling bud vase on her dresser the night before.

Had she overslept? No. The big bells of St. John the Baptist cathedral were ringing the eight-o'clock hour as she descended the stairs from her apartment to her shop one floor below.

Cara shuffled down the narrow hallway to the front of the darkened flower shop. She flicked on the wall switch, and the multitude of thrift-shop chandeliers she'd hung at varying heights from the tall-ceilinged room twinkled to light, their images reflecting from all the mirrors staged around the space. It was a small room, but she thought the chandeliers and mirrors expanded the space visually.

See? She scoffed at her own foolish sense of foreboding. All was well.

She pulled up the shades over the front windows and smiled. It was a bright, sunny Friday morning, and within seconds, her puppy, Poppy, had her nose pressed against the glass-paneled front door, watching a pair of squirrels scamper past on the sidewalk outside on Jones Street.

The message-waiting light was blinking on the shop's answering machine. She gave the machine a fond pat. Business had been slow. But it was May. Mother's Day was next Sunday, it was prom season, and wedding season, too. Things were already picking up.

And then? She felt a single bead of perspiration trickle down her back. She frowned. Why was it so hot in the shop? Even for Savannah the room seemed stuffy and overheated. Cara went to the thermostat on the wall and squinted, trying to see the reading.

She'd turned the thermostat up before bed last night, just to 81, hoping to save a little on her always spiraling electricity bill. The air-conditioning unit was temperamental at best, and her landlord was never prompt when it came to making repairs. She had a string of appointments in the shop today, and it wouldn't do to have brides and their mamas stewing in their own juices.

She fiddled with the control for a moment, holding her breath, waiting to hear the compressor click to life. When it did, she exhaled. *See? All is well.*

Before she could sit down to check her emails, the shop phone rang.

She'd known who the caller would be. "Good morning, Lillian," Cara chirped. "How's our bride today? Is she getting jittery?"

"She's still asleep, thank God," Lillian Fanning said. Never one to waste time on pleasantries, Lillian got right down to business. "Listen, Cara, I've been thinking. I know we said white candles for the altar, but with an early-evening wedding, I really believe ivory or ecru would be much more effective."

Cara crossed her eyes in exasperation. She'd already special-ordered two dozen hand-dipped organic soy *white* candles for Torie Fanning's wedding tomorrow. But it was useless to tell the mother of the bride that it was impossible to get the candles in a different color at this late date.

She heard the bell on the front door jingle and looked up to see her assistant, Bert, let himself in, a large coffee in one hand and his bicycle helmet in the other.

"Lillian Fanning?" He mouthed the words, and Cara nodded. For the past two weeks, Lillian had called Bloom at least twice a day, every day.

"I'll see what I can do," Cara said, being deliberately vague.

"Ecru or ivory, *not* white," Lillian repeated.

Cara sighed. "Of course."

"What about the flowers? Did everything get delivered? And you've got Torie's grandmother's epergne polished for the bride's table?"

"Everything is absolutely under control," Cara assured Lillian. "I've got all the bridesmaids' bouquets finished, and I'll start on Torie's this afternoon, so it will be absolutely the freshest possible. And Lillian? I have to say the two of you have made the most exquisite flower choices I've ever seen in this town."

"I should hope so, for what this wedding is costing us," Lillian Fanning said. "I'll see you at the church tomorrow."

Cara hung up and stuck out her tongue at the phone.

"Is it hot in here, or is it just me?" Bert asked, standing in front of the thermostat and fanning himself with an envelope he grabbed off a stack of bills on her desk.

"I turned it up last night before I went to bed, but I think it's starting to cool down now," Cara said.

"Well, I'm roasting," Bert declared. He looked at her closely. "You're not having chills again, are you?"

"No! I'm fine. I took the last of those darned antibiotics on Tuesday. I can't afford to get sick ever again."

Cara took Bert's hand and placed it on her own forehead. "See? Cool as a cucumber. No fever, no temp, no problem."

But Bert wasn't paying attention. He was staring at the glass door of their flower cooler. Even through the door, beaded as it was with condensation, it was a grim sight.

"Uh-oh."

Cara flung the door of the cooler open. "Oh, God."

She couldn't believe her eyes. All the flowers in all the buckets in the cooler were limp, dead, dying. Torie Fanning's bridesmaids' bouquets, so carefully wrapped in their silk-satin binding, were toast. She glanced at the thermometer hanging from the top shelf and felt like weeping. It had been at 35 degrees last night, before she'd gone upstairs. But now it was at 86.

She let the door close and pressed her face against the glass. The reassuring hum of the compressor motor was silent.

"The cooler is dead," she said. "And so are the flowers. The motor must have conked out sometime overnight."

Bert reached for the Rolodex on the desk. "I'll call the repairman. Didn't he just fix this thing like six weeks ago?"

Cara nodded glumly. "He did. To the tune of three hundred dollars. But he warned me then, he didn't know how long it would keep running. When I opened the shop I bought it off a guy whose pizza place had gone out of business. Turns out this thing is so old, you can't find new parts for it. My guy had to jerry-rig it with secondhand parts he had lying around his shop."

"What are we gonna do?"

Cara closed her eyes, hoping for inspiration. "I have no idea. All I know is, Lillian Fanning will shit a brick if she finds out about this. You heard me, I just promised her we had everything under control. The most demanding bride I've ever worked with—and this had to happen today."

She opened the cooler door again and grabbed the nearest bucket. Three dozen long-stemmed white iceberg roses were crammed into it, and their heads drooped like so many sleepy toddlers.

"Dead." She dropped a handful of roses into the trash and reached for the next bucket, and the next, repeating the diagnosis—and throwing them away.

When she was done, the big plastic trash bin was full and all that was left on the counter was one bucketful of leatherleaf ferns—"You can't kill these things, even if you tried," Cara noted—and a raggedy assortment of single blossoms that had somehow managed to survive.

Bert grabbed one of the pale blue mophead hydrangea blossoms and with his secateurs snipped off the end of the stem. He turned on the faucet in the worktable sink, let the water heat up, then filled an empty bucket with hot water. He plunged the first hydrangea in, and reached for another.

"We can save these," he said. "I'll reprocess all of them, strip the leaves, trim the stems. Put some Floralife in the water. They're not all a total loss. I bet they'll perk right back up."

Cara kicked at the trash can with the toe of her sandal, wincing in pain as soon as she'd done it. "That's twelve thousand dollars' worth of flowers, gone. Even if we save some of them, there's no way we can even put together a boutonniere out of this mess, let alone enough flowers for Torie, eight bridesmaids, and all the flowers for the church and the reception. And it's too late to get more flowers shipped from California in time for tomorrow."

Bert looked around the room, as though a new shipment of flowers might magically appear from thin air.

"What about the wholesale house? Can't you call them? Or we could run over there and see what they've got."

"Breitmueller's? On a Friday morning in May? With all the weddings and proms going on around town? They'll be picked clean by now. Anyway, they don't carry the kinds of flowers we promised Torie. Lilies of the valley? Ranunculus? Casablanca lilies? Peonies? "

"What about Lamar?" Bert asked. "I know we usually see him on Thursdays, but maybe, if you called and told him what happened . . ."

Cara blinked back tears. "Lamar's clear up in Atlanta, Bert. He's not gonna come all the way down here just to save my bacon. . . ."

Bert pointed at the phone. "C'mon, Cara. That old man loves you. He might make a special trip, if you explained what was at stake."

Cara shrugged and reached for her Rolodex. But before she could flip to Lamar's card, the shop phone rang.

She picked up the phone and looked at the caller ID, and her hand froze. The area code was one she knew by heart: 614 for Columbus, Ohio. And, of course, the caller was one she knew all too well, too.

She should let the call roll over to voicemail. Ignore it. He'd only call back, and keep calling until she picked up. Her day couldn't get much worse now. So why put off the inevitable?

Cara swallowed hard and tapped the receive button.

"Hi, Dad."

. . .

"Cara? Are you all right?" Her father's voice boomed so loudly she had to hold the phone several inches from her ear. Lieutenant Colonel Paul Kryzik's idea of a whisper was more like a shout to most people.

"Fine, Dad. How are you?"

Cara felt a knot forming in the pit of her stomach. She knew exactly why the Colonel was calling; had, in fact, been expecting this call for weeks now.

"Look, Dad, I know I'm kinda late with my payment . . ."

"I haven't had a phone call, much less a check from you, in three months now," he said. "What's going on down there?"

She swallowed hard. "We're just coming into my busiest season. Remember, I told you that? I've got a spring and summer full of weddings booked. But I've had all kinds of expenses. Buying the van, getting my website designed, finishing out the shop and buying equipment . . ."

"Our agreement was that you'd start making payments on the loan in February. You should have had plenty of money from Valentine's Day business, right?"

She felt a stabbing pain between her eyes. "We actually had a pretty good Valentine's Day. But all the profits went back into the shop. My computer died, and I had to buy a new one . . ."

"Not my problem," her father shot back. "If you'd prepared a detailed business plan, as I'd suggested, you could have anticipated that a five-year-old computer would need to be replaced. It's called a contingency plan. These things are a cost of doing business, Cara."

"I know, but . . ."

"If you've got business coming into the shop, I'd think you'd be in a position to start repaying at least the interest on your loan," he went on.

"Dad, if you'd just let me explain," Cara started.

But the Colonel wasn't interested in explanations. Not from her.

"I should have known something like this would happen. It's never a good idea to loan money to family, especially since you didn't even have a sound business plan for this shop of yours."

"That's not true," Cara said sharply. "I drew up a business plan. I did cost projections, market studies, I researched rent and utilities, I did everything I could. But how could I anticipate something like having to replace a computer? Or a deadbeat innkeeper who refuses to pay me for three months' worth of arrangements? Just this morning, I came downstairs, and my flower cooler had died. Along with twelve thousand dollars' worth of inventory I need for a wedding tomorrow. Some things are just out of my control, Dad. You of all people know that."

"Water under the bridge," he said, interrupting. "The fact is, if you can't even begin repaying the interest on a loan, after six months, your business has no hope of success. Even you can see that, right?"

"No! I can't see it. My business is building every week. We've got new clients, a few new commercial accounts. I just need a little more time to get things up and running. This wedding tomorrow, Dad? It's a ten-thousand-dollar deal." Cara hated the pleading note she heard creeping into her voice.

"For which you just admitted you don't have any flowers," the Colonel shot back. "Look, Cara. This just proves my point. You're a smart girl, and a hard worker, I'll give you that. But somebody like you has no business running a business. Take that innkeeper. You think I would have given three months of credit to a new account? Not on your life!"

Cara felt her left eye twitching, and her headache was taking on a new life of its own. She opened the drawer of her desk, found the bottle of aspirin, popped three into her mouth, and choked them down with a swallow of now-cold coffee.

She had to end this call before her head exploded.

"Dad? I'm sorry, but I really need to go now. We've got to replace those flowers I lost, and I've got another bride coming in for an appointment. I'll send you a check by the end of next week. Swear to God. And after that, I'll catch up. Monthly payments, just like we agreed. Okay?"

"No. Not okay," he said. "I know this is painful for you, Cara, but admit it, this florist thing of yours hasn't worked out. Just like your marriage. And frankly, I'm out of patience with pretending everything is okay. I'm not some ATM machine, you know. Two years from now, I'm retiring from the community college. I have to start thinking about my own welfare. Twenty thousand dollars is a lot of money at my age. I'm sorry, but I'm pulling the plug on this little enterprise of yours."

Cara's eyes widened, and her jaw dropped. "Pull the plug? What's that supposed to mean?"

"Just what it sounds like. It's over, Cara. No more stalling, no more excuses. I'm calling your loan. It's still the first week of May. Close up the shop. Call your landlord, let her know you're breaking your lease. Maybe if you give her plenty of advance notice, she'll prorate your rent."

"Break the lease?" Cara's mouth went dry. Her hands clutched the phone so hard her fingertips turned white. "Close the shop?"

From across the room, Bert, who'd given up any pretense of not listening in, looked as shocked as she felt.

"There's no reason for you to stay down there in Savannah any longer," her father continued, as though everything were settled, just like that, because he said so. "You've no ties, there, really. Leo's not taking you back, and anyway . . ."

"Leo?" Cara screeched. "Dad, I left Leo, not the other way around."

"A technicality," the Colonel said calmly. "Let's not split hairs. I think it would be better if you got a little place of your own. I could probably talk to somebody here at the school about a job, but if you think you still want to fool around with flowers, you can probably find something around town. . . ."

"Dad!" Cara shouted into the phone. "Stop. Just stop!"

"There's no need to scream, young lady," the Colonel said sternly. "I'm not deaf."

You might as well be, Cara thought. *You never hear a word I say. You never have. I'm thirty-six years old, as you dearly love to point out, and you've never really listened to me. Not in my whole life.*

"I can't discuss this right now," she managed.

There was an extended silence on the other end of the phone. And then a dial tone. Even when he wasn't speaking to her, the Colonel always managed to get in the last word. Or nonword.

Cara flung the phone onto the counter. The shop was quiet, except for the slow drip of the faucet in the sink. Bert tiptoed over, stood behind her, and placed his long, strong fingertips on her shoulders. Wordlessly, he began methodically kneading the knotted-up muscles. Poppy crept over, from her hiding place under the worktable, and tentatively placed her front paws on Cara's knees.

At least, she thought wryly, she now knew what was off. Everything. Everything was off. "I'm screwed," she whispered.

2

Cara bit her lip and did her best to blink back the tears of frustration that inevitably followed a conversation with her father. She looked over at the sad pile of flowers on the worktable. Without thinking, she reached for one of the few surviving roses. She clipped the stem end, then stripped off the remaining leaves, then added it to the hydrangeas rehydrating in the bucket.

She glanced around the shop. It was only three hundred square feet, but it was hers now. What was it the Colonel had called it? Her "little enterprise"? Not that he'd ever seen the shop. Her father had visited only once in the five years she'd been living in Savannah, and that had been shortly after she and Leo moved down from Ohio.

This was before she'd taken a job three years ago, answering the phone at Flowers by Norma. Her boss, a feisty octogenarian named Norma Poole, had been in business for thirty years. Norma's specialty was funeral and hospital flowers. Her arrangements were as tightly structured as her trademark bright orange bouffant hairdo. A cantankerous chain-smoker, Norma had nonetheless taken a shine to her young protégé, and before she knew it, Cara was not only delivering bouquets, she was actually creating them.

Not two and a half years ago, Norma had walked into the shop and plunked a set of keys onto the same worktable Cara was now using.

"Today's the day, Cara Mia," Norma said in that raspy voice of hers.

"What day is that, Norma?"

"My last day. Your first."

"Huh?" Cara gave the older woman a searching look.

"It's all yours," Norma said, gesturing expansively. "All three hundred square feet of it." She tapped her chest. "Just came from the doctor's office. He has some X-rays of my lungs that don't look so good."

"Oh, Norma!" Cara clutched the old lady's arm. "Is it . . . ?"

"Yup." Norma shrugged. "He wants me to do chemo, but I'm eighty-two, for cryin' out loud. I told him, 'No way, José.' My baby sister has a nice two-bedroom condo down in Sarasota." She smiled. "Always wanted to be able to say I was spending my last days wintering in Florida."

Cara swallowed hard. "Surely not your last days?"

"Close enough," Norma said cheerfully.

"I'm so, so sorry," Cara started. "What can I do? Help pack up the shop?"

"Why would you do that?" Norma asked. "I'm giving it to you, hon. Well, not the building. Bernice and Sylvia Bradley own that. But my lease has another year to run on it. It's October now, and the rent's paid up till January. All the equipment, and the inventory, such as it is, is paid for. And you're welcome to it, if you want the headache."

"Seriously?" Cara couldn't believe what she was hearing. She knew Norma liked her well enough—but to just give her this business?

Norma coughed for a moment, and sat down to catch her breath. "I don't have the energy to pack the place up. And it'd be a pain in the ass to try to hang around and sell everything. Not that it's worth all that much. The delivery van? The odometer quit at two hundred thousand miles, and it's a piece of crap, if you want the truth. But it's a paid-for piece of crap. If you want it, I'll get my lawyer to handle everything, get you the deed to the car, and we'll do a bill of sale for everything else."

"Uh, Norma?" She hated to broach the subject of money, but the fact was, she didn't have much money of her own. Leo handled all their finances, and he considered her job at Flowers by Norma as more of a hobby than a career.

Norma must have read her mind. "I was thinking a dollar. Would that work for you?"

"A dollar? Are you kidding? Norma, this business is worth thousands and thousands of dollars."

"And what would I do with that kind of money?" Norma's pale blue eyes peered over the rim of her sparkly-framed glasses. "The doctor says I'll be gone in a few months. My kid sister is the only family I've got left. She's fixed fine, got more dough than I ever thought about having."

"You could leave it to a charity."

"Charity!" Norma made a face and coughed again. "Charity begins at home," she said, when she'd caught her breath. "I don't have much, but I don't feel like giving what I do have to strangers." She tapped Cara's shoulder. "So. Looks like you're an instant heiress. Kind of."

Cara took a deep breath, and then another. Bert was hovering nearby, an anxious expression on his face.

"Everything okay?" he asked.

"Ask me later." She picked up the telephone and made the call she'd been about to make—right before the Colonel decided to ruin her week.

Lamar Boudreau was Cara's secret weapon. She'd met him at an industry trade show in Atlanta, not long after she'd transformed Norma's into Bloom. Every week Lamar drove his refrigerated van to a wholesale warehouse adjacent to the Atlanta airport, and filled his "bucket truck" with choice imported flowers in unusual colors and varieties not stocked by her Savannah wholesaler—tulips, lilies, gerbera daisies, freesias, and snapdragons from Holland; roses, delphiniums, and asters from Ecuador; and spray chrysanthemums and alstroemeria from Colombia. From there, he made deliveries to fewer than a dozen florists around the state.

Under normal circumstances, Lamar and his bucket truck arrived in Savannah on Wednesdays. As far as Cara knew, she was his only local customer, and she intended to keep it that way. These days most of her brides didn't want to settle for their mother's same-old carnations and sweetheart roses. They wanted the trendy flowers spotted in their favorite high-end glossy wedding magazines and, increasingly, on Pinterest. And that's where Lamar Boudreau came in.

"Lamar? It's Cara, in Savannah."

"How you doin', girl?"

"Not too good," she admitted. "My cooler conked out on me overnight, and most of those flowers you delivered Wednesday are DOA. I've got a huge wedding tomorrow. Can you help me out?"

"Aww, Cara," he moaned. "I can't be coming all the way back down there today. I got other customers besides you, ya know."

"I know, Lamar, but none you love as much as me."

From across the room Bert rolled his eyes.

"That's true," Lamar said, with a chuckle. "But don't you be telling my wife 'bout us."

"What about it? Pretty please? This is a big order, so I'll make it worth your while."

"You know how much gas my van burns up when I make a trip clear down there to the coast? Anyway, much as I wish I could help, I can't do it today."

"How far south are you coming?" Cara persisted.

"On my way to Macon next," Lamar said. "Last call of the day."

"Perfect! I'll meet you anyplace you say. I'm working with the pickiest bride on the planet, and her mother's even worse, so make sure you save the good stuff for me, okay?"

"Don't I always?" Lamar said. "I'll see you at the Cracker Barrel on Riverside Drive at two."

After tracking down the repairman and issuing dire threats about what would happen if he didn't return to the shop to get her cooler up and running again,

Cara sent Bert to the wholesale house to try to buy more stock, and spent the rest of the morning fielding phone calls and dealing with appointments and brides.

When Bert returned to Bloom at noon, Cara was waiting by the door. "I'm headed to Macon to meet Lamar," she informed him. She glanced over at Poppy, who was lounging nearby, watching her every move. "Can you do me a favor and watch you-know-who? I'd take her with me, but you know she gets carsick after more than fifteen or twenty minutes, and I haven't had enough advance time to give her the meds."

"That's cool," Bert said easily.

"And if Lillian Fanning calls again, and she will call, lie through your teeth and tell her we've got her friggin' ecru candles."

"Got it," he said.

3

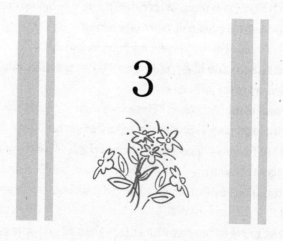

After working all night on Torie Fanning's *second* set of wedding arrangements, by Saturday morning Cara was operating on Red Bull and desperation. She would have given anything for an hour of sleep. But this was May, and she'd sleep, she promised herself, when wedding season was over.

Right now, she had a ten-o'clock appointment. She took another covert sip of Red Bull and poured two flutes of orange juice, topping it off with Sam's Club champagne.

She set the silver tray down carefully on the big worktable in the shop and beamed at today's couple, Michelle and Hank.

"All right then, you two," she said, hoping she sounded cheerful. "Let's talk about your big day!"

Michelle pushed her iPad across the zinc top of the worktable. She poised one pink polished fingertip on the screen. "This is my board for the altar centerpieces. As you can see, I'm looking for something loose and relaxed, in the blue and purple range, with greenery that's a softer silver, gray. For the containers, I'd like big ironstone pitchers like these." She tapped one picture on the screen, then slid her fingertip across the screen.

"Now. Here's what I'm thinking for my bouquet and the bridesmaids. White tea roses, white Stargazer lilies, pale, pale yellow stephanotis. Hand-dyed ribbons in the colors of the girl's dresses."

She slid over to the next board. "These are the girl's dresses. I'm having ten attendants. I would have kept it at eight, but *his* mother"—she cut her eyes sideways at her fiancé, a budget analyst named Hank—"is having a cat fit and insisting I have his sisters—and I'm sorry, honey, but Geneva is clinically obese, and LeAnne has that unfortunate red hair, so I can't have anything pink...."

She sighed heavily, then clasped her fiancé's hand and wrinkled her pert button nose. "You agree, don't you, Hank?"

Hank's hair was also what Cara thought of as an unfortunate shade of red, but he nodded agreement. "Geneva's thinking about gastric bypass. If she goes in this summer, I think we can count on her being a size sixteen by October. Anyway, pink does nothing for Michelle's coloring. So that's why we're thinking mostly blues, purples, some silver and gray for everything at the church."

"Right," Michelle agreed. "Then, at the reception, which will be in the Westin's ballroom, we'll segue into deeper, more dramatic colors."

"Show her the tablecloths," Hank urged. "Ombré! Michelle got an unbelievable deal on the fabric at this online store."

Michelle slid her fingertip and a new Pinterest board popped up. This one was labeled "Ideas for wedding receptions."

Cara Kryzik nodded and jotted down notes. "Got it. Blues, silvers, purples. No pink. Loose arrangements. Mostly white for the bridesmaids. Are we doing anything else at the church? Pew bows, anything like that? You did say it's at St. John's, right?"

"No pew bows," Hank said emphatically. "That's just so ... nineties."

Michelle snapped the cover of the iPad. "So I guess that's it for now. You'll put together a mood board for me? And a proposal? By, say ... Wednesday?"

"Wednesday will be fine," Cara said. She glanced at Bert, who'd also been taking notes throughout the two-hour meeting. "I'll email it, and then we can talk."

Bride and groom stood and left, holding hands.

The bells on the shop door jingled merrily as the couple left.

Cara rolled her eyes. "Cute couple. Controlling bride. Passive-aggressive groom. I give them three years, tops."

"Mmm-hmm," Bert said, still jotting down notes. "Less than that if she wises up and figures out she's married a raging homosexual."

Cara Kryzik raised one eyebrow. "You think?"

"Takes one to know one," Bert said.

May and June were always a blur for Bloom, but this year, Cara thought, might be the year that topped all years. If those talking-head economists wanted a real signal that the recession was over, they had only to look at her upcoming wedding calendar.

May was already manic, and it was just the first Saturday of the month. June would be even busier. Her calendar was full with showers, rehearsal dinners, and weddings.

But busy didn't necessarily mean profitable. If she could just avoid any more equipment-related disasters, she might, just might, be able to put together enough money to send the Colonel a big fat check by the end of the month.

This morning she'd delivered the centerpieces for a bridesmaids' brunch at nine, met with Michelle and Hank, and by one she was already behind schedule finishing up the flowers for the most demanding bride she'd ever worked with.

Cara wrapped a single white rose with green floral tape and inserted it into the already over-the-top centerpiece of white ranunculus, orange parrot tulips, and green and blue hydrangeas that were spilling out of an heirloom Georgian silver soup tureen destined for the buffet table.

"What do you think?" she asked, turning to her assistant.

Bert put down his scissors and gazed over the top of his wire-rimmed granny glasses at the towering arrangement.

"Baudy, gawdy, and fabulous," he decreed. "But you know our little bride Torie. More is always more with that girl."

"I know," Cara said with a sigh, selecting another flower from the dwindling bucket on the floor. "Half these flowers would be a showstopper, but I can't make Torie see that. She is determined to have the most ostentatious wedding in the history of Savannah. It's too bad we have to waste all this effort and beauty on a girl who doesn't know a pansy from a petunia."

"As though Torie Fanning would ever deign to sniff anything as incredibly middle-class as either a pansy or a petunia," Bert said.

The shop phone rang and Cara glanced over at the caller-ID screen. "Speaking of which, there's the smother of the bride now." Her hand hovered over the receiver. "I swear, if Lillian calls me with one more demand, I am going to go stark, raving bonkers."

"Think of the invoice we're going to present when this whole circus is over," Bert advised.

"No. I'm thinking of the look on the Colonel's face when he opens the envelope with his check," Cara corrected.

"Exactly," he said, nodding. "Just hold your nose and smile pretty."

The phone kept ringing.

"Brides!" Cara muttered. "If I ever even entertain the idea of getting married again, Bert, you are authorized to smack me upside the head and have me committed."

"Never say never," Bert warned.

"I'm serious," Cara said. She looked across the workroom. "Here Poppy," she called.

The curly-haired goldendoodle puppy raced over to her side and propped her front paws on Cara's knees. Cara bent down to let the puppy lick her chin. "Puppy love. That's all I need. No more men, and definitely no more weddings."

Bert pointed at the phone, which was still ringing. "Really. Don't you think you'd better get that?"

"I'm not answering," Cara said defiantly. She got up from her stool and stretched. "And I am not stuffing any more flowers in this centerpiece. The wedding is in less than five hours. We've got to get these arrangements loaded in the van and get them out to Isle of Hope before three. Whatever Lillian wants, it'll just have to . . ."

Before she could finish the sentence, they heard the tinkling of bells coming from the front of the shop. Poppy pricked up her ears and started toward the sound.

"Close the door!" Cara hollered. "Don't let the dog get . . ."

But it was too late. Sensing an opening, the seven-month-old goldendoodle, Poppy, streaked toward daylight.

"Grab her," Cara called to the startled stranger who's just entered Bloom. He paused for only a split second, pivoted, and lunged toward Poppy, managing to grab on to her collar. But Poppy, an obedience-school dropout who was as determined as she was undisciplined, easily wriggled out of the collar and was out the door in a flash, joyously running full-tilt down West Jones Street.

"Shit!" Cara cried.

"Not again," Bert echoed. "Not today."

"Sorry," the stranger said, turning from Cara to Bert, still holding the collar in his right hand. "I wanted to get some flowers sent to my sister in the hospital . . ."

"Can you help him?" Cara gave Bert a pleading look. "I'll go after Poppy. If I'm not back in fifteen minutes, start loading the van without me."

Cara sprinted out of Bloom without looking back.

"Poppy!" she called, cupping her hands over her mouth as a makeshift megaphone. "Poppy, come back!"

She passed the restored nineteenth-century town houses and elegant storefronts in her block, and dashed across Barnard Street, dodging cars as she ran.

Three tourists with cameras strung around their necks and unfolded street maps stood on the corner, arguing loudly about where to have lunch.

"No more barbecue," snapped a twenty-something girl in a tie-dyed shirt and white shorts.

"Did you see a dog run past just now?" Cara interrupted. "Curly white hair, maybe thirty pounds?"

"That way." The girl's middle-aged father pointed east. "She sure can run."

Cara continued east down Jones. She paused by the line of people still queued up for lunch outside Mrs. Wilkes' boardinghouse. "Did you see a dog run past here?" she asked breathlessly.

"Thataway," volunteered a bespectacled senior citizen with a plastic tour-company lanyard around her neck.

Cara ran on, crossing Whitaker, Bull, Drayton, and Abercorn. Her thin-soled sandals flapped against the steaming concrete sidewalks. Her face was sheened with sweat, her T-shirt glued to her chest.

"See a dog?" she asked, pausing beside a college kid locking his bike to a utility pole in front of a classroom building on the art-college campus.

"Huh?"

Twenty minutes had passed. But nobody else had spotted the puppy. Reluctantly, she started jogging back toward Bloom, breathing heavily and sweating profusely.

Bert had the van pulled around to the front of the shop by the time she got back. "Anything?"

"No," Cara said, near tears. "Look, just wait here. I'm going to take the van and see if I can spot her."

"Cara? Lillian has called back twice, and now Torie's started calling. And her wedding director wants to know why we aren't already out at the church. You know it'll take us thirty minutes to get out to Isle of Hope."

"Stall 'em," Cara said. "I can't let Poppy just wander around downtown. She'll get hit by one of those tour buses, or run over by one of the horse-drawn carriages. And even if somebody does find her, they won't know who she is, because she's not wearing her collar. Please, Bert?"

Bert shrugged and went back inside the shop to try to mollify their clients.

Cara drove east and north this time, trolling the side streets, leaning out the window of the pink-and-white-striped van, calling her puppy's name, straining for a familiar glimpse of curly white fur, but to no avail. While she cruised, her cell phone rang and pinged and buzzed, with incoming calls, texts, and emails, all of which she ignored.

She was backtracking toward the shop, turning up Habersham at East Charlton, when she saw a tall, bare-chested man dressed in nylon running shorts and expensive-looking running shoes, tugging a medium-sized, furry white dog by a piece of rope. He was walking down the lane behind Charlton.

"Poppy!" Cara cried. She veered left and into the lane.

"Hey!" she called to the man. She leaned out the open window of the van. "Excuse me, that's my dog."

He was in his mid thirties—the man, not the dog. His dark hair was pushed back from his forehead and his chest gleamed with perspiration. Even in her extreme distress, Cara noted that he was seriously ripped. The man glanced down at the puppy, then back up at Cara.

He frowned. "The hell it is. This is *my* dog."

"No." Cara put the van in park. "Honestly. That's Poppy. My goldendoodle."

"No," he said impatiently, starting to walk away. "This is Shaz. Unfortunately, this is *my* goldendoodle."

Cara climbed down out of the van and hurried after him. "That's impossible. There aren't that many dogs like this in Savannah. I had to go all the way to Atlanta to find mine. And that one *is* mine." She searched in the pocket of her shorts and held out one of the doggie treats she always carried. "Here Poppy."

The puppy looked up at Cara and wagged enthusiastically.

"Shaz!" the man said loudly. The puppy looked at him and wagged her tail even harder.

"See?"

"She does that with everybody," Cara said, desperation creeping into her voice. "She's never met a stranger."

"If she's yours, where's her dog tag?" the man demanded.

"Back at my flower shop, on West Jones. A customer came in, and he tried to grab Poppy as she made a break for the door, but Poppy managed to wriggle out of her collar." She waved the treat under the dog's nose. "Here Poppy," she coaxed. "Come to Mama."

The puppy's ears pricked up, and she lunged toward Cara, but the man pulled her back.

"See?" Cara said triumphantly. "That's Poppy."

"No," he said, wedging the now wriggling puppy firmly between his calves. "That's a cheap trick. And this is Shaz. She'd kill her grandma for a dog treat."

"If that's your dog, where's its collar?

"In my truck, back at my house. I was just taking her to the groomer, whom she hates, and the truck window was open, and she jumped out the window and took off. Come on, Shaz." He started walking away, and the puppy trotted obediently at his heels.

"Poppy," Cara called, near tears. "Come here, girl. Time to go home."

"Nice try," the man said, glancing back over his shoulder. "But I don't have time for this. Good luck finding your dog."

The puppy gave one backward look, but the man was jogging again, and the dog followed right on his heels.

Cara jumped back behind the wheel of the van. "Hey," she hollered out the open window. She beeped the horn. "Come back here."

The man jogged on down the lane, and she crept along right behind him, honking her horn every few minutes, and hollering out the window. "Stop! Come here, Poppy." She knew she looked like a lunatic, and she just didn't care.

Poppy, the little traitor, seemed quite content to follow along behind her new friend, never straying or yanking at the makeshift leash as she sometimes did when Cara took her for her morning walk.

Finally, they reached a block on Macon Street. The houses here were simpler than the grand brick and stucco townhomes farther west in the historic district. Mostly single-story wood-frame homes, they were known as freedman's cottages because they'd originally been built after the Civil War by newly emancipated slaves.

The runner paused in front of one of the least distinguished cottages on the block. Paint was peeling from the dingy white clapboards, a shutter at the window was missing several slats, and the faded aqua door seemed to be held together with duct tape. There was a wooden window box beneath the double window, but the plants were dried up and shriveled beyond recognition. The man propped his foot on the top step of the stoop and retrieved a key from a pocket in the tongue of his running shoe.

That's when he looked over and spotted Cara, parked at the curb, the van's motor idling.

"Beat it," he called.

She held her cell phone up for him to see. "Give me back my dog or I'll call the cops."

"Get away from my house or I'll call the cops myself," he retorted. He picked Poppy up in his arms and climbed the rest of the steps to the doorway. He unlocked the door. Cara jumped from the truck and ran for the minuscule porch, but he was too quick. He stepped inside and slammed the door in her face. A moment later, she heard a deadbolt lock slide into place.

"Dognapper!" Cara pounded on the door with her fist. "Give me back my dog!"

"Crazy stalker woman, go away," came the muffled reply.

She banged on the door, and looked around to ring the doorbell, but it was defunct, dangling by a single frayed wire from the dry-rotted doorframe.

Cara gave the door an ineffective kick, resulting only in a badly stubbed big toe.

"I'm calling the cops," she screamed, her lips plastered against the doorframe.

"I already called 'em," came back his voice.

She paced back and forth in front of the cottage, waiting for the police. Bert called, and she instructed him to load as many of the flowers as he could into his own car, and start ferrying them over to the church. Torie and Lillian Fanning called, too, but she let those calls go to voicemail.

While she paced, Cara studied the house, hoping the runner would somehow relent and release Poppy. The cottage was a puzzle. It sported a jaunty new-looking red tin roof, but there were cracks in the wavy glass of the front windows, and she could see that two or three of the clapboards were perilously close to falling off the house.

Cara called the police again. This time, a bored-sounding dispatcher informed her that the police had actual crimes to solve, and that an officer might not show up for another hour.

"But he's got my dog," Cara protested. "And he won't even open the door or listen to reason."

"Ma'am?" the dispatcher said. "Try to work it out like adults, why don't you?"

She disconnected and walked back over to the house. She climbed onto the front stoop and peered in through the dust-caked window. The room inside held a battered leather sofa and a flat-screen television squatting on a sheet of plywood stretched across sawhorses. The room was littered with stacks of lumber, tools, and paint buckets. There was no sign of Poppy. She would have cried, but she had a wedding to get to.

4

Did you find Poppy?" Bert asked, as she raced back into the shop.

"He's still got her locked up," Cara said. "And the police were no help at all." She was pulling her sweat-soaked T-shirt over her head as she raced for the back stairs to her second-floor apartment above the shop.

"Never mind," Bert called up after her. "I've already taken the altar arrangements, the pew bows and centerpieces out there. But we've still got the bouquets and boutonnieres and the buffet arrangements here, so hurry! I'll get the van loaded. After the wedding, I'll help you get Poppy back."

Ten minutes later, she was back downstairs, her still-damp butterscotch-colored hair pulled into a careless French knot, dressed in a floaty vintage flower-sprigged pink silk garden-party dress, and pink cowboy boots.

The ride out Skidaway Road to the Isle of Hope was a nail-biter, but they pulled up to the quaint, white wood-framed Methodist church at exactly five o'clock, with only an hour to spare before the wedding.

Cara toted the cardboard carton with the bride's flowers into the back of the church, where she was met by Lillian Fanning, her carefully made-up face contorted with anger and anxiety.

"Finally!" Lillian snapped, snatching the box of flowers from Cara's hands. "I've been having heart palpitations for the last hour. Where on earth have you been? Didn't you get any of my calls or texts?"

"So sorry," Cara responded. "The battery ran down on my cell phone. But we're here now. Bert's taking the rest of the arrangements over to the reception. Honestly, Lillian. We have it all under control."

"Mama? Is that Cara with my damn flowers?" A willowy brunette in a stunning strapless cream satin Vera Wang gown poked her head out the door of the bride's room.

"It's me, Torie," Cara said. "I was just telling your mom, everything's good."

A small, nervous woman in a pale blue dress fluttered out of the room. "Whatever you do, don't upset her any more," Ellie Lewis, the wedding planner, whispered in Cara's ear. "She's already threatened to strangle one of the flower girls."

"I'm coming," Cara said, scuttling into the room with the box of flowers held before her like a peace offering.

Torie Fanning was a gorgeous mess. Her glossy black updo was coming unpinned, and the tight-fitting bodice of her gown gaped in the back where the last half-dozen tiny satin-covered buttons refused to fasten. The dress fit snugly over her hips—a little too snugly, Cara thought—then flared out with multiple layers of spangly tulle that made the bride look like a mermaid. An overwrought, undermedicated mermaid.

"It's about damned time," Torie said.

"Sorry, sorry, sorry," Cara said. She moved behind the bride and began fastening the buttons. "You look amazing, Torie," she said, her voice low and soothing. It was the same voice she used to coax Poppy to take her heartworm meds. It usually worked well on dogs and neurotics.

"Truly. You're my most beautiful bride ever," Cara said.

"The dress isn't too tight? I think that fuckin' seamstress took it in too much." Torie inhaled sharply as Cara tugged at the last satin button, praying that it would close the gap.

"Oh my God. I can't breathe," Torie croaked.

"Perfect," Cara assured her. "You don't have to breathe. You just have to look amazing. And you do."

She placed her hands lightly on Torie's shoulders and spun her slowly around. She lifted the bouquet from its nest of tissue and handed it to her.

"Now. Isn't this worth the wait?" Cara crossed her fingers, waiting for Torie's reaction.

She'd chosen the most spectacular flowers from Lamar's bucket truck, all in Torie's wedding palette of purples, greens, blues, and pale coral. Hydrangeas, tea roses, and tiny white lilies of the valley and stephanotis made a dinner-plate-sized bouquet, wrapped in hand-dyed watery lavender silk ribbons, fastened with an exquisite platinum brooch with diamond and pearl lilies of the valley.

The bride's expression softened. The shadow of a smile appeared. Torie turned the bouquet this way and that. She touched the delicate tracery of the antique brooch with her finger. "This is pretty. Where did it come from?"

"It was Ryan's grandmother's," Cara said. "And yes, the diamonds and pearls are real. It's a signed Cartier piece. He thought of it all by himself, and he told me it was perfect—the sweetest flower for the sweetest girl in the world."

Which was a big, stinking lie, of course. One of Cara's trademark touches was to include a piece of family jewelry—a little surprise from the groom to the bride—in every bridal bouquet. She'd called Ryan weeks before the wedding to ask him to find a suitable jewel to gift Torie. And she had to admit, he'd come up with a winner.

Torie burst into tears. "That's so like him. He is so thoughtful. And I'm such a bitch! I don't deserve somebody as wonderful as Ryan."

The wedding planner's right eye twitched three times in rapid succession. She patted Torie on the shoulder. "Come on, dear, don't cry. You'll ruin your makeup."

Cara gave Torie a fond pat on the arm. "You're not a bitch. You're just a little emotional. Perfectly natural."

Another lie. Well, it was an occupational hazard. Lying to brides and their mothers.

Cara tucked a stray lock of raven's-wing hair behind Torie's ear. "All right. You're ready. Take a deep breath and try to relax. I've got to go get the rest of the flowers handed out and check on the church. You're calm now, right?"

Torie sniffed and nodded.

"Your bridesmaids' flowers are all right there too," Cara said, pointing at the box she'd put on a nearby tabletop. "Is everybody here?"

"They're here," the wedding planner volunteered. "They're just in the bathroom, touching up their makeup. I'll give them their bouquets."

"Great," Cara said. "I just want to run through the church and check on everything."

She hurried through the side door to the church and took a deep breath. The sanctuary was cool and quiet—and blessedly still for the moment. Her altar arrangements looked magnificent, spilling out of the church's own tall chased-silver urns. The candles in the Fanning family candelabras were definitely white, but she could only hope Lillian would not notice the difference. Cara buzzed up and down the aisles, straightening pew bows and picking up errant rose petals from the white satin runner.

After picking up the box with the boutonnieres, she knocked on the door of the vestry.

"It's open," a male voice called.

The scene here was the opposite of the one in the bride's room. Half a dozen men were attired in tuxes, but with vests unbuttoned and ties untied. They were puffing on cigars and handing around a silver flask, and from the slightly glazed eyes of the assembled company, it was evident that everybody had already had more than a sip of Knob Creek.

"Hey Cara, how's it goin'?" Ryan Finnerty was as calm and laid-back as his bride was overwrought. He was tall with a blocky build, with strawberry-blond hair and the Tom Sawyer freckles that went with hair that color, and a square jaw and an easy, gap-toothed grin. Ryan wasn't classically handsome, but Cara had developed just the teensiest crush on him during all the pre-wedding planning. He was friendly, down-to-earth, impossible to dislike. She wondered if he knew what, exactly, he was getting into with a high-maintenance girl like Torie.

"Goin' good, Ryan," Cara said. She handed the boutonnieres around to all the groomsmen.

"How's Torie?" Ryan stubbed out his cigar and began fastening the flower to the lapel of his jacket.

"Fine," she lied. "Excited that the big day is finally here. How are things going in here? Everybody present and accounted for?"

"We're good," Ryan drawled. "But we're waiting on my lame-ass best man to show up."

"Oh?" Cara tried not to sound alarmed. But it was getting close to show-time. "Has anybody heard from him this morning?"

The door to the vestry opened and a dark-haired man in jeans and a T-shirt strolled in.

"About damn time, Jack," one of the other groomsmen muttered.

"Aw, chill out," the newcomer said. "We got plenty of time."

Cara gasped. "You!"

He turned and his expression darkened. "You! Did you follow me out here?"

Ryan looked from Cara to the latest arrival. "You two know each other?"

"She's been stalking me all afternoon," Jack said, shaking his head.

"He stole my dog," Cara countered. "He's a dognapper."

"Ignore her," Jack said, pulling his T-shirt over his head. "She's clearly deranged."

"Dude," Ryan said. "You're late."

"Yeah, sorry about that," Jack said, looking around the cramped room. He pointed to a garment bag hanging from the back of the door. "Is that mine?"

"Hell yeah," Ryan said, glancing at his watch. "And you better get into it too. You guys are going to start hauling people down the aisle pretty soon. You're getting Mom and Grandma, right?"

"Taken care of," Jack said. He had kicked off his Topsiders and was pushing his arms through the sleeves of the starched white shirt.

The door opened again and the wedding planner coughed and waved aside the smoke. "Um, gentlemen, we've got guests arriving."

Ryan waved them out of the room. "Come on, guys. Get going. We don't need any hitches today. You know how Torie gets."

Cara saw two of the groomsmen roll their eyes, and she grinned despite herself.

If you only knew.

As the men filed past her, she checked and adjusted their ties and boutonnieres. Then she turned to the best man. He was tall and rangy, with the weather-beaten look of a man who spent a lot of time outdoors. His hazel eyes had flecks of gold beneath thick brows, which at this moment were drawn into an uncompromising frown.

"You mind?" he said pointedly, fastening the studs on his tux shirt. "I'm trying to get dressed here."

"And I'm trying to get my dog back," Cara said. "I'm not leaving this room until you agree to hand over Poppy."

"Suit yourself," he said. He unzipped his jeans and nimbly stepped out of them.

Cara blushed and looked away quickly, but the impression was made and it caused an involuntary fluttering in her chest. The starched shirttails hung just low enough to reveal an inch or two of black briefs and tanned, well-muscled thighs. This dognapper was a very, um, well-proportioned man.

"See anything you like?" Jack asked. He turned and reached for his pants, and Cara's face grew hotter as she appreciated the back view almost as much as the front. She mentally chastised herself. *Stop leering at this man. He has your dog!*

He turned around and with deliberate leisure stepped into his pants, pulling the suspenders over his shoulders, leaving the fly unzipped, she was sure, in a deliberate attempt to embarrass her. His eyes met hers, and she forced herself not to look away as he finally zipped up. Cara blushed even deeper, but stood her ground. "Please give me back my dog."

"I don't have your dog."

Restrained organ music floated from the direction of the sanctuary. Cara clenched her fists on her hips and stared at him.

He stared right back, his jaw clenched tightly. He was smooth-shaven now, his dark wavy hair brushed back from a high forehead.

"Looks like a stalemate," he said, his hazel eyes unblinking. He picked up the cummerbund, buckled it, then slid the buckle to the back.

There was a brief knock at the door. "C'mon, Jack," Ryan called impatiently. "Don't make me send Mom in there after you."

"Gotta go," Jack said, gesturing toward the door. "There'll be hell to pay if I screw up this wedding. I'm already on the bride's shit list for keeping little brother out all night at the bachelor party."

"Wait. Did you say Ryan's your brother?"

He looped the bowtie under his collar. Cara felt an irresistible urge to reach up and tie it for him, even though all she really wanted to do was strangle him with it.

"Ryan is two years younger than me. He's the nice one. I'm the asshole."

The door opened and an older woman in a floor-length peach-colored gown stuck her head in the door. "Jack! For God's sake—get a move on! Everybody's waiting on us."

Jack plucked his tux jacket off the hanger. "Keep your shirt on, Mom."

The woman gave Cara an appraising look. "Who's this?"

"The owner of the dog your son stole from me earlier today," Cara said. After a moment of hesitation, she held out her hand. "I'm Cara Kryzik."

The woman's dark hair was flecked with streaks of gray, and her head barely met her son's shoulder. Her hazel eyes crinkled in amusement. "So nice to meet you. I'm Frannie Finnerty. But why on earth would Jack steal your dog? He has a dog of his own."

"Ignore her. She's just the florist. And she's crazier than a shit-house rat," Jack said. He tucked his mother's arm through his own and steered her nimbly toward the door.

"Wait!" Cara called.

He wheeled around. "Now what?"

She grasped the ends of his bowtie and quickly tied it. The top of her head barely reached his chin, and he smelled like Irish Spring soap. Magically delicious? Or was that Lucky Charms? Make that maddeningly delicious. Then she plucked the last boutonniere from the cardboard box, grabbed the black satin lapel of his jacket, and jabbed at it violently with the long pearl-headed pin.

"Ow!" He jerked away, opened his jacket, and looked with disbelief at the tiny spot of blood blooming on his starched white shirtfront. "You did that on purpose."

"Serves you right," Cara said, jabbing again, until the flower was securely fastened to his coat.

"Jack!" His mother tugged at his arm. "Come on. Everybody else has been seated. Torie's bridesmaids are all lined up. We have to go!"

Jack narrowed his eyes and gave the florist his long-practiced stink-eye. It was wasted on her, he knew. She was a head shorter than he, but she stood her ground without flinching. Her hair wasn't quite blond and wasn't quite brown, more of an in-between caramel color, he decided. She had large, liquid brown eyes with surprisingly dark lashes that dominated her heart-shaped face. He was pretty sure she was wearing no more makeup than a little pink lipstick, and even that was wasted, since she was scowling up at him, returning his stink-eye measure for measure.

Finally, she took a step backward. "This isn't over," she said softly, under her breath.

"That's what you think," he said. And then he allowed his mother to drag him out of the vestry and into the wedding melee.

5

Cara didn't stick around the church to watch Torie Fanning pledge her troth to Ryan Finnerty. She rarely did. Weddings were her business, not her pleasure, she told herself.

Instead, she raced for the van, pausing only to give the sky an anxious look. She and Ellie Lewis, the wedding planner, had done their best to talk Torie out of an outdoor reception. It was already hot in Savannah, and tornado season to boot. Cara had witnessed way too many weather-related wedding disasters, including one memorable reception where a sudden lightning storm had pinned seventy-five black-tie and cocktail-gowned guests huddled together in terror under the Victorian wooden gazebo in Whitfield Square.

But Torie was determined to have her reception at home, on the back lawn at the Shutters, her parents' gracious old home on the bluff at the Isle of Hope, facing the Skidaway River. And amazingly, it looked as though the weather was going to cooperate. A fresh breeze was blowing in off the river, and the humidity was actually bearable.

Cara pulled the van into the long driveway at the gray-shingled Fanning house, relieved to see Bert's car already tucked beside the carriage house, in front of the caterer's trucks. The brilliant blue sky had faded to a pale lavender—one of Torie's wedding colors, of course. The setting sun sparkled on the pale green water (also one of Torie's colors) lapping at the long dock opposite the Shutters.

The Fannings' dockhouse had been torn down and rebuilt just for the wedding, and now green-and-white-striped canvas drapes fluttered from its open corners, and a large wrought-iron chandelier hung from its peaked ceiling. This was where the guests would mingle and sip cocktails to watch the sunset while waiting for the wedding party to arrive from the church.

Cara hurried across the wide expanse of front lawn, her boot heels sinking into the grass. She crossed the road and found Bert standing in the dockhouse, directing a helper who was fastening baskets of flowers to the tiki torches dotting the corners of the dock.

"Well?" he asked, turning to face her. "Is the deed done?"

"The soloist was just starting when I left. Everything at the church looked great. And Torie actually cried when I handed her the bouquet with Ryan's pin. I'd say we have twenty more minutes before the first guests arrive."

Bert nodded. "You didn't try to talk the groom into making a run for it?"

"Hah! And foul up my biggest wedding of this season? No way. Anyway, even if I had, Ryan wouldn't have run. The poor guy is totally koo-koo for Cocoa Puffs over Torie."

Bert wrinkled his nose. "No accounting for taste. So . . . what do you think?"

"I think they might just have a shot at making it for the long haul," Cara admitted. "But only because Ryan Finnerty is a total teddy bear. You?"

He shrugged. "I give them six years. Although, if she gets knocked up sooner, I could be wrong."

Cara giggled. "I've got news for you, sport. She's *already* preggers. That gown fit her with room to spare when it was delivered in March."

Bert's eyes widened. "You think?"

"I know," she assured him. "At the rehearsal dinner? She stuck to iced tea all night. And did you see the way her boobs were about to fall out of the dress? I promise you, we'll be doing baby-shower balloon bouquets for her by fall."

Cara took a brisk walk around the dockhouse, straightening tablecloths on the caterer's highboy tabletops, brushing at the stray fern frond or fallen petal. Technically, this was the wedding planner's job, but Cara Kryzik never left anything to chance.

"I'm going to head back over to the reception tent," she told Bert. "All the flowers in the baskets here have water?"

"Check," Bert said.

"And you've misted the ferns with water?"

"Not my first rodeo, boss lady."

She patted his shoulder. "I think I'll keep you."

The first thing she checked at the reception tent was the compressor for the rented air conditioner. It was humming along, she noted with relief. The only thing worse than bad weather for an outdoor function in Savannah was a nonfunctioning air conditioner—or even a heater. Again, the tent and the air-conditioning were not her responsibility, but you couldn't tell that to a finicky bride who was prone to pitch a fit over the slightest flaw in her plans.

Cara stood quietly in the entrance to the tent, taking it all in. The temperature had cooled down nicely, and her flowers, she thought, not immodestly, looked sensational.

She'd commissioned a local glassblower to create three-foot-tall vases for the centerpieces, and these were placed in the center of each of the thirty round tables in the room. The tables themselves were covered in sea-foam-colored linen flounced cloths. Spilling from each vase were arrangements of coral tea roses, blue hydrangeas, variegated Swedish ivy, and marguerite daisies. Hanging from the metal support beams of the tent, she'd rigged up five enormous ivy-covered ten-arm wire chandeliers fitted with battery-operated candles. She pulled a small remote-control pad from her pocket, clicked a button, and the candles began to flicker in the dim light of the tent.

White-coated waiters moved efficiently about the tent, polishing water and wine glasses at each place setting, adjusting and straightening the thick silver place settings and gold-rimmed dinner plates.

"Cara, hi!" Torie's caterer, Layne Pelletier, hurried to her side.

"You've outdone yourself this time, girlfriend," Layne said, gesturing around the tent.

Cara sighed. "Let's just hope our bride agrees with you."

"How can she not? It's perfection. I've been snapping pictures of the tables to put up on my own website. Your flowers plus my food—it's going to be the party of the year."

"Hope so," Cara said. "The Fannings move in some pretty lofty circles. This little clambake of Torie's could be a real rainmaker if all goes well."

"It will," Layne assured her. "Were you at the church just now? Any idea how long before everbody will start arriving?"

They heard the sound of car doors closing. "About now," Cara said. "Showtime!"

Normally, the wedding party's arrival would signal Cara's departure. If she left now, maybe she could drive back to the dognapper's house on Macon Street. Maybe there was a backyard. She could cruise down the lane and steal her dog back while Jack Finnerty was still at the wedding. Cara was heading for her van when she heard her name being called.

"Cara . . . so glad you're still here." It was Ellie Lewis, the wedding planner.

"Just leaving," Cara said. "I've checked everything in both tents, and it's all good. By the way, thanks again for referring me to the Fannings."

Ellie's face was shiny pink with perspiration. "Don't thank me yet," she warned. "The photographer wants to get some candid shots of the wedding party down at the dock, and Torie is insistent that you should be there to style things."

"I'm not a photo stylist," Cara protested. "And honestly, Ellie, I'm whipped. I've been on my feet for nearly twenty-four hours. All I want right now is a shower and a cocktail—and my bed." *And my dog,* she thought.

Ellie nodded glumly. "I don't blame you. I've had a bellyful of Torie and Mommy Dearest these past few weeks. I'd leave too, if I could. But you know how it goes—I'll be here till the bitter end tonight."

She turned and began to trudge back across the lawn.

Cara had her hand on the van's door handle, but when she saw the dejected droop of her colleague's shoulders, she just didn't have the heart to abandon ship.

"Ellie," she called.

"Yes?"

"Wait for me, dammit."

By eight o'clock, the big reception tent vibrated with life. Dinner service for three hundred guests was winding down and the eight-piece orchestra was just starting to tune up. Cara made a few last-minute adjustments to the flowers on the cake table and tiptoed toward the door.

"Cara!"

Torie's voice rose above the din of the crowd. Her mermaid skirts rustled as she cut a swath through the crowd. The bride reached out and grasped Cara's hands in hers. "You're not leaving already! The party's just starting to crank up."

"Well, yes, I was," she said, a little taken aback by Torie's sudden show of friendliness.

"But, you can't," Torie said. "I mean, of course, you don't have to stay, but Ryan and I really, really wish you would stay. You've been such a big part of all the planning for the wedding, and it would really, really mean a lot to us if you would stay and help us celebrate."

Huh?

"Well, uh," she stammered.

A large hand clamped down on her shoulder. Cara looked up to see Ryan standing beside her, his freckled face beaming with happiness—and maybe just a little extra Knob Creek bonhomie.

"What's this?" he asked.

"Honey, tell Cara she needs to stay and celebrate with us," Torie cooed.

"I was just fixin' to tell her that," Ryan said. He gestured around the tent.

"You made everything so awesome for us—now you need to stay and enjoy it for a while."

"Oh no, I really couldn't," Cara demurred. "You're very sweet to invite me, but honestly, my job is done here. And I wouldn't dream of imposing. . . ."

"It's not imposing," Ryan said. He pointed across the room. "Look. Layne's gonna hang around and party."

Layne Pelletier had shed her chef's jacket and was bellied up to the bar with a long-necked bottle of Sweetwater in her right hand. She saw Cara looking, and raised it in a salute.

"But Layne has to stay and make sure the dessert service and after-dinner drinks and the cake cutting go off," Cara protested. "That's nothing to do with me."

"That's just it," Torie admitted. "Mama and I would love it if you'd *at least* stay for the cake cutting. The photographer wants us all to have our flowers around the cake, just so . . . and nobody can make things look the way you can. . . ."

So . . . it wasn't *really* about having her stay to enjoy the party, Cara realized. It was just one more task Torie had assigned her florist. Resistance, she knew, was futile.

"Okay," she said wearily.

She fetched herself a glass of white wine from the bar, then sank down into a vacant seat at a table near the back of the tent, and watched as the party swirled around her.

Torie and Ryan's friends and family were a fun-loving bunch. They crowded the dance floor for every song, only thinning out long enough to allow Torie and Bill Fanning to have their traditional father-daughter spotlight dance to "The Way You Look Tonight."

It was nearly nine o'clock when Cara's rumbling stomach reminded her that she'd eaten nothing since breakfast. The orchestra had packed up and departed, and now a disc jockey was playing from the makeshift wooden bandstand. While the party went on, there was still a chance she could steal her dog back. Bert could just as easily style the flowers for the cake cutting.

She worked her way around the perimeter of the tent and was headed for the spot where Bert stood when Ryan spotted her.

He grabbed her by the hand and started dragging her toward the dance floor. "C'mon, Cara. They're playing our song."

"Ryan, you're sweet, but I'm the help. And the help doesn't dance at weddings."

"Sure they do," he said—just as Layne Pelletier boogied past with one of her waiters.

"Their" song was apparently KC and the Sunshine Band's "Shake Your Booty," and the next thing she knew, Cara had joined the line dance snaking its way across the dance floor, sliding, popping, and locking with the whole sweaty ensemble.

Finally, the song wound down and she began edging her way back toward Bert, but Ryan caught her by the waist.

"One more dance," he urged. The record was Harry Connick Jr.'s version of "It Had to Be You." "How're you not gonna dance to this?"

"Where's Torie?" Cara asked. "This is a song for the two of you."

"Nah. She's sitting out the next few numbers." Ryan looked around, then whispered, "She's uh, kind of, uh . . ."

"Pregnant?" Cara whispered back.

His grin lit up his face. "Yeah. It's pretty cool. She told you, huh?"

"She didn't have to," Cara said. "Congratulations."

For a guy who was built like a linebacker, Ryan was a surprisingly smooth dancer. He hummed along with the first few bars of the music.

"I wanted to thank you for everything you've done for us," he said, as they glided across the floor. "I know Torie's been kind of wound up these past few days. So thanks for putting up with all of us."

"All part of my job," Cara assured him.

"You mind me asking what's up with you and my brother?" Ryan asked. "He seemed pretty ticked off at you, back at the church."

"He stole my dog earlier today," Cara said.

"Yeah. You keep saying that. But that doesn't sound like Jack."

"Well, he did. Poppy ran away from the shop today, and when I went looking for her, I caught him dragging her down Jones Street. Now he's got Poppy, and he won't give her back."

"Why would Jack steal your dog? He's got a dog."

"He claims his dog ran away, and he spotted mine and so he stole her. But I know Poppy. There's not another dog in this town who looks like her. And he won't give her back."

"If you gave him half a chance he'd probably give you Shaz too. He's always complaining how much time she takes away from his work."

"What's your brother do for a living? Aside from stealing dogs?"

"Torie didn't tell you? Jack works with me, restoring historic properties. We're business partners."

"I saw the *historic property* he lives in on Macon Street today," Cara said, with a dismissive sniff. "No offense, but that place looks like a dump."

Ryan frowned. "Yeah, well, he sort of lost his momentum when Zoey left. Anyway, we've been working night and day to get my new house in Ardsley Park finished before Torie movies in. Jack does all the carpentry work. He's really a master craftsman."

"Who's Zoey? Not that I care."

"His ex-girlfriend," Ryan said. He was about to say more, but the song ended, and the DJ was moving through the crowd with a cordless mike.

"Torie Fanning Finnerty," he boomed. "Calling Torie and her bridesmaids. And I need all the single ladies here tonight. Single ladies—to the dance floor!"

"Thanks for the dance, Ryan." Cara managed a tight smile and began to head back to her table. But the groom grabbed her hand. "Not so fast. You heard the man. All the single ladies. That means you."

"Noooo," she wailed. "It's really not appropriate. . . ."

But her protest fell on deaf ears. Torie and her bridesmaids, eight strong, and at least sixty other women poured onto the dance floor, sweeping Cara along with them.

"Come on, Cara," Layne Pelletier coaxed, handing her an icy long-necked beer. "Time to cut loose!"

"What the hell," Cara said, taking a long swig of the beer. It went down good. Really good. And so it was that that she found herself doing her best Beyoncé moves, chanting along at the top of her lungs, "Ya shoulda put a ring on it. . . ."

When that song was winding down, Bert found her and handed her a glass of white wine. A recovering alcoholic, Bert didn't drink, but he'd apparently decided to join the fun, too, because he'd shed his staid blue blazer and tie, not to mention his shoes, and in just another minute she and Bert were breaking it down to "Brick House."

At some point, maybe after one of the other groomsmen—his name was Matt, or at least she thought his name was Matt—slow-danced with her to Ben E. King's "Stand By Me," it dawned on Cara that she was just a tiny bit buzzed.

She didn't hesitate when Ryan pulled her into the line dance for the Electric Slide. She slid and clapped and tapped and rocked and threw herself into the rhythm of the song. The dance was almost over. She was doing a pivot-turn when she came face-to-face with none other than Jack, the dognapper. She turned again, abruptly, and stumbled badly.

As luck would have it, the dance ended, and Ryan helped steady her.

"Having fun?" he asked.

Her face was flushed and her damp hair stuck to her forehead. "I am, but it still doesn't feel right. . . ."

But Ryan nimbly swung her into the next dance. The lights in the tent dimmed, and she heard Louis Armstrong's raspy version of "What a Wonderful World."

"You're a really good dancer," he said.

"Thanks, I used to . . ."

Before she knew it, Ryan was handing her off to another partner. His brother Jack.

"You!" Cara said, starting to pull away.

"Yes, me," Jack retorted. He clamped a hand around her waist, took her right hand in his, and pulled her close to his chest.

She wouldn't give him the satisfaction of breaking away. Right after this dance, she would sneak over to his place and liberate her puppy. For now, though, she floated along to the music. It was a nice song, after all, a nice senti-ment, for a nice wedding. She closed her eyes and almost managed to forget her partner's identity.

Almost. But she was all too aware of his proximity. His hand in hers was deeply callused. He was an even better dancer than his brother. One time, she raised her lashes just enough to see his face. When he wasn't scowling at her, he was downright good-looking.

The song wound down, but he kept his hand on her waist. She looked up in surprise.

"My mother's watching," he murmured. "She says I'm antisocial. Do me a favor and pretend like you're enjoying yourself, okay? For just another three minutes?"

Cara shrugged. Maybe, if she played nice, he'd relent and release her dog.

She heard a few bars of music, took a couple of tentative steps. But Jack stopped abruptly. "What the hell? Jimmy Buffett? Whose idea of a joke is this?" His spine stiffened. He dropped her hand, shook his head. "Sorry."

Without another word, he stalked off, leaving her alone, in the middle of the dance floor.

She stood in disbelief, watching him go.

6

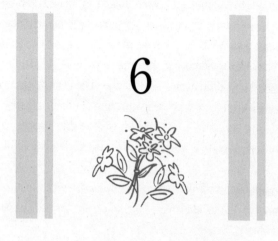

Jack hurried out of the tent, hoping to avoid the ever-watchful eyes of Torie—and his mother. By the time he made it to his truck, he'd stripped off the tux jacket, unknotted the tie, and ditched the cummerbund. He unlocked the door, slung the clothes inside, then slid onto the seat and kicked off those gawdawful shiny black lace-up shoes.

Once he was on the Skidaway Road, headed back toward town, he opened the truck windows and cranked up the radio. What a night! He'd only had one beer, but his head was throbbing. Weddings.

Shit.

All day Ryan had walked around with that goofy-ass grin on his face. And why? He'd just promised to love and obey a girl who would run his butt ragged for the rest of his life. So okay, even he had to admit Torie Fanning was one hot chick. But Ryan had dated lots of women just as hot as Torie, hotter even. Why this one?

Jack didn't get it. Never would. But then, his own history with the ladies wasn't exactly stellar.

Exhibit A: Zoey Ackerman. They'd met at a wedding. Jack had been a groomsman, Zoey was the bride's cousin. His face darkened at the memory of it. Nothing good ever happened at weddings. He'd been standing at the bar, waiting for a beer. A tall blonde sidled up, introduced herself. She was new in town, had just taken a job as a Pilates instructor at the Downtown Athletic Club, where Jack was a member at the time.

It had started as a little harmless flirtation. The next thing he knew, she'd moved into the Macon Street cottage with him. The one closet in the house was jammed with her stuff—not that Jack was exactly a snappy dresser, but it would have been good to have a hanger for his one decent pair of khakis and dress shirt.

In the beginning, it had all been good times. Zoey was great to look at, fun to be with, and yeah, the sex wasn't bad either. She termed the Macon Street cottage "adorable."

Two months in, though, everything began to change. Nothing pleased her. She hated his friends, his family, especially hated his job.

He'd come home late at night, covered in sawdust, his hair and face streaked with paint, and she'd make not-so-subtle cracks about manual labor. He had a college degree in business management, didn't he? Why couldn't he work at a nine-to-five desk job, with normal hours and sick days and profit sharing and vacation?

Nobody else had to work Saturdays or Sundays, or evenings—why did he?

He'd taken her to a job site—exactly once—to try to show her what it was he did for a living.

It had been one of those huge old Victorian mansions facing Forsyth Park. The place had been chopped up into ten apartments for college students in the 1980s, but the new owners, two retired doctors from Michigan, wanted it restored—to the standards that would qualify it for historic-preservation tax credits. He and Ryan spent six months totally rehabbing the place, gutting it down to the studs, installing all new, up-to-date plumbing, wiring, heat and air systems—then restoring the original horsehair-and-plaster walls, hardwood floors, everything.

Over the years, most of the original moldings and millwork had been destroyed, so Jack had spent hours and hours poring over photographs of houses from the same era, drawing up plans for the new moldings and woodwork, then painstakingly re-creating them. The crown moldings in the dining room, for example, included five different profiles.

Zoey had walked in with him that Saturday morning, sniffed, and wrinkled her nose. "Rat poop!"

She'd retreated to the truck and refused to ever set foot on one of his job sites again.

Maybe that's when he should have seen the handwriting on the wall. Instead, they'd hung on together for nearly a year. He probably wasn't the ideal boyfriend. He worked all the time, and when he wasn't working, he wanted to just chill at home, or maybe out at the beach. Zoey, on the other hand, wanted to go clubbing, or out to dinner, or maybe up to Atlanta to visit friends. He hated Atlanta, and he wasn't crazy about her friends, either. They'd nearly split up the night she brought home the dog.

It was January. He'd been busting his ass between two different job sites, including Ryan's house. He'd come home near midnight, to find Zoey sitting up in bed cuddling with what looked to him like a Muppets version of a dog.

"What's this?" he'd asked, eyeing the dog suspiciously.

"This is Princess Scheherazade of Betancourt," she'd trilled. "She's a pure-bred goldendoodle. Is she not the most precious thing you've ever seen?"

"Yeah, precious. What's she doing in my bed?"

In retrospect, this might not have been the ideal question to ask of a woman who was already deeply infatuated with a new puppy.

"She's mine. I mean, ours," Zoey said. Her pale blue eyes filled with tears. "I thought you loved dogs."

Christ!

"I love dogs. I think they're great. For people who have the time to spend with them. But I'm working fourteen-hour days and six-day weeks, and you're at the club all day. Who's gonna take care of her while we're at work?"

"I'll take care of her, of course, if you're going to be like that about it. But, I mean, you own the business, right? Why couldn't she go to work with you? She's great company." Zoey buried her face in the dog's fluffy coat. "Aren't you an angel? Aren't you good company?"

The dog lavished Zoey's face with a big sloppy kiss. Then it turned its big black button eyes toward Jack—and he could swear the damn thing grinned at him.

After that, the dog slept every night in the bed with them. Every night, she wedged her hot, hairy body in between him and Zoey. Every morning, he awoke to hot doggy breath in his face.

To be perfectly honest, they were at that point in the relationship where the only thing that was working was the sex. After Shaz? They didn't even have that.

Shaz. He glanced at his watch. She'd been locked up in the cottage all night. He was dead tired, but he'd need to take her out for a run as soon as he got home. It would feel good to get out of this damned monkey suit, lace up his running shoes, and work up an honest sweat.

He unlocked the front door, walked in, and stepped directly in what looked like a fresh piddle puddle.

He was shocked. Zoey had actually managed to housebreak the dog before she pulled her disappearing act. Shaz hadn't had an accident in months. And now this?

He fetched a wet rag from the kitchen and mopped up the mess. He'd sanded and stained the heart-pine floors back in the fall, but he'd never actually gotten around to sealing them. Which was a shame, because now he'd have to sand them down all over again.

"Shaz!" He glanced around the room. Kind of a depressing sight, reflected in the flickering blue light of the big screen. He'd turned on the television before leaving, something to give the dog company. He was pretty sure she liked ESPN and Animal Planet.

No sign of the dog. His stomach clenched. Had she somehow managed to get out? He'd locked all the doors earlier. He was really not in the mood tonight to go hunting for a runaway dog.

"Shaz?" He walked through the combination living-dining room, through the short hallway. He turned on the light in the bedroom. She was stretched out across the bed, with her head nesting on his pillow.

The dog lifted her muzzle and gave him a long, disdainful stare.

"Shaz!" His voice was sharp. "Come!"

Her tail thumped on the bedding, but she didn't budge.

He walked over to the bed and grabbed her by her collar. "Come on girl. Off the bed. You know the rules. No dogs in my bed."

It was a new rule, one he'd instituted as soon as Zoey walked out. Shaz had a big, oversized beanbag bed in the corner of the bedroom, and most nights, she was content to sleep there.

"Shaz?" His voice was stern. "Off!"

Thump. Thump. Thump.

"Did you pee on the floor, Shaz?"

Thump. Thump. Thump. She seemed downright proud of it.

He sighed, changed into a clean T-shirt and shorts, and laced up his running shoes. "C'mon, girl. Let's go work the kinks out."

Shaz blinked. She yawned. But she didn't budge.

Bert glanced over at Cara, who leaned against the window on the passenger side of the van.

"I'd say the wedding was an unqualified success, wouldn't you?"

"Mmm-hmm," Cara said, her eyes half closed. "Thanks for being my designated driver. I'll take you back out to the Fannings' in the morning for your car."

"Lillian actually hugged me tonight. So did Torie."

"Mmm-hmm."

"I gave out a bunch of our business cards at the wedding. Three of Torie's bridesmaids are engaged."

That got her attention. She sat up straight for a moment. "Really? Which ones?"

"Alison? The little blonde. And the taller blonde? The one they call Chatty? Oh, and Brenna, the supertanned brunette. She actually got engaged tonight, to one of Ryan's fraternity brothers."

"That's great," Cara said. "Anybody mention actual wedding dates?"

"Not to me," Bert said. "But all three of them swore they want you to do their flowers."

"I just hope they call," Cara said. "We don't have a lot lined up for the fall."

"We will," Bert said, ever loyal. "You always get panicky this time of year, and we always have more work than we can handle, come fall."

"You never can tell, though," Cara cautioned him. "Remember how dead it was last October?"

"And then we had weddings booked every weekend in November, through May," Bert said. "Can't you just relax a little? Everything is going to work out."

"I can't afford to relax," Cara said. "I owe the Colonel twenty thousand dollars. And on top of that, I checked my email back at the wedding, while you were out breaking it down on the dance floor. Bernice Bradley emailed me to let me know she wants to renew our lease. I've been going month to month for a while now—and when we renew, our rent is going up to nearly double what we pay now."

"What? That's crap! The Bradleys haven't touched the place in years. Your ceiling leaks upstairs, and the plumbing keeps backing up...."

"I know," Cara said, shaking her head. "But they've got me by the short hairs. They know it's a great location. Where else am I going to find that much square footage downtown—and with its own parking space? And with the apartment upstairs, it's perfect for me."

"I think you should call their bluff," Bert said, steering the van down Skidaway Road. "Call your real-estate agent, ask her to put out some feelers for another location. Let the Bradleys get wind of that. Look at all the improvements you've made to their property. You're probably the best tenant they've ever had. I bet they'd hate to lose you."

"But I'd hate it even more—if I have to move. It's perfect visibility—so close to the biggest downtown churches."

"What about that storefront on Bull? Where the antique shop used to be? Now, that's a great location. Tons of traffic."

"And no parking. I looked at that space the last time it became vacant. There's a reason why no business stays there longer than a year. If my brides can't find a place to park, they'll drive right on up the road to another florist shop."

"Never," Bert said. "These girls want a Bloom wedding. You've got the look they love, Cara."

"Today," she muttered. "But all that can change in the blink of an eye. These brides are all incredibly fickle. Everybody wants the next cool, hip look. And if I don't stay right on top of my game, I'll be yesterday's news."

She'd dozed off. It was nearly midnight. Bert parked the van in the space in back of the shop, then reached over and gently shook her shoulder.

"Cara? We're home."

She yawned and looked out the window at the poorly lit lane. "God. For a minute there, I almost forgot about Poppy. That horrible man still has her."

Bert cocked one eyebrow. "You seemed to be having a nice time dancing with that horrible man, earlier this evening. You two were getting pretty close, it looked like to me."

"He's a lunatic," Cara said. "Did you see what he did? Left me standing in the middle of the dance floor! One minute we were dancing—and the next, he just stopped cold. Walked off and left, after mumbling something about Jimmy fucking Buffett."

"I did see him leave. I figured you'd picked a fight with him," Bert said.

"I never said a word. I thought he might relent and hand Poppy over to me if I played nice. Dumb idea."

"What can you do now? I mean, if he won't give her back?"

"I'll take her back," Cara said, yawning. "He stole her from me, so I'll steal her back from him."

"How exactly do you steal your own dog?" Bert asked.

"Not sure," she admitted. "But I'm going over there to case the joint. Just as soon as I chug a Red Bull."

"Right now? It's midnight, Cara. What if he calls the cops?"

"He won't. And they won't come anyway. Remember, I tried to get them involved earlier, and they flat refused."

"I think you'd better wait till morning. I know that block. It's kind of sketchy at night. And what if his neighbors see you and think you're trying to break in? You'd be the one getting hauled off to the pokey."

"You could go with me. Ride shotgun?"

"Sorry. No can do. I've got plans tonight."

Cara gave him an appraising look. "What kind of plans?"

"I'm meeting somebody for a drink."

"Somebody. As in a guy?"

"Maybe."

"Bert Rosen! Are you hooking up with somebody you just met tonight? At the wedding?"

He looked insulted. "It's not a hookup. It's just a drink. An innocent drink."

"Who is he? Do I know him? Did I meet him?"

"You don't actually know him, but you did meet. He's actually one of Ryan's fraternity brothers."

"You're kidding." Cara giggled despite her weariness. "You're telling me one of Ryan Finnerty's frat-tastic macho buddies is actually gay?"

"Shh. He's not officially out. At least not to Ryan."

Cara opened her door and climbed down out of the van. "If you won't go with me, I guess I'll have to wait until tomorrow morning. But I'm telling you right now, if he doesn't hand over Poppy—I might do something radical."

"Go get some sleep," Bert advised. "I'll go over there with you myself in the morning before we go get my car and we'll storm the castle together."

It was the first night she'd spent alone in her apartment without Poppy, and now the apartment was eerily quiet without her.

Cara undressed quickly. She washed her face and pulled on a well-worn oversized T-shirt and climbed into bed. It had been a long, busy day, and she was exhausted, but she couldn't sleep. The bed seemed too big without Poppy stretched out on the other side of it. So she got up and arranged herself on the sofa in her combination living-dining room.

The living room's big bay window looked out on the street. She heard cars driving slowly down the brick street, heard doors opening and closing, her neighbors, two SCAD art students, laughing and talking as they came home from one of their customary late nights.

Finally, she drifted off to sleep, maybe around three? She wasn't sure.

Sunday. It was the one day of the week Jack Finnerty allowed himself the luxury of sleeping in. He was asleep, in a near-coma stage, when his cell phone rang. Blindly, he reached toward the packing-crate nightstand. The phone fell to the floor, but it kept ringing.

Jack leaned over the edge of the bed and groped around on the floor. Finally, his fingers closed on the phone. He thumbed the On button. Three-thirty in the friggin' morning. The number on the caller ID wasn't familiar. A wrong number at three-thirty in the morning? He tossed the phone back onto the nightstand, turned over, and tried to go back to sleep.

But the phone was ringing again. He snatched it up, prepared to give this loser an earful. He wasn't prepared for what he got instead.

It was Zoey.

"Dammit, Jack," she cried. "What the hell are you thinking?"

"I'm thinking it's nearly four in the fuckin' morning," Jack said, his voice thick with sleep. "What do you want, Zoey?"

"I want to know why you didn't let me know you managed to lose Scheherazade," Zoey demanded.

Jack rose up on one elbow and looked over at the dog asleep on her bed, not far from his own. Well, really his bed was nothing more than a mattress and boxspring. But still.

"Shaz is right here," he said, yawning. "Have you and Jiminy Cricket been getting into some of that California weed?"

"His name is Jamey, and for your information, just because he's a musician, does not mean that he is a dope fiend, not that it's any of your business," she retorted. "And I'd just love to know how my dog can be in two places at one time."

"I still don't know what you're talking about," Jack said, flopping backward onto the bed.

"I got a call earlier tonight from Dr. Katz's office, telling me that somebody found Shaz running loose on Victory Drive. Thank heavens, some good Samaritan picked her up and took her to the vet's office. They recognized her immediately, of course, but then they checked the microchip just to be sure, and they called me."

That got his attention. He sat straight up in the bed and turned on the lamp. Now the dog was awake, too. Her ears pricked up, and her nose was quivering, as though she knew she was being discussed.

"Zoey? Are you telling me that the dog sitting right here in this bedroom is not Shaz?" He buried his head in his hands. The dog edged closer and licked his ear.

Her voice was shrill. "I don't have any idea who or what you've got in your bedroom, Jack Finnerty, but yes, I am telling you that Scheherazade is being boarded at Dr. Katz's office tonight. The vet tech said it's a miracle she didn't get hit by a car, crossing all that traffic on Abercorn Street. No thanks to you."

"You're saying Shaz is at the vet's office?"

"Jack! Have you heard a single word I've said? Yes! I am telling you Dr. Katz has Shaz. See? You never listen to me, Jack. This is just one more example. . . ."

He turned his head and was staring directly into the dog's unblinking eyes.

"Poppy?"

The dog tilted its head and thumped its tail on the scarred wooden floor.

"Christ," Jack moaned. "You really are Poppy."

"Have you got a woman there, Jack?" Zoey asked.

As if.

"None of your damned business," he growled.

"Scheherazade is a very valuable dog, Jack," Zoey went on. "The breeder said once she's old enough to breed, her puppies could fetch as much as two thousand dollars. So I don't appreciate your letting her wander around town without so much as a collar."

"I didn't let her *do* anything," Jack said. "I was taking her to that groomer of yours, who she detests, by the way, and she jumped out the window of my truck. I went looking for her and found another goldendoodle wandering down the lane behind West Charlton. I naturally assumed she was Shaz, so I tied a rope around her neck and walked her back home. What I didn't know, since you couldn't be bothered to tell me, was that I'd actually dognapped somebody else's dog. A very angry somebody, who tried to sic the cops on me."

"Not my problem," Zoey said airily.

"Actually, it is your problem, since Shaz is your dog," Jack pointed out.

That shut her up. At least momentarily. Any other woman would have been feeling painfully guilty by now, for abandoning her lover and her seven-month-old puppy, to run off to California the day after hooking up with a Jimmy Buffett impersonator she'd just met at a bar on River Street. A guy who called himself Jamey Buttons, for God's sake.

But Zoey was not just any other woman.

"You told me you wanted a dog," Zoey said accusingly.

"And you told me you loved me and wanted to have my children someday," Jack said. "And just for the record? The dog I wanted was a black lab, not some funny-looking designer dog."

"I'm not going to let you put a big guilt trip on me, Jack," Zoey said. "I actually wanted to let you know that Jamey has a gig playing on a cruise ship out of Fort Lauderdale for the next three months, and I've signed on to be the ship's Pilates instructor. I'll send for Scheherazade when we get back. Probably in August."

"Yippee," Jack said bitterly. "Bye, Zoey."

"Wait, Jack," she said quickly. "Don't forget, you've got to pick Shaz up by noon, or pay an extra day's boarding fee. As it is, you already owe them seventy dollars."

7

Jack tried, but couldn't get back to sleep. Poppy was no help. She rested her muzzle on the edge of the mattress, watching him with her big, sad puppy eyes. He turned away, facing the wall, but he could feel Poppy's warm breath on his neck.

Finally, he relented. He flipped back over and scratched under her chin. "There. Okay? Now can we get some sleep around here?"

Maybe he couldn't sleep because he was dreading the coming morning. And seeing Poppy's owner again.

The woman was a pistol, for sure. Her name was Cara Kryzik, Ryan told him. She wasn't bad-looking, if you went for that kind of look. Which he didn't. He'd always enjoyed blondes: tall, cool, athletic blondes. Like Zoey.

This Cara person, on the other hand, was the opposite of his type. She had shoulder-length, flyaway not-quite-brown, not-quite-blond hair. Big brown eyes that glittered dangerously when she was pissed off, a heart-shaped face, high cheekbones, and full, pink, lips that reminded him of overblown roses.

She dressed funny, too. That night, at the wedding, she'd worn an old-fashioned-looking pink silk rig that looked more like a nightgown, with its lacy inset bodice. She'd somehow managed to look sexy and demure at the same time, although he totally didn't get how that look worked with pink cowboy boots.

Every time he'd turned around at the reception, she'd been right there in his face, telling him off, demanding that he return her dog.

His lamebrain brother, Ryan, found the whole scenario highly entertaining. But then, Ryan had notoriously eccentric taste in women. Take Torie, for instance.

"She's worth the trouble," Ryan said, when Jack pointed out the differences in their personalities. "I like a woman with fire." Especially, he'd added, "in bed."

It had been Ryan who'd coaxed Cara into dancing, despite her protests. His brother was a consummate party animal. He'd danced with almost all the women at the reception, including the seven-year-old flower girl, most of the bridesmaids, and their arthritic aunt Betty.

And he'd forced Jack onto the dance floor, too.

"You're my best man," he'd informed Jack, who would have preferred to melt into the woodwork. "It's on the list of duties. Right up there with planning the bachelor party and making the first toast."

So Jack had danced with their mother, he'd danced with Aunt Betty, he'd danced with Torie, and he'd even, at one point, been tricked into dancing with Cara Kryzik.

Torie had dragged him from the safety of the bar to do some stupid line dance, and he'd somehow ended up right beside Cara, who glowered at him with undisguised venom. Two dances later, Ryan shoved him into Cara's clutches.

It was a slow dance. She was a decent dancer, and she actually felt pretty good in his arms, with his hand sliding over the smooth pink silk, and the warm, sun-browned skin of her back and bare arms. Her figure was full and rounded in the right places. She wore the lightest of perfumes and her hair smelled faintly of cherries.

But then it happened. Louie Armstrong's wonderful world ended, and the DJ was playing "Come Monday."

He felt his face flush and his feet grow leaden. She'd looked up at him in shock. And that was that. Jimmy fuckin' Buffett. He'd fled like a thief in the night.

Smooth move, he told himself now, reliving that moment. Real smooth move, Ace.

So, just to recap. He'd stolen this woman's dog. Called the cops on her, accused her of stalking, insulted her, and then abandoned her in the middle of a dance.

She, in turn, had called him a jerk and a liar. She was moody and dressed weird, and according to Ryan, she was just coming off a lousy divorce and seemed to hate all men, with the exception of her gay assistant.

He flopped over on his other side, facing away from the still-vigilant Poppy. Tomorrow morning, first thing, he would have to return the dog and face her wrath.

8

Cara heard a buzzing from somewhere far away. Still dead asleep, she flung an arm in the general vicinity of the nightstand, searching for the alarm, to shut it off. She slapped wildly in the direction of the clock, but the buzzing wouldn't stop.

Annoyed, she flopped over, opened one eye, and stared at the clock. It wasn't buzzing. And she hadn't set it. But something, somewhere, was buzzing. And at eight o'clock on a Sunday morning. Her doorbell?

Cara jumped out of bed, wide-eyed and startled. Who would be ringing her bell that early on a Sunday?

She stumbled over to the window and looked down at the street below. A man stood by the recessed entry to the apartment. He had a big, fluffy white dog on a leash.

Poppy!

Cara flew down the wooden staircase, barefoot, dressed only in her sleep shirt. She unlatched the chain guard and flipped the deadbolt.

Jack Finnerty stood on the street just outside her door. He wore paint-spattered jeans, a faded T-shirt, and a look that could best be described as sheepish.

"Uh, well, here's your dog."

"Poppy!"

The dog stood up on her hind legs, put her front paws on Cara's hips, and shook all over with joy. Cara wrapped her arms around the dog. "I missed you! You bad, bad girl. I missed you so much. I hardly slept last night, worrying about you."

"Yeah, uh, she didn't get much sleep either," Jack volunteered. "Look, I'm really sorry about this. I've been a jerk. I should have listened to you yesterday."

"Yes," Cara said severely. "You should have. And yes, you were a jerk. And worse."

"You're right," he said, staring down at his shoes. "And I apologize."

"Where's your dog?" she asked, sticking her head out the door and looking around.

"At home. Now. After she jumped out of my truck yesterday, she made it all the way to Victory Drive and Abercorn. A woman managed to corral her and she took her to the vet, and they recognized her. Shaz is chipped, so they read the chip, just to be sure, and called the owner."

"You," she said accusingly.

Jack winced. "My ex. Shaz technically belongs to her. But she's out in California, so Shaz is mine. Sorta. The vet called Zoey yesterday to let her know Shaz had been found. But Zoey, being Zoey, decided to torture me by not calling me until three this morning."

Cara looked him over. His hair was mussed and there were dark circles under his eyes, so it was apparent he'd gotten about as much sleep as she had.

"Look." Jack's voice was low. "I really am sorry. Truly. Your dog looks almost exactly like Shaz. But if I hadn't been such a prick, I would have looked closer and realized I had the wrong dog. Especially since when I got home last night, I discovered she'd peed all over my hardwood floors. Shaz is housebroken. Your dog, on the other hand, is fairly neurotic, but I guess you already know that."

"Neurotic! She is not," Cara said sharply. "And Poppy is housebroken. She never pees at home. She was probably traumatized by being dognapped. And then left alone in a strange house for hours and hours."

"Whatever," Jack said. "I better get back to Shaz. She's been penned up in a crate at the vet's office all night, and right now she's probably not too happy with me either."

"Thank you for bringing Poppy back," Cara said coolly. "She's home now, and that's all that matters."

"Have you had her microchipped?" Jack asked.

"No. I keep meaning to, but running my own business . . ."

"You should do it right away, especially since she seems to be such an escape artist," he suggested.

"I know how to take care of my own dog," Cara said, bristling. "Maybe you should do a better job of taking care of your own, especially since she got all the way to Abercorn and Victory."

"Riiight." Jack's lips were clamped tightly in anger. "Anyway, see ya."

She took great satisfaction in slamming the door in his face. "Not if I see you first, jerk," she muttered. Poppy whined, and Cara knelt down on the floor and hugged her tightly. "Don't ever do that again, you hear me?"

Still kneeling, she gazed out the sidelights as Jack walked rapidly down Jones Street.

"Horrible man," she told Poppy. "I feel sorry for his real dog. No wonder she ran away from home."

She sniffed the top of Poppy's head and scratched under her chin. In addition to her puppy smell and the special rose-scented dog shampoo Cara bathed her with, there was a whiff of something else. Cara sniffed again, and recognized the scent.

"Sawdust?" she said, wrinkling her nose and holding Poppy at arm's length. "Really?"

9

There were days when Cara hated Savannah. No matter its lofty ambitions of being the Paris of the South, Savannah was still a very small town. Everybody who counted in the town's complicated social structure knew everybody else—and their business.

She chafed at Savannah's insularity, its petty small-town politics, and its collective suspicion of anything or anybody new or "from away." She'd tried hard to lose what she thought was only a faint Midwestern accent, but whenever she spoke to a local they invariably demanded to know where she was from.

On the other hand, sometimes that economy of scale worked in her favor. It had taken months for word of mouth to spread about Cara's flowers, and even then, it had only happened courtesy of a timid little bride named Kristin Marie Manley.

Somehow, Kristin had stumbled across Cara's cluttered little flower shop, back when she was still transitioning from Flowers by Norma. She hadn't even put up her pink and white awning, or changed the sign, so as far as the world knew, good old Norma Poole was still turning out big, bunchy arrangements of gladiolus and leatherleaf ferns.

Kristin was newly engaged to the son of a prominent Savannah banker. She'd been raised by her widower father, and the two of them were clueless about what was involved in putting on a big society wedding. So Cara had taken her in hand, spent hours and hours with her, and with a laughably spare budget had still managed to pull off one of the prettiest, most meaningful weddings she had ever planned.

As luck would have it, Kristin's new mother-in-law, Vicki Cooper, loved the flowers she'd done for her son's wedding, and absolutely adored Cara. Vicki was on the board of half a dozen Savannah charities and foundations, and within a year of Kristin's wedding to Cason Cooper, thanks to Vicki, Bloom was finally, slowly, starting to blossom.

Vicki, bless her generous, loudmouthed soul, was the gift that kept on giving.

Torie Fanning had been a Vicki connection—and on this steamy Monday morning in May, Cara had an appointment with yet another of Vicki's acquaintances.

Cara had heard from Vicki just the previous week. As usual, Vicki was on her way to yet another of her endless meetings.

"Listen, Cara, sugar, you're going to be hearing from a dear friend of mine, and I just want to give you a heads-up. Marie Trapnell's daughter Brooke just got engaged to the oldest Strayhorn boy, Harris. You know the Strayhorns, right?"

"Mmm, the name is familiar. Do they have something to do with shipping?"

"You could say that. Honey, Mitchell Strayhorn *is* Strayhorn Shipping. And of course, the Trapnells have been around Savannah since forever. I adore Marie Trapnell, and I know you'll be extra nice to her, 'cause she's goin' through kind of a hard time right now. Okay? Gotta scoot. Stay sweet, you hear?"

Cara fixed a pitcher of geranium-scented iced tea, filled two tumblers with ice, and arranged a few sugar cookies on a silver tray on her worktable. She placed her photo album on the table, then went over to the cooler and grabbed a handful of flowers—some daisies, a sprig of blue verbena, and some red bee balm.

These she clipped and stuffed in the sterling bud vase that had been her grandmother's.

The bells on the shop door tinkled, and a pale, nervous-looking woman stood looking uncertainly around the room.

"Mrs. Trapnell?" Cara hurried toward her, but Poppy bounded into the room, nearly knocking the poor woman on her butt.

"Poppy, down!" Cara cried. "Bad girl!"

"Oh, she's all right," the woman said, her voice soft. She stroked Poppy's ears and looked up at Cara. "What a beautiful dog. What breed is she?"

"She's a goldendoodle. A very disobedient, undisciplined cross between what's called a cream English golden retriever and a standard poodle," Cara said. "But please don't judge the breed by Poppy. I'm afraid I haven't been very effective at training her."

"She's just high-spirited, is all." The woman extended her hand. "I'm Marie Trapnell. Vicki Cooper's friend? And you're Cara—how do I pronounce your last name?"

"'Krizzik'—the 'y' is soft," Cara said. "It's always good to meet one of Vicki's friends, Mrs. Trapnell. She seems to know everybody in Savannah, doesn't she?"

"Please, call me Marie. Yes, Vicki does know an astonishing number of people. I don't know how she juggles all her charitable and social commitments. I get exhausted just looking at one week of her calendar."

Cara guided Marie Trapnell to the worktable, seated her, and poured two glasses of iced tea.

"So," she said, once Marie seemed comfortable. "Vicki tells me your daughter just got engaged. What an exciting time for you."

Marie's face flushed softly with happiness. Now that she was sitting across the table from her, Cara realized the mother of the bride was probably much younger than she'd initially estimated. She was fair-complected, with intelligent brown eyes, a short, straight nose, and poker-straight shoulder-length graying brown hair pushed back from her high forehead with a tortoiseshell hair band. Her clothes were obviously expensive—a little nothing sleeveless cotton shift in a sedate pastel print, low-heeled pumps, and a Ferragamo hand-bag. She wore pearl stud earrings, but no other jewelry.

"Brooke wanted to come with me to meet you, but she had a client meeting she couldn't get out of. She's a second-year associate at Farrell Wynant Hanra-han," Marie said.

"Have they set the wedding date?" Cara asked, opening her day planner.

"Oh yes," Marie said. "And that's what's giving me heart palpitations. They're getting married in less than eight weeks."

"Oh my," Cara said. "That doesn't give us much time, does it?"

"It gives me *no* time," Marie agreed. "I've tried and tried to get Brooke and Harris to move the date at least to October, but Harris is adamant. July sixth it is, and he refuses to discuss any other date."

"Well . . ." Cara turned to the July page of her calendar. She had weddings every Saturday of the month, and several big debutante parties later that month. But a big black X had been drawn through the notes she'd scribbled there.

"Ahh, yes," Cara said, tapping the X with a fingertip. "I did have a wedding scheduled on the sixth, but I'm afraid it's been called off."

"Oh." Marie looked startled. "Oh, how sad."

Marie would never know just how sad Cara was about that canceled wed-ding. Hannah Draper's daddy had major bucks, and only one daughter. But just two weeks earlier, Hannah had come home from her senior year at Welles-ley and announced a change of plans. Hannah, it seemed, had discovered her true sexual leanings, and was deliriously in love with her field-hockey coach.

Thank God, Cara was thinking, she'd been firm about that nonrefundable fifty percent deposit on the flowers. And thank God, again, that this new bride wanted the only open Saturday she had for July.

"Was your daughter able to book a church on such short notice?" Cara knew that all the big downtown churches, Christ Church, Independent Presby-terian, St. John's Episcopal, Wesley Monumental, First Baptist, and the Cathe-dral of St. John the Baptist, were all always booked up for summer weddings as far as two years in advance. She knew of at least one bride, Leigh-Anne

Grady, whose mother had booked her wedding at Christ Church two months before dear Leigh-Anne had actually gotten engaged.

Marie fiddled with one of her pearl earrings. "The church isn't the problem. We're actually going to have the ceremony and the reception at Cabin Creek— the Strayhorns' plantation in South Carolina."

"Ahh," Cara said, trying to contain her excitement. She'd seen photos of Cabin Creek in numerous magazines. It was a working rice plantation on twelve hundred acres, just across the river from Savannah. From the photographs it looked like the main house would make Tara look like a bait shack.

In her mind, Cara was already designing the flower arrangements for Cabin Creek's high-ceilinged entrance hall. She'd have to meet the bride very soon, to discover her flower and color preferences. Was she a brunette like her mother?

"Um, Cara?"

"Oh, sorry. Marie, I've got so many questions. When do you think Brooke will be available to meet with me? And what about Harris? And his mother? Since it's their home, will they want to be consulted?"

"Harris?" Marie looked blank. "Do you usually talk to the grooms? I guess it didn't occur to me. . . ."

"It just depends on the couple. Some grooms like to be consulted on every detail of the event, while with others—and I will say this is the majority—all they care about is what kind of beer is served at the reception."

"Well, uh, Harris probably falls into the latter group," Marie said. "Anyway, he travels a good bit for business, and according to Brooke, all he cares about is that everything is tasteful. Libba Strayhorn, that's Harris's mother, has already said she's happy for me to plan everything." She gave Cara a dubious shrug. "Libba is very horsey. According to Harris, she'd live in the stables at Cabin Creek if she could."

"I have to admit, it's sort of overwhelming," Marie went on. "I've never had to plan a wedding before. I eloped, you see. Anyway, I'd really hoped Brooke could join us this morning. To tell you the truth, I didn't even know where to begin. I was just talking to Vicki about that last week—we're both on the literacy-council board, and she insisted that you would be the perfect person to help us."

"Vicki has been very kind to me," Cara said. "I've done weddings for several of her friends in town."

"That's what she said. In fact, I was at Torie Fanning's wedding Saturday night. I thought everything was absolutely beautiful."

"I'm glad," Cara said. "Maybe we could start there. Was there anything in particular at Torie's wedding that you liked—or even disliked?"

"Well . . . I loved all those hydrangeas. So old-fashioned. But Brooke is a very modern girl. I'm not sure she'd share my opinion."

Cara flipped open the cover of her photo album. "These are photos of some of my weddings over the past few years. Most of these are in my portfolio on my website, so hopefully, you and Brooke could look through it and see if there are any flowers or styles or colors that speak to you."

Marie nodded. "That sounds like a good idea. All I have to do is manage to get Brooke to slow down for an hour or so to think about the wedding."

"What about her gown?" Cara asked. "It would be helpful if I had a photo of it—and also of her bridesmaids' gowns."

"Her gown." Marie said it like a sigh. "She hasn't bought one yet."

"Really?" Cara raised one eyebrow. "Is she aware that it can take as long as three months to order a gown, get it delivered and fitted?"

"How well I know," Marie said. "This daughter of mine—she can be unbelievably stubborn. She's looked in magazines, shopped in Atlanta, tried on dozens and dozens of gowns, but so far she says the dress—the magic dress, she calls it—hasn't grabbed her. I want to grab *her*—around the throat," she said apologetically.

"Can she wear a dress off the rack?" Cara asked, which was a tactful way of asking if the MIA bride was a standard size.

"She's a size six, so I don't think it will be too hard to fit her," Marie said. "But I'd feel so much better if she could just choose something . . . anything."

Cara scribbled a note to herself on her notepad, then looked back at Marie. "Bridesmaids? How many?"

"One. Just one maid of honor. Harris's sister Holly."

"Does Holly have a dress? Do we know what color?"

Marie rolled her eyes. "Brown. For a July wedding. It seems all wrong to me. Does a brown dress sound as awful to you as it does to me?"

"Wellll . . ." Cara flipped a couple of pages of the photo album. "It depends on how brown the brown dress is. For instance, the right shade can be flattering—and brown is a wonderful foil for pale pink flowers." She tapped a fingertip on a photo of a wedding she'd done the previous October. "See?"

Marie opened the gold clasp of her pocketbook, pulled out a pair of horn-rimmed reading glasses, and peered down at the photo. "Oh. Hmm. But this was a fall wedding, wasn't it? And the girl—the bridesmaid—she was a blond. Holly is a strawberry blond."

"You've got a point there," Cara said. "But can you talk Brooke and Holly out of a brown dress for a July wedding?"

"Probably not."

"Then we'll figure out a way to make it work."

Marie smiled and closed the book. "Vicki was right. I do like you." She bit her lip and looked out the window of the shop.

"But?" Cara asked, waiting for the other shoe to drop.

"It's not up to me. Not completely."

"Of course, I understand totally," Cara said. "When do you think Brooke can make time to meet with me?"

"Not Brooke," Marie said quietly. "Her father."

10

Marie Trapnell was flipping the pages of the wedding photo album, avoiding Cara's eyes.

"Gordon—my ex-husband—has been very clear that he wants to be completely involved in the planning of Brooke's wedding."

"That's very . . . sweet," Cara said, trying to tread carefully. "I guess he and Brooke must be very close?"

"At one time Brooke was an absolute daddy's girl. Since the divorce, well, Brooke is conflicted. She feels loyalty to me, I think, and she's still angry at her father. And her new stepmother."

Marie's eyes flickered with something resembling emotion. "We are *all* still angry at Gordon. Nevertheless, Gordon is adamant that if he is to pay for this wedding he has to have complete veto power."

"I see." Cara had done lots of weddings for brides and grooms with divorced parents. It was never particularly easy, but the upcoming Trapnell-Strayhorn nuptials were already sounding like a major pain in the posterior.

"Would your ex-husband like to meet with me? Or would he prefer to wait until we come up with some kind of a proposal and a budget?"

Marie was fidgeting with her other earring now. "I should warn you,

Gordon is interviewing other florists. He seems to think that's how you plan a wedding. Brooke has tried to reason with him, but, well, Gordon does things his own way."

"I appreciate your letting me know that." Cara closed the photo album. "To be honest, Marie, I have a pretty busy summer coming up. I appreciate your honesty, and your interest in working with me, but if your ex wants to hire somebody else, well, maybe I'm not the right person for you."

"No!" Marie's voice was sharp. "You're the exact right florist for our wedding. Please don't bow out. I've seen your photo album, I was at Torie's wedding. I know you'll give Brooke something lovely and memorable. I'll have Brooke look at your website, but I know she'll love your work. And then, maybe she can talk some sense into her daddy. If he'll listen to anybody, he'll listen to her."

"Of course," Cara said. "Talk it over with Brooke. Have her look at my portfolio. But do keep in mind that time is really running very short for a July wedding. If I'm going to do a good job, I'll need some kind of a commitment from you—by the end of the week. Does that sound reasonable?"

"Very reasonable." Marie stood and straightened the nonexistent wrinkles in her dress.

Cara nodded. "Just out of curiosity—do you happen to know what other florists your ex-husband is interviewing?"

Marie chewed her bottom lip. "It's just one florist. Somebody Patricia met at a wedding in Charleston. I don't actually know his name. Just that he's very well known, and considered very chic. I believe he's just opened a shop here in Savannah. I think he and Patricia have become bosom buddies."

"And Patricia is?"

Marie's brown eyes narrowed. "Gordon's new wife."

As soon as the would-be new client left, Bert popped his head out of the back room, where he'd been getting hospital orders ready for delivery. He rubbed his hands together in the manner of a cartoon villain. "Oooh. Drama."

Cara laughed. "Which I don't especially need in my life right now."

Poppy edged over to Bert and rubbed up against his legs.

"Hello, Miss Thang," Bert said, obligingly scratching the dog's ears. "When did you come home?"

"Yesterday morning. It seems her captor discovered his own dog at his vet's office. He showed up here at eight yesterday morning, looking pretty embarrassed."

"Good for him," Bert said. "Poppy doesn't seem any worse for the wear, right?"

"Guess not," she admitted. "I had to give her a bath just to get rid of the smell of sawdust. And I don't ever want to go through a night like that again."

"Tell me about our new client. Obviously, I was eavesdropping from the back room. But I came in late. Who is she, and where did she come from?"

"Another of Vicki Cooper's friends. Her name is Marie Trapnell, and her daughter is marrying one of the Strayhorns."

"Big money marrying big money. Me likey," Bert said. "But the ex-husband has to approve you? And he's interviewing another florist? What is up with that?"

"Sounds like another control freak. Which I would just as soon avoid. Marie seems like a very nice person, but I honestly won't mind when they choose somebody else."

"Wait just a second," Bert protested. "Why wouldn't they choose you?"

"You heard the woman, right? The daddy wants some hotshot florist from Charleston. I guess this guy just decided to expand into Savannah."

Bert moved over to the laptop, and his long, tanned fingers began to fly over the keyboard. "Hang on, I'm Googling."

A moment later he looked up. "Well, his name is Cullen Kane, and from the look of his website, he has quite the business. Big-ass shop on Tradd Street, and he's had lots of events published—*Town and Country, Charleston Magazine, Garden and Gun,* and on and on. He just expanded to Savannah last month. Opened a little outpost on Habersham Street."

Cara's curiosity got the better of her. "Let me see that thing." She peered over Bert's shoulder at the website. The opening page was an extreme closeup of a mouthwateringly beautiful all-white bride's bouquet, featuring velvety magnolia blossoms, crinum lilies, orange blossoms, and stephanotis.

She paged over to Cullen Kane's portfolio, which featured dozens of achingly gorgeous photographs of his flowers showcased in all kinds of settings.

Bert clicked the mouse on the About Us tab of the website, and read his bio aloud in a deeply accented Southern cartoon voice that made him sound like Foghorn Leghorn.

Cullen Kane is a native Charlestonian. He received his undergraduate degree in English Literature from the College of Charleston. Cullen spent his senior year abroad in England, where he met and studied floral design for three years under famed horticulturist Rosemary Verey. Returning to the States, Cullen settled in Napa Valley, California, where he became the in-house floral designer for Valleyview House, the largest private event venue in Napa. In 2008, Cullen returned home to Charleston, where he opened Cullen Kane Floral Design Studio.

"Here's a photo of him," Bert said, tapping the laptop screen.

"Oh shit," Cara said.

The photo of Cullen Kane showed him lounging in an artistically weathered Adirondack chair, with a stretch of the low-country marsh in the background. He was dressed in an open-necked white dress shirt, with a celadon-green sweater knotted casually over his shoulders. His glossy blond hair was worn stylishly long, he had a small goatee, and his hand rested lightly on a Cavalier King Charles spaniel in his lap. He was a candy-coated cinematic version of everything a Southern gentleman should look like.

"I'd hire him if I weren't me," Cara said glumly.

"He's certainly yummy-looking," Bert agreed. "You know, if you go in for that kind of screamingly effeminate, highly overqualified overachieving type. But if he's such a hotshot in Charleston, why would he want to open shop in Savannah?"

"To make my life a living hell," she said.

Bert laughed. "That's right, Cara. Cullen Kane hasn't even met you and he's already conspiring to put you out of business and ruin your life. Are we feeling just the teeniest bit paranoid this morning?"

Monday was technically Cara's day off, but she hadn't hesitated to schedule the appointment with Marie Trapnell.

Now Poppy was standing by the door, scratching to go out.

"I'll take her if you like," Bert offered.

"Thanks, but it'll do me good to stretch my legs," Cara said. She grabbed Poppy's leash and clipped it to her collar, which she'd already shortened by a notch.

"Now listen," she told the puppy, who was already straining at her leash as they exited the shop. "Slow down. Heel. We've really got to work on this obedience thing, you know."

It was a spectacular late-spring morning. The sky was blue, and a slight breeze stirred the Spanish moss draping the live-oak trees.. She gave Poppy a little slack in her leash and the dog gamboled along happily down the street. Cara heard feet approaching rapidly from behind.

"On your left," a gruff voice called out. She stepped to the right just in time to avoid being mowed down by a sweaty male jogger wearing a white T-shirt and red running shorts. He had a familiar-looking puppy on a leash.

Poppy gave an excited yelp of recognition and lunged for the puppy and the jogger, nearly yanking Cara off her feet.

"Poppy, heel!" Cara exclaimd. "Sit!"

But Poppy did no such thing. She strained at her leash, whining her disappointment at being kept from joining the jogger.

It was him! Jack the dog thief. She watched as he and his dog sped away down the street, without so much as a backward glance. It had all happened so fast she'd nearly missed it. But yes, the other puppy did bear a resemblance to Poppy. She was certainly a goldendoodle, and she shared Poppy's creamy coloring and curly coat.

"Come on, girl," Cara said, giving her dog an affectionate ear scratch. "Let's get a move on before it gets too hot."

She and Poppy continued their stroll, walking down Jones to Whitaker, and then south on Whitaker, where she happily window-shopped at the half-dozen little boutiques and antique shops that were some of her favorite local haunts. They continued on Whitaker, crossing over at Gaston Street when they got close to Forsyth Park.

It was late, nearly ten, but the park was still full of joggers, dog walkers, and young mothers with babies in strollers and toddlers in tow. Cara greeted several young mothers who'd been her brides not so long ago. She and Poppy did one circuit of the park, then walked over to the Sentient Bean, where she treated herself to a cold bottle of water and an orange cranberry scone and Poppy to a vegan dog biscuit.

When they were within a block of home, Poppy, already a creature of habit at seven months, did her business in her own dainty way, squatting in her customary spot between two huge camellia bushes, as though she required absolute privacy from prying eyes. Cara cleaned up after her pet, and walked back to the shop, keeping a wary eye out for joggers with goldendoodles.

Bert was finishing up a staid hospital arrangement of daisies and carnations.

"You're not going to believe it," he said, after she'd unclipped Poppy and washed her hands. "I just got off the phone with Lillian Fanning."

"And what was her complaint? Honestly, Bert, Torie's wedding was truly as close to perfection as I've ever gotten. And yet she still finds something to bitch about? I give up!"

"Not so fast," Bert said. "She wasn't calling to complain. Actually she was calling to thank you for making Torie's day so amazing. Her phone's been ringing off the hook from calls from all her friends, wanting to know who did Torie's flowers."

"Really? Lillian was actually pleased about something? That's a first."

" 'Tickled pink' were her exact words. And," he added, then paused for drama. "She also wanted to ask a huge favor."

"Such as?"

"She's giving a baby-shower luncheon for Torie's cousin Lindsay at the golf club tomorrow, and it just occurred to her that she'd love for us to whip up a few 'teensy' little centerpieces, and a corsage. I told her no, of course. There's no way we can do something like that with no lead time."

"Why would you do that? We can't turn down business, especially from somebody like Lillian Fanning."

Bert gestured toward the shop's glass-fronted flower cooler. "Look in there. We're cleaned out. I used the last pathetic little carnations for this hospital arrangement that just came in. All we've got left is some sad yellow spider mums and a few sprigs of baby's breath. Which we both know will never satisfy Lillian. She wouldn't have spider mums and baby's breath for her worst enemy's funeral. And Lamar won't be back here until day after tomorrow."

"Oh." Cara stood in front of the cooler and peered inside. Bert had a point. The dozen buckets of water in the cooler were nearly empty.

"Dadgummit. I hate giving up that kind of business. Was Lillian talking about the smaller eight-tops at the golf club?"

"Yes," Bert said. "but it doesn't matter. We don't have any flowers. You're a floral designer, Cara. Not a magician."

"How many tables?" Cara asked, reaching for her phone with one hand and her supplier's catalogue with the other.

"Eight," Bert said. "What are you thinking?"

"What color scheme?" Cara asked, rapidly flipping the pages of the catalogue.

"She didn't specify. Just something pretty and springish. You're not seriously thinking of taking this party on, are you?"

"Is the baby a girl or boy?"

"Girl," Bert said.

"Call Lillian Fanning," she told Bert. "And let her know there's been a change of plans."

Cara had her Savannah wholesaler, Breitmueller's, on speed dial.

"Wendy? This is Cara over at Bloom. How are you?"

"Fine," Wendy Breitmueller said cautiously. "What do you need, Cara?"

"Pink and white," Cara said. "Springy, youthful. With maybe some silvery gray foliage? And I need something feminine and pretty for corsages, but no gigantic orchids. Maybe some pink spray roses?"

"Mmm-hmm," Cara said, jotting down notes as Wendy listed what was available. "That sounds good. Love the idea of the tulips and the pink stocks and the foxgloves. And I'll take all the pink gerberas you've got. Can you put everything aside for me? I'll come over right away to pick everything up."

She hung up the phone and grabbed her car keys.

"Lillian is thrilled you'll do her flowers. But I think you're crazy," Bert said disapprovingly. "It's supposed to be your day off, remember? And when was the last time you actually took any time for yourself?"

"I know exactly how long it's been," Cara said ruefully. "I haven't had a real day off since the Monday before Valentine's Day last year."

Valentine's Day the previous year had been memorable, for sure, but for all the wrong reasons. It was her birthday, but because of the business she was in, Cara rarely had time to celebrate.

That year had been crazier than usual. She'd been forced to rent a second van just to get the flower deliveries covered. And when her second driver slipped and fell and broke his ankle on the third delivery of the afternoon, Cara had gotten behind the wheel of the van in his place.

She was making the last delivery of the afternoon, to a dentist's office on the south side of town: two dozen long-stemmed American Beauty roses to the dentist's wife, who ran the office, for her husband, Dr. Pratt, one of Cara's regular customers.

While Nancy Pratt was oohing and aahing over the roses from her husband in the reception area, another florist's delivery driver had walked into the office, with a huge vase of lilacs.

Lilacs? Who ordered lilacs in Savannah? Only one man Cara knew of. Her husband, Leo.

As soon as she saw the lilacs, Mrs. Pratt opened the door to the back office. "Cyndi! Flowers from your mystery man again."

Cara heard a chorus of giggles from the girls in the office—the receptionists and billing clerks and hygienists. "Our Cyndi has a mysterious beau who sends her gorgeous flowers every month," Mrs. Pratt confided.

A petite redhead in a tight-fitting white lab coat unbuttoned just enough to reveal her double-D décolletage burst through the door.

"Oh my God, is he is the sweetest thing ever?" She reached for the card stuck among the lilacs. Then she saw Cara, standing there beside Mrs. Pratt and her American Beauty roses, and Cyndi froze. She snatched the vase and disappeared into the back office.

Cara had seen enough. When she got home she picked up the huge vase of lilacs that had been left on her doorstep, and set them on the kitchen counter. She listened to the message Leo left on her voicemail. "Late meeting tonight. Sorry babe. I know you'll be dead on your feet by the time you get this, so we'll celebrate your birthday tomorrow night. 'Kay? Love you."

Leo's message had a strangely energizing effect on Cara. She went into his home office, and using a nail file, pried open the desk drawer where he kept their financial records. It was easy to find the statements for the new Visa card he'd procured for himself, easier still to find the monthly flower deliveries to Cyndi Snodgrass and the biweekly check-ins at the Airport Courtyard Marriott, visits that neatly coincided with Leo's supposed sales meetings in Atlanta.

Cara left the Visa statements on top of the desk. She dumped the lilacs onto the middle of their bed. She packed her clothes and her books and called Bert on the way over to his apartment to ask if she could stay in his guest room for a few nights.

She'd hired a lawyer and started divorce proceedings the next day, and within two weeks she'd rented the apartment over Bloom. And she'd worked every day since then, with the exception of the day after this Valentine's Day, when she'd gone to visit the breeder in Atlanta to pick out her own birthday present, her new roommate, Poppy.

"You're going to burn yourself out," Bert chided her now. "Do you realize we've got weddings every Saturday for the next six weeks, not to mention the Mandelbaums' golden anniversary party and those two huge banquets at the Westin? Plus the deb parties . . ."

"We can't afford to turn down Lillian Fanning," Cara said firmly. "Between Lillian and Vicki Cooper—if this keeps up we'll have more business than we can handle."

"We *already* have more business than we can deal with," Bert grumped.

"We can handle it," Cara said.

"Yeah, if we don't want to have a life. Which I do," he added.

"Are you referring to your new frat friend? Or the fireman?" Cara asked.

Bert winked. "You could say things are heating up with my love life." He put an arm around her shoulders. "And what about you? It's been what, a year and a half since you left Leo? You have got to stop burying yourself in work, Cara."

"Stop and smell the roses, you mean?"

"Something like that. Not all men are like Leo, you know. Some of us are actually faithful and caring and thoughtful. And fun to be around."

"All the men I know who fit that description in this town are gay," Cara pointed out.

"You never meet any new men. All you ever do is work. And you'll never meet anybody nice again if you keep up like this," Bert said.

"Has it occurred to you that I don't want to meet anybody new?" Cara tried to keep her voice light. "I'm done with men." She reached down and scooped the wriggling Poppy into her arms, burying her nose in the dog's rose-scented curls.

"I've got a dog now," she informed her assistant. "She never steals the covers. Never lies. And she would never, ever sleep with some skanky dental hygienist with short arms and big boobs. Plus, Poppy loves me unconditionally."

"Except when she runs away," Bert said.

"That reminds me," Cara said. "When I was out walking Poppy earlier, the jerk ran right past me—with his real dog in tow."

"But he did go to all the trouble to track you down here and bring her back yesterday," Bert said. "So he can't be that big a jerk."

"You don't know him like I do," Cara said. "Look, Bert. I've got to get moving if I'm going to get over to Breitmueller's for Lillian's flowers. Will you keep an eye on Poppy?"

"That's cool," Bert said. He looked down at Poppy, who was standing by the window, wagging her tail as she watched a woman walk by with a pair of dachshunds on leash. "But maybe you should think about getting Poppy microchipped. Just in case she gets out again. Right?"

"All right, all right, I will," Cara said. "The very next time I have a day off."

11

On Tuesday, Cara used one hip to bump open the door at the Savannah Golf Club at 10:45 a.m. Her face was beaded with perspiration and she was well aware that she looked a hot mess.

The previous day's pickup from Breitmueller's had been a failure.

She'd arrived at the wholesaler shortly before noon. But the buckets of flowers holding her order were nothing like what she'd been promised.

Gaudy hot pink dyed carnations, some sad-looking cream spray roses, a few Stargazer lilies, and loads of stiff yellowish baby's breath.

She marched over to the office, where Wendy Breitmueller was typing away on her computer terminal.

"Oh, hi, Cara," Wendy said, not looking up. "We pulled your order, it's back out in the warehouse."

"That's not what I ordered, Wendy," Cara said sharply. "Come on! Baby's breath? And those yucky dyed carnations? Where are my tulips? My pink spray roses? My gerberas?"

Wendy sighed. "Look, it's not my fault. Allen took a big phone order just before I talked to you, and he'd already promised all the stuff you wanted to another client. You know how it goes. This is our busy season, and unless you call up a week ahead of time and let us know what you need, you take what you get. First come, first served."

"But you promised *me*," Cara reminded her. "Not less than an hour ago. I've got a baby shower tomorrow for one of my regular clients, and there is no way I can show up at the golf club with that mess out there."

"You're welcome to walk around in the warehouse and pick out whatever else looks good," Wendy said with a shrug. Reluctantly, she got up from her computer and led Cara back into the chilled air of the warehouse.

Cara saw a huge cluster of buckets lined up near the loading-dock doors, holding what looked like a whole greenhouse full of blooms: peonies, tulips, hydrangeas, orchids, roses, ranunculus, lilies, and more.

"That!" Cara said, pointing. "That's what you promised me."

"Sorry, like I told you, it's all spoken for. Allen's new customer."

"Wow. All that for one client?"

"He's got two shops. Been open in Charleston for a while, and now he's moved over to Savannah too. And he's just as particular about his flowers as you."

Cara felt a twinge of jealousy. "Are all these flowers for Cullen Kane?"

"Sure," Wendy said. "You know him?"

"Just of him," she said. "I guess he has some pretty fancy clients."

"I'd say so," Wendy said.

Cara was still looking at all those flowers by the loading dock. "Wait a minute, Wendy. He's got *tons* of pink tulips. But I didn't get any. And I specifically ordered three dozen."

Wendy shrugged. "Nothing I can do about it, Cara."

"Since when?" Cara asked. "You're the owner. Come on, Wendy. You know this isn't right. I might not order as many flowers as this new guy, but I've been a good customer. You can't just short me like this. At least split the order with me."

"Oh, Cara," Wendy sighed.

Cara could sense she was softening.

"Wendy? Don't do me like this. Please? I need those tulips."

She shook her head, then gestured toward the buckets of flowers, looking furtively around the warehouse. "I can spare a dozen of these pink tulips."

"Two dozen," Cara said, not too proud to beg. "I've got all these tabletops at the golf club."

"Eighteen," Wendy said. "Take 'em, but be quick about it. I don't want Allen to catch me raiding his customer's order. I'll adjust your bill. Now shoo, before I change my mind."

Cara spent all Tuesday morning scrounging up enough greenery to fill in for the missing flowers for her centerpieces—snipping asparagus ferns from one friend's garden in Ardsley Park, Meyer lemon leaves from a client's courtyard, and silvery-gray lamb's ears from the hip-pocket-sized container garden she tended behind the shop. She made a trip over to Whole Foods and bought four fat pots of pink hydrangeas, wincing at the cash register while she paid retail prices for the flowers.

She'd even made a quick trip out to Wilmington Island, where she knew of a thick patch of blue plumbago growing in the Publix shopping center parking lot. She'd parked her car right by the patch, snipped a big batch, then fled like a thief in the night. It wasn't really stealing, she'd told herself. The plumbago needed trimming.

All that foraging put her behind schedule—she'd intended to get to the golf club by ten. She had her arms full—a huge cardboard box containing eight square glass centerpieces, plus the corsages in their clear plastic clamshell boxes. She looked around the nearly empty lobby, wondering where the party was being held.

Lillian Fanning hurried toward her. She wore a sleeveless coral sheath, matching sling-back heels, and a necklace of twined turquoise, coral, and seed pearls. "Cara!" she called. "We're back here, in the grill." Lillian looked pointedly down at the thin gold watch on her wrist.

"Hi, Lillian," Cara said. "Sorry to be a little late."

Lillian glanced over at the box. "Those look nice," she said. "I'm so glad you could do this. I know it was short notice, but after seeing all the beautiful centerpieces you did for Torie, I just couldn't settle for those dreary little half-dead flower sprigs the club puts out for luncheons."

"Happy to do it," Cara said, struggling to keep up in Lillian's wake.

The tables in the grill had already been set for luncheon. Pale pink cloths covered the rounds, and somebody, Lillian, she assumed, had placed tiny wrapped boxes at each place setting. Cara hurried around the room, depositing the centerpieces where Lillian directed.

They heard voices coming from the doorway. "Oh good," Lillian said, turning to see the first arrivals. "That's Lindsay."

"Then I'll just get out of your hair," Cara said. She unloaded the corsages onto a chair and made a beeline for the door.

She was streaking across the lobby when she heard a familiar voice call her name.

"Cara! Yoo-hoo!"

Vicki Cooper and a woman Cara didn't recognize were walking toward her.

Cara pasted a smile on her face and wiped her palms on the seat of her capris. She was sweaty and her clothes were smudged with specks of mud from her morning of greenery wrangling, and she should have stopped back at the shop to change her clothes before delivering the flowers to the club, but time had been her enemy all morning.

Vicki Cooper, on the other hand, looked fresh as a daisy in a sleeveless black silk dress, silver wedge sandals, and chunky silver bracelets and hoop earrings. Vicki's shimmery white hair hung to her shoulders. Her deep blue eyes were lightly made up and she wore a peach-colored lipstick. At sixty, Vicki looked like what Cara wanted to be when she grew up.

"Pretend you don't see me," Cara told Vicki, giving her a quick hug. "I've been playing in the dirt all morning, and I'm a big mess."

"You look fine! Cara, I want you to meet Faith McCurdy. Faith, this is our favorite florist in town, Cara Kryzik. She did all the flowers for our son's wedding, and she's an absolute genius."

The other woman was in her early sixties, dressed in a tidy shirtwaist dress, heels, and hose. "So nice to meet you," she murmured.

"Faith's nephew Tyler Carver is married to Lindsay Fanning," Vicki said. "Is that what you're doing here? Flowers for the baby shower?"

"Just delivered them," Cara said. She looked around the lobby and saw several groups of women walking toward the entrance to the grill. "And I better move along."

"Oh, don't run off just yet," Vicki protested, catching Cara by the arm. "Faith, you go ahead on. I'll be along in a minute. I just want to chat with Cara for a moment."

Vicki drew Cara to an alcove on the far side of the lobby, gesturing for her to sit on a settee looking out on the golf course.

"I won't take a minute of your time," Vicki started. "Just wanted to check. Did you hear from Marie Trapnell?"

"I met with her yesterday. Thanks so much for the referral."

"Well?" Vicki raised an eyebrow expectantly.

"It's . . . complicated," Cara said. "Marie is very nice, and we hit it off immediately. But it sounds as though her ex-husband is the one who is really running the show. She says he's got another florist in town he's very interested in working with. I told her I understand . . ."

"What?" Vicki's voice echoed through the high-ceilinged room. "Are you telling me Gordon Trapnell now fancies himself as an event planner?"

Cara looked around the room, uneasy at discussing a client's private life, even if the client might not even turn out to be her client.

"According to Marie, Mr. Trapnell wants to be involved in every aspect of his daughter's wedding."

"Oh, puh-leez," Vicki drawled. "Gordon doesn't care a thing in the world about this wedding. He just wants to make a big show of being the adoring daddy to his darling Brookie, because he's eaten up with guilt over his shabby treatment of poor Marie. Which he should be. But Brooke's a smart girl. She has no illusions about Daddy Rat."

"This doesn't sound like something I need to get in the middle of," Cara demurred.

"What exactly did Marie tell you—about the circumstances of her divorce?" Vicki asked, leaning forward. "Come on, you can tell me. It's not like it's a secret."

Cara shrugged. "She didn't get into the details. She just said she thinks Brooke feels torn—between loyalty to her mother, and anger at her father. Something about the second wife?"

"Patricia," Vicki said. "Or Patti, as she used to be called before she decided to reinvent herself. Patricia Showalter Linencamp Trapnell. Do you know her?"

"No."

"You haven't missed much," Vicki said. "What a remorseless little tramp she is. And when I think about how she had all of us fooled . . ."

Cara twisted around in her chair. She really needed to get back to the shop. And she didn't want to be seen slinging mud with Vicki Cooper right in the middle of the golf-club lobby. It just didn't look right.

"I know, I know, you think this is all just petty gossip," Vicki said. "But you know me, Cara. I never gossip."

Cara struggled to keep a straight face.

"How did you leave it with Marie?" Vicki asked.

"I just asked if she could let me know by Friday whether or not her ex had decided to hire this other florist his new wife, Patricia, knows."

"Oh yes, Cullen Kane, boy wonder. Patricia's new best friend. I hear they're practically joined at the hip these days. And that's who Gordon wants to hire to do the flowers for Brooke's wedding?"

"I think so," Cara said. "Although Marie did say her ex might want to interview me."

"Absurd!" Vicki said. "Gordon doesn't know the first thing about flowers. This is all Patricia's doing."

"I might just go ahead and bow out," Cara said. "After all, if they really want Cullen Kane . . ."

"Don't you dare!" Vicki said sharply. "This is all just a control issue. Gordon wants to prove that he still has Marie under his big fat thumb, that's all."

"Still, if he's paying for his daughter's wedding, you can't blame him for wanting to be consulted."

"Marie doesn't need Gordon's money to pay for Brooke's wedding. She inherited more money than he'll ever think about having, from her grandfather when he passed away last year," Vicki confided.

"I've known Gordon for years and years," Vicki said now. "Patricia too, for that matter. And I hate what the two of them have done to Marie. She's a shell of her former self, Cara. Would you believe, she used to be a senior vice president at one of the biggest ad agencies in New York? She's twice as smart as Gordon ever hoped to be, but gave up her career after she married that goober. Even after she had Brooke, Marie was a powerhouse. Headed up the development committee for Brooke's school that raised a five-million-dollar endowment fund, was on the board of the library, she helped get the book festival started here, chaired the United Way campaign . . ."

"Really?" It was hard for Cara to reconcile the image of a powerful business executive with the nervous, uncertain woman she'd met the previous day.

"The divorce shook her to the core," Vicki confided. She made a face. "When I think of that weasel Patricia, pretending to be Marie's dear friend all those years—it literally makes me sick. You think you know somebody, right? And then they turn out to be a devious, backstabbing bitch."

"You were friends with this Patricia?"

"Honey, we all ran around in the same crowd. Brooke and my Cason started preschool together. Patricia's twins from her first marriage were a year older, and anyway, after Patricia split with Billy, her second husband, she shipped the boys off to military school and that was the last we saw of them. I never liked Patricia, her pretensions were always a little much as far as I was concerned—but our husbands were business associates and golf buddies. You know how that works in this town."

Cara did know.

"When Patricia snaked Gordon away from Marie, she did more than just wreck a marriage. She broke up our supper club—couples were taking sides, of course, and it wasn't fun anymore. Our book club dissolved—Marie was the glue, and after she quit coming, because of Patricia, we never got back on track. I know it's selfish of me, considering what Marie has been through, but

really, even though it's been four or five years, I'm still so mad about book club
I could spit!"

As she talked, Vicki was idly watching the flow of traffic in the country-
club lobby. Men in golf and tennis togs filtered in, heading for the men's card
room; young mothers with small children in swimsuits came in from the pool.
Vicki's eyes widened.

"Well I'll be damned," she said, her voice low. "Speak of the devil."

Cara casually glanced to her left. Two women were walking in, their heads
bent together in conversation. They headed toward the main dining room.

"The blonde? With the face transplant? That's Patricia," Vicki murmured.
"I don't know the gal she's with. Probably one of her new friends from Charleston. She pretty much burned all her bridges here, so she had to go trawling up
there for some new besties."

Patricia Trapnell was scanning the room as she walked. She spotted Vicki
Cooper, gave her a bright smile and a finger wave, then turned back toward
her friend.

"She knows better than to try to speak to me," Vicki said bitterly.

Cara saw an opening and went for it. "Thanks for the backgrounder on the
Trapnells, Vicki. It's probably a good thing to get the whole story before I meet
with the husband. But I have a feeling this is all going to be moot, if Patricia is
that close to Cullen Kane."

She stood up to leave, but Vicki seized her by the arm.

"Look, Cara. I know you don't want to get involved in some messy intra-
marital showdown. All I'm saying is, don't back down just yet. I'm thinking
Marie is about to get fed up with Gordon's dictatorial bullshit. And when she
does, she's going to want Brooke's wedding to be everything that girl has
dreamed of since she was in pigtails. You're the one who can give her that.
Right?"

"Maybe," Cara conceded. "Guess I'll just have to wait and see how the
interview goes."

12

The courtyard garden behind the little shop on Jones Street was what convinced her not to leave when Cara was considering moving the shop after she inherited it from Norma.

Cara told herself that she stayed out of convenience. Plus, there was the space itself—high-ceilinged and airy, with a wide front window looking out on the street, a serviceable office nook, and a nice-sized workroom that could be curtained off from her showroom. There was space in the showroom for her flower cooler, and shelves that held the various unusual and vintage containers and knickknacks she sold in addition to her flower arrangements. There was a dedicated parking space out back for the delivery van. And the block itself was a good one, on tree-shaded West Jones Street, surrounded by private residences as well as a handful of discreet businesses: a trendy women's boutique, a gift and card shop, and a pair of antique shops.

On the downside, she'd had to put hours and hours of sweat equity into transforming the place from Norma's to Bloom: sanding and refinishing the floors, painting the exposed brick walls, and having display shelves and tables built. It was only when her costs began to mount up that she'd had to go to her father, hat in hand, to beg for a loan.

She might have been okay after that, if life hadn't happened. If the van hadn't needed a whole new suspension. If the computer hadn't died, if she hadn't had to pay for expensive photography to showcase her portfolio on her website. If. If. If.

Still, most days, she was at peace with the decision to stay on Jones Street and live above the shop. And the thing that that made her heart really sing about her new home was that pocket-sized courtyard garden. It was surrounded by a high wall of aged Savannah gray bricks, and the design was simple, two narrow rectangular planting beds outlined with more brick and a border of dwarf boxwoods.

A brick walkway bisected the space, and there was a small brick-paved patio.

When she'd inherited the lease from Norma, the beds were overgrown with chickweed, privet, wild onions, and morning glories that spilled over the borders and onto the basketweave brick walkway. A ginormous wisteria vine with a trunk the size of her waist had taken up occupancy in the right rear corner of the courtyard, and its tendrils had wound their way clear around the brick walls and up a neighbor's two-story-high camellia.

Busy with remodeling the downstairs, she'd had no time to spend on that garden, until her marriage crumbled and she'd retreated to the apartment on the top floor of the building.

Cara had barely unpacked her clothes before starting her assault on the garden. Every morning at daylight she had donned jeans and work gloves and headed out to the courtyard to do battle for a couple of hours before going to work in the shop. She hacked down most of the wisteria and weeded the borders for what seemed like weeks. Her hands were left blistered, and callused, and every night when she soaked in the claw-foot bathtub in her upstairs apartment, she got a kind of grim satisfaction from viewing what she saw as the battle scars from a failed marriage.

Leo called. He texted. But when he dropped by the shop, Bert gave him the cold shoulder and glared at him with undisguised loathing. Leo suggested counseling. That's when Cara suggested he get their house listed and sold, because she needed her share of the equity to grow her business.

Leo gazed at her with his round blue eyes—the ones she'd gazed into on her wedding day, when he'd promise to love her forever. "It was a mistake. All right? How many ways can I tell you I'm sorry? Didn't you ever make a mistake you came to deeply regret?"

"Yes," Cara said gravely. "Marrying you. Believing you would be faithful was a mistake. That's my big regret."

When she'd cleared out the invaders in her courtyard, she'd been thrilled to find the bones of a lovely old garden. Hiding in the shadow of the wisteria she found a beautifully mottled marble birdbath with a bowl shaped like a sunflower. With Bert's help, she'd dragged it into the center of the courtyard and dug out a circular bed and planted lavender, rosemary, creeping thyme, and three different varieties of scented geraniums at its base.

As the weather warmed up and spring arrived in Savannah, she was thrilled when an unnamed heirloom rose she'd pruned back sprouted new canes and brought forth a froth of delicate white blossoms with orange-tipped centers.

When one of her elderly spinster Jones Street neighbors died, Cara went to the estate sale and bought two huge old terra-cotta pots, which she dragged home in a rusty little red wagon she'd found in a trash pile down the lane. She dumped out the hideous cast-iron plants that had filled those pots for decades, and in their place she planted a pair of lemon trees.

She planted banana trees in the far corner of the beds and underplanted them with hostas, ferns, and ruffly bicolored caladiums.

Leo called one day to tell her the house was under contract. The next day, when she knew he'd be at work, she drove the van over to the house, and let herself into the back gate. With Bert's help, she loaded up the only furniture she really wanted from her previous life, a pair of teak Luytens benches that had been a wedding gift from her father.

She doubted Leo would notice they were missing. The only time he went into their backyard was to mow the grass or practice his backswing.

Cara searched the Savannah Craigslist ads for weeks before she finally found a square teak outdoor table. She added a market umbrella and placed her benches on either side of it.

When spring came, even if it was raining or storming, Cara stole away to her courtyard garden for an hour or two. She'd light one of the red-currant candles she sold in the shop and then have her dinner sitting at the table. She sipped wine while she plucked weeds or snipped herbs, or just sat, with Poppy at her feet, watching the stars, listening to the rustle of the birds in the treetops.

Sometimes Bert would join her. He'd donated a pair of weather-beaten Adirondack chairs to the garden. They would sit back on the chairs, not talking. Cara would sip her pinot grigio and Bert, a recovering alcoholic, would occasionally sneak a joint—although this was not something she actually approved of.

"Gimme a break," Bert would say, closing his eyes, tilting his head skyward and blowing smoke through his nostrils. "I quit drinking. You can't make me give up all my vices."

Thursday night, after putting together dozens of Mother's Day arrangements for delivery, Cara and Bert were sitting in the courtyard garden. Bert slapped at a mosquito and sighed. "Here it comes. Skeeter season. Makes me want to move to Maine. I hate those little fuckers."

"They have stinging black flies in Maine, Bert," Cara pointed out. "And mud. Months and months of mud. Not to mention snow."

"Never mind," he said lazily. "So—did I hear right? You're actually going to interview for the privilege of doing that Trapnell wedding?"

"Yessss," she said, already regretting what she thought of as her capitulation. "I really like Marie Trapnell. And Vicki Cooper tracked me down at the golf club Tuesday and begged me to at least consider taking the job if they offer it. Brooke's father, Gordon, called me today to set up an appointment for 'a chat.' He wants me to see the Strayhorns' plantation house, so I can get an idea of where the wedding is being held. So yes, I'm going over to Cabin Creek tomorrow, hat in hand, to present my ideas for the wedding."

"Want me to tag along?"

"Normally, I'd love to have you accompany me. It looks pretty fancy, don't you think, to introduce you as my assistant and have you carry my photo book and bow and scrape like a minion?"

"Bowing and scraping? Not in my job description."

"Anyway, I need you at the shop tomorrow to finish up with the Mother's Day orders. And don't forget, we've got Laurie-Beth Winship's wedding Saturday. But don't worry, I promise to bring back a full description."

13

Somebody, at some point in the Strayhorn family history, had a puckish sense of humor. Cabin Creek? Cara drove slowly down the bumpy crushed oyster-shell drive. Age-blackened live oaks dripping with thick curtains of Spanish moss shaded both sides of the roadway, their trunks dotted with clumps of dark green Resurrection ferns, and the trees were underplanted with hedges of azaleas, past blooming, but still lovely. A rail fence separated the drive from a vast green pasture, and a trio of horses grazed outside a weathered barn. At the end of the quarter-mile drive, a weathered cypress sign was nailed to one of the trees.

SLOW DOWN. SMALL CHILDREN. LARGE DOGS. OLD MEN.

The house loomed ahead. Cara had read up on Cabin Creek in a book about low-country plantation homes. The property had been a land grant from King George III, but the original homeplace, described as a two-story wood-frame cabin, had burned in the early 1800s, and the Strayhorns, who'd done well with cotton, rice, and indigo, built themselves a showplace to display all that wealth.

Cabin Creek was no longer a cabin. Not by any stretch of the imagination. The main house was a three-story Greek Revival beauty, with a two-story-tall portico supported by four thick Doric columns. A widow's walk topped the portico. Large wings sprouted from each side of the main house, and the estate was set on an expanse of deep green lawn, with foundation plantings of carefully clipped boxwoods.

Cara followed the drive around to the right side of the house, as Gordon Trapnell had instructed, where she found a gravel car park adjoining a low three-bay garage. She parked her own car next to a sleek silver Jaguar, and walked around to a smaller side entrance marked by a pair of miniature versions of the front columns.

Before she could ring the doorbell, the door opened. A stocky middle-aged woman dressed in faded blue jeans and a grubby T-shirt pushed open the screen door. An army-green ballcap with an embroidered Cabin Creek logo shaded the woman's round, ruddy face.

"Are you the florist?" she asked.

"Uh yes," Cara said, taken aback. Funny way for a butler to dress.

The woman extended her hand and opened the door wider. "Great! So glad to meet you. I'm Libba Strayhorn. Come on in. I was just getting ready to go out to the stables, but Gordon and Patricia are inside. I'll show you the way, then let you all talk."

They were in what was obviously used as a mudroom by the Strayhorn family. It was high-ceilinged, with a marble floor, but simple wooden benches lined each side, and wall-mounted hooks held jackets and coats. Muddy boots were lined up beneath the benches, and a pair of shotguns rested casually in one corner.

Libba walked quickly, the soles of her riding boots clacking against the marble floor. Cara followed her through a pair of double doors into a formal parlor with an immense fireplace mounted by a fancy gilt-framed mirror. Stiff brocade-covered Empire-era settees and armchairs faced the fireplace. Libba didn't slow. Instead she led Cara through yet another doorway, into a cypress-paneled library.

Gordon Trapnell and his wife were sitting at a felt-topped game table near the fireplace. "Cara?" he asked, standing to shake her hand.

He was short, maybe only an inch or two taller than Cara, with thinning dark hair, carefully combed across his high-domed head, and a neatly clipped mustache. He wore silver wire-rimmed glasses, a pale pink logoed Polo shirt, and dark dress slacks.

"Yes, hello, Mr. Trapnell."

"Call me Gordon." He turned toward the woman seated to his right and beamed. "And this is Patricia, my wife."

Cara had only caught a glimpse of Patricia Trapnell at the golf club earlier in the week, just a blur of blond hair and cheekbones.

Patricia's silicone-plumped lips widened into what she probably thought was a smile. But her skin was stretched so tightly over the high cheekbones, it really resembled more of a grimace. Her pale blue eyes had an almost Asian tilt. Her face was skillfully made up, and her blond hair gleamed in the low light of the library. She was dressed in a cobalt-blue silk blouse.

"Hello, Cara," she said, her voice husky. "We've heard so much about your work. And of course, we loved what you did for Torie Fanning's wedding last week. Please sit, and tell us about your ideas for Brooke and Harris."

"I'm going to leave you experts to it then," Libba Strayhorn said, and she hurried out of the room.

Cara took a deep breath and opened her iPad. "These are a few ideas I came up with for the church, and the reception," she said, tapping an icon on the screen that read "Trapnell Wedding."

"Of course, everything is very preliminary," she said. "I was able to find pictures on the internet of the ballroom and the chapel here at Cabin Creek, but it would still be helpful for me to see them in person, just to get a sense of the scale of the spaces."

"Of course," Gordon Trapnell said. "We can walk around and show you the layout after we chat. Libba has graciously given us the run of the place."

"I forgot to ask Marie—how many guests?"

Patricia sighed deeply. "That's been a matter of controversy. Brooke and her mother have some quaint notion about a small, intimate affair. But they totally overlook the fact that with Gordon's and my extensive social and business contacts, not to mention the Strayhorns,' we're talking about three hundred people minimum—and that's cutting the guest list right to the bone."

"To the bone," Gordon said, nodding agreement.

"And do you have a budget in mind?" Cara asked.

"Not really," Patricia said. She gave Gordon a warm smile, then reached over and squeezed her husband's hand. "How do you put a price tag on a father's love for his only daughter?"

"Exactly," Cara replied.

Really? This is about demonstrating love for Brooke? Not about showing your "extensive business and social contacts" just how much money you have to throw around on an overblown wedding your kid doesn't even really want?

Cara tapped an icon marked "Centerpieces." "Since it's a July wedding, I thought we might stick to cooler colors, blues, greens, white, cream, maybe some lavenders and silvers." She glanced from Brooke to Gordon. "Are those colors Brooke likes?"

Gordon glanced at his wife for guidance. Patricia rolled her eyes. "Brooke doesn't really have much of a sense of color at all, bless her heart. Or style, for that matter. As far as I can tell, she wears navy blue or black suits to work, and she lives in running clothes on the weekend."

"Oh."

"*We* thought, that is, Gordon and I thought, it might be exciting to do something really dramatic with the tables. We were at a wedding in Charleston last month, that was simply *stunning.* The designer had spent time in India, and he designed these amazing pierced brass vessels and low tables, with piles and piles of cushions and Oriental rugs, and there were no flowers at all, just flickering lights, and piles of exotic fruits, pomegranates and what have you, and the tablecloths were embroidered, with mirrors..."

"No flowers?" Cara said blankly.

Then what the hell am I doing here?

"But we wouldn't want to copy that look, not exactly," Patricia added hastily. "And anyway, that was just to give you an idea of the kind of emotions we'd like to elicit with our event."

It's a wedding, Cara thought. *And it's not actually your wedding. It's Brooke's and Harris's.*

"What we're looking for, Cara, is something absolutely original," Gordon said.

"Something that hasn't been done in Savannah. None of those tired old postdeb looks you see all the time," Patricia added. "And to be perfectly honest, Cara, we have looked at a presentation by another designer which was beyond amazing. So I guess what Gordon is asking from you, is to be amazing."

Cara looked down at her iPad. *Screw this. Be amazing? That's your design mandate?*

She willed herself to smile. "Would you like to look at some of my ideas now?"

Patricia scrolled rapidly through the photos and sketches Cara had assembled, and five minutes later, handed the iPad back.

"Interesting," she said. "Lots of silver vases and such. Very traditional though, wouldn't you say?"

"Well, yes. I assumed that since the wedding and reception were being held in a historic home, you'd want the flowers to fit in with the setting. But I'm not necessarily tied to any one look. We do lots of cutting-edge weddings. In fact, tomorrow, we're doing the décor for a wedding in an old cotton warehouse down on River Street, and the bride requested an industrial, steampunk look, with some goth elements mixed in."

"Goth?" Gordon looked to his wife for interpretation.

"Oh, you know, Gordie. Those kids who wander around with their faces made up with white powder and black-lined eyes and lips, like something out of a Halloween fright show."

"People do that at weddings? Adults?" He shook his head. "Thank God Brooke was never into that sort of thing."

Cara couldn't help herself. There was no way these people were going to hire her, so why not have a little fun with them? "Instead of tablecloths, we're topping the tables with long sheets of rusted corrugated tin, from old farmhouses. And we're doing centerpieces with all black flowers, and animal skulls."

Patricia's pale eyes bugged out slightly. "Not . . . real animal skulls."

"Oh sure," Cara said cheerfully. "The groom is a big hunter, so he's collected things over the years from his own kills and walks in the woods. I've managed to incorporate rattlesnake rattles in the bride's bouquet, strung on strips of deer rawhide. Plus, I've been buying additional skulls and antlers online for months now."

"Dear God," Patricia said faintly. She looked a little ill.

"And we're having a tattoo booth," Cara added. "I've designed a custom tattoo that combines the bride's and groom's initials and their wedding date. It's the first one I've designed, and I'm really very proud of how it turned out."

"Who in hell *are* these people?" Gordon demanded.

"Laurie-Beth Winship?" Cara said. "She's marrying Payton Jelks."

"That's not Frank and Elizabeth Winship's child, is it?" Patricia asked. "I know they have a daughter, but Laurie-Beth was in Brooke's debutante class. Surely they wouldn't sanction something like that. . . ."

"It is," Cara said. "Do you know the Winships? I just love them. So adventurous. Elizabeth has already promised that she'll get tattooed tomorrow night, but I think Frank is a little squeamish about needles, so he's just going to do the henna thing. You wouldn't think a radiologist would be, would you? Squeamish, I mean."

"Dear God." This time Gordon and Patricia said it as a duet.

14

Cara climbed uneasily to the top of the scaffolding, eight feet off the ground. She aimed the can of black spray paint at the age-blackened brick wall and began writing, in big, looping letters.

LUV WILL KEEP US 2-GETHER.

She looked down at Bert, who was holding the piece of paper that acted as their script. Bert, it turned out, was afraid of heights. The next time she hired an assistant, she vowed, she would have to ask prospects about their phobias. But for now, it was what it was. "What next?"

"Mmm. Says here 'Laurie-Beth (heart) Payton.'"

Cara walked a few paces down the catwalk, and clambered up to the next level, the paint can tucked into the waistband of her jeans. She painted the next phrase, walked four feet to the left, and looked down. "Next?"

Bert had to crane his neck to see her. He cupped his hands to form a make-shift megaphone. "'You are the sunshine of my life.'"

She remembered that one. It was the title of Laurie-Beth's parents' favorite song from their own courtship. She sprayed the phrase on the wall, using the last little bit of the spray paint. She tossed the can to the ground and began the slow climb down.

Bert still had his eyes tightly closed when she reached the concrete floor. "You can look now," she said, touching his arm.

He did. The two of them walked around the cavernous warehouse, surveying their handiwork.

"Fanfuckintastic," Bert said.

And Cara, despite all her initial misgivings, had to agree.

Laurie-Beth Winship had read one too many wedding magazines, stayed too long on Pinterest. Despite her mother's tearful pleas for a nice, traditional reception at the Oglethorpe Club, or the Chatham City Club, Laura-Beth had proclaimed she wanted a "real" venue for her wedding.

Unable to find a wedding planner willing to execute her vision, Laurie-Beth had appointed Cara her de facto "imagineer."

This cotton warehouse belonged to one of Elizabeth Winship's great-uncles, but it hadn't been used in at least thirty years. They'd had to hire a commercial cleaning crew to come in and steam-clean the brick walls and pressure-wash the grease-soaked floors. After that, the one existing bathroom, which consisted of nothing more than a urinal and a sink, had to be gutted and rebuilt into a proper unisex facility—while still keeping to Laurie-Beth's "industrial" look.

It would have been cheaper, Cara thought, to just build a new warehouse. But she kept that thought to herself, and gamely soldiered on, buoyed by the thought of the handsome fee the Winships were paying her.

So here they were, on the Friday night before the Winship-Jelks wedding. It was nearly midnight, and she and Bert had been working all evening. They'd hung miles of safety lights, spray-painted graffiti on everything that didn't move, and strung canvas painters' dropcloths from those rusty steel girders to form a backdrop for the newly built bandstand constructed of old wooden pallets Cara had liberated from the back of a nearby building supply.

The oversized wooden cable spools that would act as cocktail tables had been wheeled into place, and tables, improvised from corrugated metal spread over sawhorses, were arrayed around the dance floor.

"You really think the flowers are okay?" Cara asked Bert.

He shrugged. They'd cleaned out two local feed and seed stores of every galvanized bucket, tub, and horse trough in stock. These were now filled with leafless branches that had been spray-painted black, and strung with white lights and chains made of beer-can pop-tops. On every tree, Cara had wired bunches of carnations, dip-dyed in bloodred and black.

More dyed black flowers filled recycled aluminum cans on the tabletops, which were interspersed with Cara's carefully curated assortment of animal skulls.

"It's sure as hell original," Bert said. "And that's what she wanted, right?"

"If Tim Burton married Alice Cooper, I think this is what their wedding would look like," Cara muttered. She yawned. "Let's go. I'm dead on my feet, and we've got another loooong day tomorrow."

She pulled the van to the curb in front of Bert's apartment on St. Julian Street. "See you in the morning."

"Hey. You never told me how your meeting with the Trapnells went," Bert said, his hand on the passenger door.

"It went. The plantation? Cabin Creek—it's unbelievable. If it weren't for the bride's father and stepmother, I'd love to design a wedding in that house. But those two? Gordon and Patricia?" She made a face. "It's the first time I've ever hoped *not* to get hired."

"Then why bother to talk to them?" Bert asked. "We're not exactly hurting for work, Cara."

"I know, I know. I keep telling myself that. But I really liked Marie, the mom."

"That's your problem, Cara," Bert said, interrupting. "You like *everybody*. You get sucked into their dramas, become a part of their family, and then get stuck in the middle of their shit. You're a florist, honey, not a family therapist!"

"You're wrong. I absolutely don't like Gordon, and it took me about five seconds to decide I detest Patricia. But Marie—she's a different story. She's sort of a lost soul, and I just get the feeling Patricia will totally mow her and Brooke down, if I don't get the job. But don't worry. They are so *not* going to hire me. I told them about everything we had planned for Laurie-Beth's wedding and they were really and truly appalled. Anyway, Patricia is totally gaga over this Cullen Kane guy from Charleston."

"Oh yeah, *him*," Bert said, with a sneer. "Just what Savannah needs. Another flower fairy."

Cara laughed and gave his shoulder a gentle shove. "Go on, get out. We've both got to get our beauty rest. See you in the morning."

15

Cara caught sight of the stranger just as she was finishing the last details of the elaborate arch she'd constructed out of fallen tree branches, Spanish moss, deer antlers, grouse feathers, ivy, and dried hydrangeas. Since it was where Laurie-Beth and Payton would stand to say their vows she wanted to make sure an errant antler wouldn't fall off and bonk the couple on the head. Concussions were never fun at a wedding.

She'd arrived at the cotton warehouse late Saturday afternoon, already behind schedule.

He was standing just inside the propped-open door of the warehouse, his arms crossed over his chest, and a late-afternoon ray of sunlight seemed to catch and illuminate his blond tresses, almost like a halo. He wasn't a guest; the wedding wasn't for another two hours, and anyway, he was dressed casually, in designer jeans—7 For All Mankind, she was sure, a silky black T-shirt, and black motorcycle boots. He had deliberate beard stubble, piercing green eyes, and he was tall enough and slender enough to be a runway model.

But she knew he wasn't. The hair was the giveaway. She'd seen it on his website.

He was watching her, spying on the competition, and he didn't care if she knew. Should she confront him, ask him to leave? But that would make him think she had something to hide. She decided to ignore him, for now anyway.

Cara stood on the top rung of her stepladder, and steadied herself with both hands on the side supports of the arch. She made another pass with the picture wire, looping it around and around Payton Jelks's prized ten-point antlers, which she'd secured to the top of the arch, then tying it off on the backside of the arch, where it wouldn't be seen.

She reached into the bag of extra feathers and dried flowers she'd slung over her left shoulder, pulled her glue gun from the holster she'd rigged on her belt, and went to add another cluster of dried hydrangea blooms, leaning ever-so-slightly to the right. Which was a mistake. It was like a slow-motion cartoon. She tried to counteract the wobble, inching to the left, but she overcorrected, and it was too late. She grabbed for the right tree branch. Also a mistake. It came away in her hand, and she tumbled to the concrete floor.

And her arch, her gorgeous, forest-fantasy arch, came tumbling right down around her.

She fell flat on her ass, but instinctively shielded her head with her arms, as antlers and branches and feathers rained down around her. She felt a sear on her calf, felt the hot glue gun ricocheting onto the floor.

"Shit!"

He was at her side in a moment, kneeling down beside her, pulling her to a sitting position.

"Hey! Are you okay?" He brushed feathers and moss and dried hydrangea petals from her hair and shoulders.

"Shit!" she repeated, looking around at the ruins. "Shit. Damn. Hell. Piss."

He laughed, throwing his head back, displaying a set of perfect white teeth in contrast to his perfect golden tan. Actually, he was prettier than a runway model. He looked like something off the cover of a paperback romance novel. Biker boots and all.

"At least you didn't get impaled in the throat with an antler."

"At least," she said sourly.

"Can you stand?" he asked, extending a hand to help her up.

"Guess I'd better, if I'm gonna get this thing rebuilt before seven." She took his hand and managed to stand. Her tailbone was already starting to throb, her right shin was bleeding, and she could see a bruise blooming on her right elbow, where she'd tried to break her fall.

"Thanks," she said.

"I'm sorry about your arch," he said. "It was really looking pretty kick-ass."

"I know," Cara said. "Was."

He hesitated for a moment. "I could help you put it back together. You know, if you want."

Did she? Did she want his help?

"I'm Cullen Kane," he said. "The new kid in town."

"I know," she said.

"And you're Cara Kryzik," he said. "Bloom. I'm a big fan of your work."

"Thanks," she said, feeling her face redden. Was he being facetious? How would he know what her work looked like? Unlike him, she'd never had a wedding published.

"I was a guest at that wedding you did last weekend. Lillian Fanning's sister-in-law used to be married to my cousin."

"Really?" She hadn't noticed him at the Fanning wedding, but then, she'd been so distracted, what with Poppy and the creep who'd dognapped her, that that shouldn't have been a big surprise. Cara arched an eyebrow. "I'm surprised Lillian didn't ask *you* to do Torie's flowers."

"Gawd forbid," he drawled. "I've known Torie since she was in diapers, and she was hell on wheels even back then."

Cara wasn't sure whether to agree or take the high road. "Torie was a ... challenge," she allowed.

He smiled. "Tactful and talented. Anyway, I really did love what you did at their wedding. I'm sure Torie and Lillian were insisting on some blown-out Versailles-style designs. You did a nice job of reining them in, but still giving them what they thought they wanted."

"Well ... thanks. Thanks very much. I appreciate the compliment, coming from somebody in the field."

"Not at all." He gestured at the pile of branches. "I really would be happy to help you resurrect your arch. I'm pretty handy with a cordless drill and a glue gun."

"Oh, I couldn't," she tried to demur. But the minutes were ticking away. It had taken both her and Bert an entire day to build the damn thing back at the shop.

"Professional courtesy," he said, bowing from the waist. "I insist."

True to his word, Cullen Kane was a whiz with power tools. With the extra set of hands, they were able to get the branch structure rebuilt in only thirty minutes. This time, though, at his suggestion, they added bracing with some extra branches she'd brought along. He tugged hard on both sides, and then at the top of the arch, and this time around, there wasn't the slightest wobble.

He was so tall he didn't even really need the stepladder to wire the antlers to the top of the arch. So Cara worked on the side supports, attaching the antlers and feathers and flowers, while he positioned the ten-point antlers precisely at the top of the arch, adding sprays of dried flowers and feathers in a carefully contrived medallion shape, even fashioning a rough bow with a long strand of ivy, before applying more festoons of Spanish moss.

"Dammit," Cara muttered under her breath, looking up at his composition.

"Too much?" He stood back.

"No. Much better. Dammit."

"It was your vision," he said. "All I did was follow directions."

He was really insufferable. She should hate him. And she kind of did hate him, making her grateful for his help.

She glanced at her watch. "Oh! I've gotta get out of here. Gotta get home and shower and change before the wedding party starts arriving." She held out her hand. "Thanks for helping out. You were a lifesaver."

He shrugged. "It was the least I could do, after you caught me spying ."

She took a half step backward. "I suppose Patricia Trapnell told you they'd interviewed me for Brooke's wedding."

"She did. That's Patricia. She loves intrigue. Loves to pit one person against the other."

"I'm really not your competition," Cara told him. "I think they only interviewed me as a courtesy to Brooke's mother. Our styles seem . . . very different."

"Not so different," Cullen said, flashing those beautiful teeth again. "We're both perfectionists."

"There is that," Cara admitted. She grabbed a broom and started sweeping up the stray bits of moss and flower petals.

"Good luck with the wedding," Cullen said, realizing he'd been dismissed.

"Thanks," Cara said. "And good luck with yours."

He arched one eyebrow in an implied challenge. "We'll see, won't we?"

16

The wedding party looked to Cara like a group of trick-or-treaters who'd gotten lost on their way to Halloween. The bridesmaids wore matching short black spandex dresses that resembled overgrown tube tops, over black fishnet hose and short black bootees. The groomsmen wore black leather pants, and T-shirts with custom screen-printed designs featuring snarling befanged monsters.

The bridegroom was dressed in black leather pants, too, but instead of a screen-printed shirt he wore a metal-studded black leather vest over his bare chest. And he'd shaved his head for the occasion.

Laurie-Beth Winship's choice of a wedding gown was equally quirky—she'd designed it herself, with a bodice made of her grandmother's tightly laced 1950s corset, and a skirt made of layers of another grandmother's Irish lace curtains—but somehow, the wacky creation totally suited her pale complexion and long red hair.

It was a remarkably relaxed group. There were no hysterics, no panic attacks, no death threats issued. Even Payton, the edgy investment banker/punk rocker groom, seemed to be having a good time, as he and Laurie-Beth held their two-year-old son, Levi, between them as they swayed to "Brown-Eyed Girl."

Best of all, the wedding arch stood firm throughout the ceremony, even when little Levi managed to yank off one of the deer antlers while his parents were saying their vows.

It was actually a very original party, Cara decided, happy that she'd made a deal with the wedding photographer to document everything for her look-book at the shop. Although most of her Savannah brides still clung tightly to tradition, the Winship-Jelks wedding would show that she could deliver the goods no matter how outrageous the request. She was getting positively misty-eyed, sipping her second glass of blanc-de-blanc champagne, leaning against one of the steel support columns, watching the swirl of black-clad guests, as they laughed and danced and table-hopped around the cavernous warehouse, the multiple bloodred candles sending their shadows dancing across the rustic walls.

"I notice you're not wearing black tonight," came a low voice in her ear. "Even though the bride decreed an all-black dress code for her guests."

Cara recognized the voice at once. She didn't bother to turn and address him face-to-face. "I'm not a guest. I'm just the florist."

He stood so close she could smell his pine-scented soap, feel the tickle of his beard on her bare shoulder, which sent a delicious shiver down her spine, which she instantly regretted.

"And yet, here you are. What color would you call that dress of yours?"

She looked down at the vintage orangish-pink silk cocktail dress she'd found on eBay. It was an old favorite that she'd worn to half a dozen weddings since buying it. It was obviously homemade, with sweet pinked seams, a metal zipper sewn into the side seam that dated it to the sixties, thin spaghetti straps, and hand-appliquéd daisies around the hem of the frothing full skirt.

"Hmm. I guess I'd call this coral."

"Kinda pretty," he said grudgingly.

"Kinda?" Now she did turn around. What she saw made her raise one questioning eyebrow. Jack Finnerty had ignored Laurie-Beth's blackout edict, too. Instead, he wore a blue seersucker suit, a pale yellow button-down shirt, no tie, and battered brown Topsiders on his sockless feet. "You sweet-tongued devil, you."

He was sipping a Moon River pale ale from a plastic cup. "I gather you did all these, uh, arrangements tonight. Mind if I ask what's with all the black flowers and skulls and heavy metal?"

Her smile was tight. "The bride and groom tell me their dreams. I make it happen."

She sipped her champagne and wished he'd go away.

"Do you do all the flowers for all the weddings in Savannah?"

"Just the cool ones. Do you come to all the weddings in Savannah?" she countered.

"Not all of 'em," Jack said. "I guess I get around. It just happens I went to school with Laurie-Beth's older brother. And Laurie-Beth and I went out a couple times. You know, way back in the day before she met Payton."

"You went to school with Austin?" Cara asked.

"Technically. He was a couple years ahead of me in school, so we never hung out together much."

"I see," Cara said, gazing across the room at the brother in mention, Austin Winship, a towering six-foot-five presence, who at that moment seemed to be in danger of teetering facedown onto the grits bar the caterer had set up in the far corner.

Jack followed her eyes. "Ol' Austin seems to have gotten pretty caught up in the spirit of the wedding festivities. Is he actually a real justice of the peace or something?"

"Oh, no," Cara assured him. "Payton was dead set on not having a real minister for the wedding, so Austin got himself ordained into some nonde-nominational denomination, just for tonight."

"Is this one of those peyote-eating churches, by any chance?" Jack asked. "Because even a casual observer, like myself, can tell that Austin seems to have ingested some kind of pharmacologically enhanced substance."

That did make Cara laugh. "He showed up pretty glassy-eyed tonight. And

I'm assuming that high-pitched giggle that he kept breaking into during the ceremony isn't part of his day-to-day persona?"

"As I said, we weren't really friends," Jack said. "Austin missed his senior year at Country Day because his parents enrolled him in what was billed as an 'alternative school' out in Oregon."

"Rehab," Cara said.

"Exactly," Jack agreed.

There was an uneasy lull in the conversation. Cara found herself wishing he'd go away and simultaneously hoping he wouldn't.

Jack Finnerty made her nervous. He'd made her nervous every time she looked out the window of the shop over the past week and caught a glimpse of him running past, with Shaz trotting alongside. It made her nervous to realize how much time she spent gazing out that same window, hoping for a glance of him. And it made her desperately anxious when she found herself driving past his hovel on Macon Street, telling herself she was simply taking a short-cut to the Kroger, which was actually not a shortcut to the grocery store.

Jack Finnerty was taking up way too much space in her head. He'd looked so remotely elegant and reserved—and unbearably snotty—in his tuxedo the previous Saturday. And then when she'd opened her door Sunday and found him all sweaty and buff, standing on her doorstep with that look of chagrin on his face.

And now, damn him, he'd turned up here tonight, in his stinking seersucker suit, striking just the right note between hopelessly preppy and effortlessly casual. He was just a guy, one of these obnoxious Savannah guys who knew everybody and fit in everywhere without even trying.

He had to know the effect he was having on her, standing so close she swore she could see a bit of sawdust clinging to the lapel of his jacket. It was all she could do to keep herself from reaching out to dust it off. She could even see a place on his chin where he'd nicked himself shaving, a tiny dot of dried blood standing out from the dark stubble. She clasped her hands behind her back, just in case.

"How's the dog?" Jack finally asked.

"Poppy? She's fine. Happy to be home."

"Any more accidents?"

He was being deliberately annoying. Cara frowned. "I told you, she's housebroken."

Which wasn't completely true. If Cara left her alone for more than a few hours, Poppy would sometimes stand by the door, waiting for her to come home, even though there was a dog door that would let her out into the court-yard. Sometimes, Bert told her, Poppy would lie down in front of the shop door, staring at it, as though willing her to come back through it. Cara believed Poppy peed on the floor as revenge, or out of separation anxiety.

Was she really raising a neurotic puppy?

She gave Jack a sharp look. "How about your dog. Shaz? I'm guessing she hasn't run away lately?"

"No," Jack said. He leaned in even closer, his breath tickling her face. She took a half step backward. "Listen. Let me ask you something about Poppy. Would you say she's moody?"

"Moody? No." Cara laughed. "Why, is your dog moody?"

"She's just not very . . . peppy. I thought all puppies were kinda bouncy and off the wall and crazy. But that's not Shaz. She's pretty quiet. Seems to sleep most of the day. And when I come home from work, she kind of looks at me. Like, 'What? You're back? Who cares?' When I get ready to go out for a run, I almost have to drag her out the door. I was thinking maybe it has something to do with the breed."

For just a moment, she was tempted to suggest that maybe it had something to do with *him*. But no. He seemed seriously worried about Shaz, and she was touched by his concern.

"I don't think goldendoodles are particularly moody. I mean, yeah, Poppy sometimes lets me know she misses me when I'm working late, or not paying her proper attention, but mostly, she's a happy camper. And if I don't walk her at least twice every day, she lets me know I'm being a slacker."

"Hmm," he said.

"Is there a chance Shaz is depressed? I mean, has anything changed in her routine that would make her want to run away?"

. . .

Jack took a long swig of his beer. Hell yeah, he wanted to tell her. Everything had changed in Shaz's routine. His, too. The minute Zoey walked out the door, it had all changed. He would have liked to have left, too. But he had bills to pay, and obligations to his brother, and their business. Anyway, where would he have gone?

It wasn't that he actually missed Zoey that much. They hadn't gotten along for months before she left. They quarreled constantly. Zoey couldn't understand why they couldn't travel, cut loose, have some fun. Couldn't he get a real job in a real office, instead of coming home late every night, dirty and sweaty, his hands and hair spattered with paint, his clothes leaking sawdust with every step he took?

He couldn't really blame her for resenting him. He'd had a good job as an insurance broker when they met a year previously. He drove a new BMW 750, had a sleek glass and chrome loft in a new development down by the river. He'd walked away from all of it, only two months after Zoey moved in, selling the loft to buy the crappy little freedman's cottage on Macon Street, trading in the Beemer for a used F-150 pickup, leaving behind his slick suits for painter's pants and a tool belt when he and Ryan started their historic-restoration business.

Jack had bedgrudgingly accepted Zoey's crazy designer dog, christened with a name he couldn't even spell. And then she'd taken off, leaving him and Shaz trying to figure out where it had all gone so wrong.

He glanced over at Cara's empty glass, deciding to save her the dismal details of his dismal home life. "Is that champagne? Can I get you another? Or maybe you wanna dance?" He hoped he didn't sound too eager. In fact, he halfway hoped she'd tell him no. Then he'd have an excuse to go home and drink some real liquor. Maybe he'd even think about hanging some doors, or finishing the tile in the hall bathroom.

"After Torie's wedding, I didn't think you liked to dance," Cara said.

"Oh." He looked away, his hands in his pockets, looking bored. "I'm okay with dancing. It was just that song. It's stupid, I know. . . ."

"Torie told me," she said, her voice gentle. "About your girlfriend."

"Torie talks too much," he snapped. "How about that drink?"

But now the bride and groom were making their way to the cake table. Laurie-Beth had commissioned a sculptor friend to make figurines of her and Payton, authentic down to the tiniest real flowers in her bouquet, for a cake topper. The caterer had asked Cara to stick around for the cake-cutting ceremony so she could help remove the sculpture before it came under attack from the Confederate-era sword Payton planned to use.

"Sorry, can't," Cara said, giving him a smile he hoped was full of regret. "I'm still on duty."

She hurried off in the direction of the bride and groom, leaving Jack Finnerty staring at her back, at her bare shoulders, and her neck. She really did dress oddly, and yet, he thought she was by far the prettiest girl in the room that night, with her windblown butterscotch curls tied up with a pink satin ribbon. Her pink-orange skirt billowed out from around her tightly belted waist, and she reminded him of a tropical hibiscus blossom. Begging to be picked.

17

Bert was lounging on a low brick wall outside the warehouse, smoking a questionable substance with Austin Winship. When they saw Cara approaching, they giggled in unison, threw down the butts and stamped them flat. Austin drifted down the cobblestoned walkway toward River Street, where yet another party beckoned.

"Heeyyyy, Cara," Bert said, in a singsongy voice. "Is the reception over already?"

"It is for me," she told him. "Do you want a lift back to your place?"

Bert looked off toward the river, where they could hear faint strains of loud rock music, and laughter, but Austin had already disappeared.

"I guess," he said.

She left the van's windows down for the short ride back to Bert's apartment on St. Julian Street, which was only a few blocks away from her own place.

"I saw you talking to your favorite person," Bert said, giving her a sly sideways look.

"Jack Finnerty? He's not so bad."

"Certainly not bad-looking," he said. "Kind of a coincidence that he'd show up at two weddings you were working, two weeks in a row, don't you think?"

"He knows a lot of people," Cara said. "He went to school with Laurie-Beth's brother. And he knows Payton's brother too."

"Interesting," Bert said. "What were you two chatting about?"

"Nothing, really. Our dogs. He thinks his dog is depressed."

Bert giggled. "Maybe his dog needs some puppy uppers."

She rolled her eyes in the dark.

"So. Is he married? Seeing somebody?"

"Not married. Had a bad breakup with his girlfriend a few months ago. And before you start, Bert, I am *not* interested."

He feigned a look of innocence. "I'm not saying a word."

"You were thinking it," Cara said. "I could hear you loud and clear."

"Would it hurt you to have a life after Leo? To start seeing a nice, good-looking guy, who also happens to have a dog?"

"Yes," Cara said crisply. "It would. Now let's drop it, shall we?"

He waved his hands wearily. "Whatever. You're the boss."

She pulled the van alongside the curb outside his apartment. Bert got out and walked unsteadily over to the driver's-side window and leaned in.

He lightly touched her shoulder. "Don't be mad at me, okay?"

"I'm not mad. But you're wasted. Why don't you get some sleep?"

"I am *not* wasted. A little buzzed maybe, but definitely not wasted. So, I just want to tell you one more thing. And it's going to make you mad at me, but I'm telling you anyway. The guy was watching you. All night. But not in a creepy way. I saw him looking around, during the ceremony, and when he finally spotted you, he got this dippy smile on his face."

"You're imagining things," she told him. "Go to bed, okay?"

"Oh-kay. But remember, you heard it here first."

She was a block away from Bert's apartment, humming along to the radio, when she realized, much to her chagrin, that she had a big dippy smile on her own face.

18

Cara was on the phone with a customer when she heard the shop door open. It was only 8:30 a.m., but Bert was out on a delivery, so she was manning the store by herself. She placed a hand over the receiver and addressed the visitor. "Be with you in a minute."

While her phone customer droned on and on about the exact right shade of red she wanted for the roses she was sending her recuperating granny, Cara sized up her visitor, who was wandering around the shop, examining some of the "make and take" arrangements in the walk-in cooler.

She was a bride, obviously. In her late twenties, tall and slender, with skin so pale it was nearly opaque, and fine, dark hair gathered into a hastily styled ponytail tied with a scrunchy. A scrunchy? Cara didn't even know those still existed. The bride wore very little makeup and was dressed in a navy-blue suit and white silk blouse that fairly screamed job interview. The earpiece from her phone dangled from one ear, and she clutched a briefcase under one arm. Every once in a while, she glanced furtively down at her watch. The diamond solitaire on her left ring finger was impressive, at least two carats, Cara thought, and her pulse quickened. She needed to finish up with the sixty-dollar red rose order and get with this bride.

When she'd finally managed to persuade her caller that she'd only use the very freshest, loveliest, long-stemmed roses for her arrangement, she put the phone down with a sense of relief.

"Good morning," she said, hurrying around from behind her worktable. "Is there anything special I can help you with?"

"No. Well, yes, I mean, are you the owner? Cara? I think my mother's already been in to see you. I'm getting married in July, and we thought, I mean, well Vicki Cooper raved about the flowers you did for their wedding and..."

"I'm Cara. And you must be Brooke Trapnell. Is that right? Marie's daughter?"

"That's right." Brooke nodded. A faint blush crept over her face. "I understand you met with my father and stepmother too?"

"Yes," Cara said. "Just last week. I met them over at Cabin Creek. What a beautiful spot for a wedding. You must be very excited."

Brooke was busy looking around the shop. She traced the tip of a white phalaenopsis orchid with her fingertip. "This is so pretty. What kind of flower is it?"

"It's a phalaenopsis," Cara said. "Do you like orchids?"

The girl was still concentrating on the orchid. "Hmm?" She looked up at Cara. "I'm sorry. What were you saying before?"

"Just that you must be getting excited. With your wedding only a few weeks away."

The girl nodded, her face serious. "Patricia printed out this timeline thing from one of the wedding websites, and according to it, I'm already hopelessly behind schedule. On top of everything else, I've got a big trial scheduled a week before the wedding. I'm actually starting to feel pretty panicky."

"Oh, no. Don't be panicky," Cara said. "That's my job. Your job is to look beautiful and enjoy your special day."

Brooke gave her a dubious look. "Half the girls I know have gotten married this past year. I've been a bridesmaid six times just since September, and it's been hell. Every single time. Have you ever seen a bride who wasn't panicky?"

"Well, there was this one girl this past weekend," Cara admitted. "But she was probably the exception to the rule."

"One of my friends, Melanie Eaves? Maybe you know her? Her caterer went out of business two weeks before the wedding. Mel got so stressed her hair was falling out in big clumps. She lost so much weight they finally put a feeding tube in her stomach."

"Oh my."

"And this other girl? She was a year ahead of me in law school at Georgia? Samantha Epstein? She ended up going so far over budget, her parents were fighting like cats and dogs, and they ended up filing for divorce. Like, the week before Samantha's wedding. Her father refused to go the reception."

"That's too bad," Cara said.

"Yes, well, at least that won't happen with my parents. Patricia already took care of that, didn't she?"

"Ummm," Cara said, stalling.

"Anyway." Brooke stole another glance at her watch. "Oh, God, look at the time. I promised my mom I'd come by and see you. About the flowers. She said you'd need to talk to me?"

"Yes," Cara said. "Usually I like to spend some time with the bride, to talk about what type flowers you like, color preferences, style. Maybe you have a Pinterest board, or some pictures from the wedding magazines you've been clipping, something like that?"

Brooke shrugged. "Not really. I guess I'm not much into that kind of stuff. Whatever you and Mom come up with, I'm sure I'll like."

This was a first for Cara. A bride who didn't have pages and pages of carefully clipped or pinned wedding photoraphs. Earlier in the spring, she'd done flowers for a bride who'd actually been scrapbooking her future wedding since the age of twelve.

"No favorite color or flower?"

Brooke flicked the phalaenopsis blossom. "This is pretty."

"That's a start," Cara said. "We can do some really pretty arrangments with orchids. Probably not just orchids though, right? I'm thinking maybe something very simple and natural-looking?"

Brooke nodded vigorously. "Yes. Definitely simple. I don't want anything too . . ." She waved her hands in the air. "Too fluffy. Or show-offy. Do you know what I mean?"

Yes, Cara thought, *I do: the exact opposite of what your father and step-mother are envisioning.*

"Anything else?" Cara asked. "Besides orchids for your bouquet? What about your attendants? And the groom and groomsmen? Any particular flower your fiancé likes—or hates?"

"Harris?" Brooke shrugged. "He's a guy." Her face softened. "A sweetie, but he's probably even more clueless than me when it comes to something like this. As far as Harris Strayhorn is concerned, as long as we have an open bar and some kind of barbecue at the reception, he'll be happy."

"Like a lot of grooms," Cara said, laughing. "I can help you figure out the boutonnieres—maybe in Harris's school colors or something? And we'll need to talk about flowers for the reception, as well as the chapel at Cabin Creek. Patricia showed me the dining room, which is lovely. But Patricia wasn't clear on whether you'll be doing a seated dinner or a buffet, so that's something we'll need to talk about. . . ."

"All that?" Brooke twisted the solitaire on her ring finger with her right hand. Around and around, looking down at it and then back up at Cara. "Just, I mean, can't you make all the flowers sort of all look like the same thing?"

Cara heard a faint ringing coming from the vicinity of Brooke's jacket pocket, prompting the girl to start patting all the pockets of her jacket, searching for her phone.

"Oh geez. I have to take this. It's the office. Hello?" Brooke's eyebrows drew together, her narrow shoulders hunched over. "Right. Yes. Absolutely. I'm on my way in right now. I can do a conference call in ten minutes. Will that work?"

She was heading for the door, already immersed in business.

Cara cleared her throat, and Brooke turned.

"Look. Just talk to my mom, would you? The two of you can work it out much better than I could."

"What about your father?" Cara asked. "I think he and your stepmother have some ideas. . . ."

"No!" Brooke said sharply. "Patricia already took over my dad. She doesn't get to take over my wedding too. I won't let her."

"Well okay," Cara said. "But they have another florist in mind. I'm actually not certain they plan to hire me."

"It's my damned wedding," Brooke said, her jaw clenched. "And my mother and I am hiring you. Period."

She threw open the shop door and hurried down the sidewalk.

19

The siege by Trapnells descended upon Cara Kryzik at 6 p.m. on Wednesday, right at closing time.

Brooke and Marie Trapnell arrived at the door, just as she was wheeling in the old-fashioned wooden garden cart full of potted plants from the sidewalk.

Brooke wore a black lady lawyer dress with a black-and-white-striped jacket, and an expression of pure misery. Her mother was dressed more casually, but the expression was almost identical to Brooke's.

"Brooke, Marie, uh, well, how nice to see you," Cara stammered. She heard a car door slam then, and glancing over, saw Patricia Trapnell step out of the silver Jaguar parked in a no-parking slot at the curb.

Her head whipped from the stepmother to the mother and daughter.

"Hi, Patricia," Cara said. She felt her scalp prickle, and wondered if this was what the sensation of fight-or-flight was like.

"You're about to close, aren't you?" Brooke said. Brooke glared at Patricia, who'd joined them on the sidewalk. "I *told* you, she closes at six."

"But not for you," Cara said quickly.

"Of course not," Patricia said, her voice silky, as she neatly sidestepped Marie and Brooke. "We're so sorry to catch you like this, on the spur of the moment, but as I was just explaining to Brooke, if we're going to pull off this wedding, we simply have to start nailing down the details. Now."

Patricia reached into the large buff-colored calfskin bag that dangled from her shoulder. Cara, who told herself she only read *In Style* magazine to keep up with wedding trends, recognized the handbag as the $3,500 Fendi bag she'd drooled over in a recent issue.

"Here," Patricia said, thrusting a document into her hands. "This is the game plan we've finally managed to hammer out."

"Game plan?" Cara said dumbly, glancing down at the multipage dossier.

"For our wedding, of course," Patricia said.

"*My* wedding. Mine and Harris's," Brooke said.

"Which her father and I are paying for," Patricia added.

Marie coughed quietly.

"And her mother, of course," Patricia said, giving Marie a curt nod.

"Does this mean you want me to do the flowers?" Cara looked directly at Brooke.

"Yes," Brooke said, nodding vigorously. "And everything else, too. Flowers, food, all that stuff. Can you?"

"Brooke, I'm flattered to be asked, but, I'm not a wedding planner—I can give you the name of several people locally who'd do a wonderful job. I work with most of them. . . ."

"That's what I suggested," Patricia said. "What we need is a professional planner to pull together all our vendors, the photographer, the caterer, the cake baker, the band, the valet-parking people . . ."

"I want Cara," Brooke said. She crossed slim, freckled arms over her chest, and in that moment, Cara found new admiration for this bride who'd suddenly acquired a backbone. "She's done tons of weddings for lots of girls I know, right?"

"Well, flowers for the weddings," Cara said cautiously.

In fact, she'd been a de facto wedding planner lots of times, mostly for small weddings, as a favor to her budget-minded brides. And she'd complained, privately, to Bert, that she might as well have charged for the service, though she never had.

"See!" Patricia said. "Brooke, we're not talking about some little cake and punch affair at the American Legion hall. Your father has budgeted two hundred and fifty thousand dollars."

Cara was about to agree with Patricia. Why get in over her head?

But then the figure she'd just mentioned floated before Cara's eyes. A budget of $250,000. Not just a measly $10,000 for flowers. A quarter of a million smackers. Of which she, as the wedding planner, could expect to be paid twenty percent.

Suddenly, dollar signs danced merrily in the humid afternoon air. That much money could wipe out her debt to the Colonel. No more phone calls, emails, or terse text messages. No more ramen-noodle dinners. She could buy a new cooler for the shop, get a reliable car. Her mind swirled with all the possibilities.

Why shouldn't she plan Brooke's wedding?

"Look," Cara said, "we don't have to stand out here in the heat, debating this. Why don't you all come inside and sit down? I'll make us some iced tea—or we can even have a glass of wine, if you like, and we can discuss the pros and cons."

Cara found the pitcher of peach iced tea in the fridge, glancing longingly at the bottle of pinot grigio on the rack in the door. When this ambush was over, she promised herself, that bottle would be empty.

While the ladies sipped their tea, Cara skimmed over the "game plan." Brooke jiggled her foot impatiently and pulled out her phone, texting a mile a minute.

The first line of the document was a surprise. "Two hundred fifty guests? Really?"

"I know," Brooke said, not bothering to look up from her phone. "Crazy, right? And you should see the list. People I've never met. People I haven't seen since, like, ever. If it were up to me, we'd have fifty, tops."

"It's not up to you, though, is it?" Patricia set her tea glass down on the tabletop with a clatter.

Marie looked up at the ceiling and hummed under her breath. This discussion, Cara sensed, had been going on for hours, if not days.

"Apparently, not," Brooke muttered.

Cara read on. "Passed appetizers during cocktail hour. Seated dinner. . . . Will the dining room at Cabin Creek hold two hundred fifty people?"

"Easily." Patricia said. "According to Libba Strayhorn, they can open up the doors between the dining room and the twin parlors and entrance hall and easily accommodate that many."

"It'll be awful," Brooke said. "A mass of hot, sweaty, hungry, overdressed social climbers, all pawing at me and grabbing for the last piece of shrimp."

"Brooke . . ." Marie gave her daughter a warning look.

"So . . ." Cara did some quick math. "Maybe do cocktails and apps in the entry hall as people are entering. We'll have scattered high-top tables around the perimeter of the room. For flowers—maybe just some bud vases on the high-tops?"

"Whatever." Brooke was texting again. Marie reached over and gently took the phone from her daughter's hand.

"Do you have a caterer in mind?" Cara asked, directing the question at Marie.

"Well . . ."

"Simple Elegance does all the best events in town," Patricia put in. "They did an amazing job for a dinner for us a few years ago."

"Your wedding dinner?" Brooke shot her stepmother a malicious smirk.

Patricia had the grace to blush. "Well, yes, as a matter of fact."

"They're *not* doing *my* wedding reception," Brooke said.

"We've got lots of fabulous caterers in Savannah," Cara said, desperate to fill that awkward moment. "I work with Layne Pelletier of Fete Accompli a lot. In fact, she did Torie Fanning's wedding."

"That food at Torie's wedding was wonderful," Marie said. "Especially that salmon tartare thingy on the corncakes."

"Harris adores salmon," Brooke said. "Let's go with Layne."

"She's good, I suppose," Patricia allowed. "I know the Fannings were pleased with what she did."

Cara looked back at the "game plan." "Okay, well, this does look like a fairly ambitious event. Full bar with premium brands, wine service with dinner . . ."

"*My* friends all drink beer," Brooke said pointedly. "But, whatever. . . ."

"Dancing after dinner," Cara went on. "Disc jockey?"

Patricia's waxen face took on something close to a look of pain. "An orchestra," she said. "If the kids want to have a DJ, they can do that at the after-party."

"We might be hard-pressed to book an orchestra at this late date," Cara warned. "In fact, it might be tricky to get the best vendors, working this close to the date, especially Layne. She usually stays booked up months and months ahead of time."

Patricia reached back into her Fendi bag for her phone. She tapped a button, looked up at the others. "I'm calling Carlos at Simple Elegance. We have a relationship. I'm sure if the others are busy, he'd be willing to accommodate us."

"Patricia!" Brooke glared at her stepmother. "Cara is our wedding planner. Can't you just let her figure this out?"

The older woman sighed, shrugged, put the phone away.

"I'll start making calls right away," Cara said. "If we can't get Layne, I do know Carlos at Simple Elegance, as well as several other people. But again, no promises."

Marie glanced over at Brooke. "Honey, couldn't we could just wait until fall, October, say?"

"No." Brooke shook her head vehemently. "I've got another huge civil trial coming up this fall. Harris has a conference in San Francisco. It's July or nothing." She glanced from Marie to Patricia. "July sixth. It's the anniversary of our first date."

"Impossible," Patricia muttered.

"I'll make it work. Somehow," Cara said. She sounded more positive than she felt. A big-budget wedding in six weeks? Was she nuts to think she could pull it off?

"Great," Brooke said. She took a last sip of iced tea, draining her glass, and stood. "I'm meeting Harris for dinner in ten minutes. I'll let all of you deal with the rest of the details." She put her hand lightly on Marie's shoulder. "Okay, Mom?"

"Wait!"

The others looked at Cara in surprise.

"Your wedding dress? You've ordered one, right? I really need to take a look at it, and I definitely need to talk about your preferences for flowers for your bouquet and the reception."

Patricia gave a derisive snort.

"She actually did buy a dress," Marie said quietly. "It's lovely. Very simple, very flattering for Brooke's figure."

"Do you have a photo?" Cara asked.

Brooke frowned. "No photos. But the dress is out in Mom's car."

"You bought a wedding gown off the rack?" Patricia shuddered. "Do I dare ask where you got it?"

"Some bride place in Atlanta," Brooke said carelessly. "Mom can show you." She started for the door.

"Brooke, honestly!" Marie called after her. "Cara really needs to get these things settled. Can't you call Harris and tell him you'll be a little late?"

"You can deal with all that stuff," Brooke said. "You know what I like, Mom. Just no orange. Or purple. Or red. Or yellow."

With that, she stepped out of her black pumps, slipped on a fair of flats, and was out the door, striding down the sidewalk without a backward look.

Which left Marie and Patricia sitting at the worktable in Cara's shop, separated only by a space of about three feet. Things got very quiet. Too quiet.

Cara jumped up. "Wine anybody?"

"Definitely," Marie said.

"Unless you've got the makings for a dry martini," Patricia said hopefully.

20

By Friday morning, she'd not only gotten the signed contract for the Trapnell wedding, she had a $12,500 deposit check in her hot little hand.

"Awesome," Bert said, when Cara showed him the check. "So, now you're a full-fledged wedding planner?"

"As far as the Trapnells are concerned, I am."

"We're rich," Bert said. "Wanna take your favorite assistant out to lunch?"

"You can have half my tuna sandwich if you like. We're not rich. We're not even solvent. Yet." She nodded toward the pile of bills on her desk. "It took six hundred dollars to replace the compressor on the cooler. I spent close to five thousand dollars replacing the flowers for Torie's wedding, which ate up half my profit from that wedding. And if I don't pay my phone bill by two p.m. today, they're going to cut off our service."

"And then there's the Colonel," Bert said.

"There's always the Colonel," Cara agreed. "He gets paid first—ten thousand right off the top."

"I thought he told you he wanted the whole magilla—twenty thousand," Bert said.

"I don't *have* the whole magilla," she reminded her assistant. "But I get the rest of the Trapnell deposit two weeks before the wedding. If the sky doesn't fall on my head between now and then—I should be able to fork over the rest of his money."

"Sounds like a plan," Bert said. "Speaking of—are we okay for Maya's wedding tonight? She's not one of our usual angsty brides, but she did text me this morning and ask if everything was okay."

Maya Gaines wasn't her typical Bloom bride. She was just out of design school at SCAD, and her flower budget was nearly nonexistent. Cara had agreed to take the job as a favor to Bert, who'd known the bride since elementary school. But also because Maya was hip and cute—and just plain nice. The ceremony—and the reception—would be at the Knights of Columbus hall just a few blocks away on Liberty Street.

"We should be fine," Cara said. She pointed to the buckets in the cooler, which she'd filled with inexpensive "filler" flowers she'd picked up earlier in the morning at Sam's Club.

"That's all the stuff you'll need for the boutonnieres," she said. "Get started on those, and I'll run over to Breitmueller's to pick up the rest of Maya's order. You can make the bouquets when I get back, and I'll start on the table arrangements." She looked around the workroom. "Did you pick up the Mason jars?"

"And the raffia, and the Twizzlers," Bert said. "So, you're really going to plunk red licorice sticks in those flower arrangements?"

"Along with red striped Pixy Stix," Cara said. "They're the bride and groom's favorite candies. They're Maya's colors. And they're cheap."

"I guess," Bert said, looking dubious.

"You mark my word. By tomorrow morning, those Mason-jar arrangements with Twizzlers and Pixy Stix are going to be all over Instagram and Pinterest."

Cara was at the wholesale house, watching her sales rep total her tab, carefully adding up each item with her pocket calculator. Even an innocent ten-dollar overcharge could throw Maya's tiny budget out of whack.

Without warning, Cullen Kane sidled over. He was wearing a loose-fitting blue linen shirt and white jeans, with a cluster of silver and leather bracelets on his right wrist. Cara, on the other hand, was wearing a faded orange sundress and rubber flip-flops.

He stood a little too close, invading her personal space.

"Hi there," Cara said, taking a half step backward. "How are you?"

"Fine. But not as fine as you, apparently. Congratulations. I hear you're doing the Trapnell wedding."

She blinked. "Where'd you hear that? I just signed the contract last night."

"Patricia's a dear friend," Cullen said. "We talk every night. I don't mind telling you I was a little surprised. She felt badly about it, but it's not as if I need the work."

"Of course not," Cara said.

Cullen came even closer. He smelled like Clinique moisturizer. He was so close she could see that he was actually wearing guyliner. Skillfully applied, yes, but it was still eyeliner.

"Any guesses why Brooke got her way and hired you?" he asked.

"Because it's her wedding, and I'm good at what I do?"

"Don't be naïve," he snapped. "Brookie is still pissed off that Gordon left Marie for Patricia. She can't get it into her head that after years of being trapped in a loveless marriage, Gordon actually had the balls to be with a real woman."

"A real woman named Patricia."

"Exactly. Yes, Patricia. Who in no way broke up that marriage. Anyway, it's been ages, but Marie still can't deal, which means that her daughter can't deal. And Brookie, PS, doesn't actually give a rat's ass about flowers, or any of this. So she's torturing Gordon with all this wedding crap, just to get back at him. It's all about retaliation with that girl."

"Thanks for the backgrounder," Cara said. "Or, at least, your theory of the background."

"And I hear you've now signed on as wedding planner too. Quite a coup. Let me ask. Have you ever actually planned an entire wedding before?"

She felt her face grow hot. "Obviously."

"A wedding with a two-hundred-and-fifty-thousand-dollar budget? With a high-profile client like the Trapnells and Strayhorns? Were you aware that Patricia's been in contact with *Town and Country* to have the wedding covered by them?"

Cara's mouth went dry. Patricia hadn't bothered to mention she was angling for a glossy society-magazine story about her stepdaughter's wedding, but she shouldn't have been surprised. The woman was dying for attention.

"As far as I'm concerned, all my weddings are high-profile," Cara said. "All my brides are incredibly special to me, and I try to give each one exactly the day of their dreams. No matter what the budget."

"How sweet," Cullen purred. He glanced over at the table where her order had been assembled.

Cara's buckets held bunches of cheerful Shasta daisies, red zinnias, yellow gerbera daisies, and Queen Anne's lace. A grand total of $867, by her calculator.

"Looks like you're doing a children's birthday party," he observed. "Let me guess. Circus theme?"

She chose to ignore the taunt. Instead she pointed at the masses of flowers covering the counter next to hers. It was piled high with exotic flowers, all in vivid tropical shades of orange, purples, hot pinks, and lime green.

"Gypsy wedding?" she asked.

He smiled blandly. "Just a dinner party Patricia is throwing tonight for Alexandra Skouras. Do you know her? She's the new head of marketing for General Mills. She and her husband Creighton just bought a second home over at Palmetto Bluff."

"Never met them," Cara admitted. Or heard of them, she wanted to say.

Her sales rep had finished tallying her order, and silently handed her the receipt.

Ignoring Cullen Kane, Cara checked the total on the receipt against the one on her calculator.

"Looks fine," she told the young woman, whom she hadn't worked with before. "Just put it on my account, please."

"Name?"

"Cara Kryzik. It should be under Bloom."

The clerk tapped her keyboard, found Cara's name in the system, but frowned.

"Um. It looks like there's a hold on your account."

Cara felt the blood drain from her face.

"Ouch," Cullen said, under his breath. He gave Cara a mock sympathetic smile, and finally moved back to his own side of the counter. But Cara knew he was watching. And listening intently.

"That's got to be a mistake," Cara said quietly.

The girl shook her head. "I only know what's in the system. This says you've got an outstanding balance."

"Look," Cara whispered. "I paid that bill yesterday. In full."

"But it's not been entered into the system," the girl said.

"I get that," Cara said, losing patience. "But the check is probably in your accounting office right now. Maybe it hasn't been posted yet."

"Probably not." The girl shrugged and looked meaningfully over Cara's shoulder, at another florist, who was hovering nearby with a bucketful of pink and white carnations.

"Okay. So what are we gonna do?" Cara asked. "I'd just write you another check, but I didn't bring my checkbook with me. I literally just ran over here to get these flowers for the wedding I'm doing tonight. I can come back later. All right?"

"Nope," the girl said. "Sorry. New policy. I can't let you take any product out of here until that hold is lifted."

"This is crazy," Cara moaned. "I've never had this happen before. And I need these flowers."

"Sorry," the girl said, but clearly, she wasn't sorry. She wasn't even terribly interested in Cara, or her credit hold. "Next."

The florist with the carnations stepped around Cara, giving her a quick, pitying look, the kind you'd give a crazy bag lady with a shopping cart full of recycling.

But Cara wasn't budging, and she wasn't leaving Breitmueller's without her damn flowers.

"Call Wendy," she told the girl. "Please."

. . .

Thirty minutes later, they found Cara's check in a stack of unopened mail on the bookkeeper's desk.

"Cara, I'm so sorry," Wendy Breitmueller said. They were sitting in her glass-walled office, located on a catwalk overlooking the warehouse. "Obviously, Janet didn't handle that very tactfully."

"No," Cara said, remembering the looks of pity and contempt she'd been given by the other customers in the warehouse. "She didn't. I was mortified."

"She's new," Wendy said. "But I've explained to her that that's not how we handle credit issues. You have my promise, it won't happen again."

"Hope not," Cara said, standing. She looked down at her phone. Two texts from Bert had popped up while she was dealing with this latest snafu.

WHERE R U?

And then, *NEED THOSE DAMN FLOWERS.*

Wendy followed her to the office door. "I hear business is looking up. You're doing the Trapnell wedding?"

"Damn!" Cara said. "Word travels fast."

"It's a small town," Wendy said with a smile. "People talk."

"People like Cullen Kane?"

"I think he's jealous of you," Wendy told her.

"Me? I'm no threat to him."

"Anybody who gets what he thinks he wants is a threat to somebody like Cullen Kane," Wendy advised. "Remember that."

21

Bert was standing at the worktable, fastening sprigs of rosemary and dai-sies together with floral tape. He looked up as Cara came in the door, weighed down with the flowers.

"Thought maybe you'd been abducted by aliens," he said, putting down the boutonniere he'd been working on. "Everything okay?"

"Grrr" was her only answer. "Ask me later. I've got to get moving with these bouquets and arrangements."

Fortunately, Maya had chosen only two attendants for her wedding. Cara went to work first on the most important bouquet. And as she bunched together the sunny reds, whites, and yellows for the bride's bouquet, snipping their stems and stripping the lower leaves, she felt her anger and frustration melt away. She reached into the cooler and brought out a handful of lemon leaves she'd trimmed from the tree in the courtyard garden, and tucked the glossy leaves in and around the flowers, turning the bouquet in her hand as she worked, studying it to make sure it worked from all angles.

She put the bouquet down in a Mason jar of water on the worktable, stepped back, and thought. It needed a touch of drama, she decided. After another moment, she walked out the back door into the garden, and stood there, hands on her hips, surveying what she had in bloom.

Finally, she spied the happy green and yellow zebra-striped leaves of the canna plant that had been left behind by a long-ago gardener. Cara wasn't normally a fan of the lowly canna, but she'd loved this zany striped foliage the moment she spotted it among the weeds and underbrush in the courtyard. With her scissors, she cut two of the long, straplike leaves and brought them back inside.

Bert watched while she split the leaves in half lengthwise, then wound them around and around the bouquet stem, like so much living ribbon, finally fastening the ends together with a large vintage enameled daisy brooch from the 1960s.

"Ohmygod, that's awesome," he laughed, when she held the bouquet up for inspection. "It's so Maya! She'll love it."

Maya Gaines knew what suited her. She was Amerasian, petite, just over five feet tall, with a mop of shiny dark curls. Her wedding dress was a short, pale yellow eyelet frock with spaghetti straps and a yellow satin bow at the waist. Her shoes were red ankle-strap heels, and instead of a veil she wore a narrow-brimmed straw fedora trimmed with yellow ribbon and a jaunty red fabric daisy.

She hopped up and down and hugged Cara when she walked into the K of C hall and saw the tables, with their white paper toppers and centerpieces of flowers and candy. Hanging from the ceiling at random heights were over-sized red, yellow, and white tissue-paper flowers Cara had assigned for Maya and her sisters to create.

"I love it," Maya exclaimed, twirling around and touching the Mason jars. "It's what I dreamed about, only better. Twizzlers! And Pixy Stix! Wait until Jared sees these."

Cara laughed. "I really don't think Jared is going to get all that excited about Twizzlers on his wedding day."

"You don't know Jared," Maya replied. "He's a total candyholic."

. . .

The ceremony was brief, but sweet. Standing before a beaming white-haired Asian man, who Cara later learned was the bride's maternal grandfather, Maya and Jared pledged to love each other and play nice, and hold hands through every adventure life would bring them.

When they'd exchanged rings and kissed, the crowd of around a hundred in the hall roared their approval and clapped and whistled.

Cara and Bert, who'd stayed for the ceremony, exchanged a look. "What do you think?" Cara whispered.

"They'll make it," Bert said solemnly. "She's a sweetheart, and Jared's the first non-asshole she's dated. I mean, they've lived together for three years, the whole time Maya was in school."

Cara raised one eyebrow. "Forever? Really?"

Bert nodded vigorously. "Yeah. A hundred percent. I mean, I wouldn't want to jinx them, but if anybody can make a marriage work, it's those two zanies."

Cara was in line at the buffet, about to serve herself a pig in a blanket from the steam tray, when for some reason, a couple on the dance floor caught her eye. She had to look again.

Jack Finnerty! He wore a dress shirt with rolled-up sleeves, khaki slacks, and a straw fedora not too unlike the one the bride wore. In fact, most of the men and many of the women at the wedding wore hats. It was the new hipster thing, Bert had informed her. He himself was sporting a straw boater.

The girl Jack was with was nearly his height, with long light brown hair. She wore a strapless navy-blue sundress, and she danced effortlessly with Jack, laughing and chattering away as they moved through the crowd on the dance floor.

Bert stood beside her in the line and saw what she was watching. "Hey. Isn't that the dognapper? Who let him in here?"

Cara shrugged. "He literally knows everybody in Savannah. I don't know how the man has time to work, in between going to weddings every weekend."

They found a table near the back of the room; Cara sipped a glass of pinot grigio, and Bert ate what she estimated was his weight in boiled shrimp, pigs in a blanket, and Buffalo chicken drumettes.

"How do you eat like that and never gain weight?" she asked. "I bet you've eaten like, twelve thousand calories, just while I've been sitting here."

Her assistant was as tall and gangly as a strand of sea oats, six foot three, weighing maybe 140 on his version of a fat day. He'd died his blond hair purple in honor of his best friend's wedding, and he wore skinny white jeans, a red shirt, and a narrow yellow tie, loosened at the neck. Bert patted the vicinity of his belly. "I don't know. I just like food. I guess I like it as much as I used to like Scotch. So now, I eat instead of booze."

"You're an exoskeleton, I swear," she countered.

They stayed until the bride and groom cut the wedding cake, which in their case was actually a huge Key lime pie, and then Cara tried to leave. She'd already stayed longer than she'd planned, lingering only because she was enjoying attending a wedding with a happy, carefree bride and groom—a rarity in her business.

"C'mon," Bert protested. "Stay awhile. You haven't even danced with me."

"You dance? With women?"

He looked around the room. "Sometimes. When there are no other attractive options."

"Am I supposed to be flattered?"

Still, she allowed him to lead her onto the dance floor, where she tried, mostly unsuccessfully, to match the rhythm of the weird technopunk song the disc jockey was playing.

"I give up," she said finally, after the third time her sandal-clad foot had been thrashed by another dancer.

She was headed back to her table when a hand touched her elbow. "Quitter."

Cara turned and found herself facing Jack Finnerty, who was suddenly solo.

"It's this music," she said. "I'm only thirty-six, but I totally don't get it. There's no beat, no rhythm."

"There probably is," he corrected her. "But I think it's like high-pitched tones only dogs can hear. You have to be under thirty to appreciate this music."

She gave him a rueful smile. "Your date seems to get it."

"Date?" He looked around.

"Your dance partner? The girl you were with earlier?"

As soon as she opened her mouth she regretted it. Now he'd think she was watching him. Which she had been, of course.

"The pretty girl in the blue dress?"

"Meghan? You thought Meghan was my date?" He chuckled. "Wow. That really makes me feel like a dirty old man."

"Aren't you?" She was making a beeline for the table, intent on getting her handbag and going home.

"Meghan's my little sister," Jack said. "Wait until I tell her you thought I was with her, like with her."

Cara narrowed her eyes. "You're telling me you have a sister? She wasn't at Ryan and Torie's wedding. I know, because she's so striking, I would have noticed her."

"She was still in school. She just finished a semester abroad in Scotland," Jack said, amused. "Had finals the week of the wedding."

"I see," Cara said, looking around to try to spy the girl again.

"Also?" He lowered his voice conspiratorially. "Meghan and Torie aren't what you would call best friends."

"Do I dare ask what you're doing here tonight?" Cara asked. He'd followed her to the table and was standing by her side, obviously not in a hurry to leave.

"You want a beer?" he asked, deflecting her question. He snapped his fingers. "No. Wait. You drink wine. Pinot, right?"

"Riiight. But I was just leaving."

"Why? The night's young."

"But I'm not. Remember? I stayed longer than I planned as it is. I've got to be back here in the morning to clear out the flowers and things, and then I've got an early appointment over in South Carolina. Besides, since I've already owned up to being a geezer, I gotta tell you, this music is giving me a headache."

He smiled. "Grab your purse and follow me."

Bert was dancing with the bride. She managed to catch his eye and gave him a signal indicating her exit.

She followed Jack as he threaded his way through the swirl of thrashing dancers out the door and onto the street outside.

It was cooler there, and a cluster of partygoers stood around on the sidewalk, smoking and talking quietly.

"Better?"

She nodded.

"What about that drink?" he asked.

"What about your little sister?"

He shrugged. "Meghan won't mind. She didn't want to show up at Maya's wedding without a date, but now that the party's revved up, she'll never miss me."

"So she's a friend of Maya's? Or Jared's?"

"Both. Maya used to babysit her. And Jared used to work for Ryan and me."

Cara shrugged. It was only nine o'clock. "Where did you have in mind?"

"How about Doyle's? It's just down the block. We can walk if you want."

"All right," she agreed.

Doyle's Pub was a fairly new place, near the DeSoto Hilton on Liberty Street.. It was busy, but the hostess led them to a booth in the far reaches of the room and a waitress came and took their drink orders.

Sliding onto the bench opposite hers, Jack looked around the room appreciatively. "I remember when this was the old Shamrock Shop. My grandmother always bought all her birthday cards here." He pointed to the far wall, where the bar was located. "And that was the candy counter. All the St. Vincent's girls would come in here to buy candy and Cokes after school. Which meant the BC guys showed up too. It was a happening place."

"Still happening," Cara said, looking around. "I know they've been open at least a year, but this is actually the first time I've been in."

"Did you ever come in here, back in the day? Where'd you go to high school?"

"Not here," Cara said. "I'm an Air Force brat. I went to six different schools between elementary and high school, but I finished up in Columbus, Ohio."

"I figured." He nodded. "Not much of a Southern accent."

"I'm working on it. I've learned to say 'fixin' to' and 'crank the car' and 'carry me to the store,' but that's as far as I've gotten."

"You should hang around my aunt Betty," Jack said. "Born and raised here, never lived anyplace other than Savannah. Half the time, even I can't understand what she's saying."

The drinks came then. He seemed to be studying her, waiting for something. It was making her nervous. *He* made her nervous. Fidgety.

Say something, she told herself. "How's your . . ."

"How's your dog?" he blurted out, at the exact same time.

They both laughed.

"You start," he said. "How is Poppy? Over her trauma?"

"She's good," Cara said. "How about Shaz?"

"Not as depressed. I've started taking her to job sites with me now, and she's kinda into that. Although Torie's not crazy about having her at the house—she thinks Shaz intimidates Benji."

"Benji?"

"Torie's dog. Some kinda purse puppy. I don't know what kind of dog he is. Ryan calls him a shih tzu."

"But not in front of Torie."

"No."

"I'm lucky Poppy can just come downstairs to the shop with me most of the time. When I'm not there—is it weird that I leave the television on for her to watch?"

"Don't ask me. I leave the Animal Planet on for Shaz. Or Sports South."

"Poppy loves that too," she confided. "That and Disney."

They sipped their drinks. Cara decided it was her turn to study him. See if she could make him feel as fidgety as she felt.

He was easy to look at. Intelligent hazel eyes with crinkle lines at the corners, that made her think he laughed a lot when he wasn't around her. He had the dry, weather-beaten skin of somebody who worked outside, a trace of five-o'clock shadow on his strong jawline. He'd taken off his hat, and his dark hair was a little matted, but he wasn't the kind of guy who'd be self-conscious about that. His hands, clamped around his beer stein, were strong, sun-browned, callused.

Ryan told her that Jack was getting over a bad breakup. Torie had told her about the Jimmy Buffett impersonator. *Why would anybody leave somebody who looks like Jack Finnerty?*

"Kinda weird our dogs look so much alike," Jack said. "I've been wondering about that."

"You don't see that many goldendoodles in Savannah," she agreed. "I had to go to Atlanta to find Poppy's breeder. Where'd you get Shaz?"

"I think Zoey got her in Atlanta."

"You think?"

"We'd talked about getting a dog, in kind of an abstract way. Like, we were running in the park one day, and she said, 'We should get a dog.' And I said, 'Yeah.' And a few weeks later, I come home, and there's Shaz. Don't get me wrong. I like dogs. I love 'em. But it would have been nice if she'd discussed it with me."

He sipped his beer. "It wasn't the best time to bring a puppy into the mix. Relationship-wise. We weren't really getting along anyway. So I was pissed at her, and she was pissed at me for being pissed about the dog. And we were both pissed when Shaz pissed on the floor, which totally wasn't the dog's fault. She was a puppy! It went like that. Anyway, we split up. Probably just as well."

"If it was her dog, I'm surprised she didn't take Shaz."

"Not as surprised as me." They both laughed at that. "She was with one of her girlfriends at a bar on River Street, she met this guy, he was playing there. I guess they hooked up right away...."

His face darkened at the telling. "He's a Jimmy Buffett impersonator, for God's sake."

"Oh my."

"That was a Friday night," he went on. "It was late March. Ryan and I were working crazy hours, trying to finish this Victorian house on Huntingdon Street. A total gut job. So I worked all day Saturday and Sunday too. When I got home that night, we had this big blowout of a fight about it. And again, in hindsight, I know now it wasn't about the dog, and it wasn't really about me working too much. At some point, I realized I needed to cool off. So I got in the truck, and I went back to the job site, and I actually slept in the truck that night, because I was too pissed off to go home. . . ."

"And that was it?" Cara asked.

"Yeah. How lame is this? I go back home the next morning, to shower, and she's gone. Packed up most of her clothes and crap, and just headed out on the road with this character, who calls himself . . . get this . . . Jamey Buttons."

Cara groaned. "And she left Shaz behind."

"And me. Now I'm like the opposite of what the song says. Come Monday, *nothin'* was all right."

22

There was a votive candle in a jar on their table, and the small flame lit Cara's face in shades of pinks and peach as she leaned in, listening to him tell the end of the Jack and Zoey story. She had large, expressive brown eyes, and her nose had a weird little indent at the very tip, and her hair, which she'd worn up, was falling down, strands lightly touching the bare skin on her shoulders. Her lips were the color of ripe peaches. Or was that just the candlelight? She was wearing the same orangey-pink dress she'd had on the night of Ryan's wedding.

Why am I telling her all this? Why does she care? Why do I care?

He cared because he'd been deserted, left behind. Because Zoey had found somebody else. Somebody better. And let's face it, he cared because she'd beat him to the punch, leaving him before he could leave her.

But why should Cara Kryzik care about any of this? Maybe . . . because she'd been hurt, too. At least, that's what Ryan had said. She was a good listener. Zoey never listened worth a damn. You'd start telling her something, and she'd interrupt, stepping all over your sentences, making you forget what you were talking about, turning everything around, until, inevitably, whatever you were about to say was somehow about her. Her day. Her crappy job. Her. Her. Her.

"Do you miss her?" Cara was asking.

"Who? Zoey?" He would have shrugged off the question, but there was something about this girl that made him speak the truth, even when it was painful.

"Maybe. Yeah, okay. Sometimes. And then she pulls some stunt, like letting hours go by before letting me know that Shaz has been turned in to the vet's office, and I've abducted somebody else's dog."

She nodded.

"What about you?" he asked softly. "Ryan tells me you're divorced. Pretty recently?"

Cara bit her lip and looked out the window. "Last April. Hard to believe it's been a year."

"Miss him?"

"No." She fairly spat the word.

"Really? Never? How long were you married?"

"It would have been five years, but we split last year on Valentine's Day."

Jack grimaced. "Brutal."

"It was also my birthday."

"Shit," he said softly.

"Exactly. He was a shit. Which is why I now have a dog."

"A female dog," Jack observed.

Cara took a long sip of wine and then a deep breath. "Hate to say it, but I'd better start thinking about heading home."

"Really?"

Jack could have kicked himself. He'd struck a nerve, asking about her ex. What was he thinking? Never, ever, ask a girl about an ex. Was he that out of practice?

He put some money on the tabletop and stood, holding out a hand to steady her, as she pulled herself from the narrow booth. Her hand was small and warm, but her fingers were long, like an artist's.

When she was standing, he released her hand, but rested his own, lightly, on the small of her back, as they made their way to the door. Doyle's was packed now, with a din that drowned out anything they could have said, until they were back outside on the sidewalk again.

"Can I give you a ride home? My truck's just parked over on Liberty."

"Thanks, but I've got the shop van parked in the lane behind the K of C."

"Oh."

His face fell, and Cara was secretly glad. They'd had a drink together. Just one. But she was starting to like him. Okay, she'd started liking him the day he brought Poppy back home, and apologized. And she thought just maybe, he kind of liked her.

"You could walk me back over to the van," she offered. "I'm no fraidycat, but I definitely don't like walking in these dark downtown lanes at night."

"Good thinking," he said. "You never can tell what kind of lowlifes are wandering around down here on a Friday night." As they moved down the sidewalk, she hesitated, but then reached over and tucked her hand through his arm. "For safety," she said gravely. "Because you really never can tell."

He squeezed her hand, and gave her a sideways glance, and her smile was warm, as though they both shared some exciting new secret.

He could have covered the two blocks to the K of C hall in less than five minutes. Instead, he took his own sweet time. He *strolled*. It was a typical May night in Savannah, in the mid-eighties, and the scent of her light, flowery perfume wafted in the warm evening air.

She was walking slowly, too. "I'm a house voyeur," she confessed, as they passed a stately town house. "I love walking around downtown, peeking in the lit windows. I want to see what kind of furniture people have, the pictures hanging on their walls, their wallpaper. My ex used to accuse me of being a peeping Tom. You ever do that?"

"No. Okay, occasionally. But I'm trying to see the molding profile, the staircase details, the old hardware, and the window casings."

"I'm even worse when it comes to gardens. I'm forever riding down lanes, hoping for a glimpse into somebody's courtyard. Someday, somebody's probably going to see me peeking through their fence and sic the cops on me."

"Like I tried to do after you followed me home a couple weeks ago?"

"I guess it's lucky for both of us the cops had better things to do that night," Cara said. They walked past Liberty Street and entered the lane that ran behind the Knights of Columbus hall. Jack took the opportunity to put a protective arm around Cara's shoulder. Just in case.

"This is me." The pale pink striped Bloom van was parked near the K of C's back door. They heard music from inside. A group of men were standing just down the lane, talking loudly, their lit cigarettes making an arc in the inky night. They heard a loud metallic clatter, as something was tossed against a battered trash can.

"Party's still going," Jack said, nodding in that direction. "I think I recognize a couple of those guys from the wedding. Tommy Hart, the guy in the black fedora? He used to date Meghan."

"I hope Bert's gone home by now," Cara said. "He's been sober two years now, and I shouldn't worry about him, I know, but it can't be easy for him, being around parties and booze all the time, every time we do a wedding."

"Want me to go inside and check on him?" Jack offered.

"No. He's a grown-up. I don't want him to think I don't trust him. What about you, will you go back inside, to find your sister?"

Instead of answering, he pulled his phone from his pocket and showed her the screen. There was a text message—

Gone out with the girlz. Don't tell Mom.

He grinned. "That's Meghan for you."

Cara reached in her bag for her keys, and he moved closer beside her, with his hand on her arm, and she realized, with a start, that he was probably going to kiss her. A little frizzle of electricity shot up her spine, as she realized she hoped he would.

She found the key and fit it in the lock. His hand touched her cheek, lightly, and he leaned down.

"Hey, asshole!" A man's voice echoed in the lane. They heard glass splintering against concrete, and more voices.

"Drunks," Jack said, shrugging.

"What the fuck? Man, that's not cool!"

Jack jerked his head around to see what was happening.

More glass shattering. Shouts.

A door opened from a town house at the entrance to the lane, spilling light into the lane. They could see four men, clumped together, and a fifth man, sprawled on his back on the broken asphalt.

A shrill woman's voice called from the back of the house. "Whoever's out there I'm calling the cops. I mean it, I'm calling them right now!"

"Fuck you, bitch." Coarse laughter. But the men slunk off into the darkness, like so many feral cats. All but the one, who was still on the ground, clutching his black fedora, curled up now in a fetal position. Even from where they stood, they could hear his groans of pain.

Jack sighed. "I better see if he's all right."

"Tommy?" Jack crouched over the fallen man. "You okay?"

Dumb question. Tommy Hart was definitely not okay. His nose was already a bloody, swollen pulp, and his left eye was closed, a ring of purple already blooming.

He helped the younger man to a sitting position.

Tommy held both hands to his face. "I'm fuuuuucked up."

"I see that," Jack said. "Did they hit you anywhere else?"

"No maan. Just my faaace." The words were slurred. "I think my nose is broke."

They heard the loud wail of a police siren.

"Will he be okay?"

Jack turned, and was surprised to see Cara, kneeling on the filthy, glass-strewn asphalt, at his side.

"His nose is probably broken," Jack said succinctly.

Before he could say anything else, Tommy Hart, improbably, staggered to his feet. "I gotta go, man." He swayed, and it looked, for a moment, that he might fall down again. Blood dripped down the front of his face, onto his white shirt.

"Whoa," Jack said. He wrapped an arm around Tommy's shoulder. "You need to get your nose looked at."

"Yeah. Later." Tommy tried to pull away, but Jack held his ground.

"Where do you think you're going?"

"I got to go," Tommy insisted. He glanced toward the end of the lane. "Cops. I don't need to be messing with the po-po." He tried again to free himself from Jack's grasp. "Come on, Jack. I'm okay."

"You're not okay," Jack repeated. "You're shitfaced. You can't drive like this."

The sirens were growing closer.

Tommy moaned. "I can't get another MIP. They'll pull my driver's license. I'll lose my freakin' job. My old man will kill me."

"Come on, then," Jack said. "Let's walk." With his arm around Tommy's shoulder, he force-marched him in the direction of the K of C hall.

Cara followed, unsure of her next move. She hesitated, then picked up the battered black felt fedora she found lying on the ground.

Jack banged hard on the K of C's kitchen door, and a frightened-looking Hispanic man yanked the door open a few inches.

"Incoming," Jack said. Silently, the porter held the door open wide enough for them to pass.

Jack shoved Tommy onto a rickety kitchen stool, went to the commercial ice machine, and scooped up a handful of ice, which he wrapped in a white terry dishcloth.

"Jesus!" Tommy yelped, as Jack held the cloth to his battered nose.

"How'd you get here tonight?" Jack asked.

"Huh?"

"Do you have a car here?"

"Yeah. Of course. I'm parked on the square." Tommy looked up at him through his good eye. "I can drive."

"Nuh-uh," Jack said. "You can't hardly walk. No way I'm letting you get behind the wheel of a car. You still living at your mom's place? On Wilmington Island?"

"I ain't saying."

"Fine," Jack said. "I'll just drop you off at the ER at Memorial. Let them deal with you."

"No! Okay. We're still in the same rathole in Spinnaker Cove."

"That's better. You ready to roll?"

Tommy shot Jack a hopeful look. "I could use a drink. For pain."

"You could use a kick to the head," Jack said. "You're underage, probably got, what, a couple minor-in-possession citations already? And you think I'm gonna pour you another beer?" He pulled the boy to his feet. "Let's go."

Tommy stood, unsteadily.

"Keys?" Jack held out his hand.

"Fuuuuck." Tommy dug them out of his pants pocket and handed them over,

Cara followed them to the front of the hall. It was nearly ten, but the party raged on. In the middle of the dance floor, Maya and Jared danced alone, bodies pressed close together, performing what Cara thought was a fairly credible tango.

On the sidewalk, Jack turned and gave her an apologetic smile. "Sorry. But this kid's mom is an old family friend. Tommy's not a bad guy, but he seems to attract trouble. I better get him loaded up. Want me to drive you around to your van?"

She looked over at Tommy, who'd draped himself over a parking meter, head resting on his chest. He seemed to be humming something.

"No need. Now that the bad guys are gone. What about you? You're driving him all the way out to Wilmington Island? I could follow you out, give you a ride back."

"Thanks, but no," he said. "I'll catch a ride back to town."

"You're sure?"

He touched her cheek lightly, his voice full of regret. "No. But that's another story."

Suddenly, with no warning, he pulled her close, his arms wrapped around her waist. He kissed her quickly. She'd had exactly two glasses of wine, but she felt dizzy, so she pulled him closer. His tongue slipped through her lips . . .

"Blllleeeechhh."

Tommy was crouched on the curb, his head between his knees. "Blllleccchh."

Jack released her, reluctantly. He shrugged. "Kids. Okay if I give you a call next week?"

She gave him another quick kiss. "You better."

23

The South Carolina low country was a sea of green and gold, contrasted against a pure blue sky. Wildflowers bloomed in muddy ditches, and carpets of red clover paved the higher ground along the roadway.

As always, in her mind, Cara was composing arrangements. She could see a small jelly glass filled with those lowly ditch daisies, wild violets, and red clovers, with slender stalks of sweet grass spiking and spilling over the sides of the glass.

Brooke Trapnell had professed no real interest in flowers, but she did have definite color biases. With her dark hair and fair skin, tones of silvers, blues, pinks, and lavender might be nice. She'd nixed purple, but lavender wasn't really purple. When she got back to the shop, Cara decided, she'd put some flowers together, snap a picture, and text it to Brooke. Texts, she'd already discovered, were the best way to communicate with this busy bride.

So much to get done for this wedding, in such a short time span. Thankfully, she'd already gotten commitments from Layne at Fete Accompli to cater, and found two of her favorite photography studios that had openings for July 6. She'd emailed links to both photographers' websites to all parties, and as soon as Brooke, or more likely, Marie, got back to her, she'd get that nailed down.

Patricia Trapnell had already sent audio clips from the orchestra she was determined to hire, and since there was no obvious reason to veto them, Brooke had reluctantly agreed, so Cara had called the orchestra's booking agent that morning, and their contract was sitting on her desk back at the shop.

It was a forty-five-minute drive from Savannah to Cabin Creek, and for the rest of the journey, Cara puzzled not over flowers or canapés, but the more interesting and confusing topic of Jack Finnerty and his behavior the night before.

She really didn't know what to make of this man.

He could have left his sister's old friend in that alley the previous night. Could have walked away with Cara, maybe sweet-talked his way into her apartment, and who knows, eventually her bed. Yes, she'd fantasized about that. He could have allowed the underage drunk to get picked up by the police. It would have saved a lot of time and trouble if he'd just walked away. But he hadn't.

Leaving his own truck where it was, Jack had cleaned the kid up as best he could, loaded him into his beat-up Camry, and driven him all the way home. And then—he'd texted Cara to make sure *she'd* gotten home all right.

What kind of guy did something as kind and caring as that? Her brow furrowed. Was he really that sweet, or was he just trying to impress her?

Libba Strayhorn was standing in front of the magnificent plantation house, an incongruous figure in her faded ball cap, brown riding pants, blue work shirt, and scuffed leather riding boots. She had a black and white dog at her heels as she walked back and forth among the boxwood borders, leaning down to pull up weeds.

She waved as Cara drove around to the car park, and walked around to meet her.

"Hey there!" Libba greeted her. "I hear you're the one who's going to make this whole wedding happen. Congratulations!"

She leaned in and stage-whispered. "Just between you and me and Rowdy here, I'm glad it's you. That other fella was just a little too fancy for my tastes."

"I'm glad you're glad," Cara said. "And thanks again for agreeing to let me come out today and walk through the house again. Are you sure you have time to do this with me?"

"Plenty of time," Libba assured her. "The horses are exercised, and I've got the whole day free for this. Mitch is out of town on business, but as he likes to say, his only role in this wedding is to smile and nod and stay sober."

They walked through the front door, into the high-ceilinged entry foyer, with its hand-painted Chinese-motif wallpaper and black-and-white-checkerboard marble floor. A spectacular antique gold-leafed Chippendale mirror took up most of one wall of the foyer, and Cara eyed it apprehensively.

"You know, Libba, the plan is to have cocktails and passed appetizers in here as the guests arrive. I think we're expecting about two hundred and fifty people. It could be quite a crush. I know this mirror must be an old family piece, and I'm a little worried somebody could accidentally jostle and damage it. Do you think that's something you might want to move to storage during the reception?"

"I don't see why," Libba said, giving the mirror a fond pat. "This thing's been in this hall for at least a hundred and fifty years. It withstood Union forces, who camped out here during the war, and even worse, all those generations of rambunctious Strayhorn boys, including Mitch and Harris. Anyway, we couldn't move it if we wanted to. It's bolted to that wall."

"Great," Cara said. "It's so stunning, I'd hate to lose it. I was thinking we could leave a big silver bowl on that console table for guests to drop cards and gifts."

"Okay," Libba said. "You're the boss. What else do you want in here?"

"Nothing, really. We'll bring in rented high-top tables and scatter them against the walls, so people will have a place to rest their drink glasses."

She and Libba passed from the hallway into the double parlors, and discussed the placement of tables and chairs, and the bride and groom's table.

They went into the kitchen, which was huge, but surprisingly modest for a house of Cabin Creek's grandeur. The cabinets were vintage forties, metal, with tiny patches of rust beginning to show through at the edges, the counter-tops yellow formica, and the floors were worn yellow linoleum tile.

"Mitch is all het up about ripping this old stuff out and putting in a com-pletely new kitchen with all the modern bells and whistles. He's the cook in the family," Libba confided. "He's got his eye on an eight-burner restaurant range and one of those double-door glass-front fridges, marble countertops, the works."

"Sounds like a dream," said Cara enviously. "The kitchen in my tiny apart-ment downtown would fit inside your pantry."

Libba shrugged. "Personally, I don't see the point. Holly has her own apart-ment in Savannah, and Harris and Brooke have their own place there too. It's just Mitch and me here most nights, and this old stuff has worked fine for the forty years we've lived here, but then again, someday, we hope, Harris and Brooke will be living here, with a passel of kids, and they'll appreciate a kitchen like that."

"You wouldn't try to do the kitchen before the wedding, right?" Cara asked.

"Oh no," Libba assured her. "Maybe in the fall, when things quiet down."

"Good. You've got a lot of counter space, which is great, because our caterer is going to need every inch of it. Layne is going to want to run over here to take a look at the space too, but she's already said she may want to bring in an extra fridge, and maybe even an extra cooktop, but I think there'd be room for that if we move out the table and chairs in your eating nook. Would that be okay?"

"Sure," Libba said. "As long as we have a place to get a cup of coffee and a bowl of cereal in the morning, Mitch and I are fine."

As they moved through the house, Cara marveled to herself at the good nature and calm radiated by this mother of the groom. In less than five weeks, her home would be invaded by a huge, lavish wedding complete with 250 guests, but she seemed totally unfazed by any and all requests Cara made.

"Can we take another look at the ballroom?" Cara asked, as they neared the back of the house.

Libba nodded. "Hasn't been used since Harris's twenty-first-birthday party. I guess you've noticed Mitch and I aren't really big on entertaining. We enjoy it when we do it, but mostly, we're out here in the country, keeping to ourselves with the horses and dogs. Or, I am. Mitch is happy as long as he's got his big-screen TV, twenty-four-hour cable sports, and an easy ride to the airport when he needs to travel, which he does a lot for his business."

The ballroom was another grand, high-ceilinged room in a wing that had been added on to Cabin Creek, Libba told her, in the 1950s. "Mitch's grand-parents had it built for his parents' wedding. Back then, there was nothing around here where you could have a big party, no country clubs or hotel ball-rooms, nothing like that."

"It's lovely," Cara said. Floor-to-ceiling windows ran down both sides of the long room, and there was a low platform at the far end. "Perfect for the orches-tra," Cara said.

Libba rolled her eyes. "They sure are getting grand with this wedding. I wouldn't even know where to start to look for something like that."

"It's a lot," Cara agreed. "But Patricia has tracked down a ten-piece orches-tra out of Charleston. I've heard some clips of their work, and seen some You-Tube videos. They play all the standards, great dance music, all the way up to the nineties."

"What's Brooke think about all this fuss?"

Cara studied the other woman. "I can tell she's not crazy about it. And to tell you the truth, I don't understand why she bowed to Gordon and Patricia in all this."

"I can tell you. Because her daddy bribed her," Libba said with a snort. "Offered to pay off her law-school loans if she'd agree to a big to-do."

"Ahhh. That explains a lot. Don't get me wrong, I'm thrilled to have the work, Libba, but the last time I was out here meeting with the Trapnells, I got the distinct impression that Patricia was planning on hiring Cullen Kane."

"She was. But then Brooke dug in her heels and insisted they hire you in-stead. I think it was all about tweaking her stepmother—although you didn't hear me say that."

"What's Harris think about all the wedding plans?" Cara asked. "Do you know, I haven't even met him yet?"

"Those kids stay so darned busy, I don't know how they even had time to get engaged," Libba said. "Harris is pretty easygoing. He does love a party, though. I think whatever Brooke decides will be fine with him."

Cara looked around the ballroom. Although the architectural details were good, it was apparent that the room hadn't been used in years. The white paint on the walls was yellowing, and the wood trim on all the window casings was peeling. The highly polished oak floor was scuffed, and the fussy crystal chandeliers were coated with dust and grime.

Libba noticed Cara's appraisal. "Needs some spiffing up in here, that's for sure. I'm gonna have the painters in, and we'll have the floors stripped and buffed. Guess I'm gonna have to bribe my housekeeper to see about those old chandeliers."

"Some freshening up, and it'll be glorious," Cara assured her.

"What were you thinking about parking all the cars?" Cara asked, as they walked back toward the front door. "We'll have valet-parking people, of course, but we'll need to figure out where to put the cars without trampling all your landscaping."

In answer, Libba flung the front door open and pointed to a pasture on the west side of the house. "Plenty of room over there. It's higher ground than the east side of the property, so even if it does rain that night, it should drain quickly."

As they crossed to the pasture, Cara was glad she'd dressed casually for the trip, in jeans and tennis shoes. Already, she'd sidestepped one horse plop.

The two women leaned over the barbed-wire pasture fence. Two horses, one black, one brown, grazed nearby in the tall grass.

Libba whistled softly, and both horses raised their heads, then ambled over, to accept their owner's head pats and soft praises.

"We'll move these guys over to the other pasture the week before the wedding," Libba said. "And don't worry, I'll get one of the men to make sure the pasture is thoroughly shoveled out and the grass mown. Don't want Patricia ruining her Jimmy Choos on the big day."

Cara pointed at a weathered silver barn at the far end of the pasture. "Is that your stable?"

"Not anymore," Libba said. "That building down the pathway from where you parked the car, that's the new stable. Mitch had it built as a fiftieth-birthday present for me. Those horses live better than we do now," she said proudly.

Cara had a glimmer of an idea. "What do you keep in the old barn, then?"

"Random crap," Libba said, grinning. "Why do you ask?"

"Well . . . sometimes, especially with a big, formal wedding, brides and grooms like to have an after-party, for the guests of their own generation. Sort of a place everybody can cut loose. We bring in a DJ, and the bride and groom usually change into casual clothes. Sometimes, we do a midnight buffet. Just something fun. We've done wienie roasts, barbecues, in cold weather I've seen couples have bonfires with spiked hot chocolate and s'mores . . ."

"We could probably do something like that in the barn," Libba said slowly. "Want to take a look?"

It took both women tugging on the old barn doors to yank them open, their rusted hinges squealing in protest.

Cara's eyes took a moment to adjust to the dimness. The barn was redolent of mildew, leather, old hay, older manure, but somehow it was a rich, pleasant, promising scent. She craned her head and stared up at the high, peaked ceiling, where pinpricks of daylight shone through the rusted tin roof.

It looked like the barn had become home to anything and everything the Strayhorns owned that was too broken to use but too valued to discard. Cardboard boxes were stacked in corners, there was a profusion of tools, tires, old saddles, unidentified agricultural machinery, discarded appliances, broken furniture, and even a faded red Mustang, sans tires, perched on jacks. Everything was coated with a thick film of dust, and the overhead corners were festooned with cobwebs.

"That's Mitch's first car," Libba said, pointing at the Mustang. "He swears he's going to restore it someday. Maybe when he retires. We'll see. The man doesn't know the first thing about cars or engines." She turned slowly and pointed out other family mementos. "Harris's crib. The first dryer I ever owned. My mother-in-law's favorite riding lawn mower." She turned to Cara with a sheepish grin. "See? Random crap. Living this far out in the country, it's easier to just stick stuff in the barn than it is to have it hauled off to the dump.

"Mitch would love to have everything in here cleared out. Except the Mustang. That's the holy of holies. But everything else?" She shrugged. "Time to let go of all of it."

"Except Harris's crib," Cara guessed.

"Precisely."

Libba was walking around the barn, examining the walls. "Don't know how long this thing has been standing. Mitch's mom said it was here when she moved to Cabin Creek. And we did keep the horses here for years." She glanced up at the glints of daylight.

"Have to get a new roof. Otherwise, I think this thing could probably stand another seventy-five years."

It was a big barn, and roofs, Cara knew, were expensive.

"Is that something you'd want to undertake? With all the other expenses with the wedding?"

"We'd have to do it sooner or later, if we want the barn to keep standing," Libba said. "Which we do. Only problem is, getting somebody reliable over here to do the work. With the economy like it's been, you'd think people would be eager for a job, but that's not how it is out here. The last work we had done here? I wanted to rip out the old tub in our master bath and put in a nice big glass-walled shower. Like you see in all the magazines." She snorted in disgust. "The jacklegs we hired took six months, screwed it up so bad, Mitch kicked 'em out before the tile was even grouted. We still can't use that shower."

"I might have an idea," Cara said slowly. "I know a contractor in Savannah . . . all they do is historic-restoration work. I suppose that would include roofs. . . ."

"I'd love to talk to them. Maybe they could take care of the other stuff we want to do before the wedding too. See about those leaky windows in the ball-room, get the barn fixed up."

"It's the Finnerty brothers," Cara said. "I just did a wedding for Ryan Finnerty, the younger of the two brothers. He married Torie Fanning."

"Finnerty? From Savannah? We know the Finnertys. Been knowing 'em for years. I didn't realize they were contractors."

"I can get you their number. They haven't done any work for me person-ally, but I'm sure it would be easy enough to check their references."

"I wouldn't worry about references with those boys," Libba said. She nod-ded emphatically. "I'll call their mom tonight." She looked pleased with herself. "Yes sir. Fix this place up nice."

"Would you keep horses here again?" Cara asked.

"No. We've got the new stables for them." Libba's face took on a wistful quality. "This old barn has a lot of good memories for our family. Holly and her friends played house up in the loft. Harris and his buddies would play out here, on rainy days. It was their secret clubhouse, their army fort. He was in a kind of garage band in high school. They were awful! I wouldn't let 'em play in the house, so they practiced out here. Mitch said he and his brothers did the same thing when they were kids." She turned to Cara.

"Someday, I hope, we'll move Harris's crib back into the big house. And this barn will be full of my grandbabies, playing hide-and-go-seek, and pirate and bad garage rock.

"That is," she said, pulling a face, "if Harris and Brooke can slow down enough eventually to give me those grandbabies while I'm still young enough to enjoy them."

Cara reached out and squeezed Libba's hand. "I hope they will."

Libba sighed, and the two women picked their way through debris toward the door.

By now, both their faces were coated with a sheen of perspiration.

Libba mopped her forehead with a blue bandanna. "You can see how hot it is in here right now, and it's only May. How are we gonna get this place cooled down enough come July?"

"It's actually not that difficult," Cara said. "We do tons of weddings in tents and all kinds of outbuildings these days. We'll rent generators and big air-conditioning units."

"Really?" Libba looked impressed. "You can air-condition a barn?"

"I did the flowers for a wedding in an airplane hangar last August," Cara assured her. "With enough money, you can do just about anything."

"One thing we know," Libba said with a laugh. "Gordon Trapnell has more than enough money. And he's bound and determined to spend it on this wedding. But you know what? I don't want to rent air conditioners. Let's just buy us a new system. That way we don't have to give it back. And I don't have to feel beholden to Gordon or Patricia."

24

Jack ran past the town house on Jones Street three times the following Sunday morning before he finally worked up the nerve to stop.

"This is stupid," he muttered, slowing to a walk, as he approached the house. He looked down at Shaz, who was panting heavily. "I could just tell her you need a drink. She might turn me down, but she would never turn away a thirsty dog."

Shaz seemed to agree. In fact, as soon as they got in front of the stoop leading up to the shop, she abruptly sat, and refused to be moved, no matter how hard Jack pulled on her leash.

He wound the leash around the wrought-iron window box beside the door and rang the bell, shifting nervously from one foot to the other as he waited.

"We'll just act like we were passing by, and decided to stop on the spur of the moment."

Five minutes passed. He looked down at Shaz, who didn't seem perturbed by the delay. "Maybe she's at church."

Shaz gave him a baleful stare.

"She could have gone out to brunch. Like a date or something. Or out of town for the weekend. " They heard a short, excited bark then, coming from the other side of the door. Shaz stood now, her ears pricked in excitement.

Finally, the paper shade on the glass shop door was pulled up. Cara Kryzik looked out at them, bemused. She wore shorts and a tank top and her hair was wrapped in a towel.

"Or maybe she was in the shower," Cara said, opening the door. Poppy stood directly behind her, peering around her legs.

Jack felt his face redden. "You heard, huh?"

She pointed upward. He took a step back, off the stoop, and saw the open window directly above the stoop. "My bedroom. When that window's open, I can hear everything out on the street. It can make for some pretty interesting nights."

"You don't have air-conditioning?" It was the best comeback he could think of.

"Not right at the moment," Cara said. "It's on the blink, which is not at all unusual. I've been calling the landlord for two days, but she hasn't called back. If I don't hear from her by tonight, I swear, I'm gonna buy myself a window unit and deduct the cost from my rent."

"You should," Jack agreed. "It was in the high eighties last night."

"It was in the low nineties upstairs," Cara said. "Did I hear you say something about some water for Shaz? And how about you? I could fix us some iced coffee?"

As she'd promised, the interior of the shop was steamy. While Cara disappeared into a small kitchenette, he looked around.

It was a small room, no bigger than his living room on Macon Street. But she'd hung a dozen old mirrors on the exposed brick walls, and they made the room look larger. There was a large zinc-topped worktable, a small antique table with three chairs in a bay near the front window, a glass countertop with a cash register, and a large glass-doored cooler full of buckets holding flowers.

An alcove hid behind a half-opened curtain, and he could see a desk stacked with papers, a computer, and a phone.

"How's your friend Tommy?" Cara called from the kitchen.

"Alive."

"Thanks to you."

"He was passed out cold by the time I got him home. It was all I could do to unload him from that Camry and dump him on a lawn chair under the carport. He left a pretty sheepish message on my answering machine the next day. I think the experience might have helped him sober up—and grow up—a little."

"And how did you get back to town to your truck?"

"I texted Ryan and he gave me a ride."

Cara came out of the kitchenette holding two tall frosted glasses of iced coffee. "Let's take the drinks and the dogs out to the courtyard garden. I've got dog bowls out there, so Shaz can have that water you promised."

He followed her down a narrow hallway, passing a stairway that led to the upstairs apartment, and a closed door that he guessed held a bathroom.

The garden was a surprise. There were a pair of tall palm trees at the back of the garden, and these were underplanted with lush banana trees, hydrangeas, hostas, ivy, ferns, and a dozen more plants whose names he didn't know. A walkway of mottled Savannah gray bricks bisected the planting beds. She set the drinks down on a teak table shaded by a large market umbrella, and motioned for him to take a bench opposite the one she sat on.

"Nice," he said appreciatively. "But I guess it makes sense you'd have a great garden, you being a florist."

"It's my escape hatch from reality," she said. Poppy found a place in the shade of the umbrella, while Shaz roamed around, sniffing the plants, until finally spotting the aluminum bowl of water near the hose bib.

Jack took a sip of the coffee, but he was still studying her garden. There was something different about it, and it took a moment before it dawned on him.

"No color," he said, nodding slowly. "Except white. It's all white and green. And a little bit of yellow."

"That's right. I'm around color all day. I love it, but when I get away from work, my eyes need to rest. I find green and white really soothing."

"Very soothing," he agreed. "And it feels a lot cooler than I'd expect."

"That's the plan."

He cleared his throat. "I had a call from Libba Strayhorn yesterday. She wants to talk to us about doing some work over at their place in South Carolina. I guess I have you to thank for that."

"She's a nice lady, and they've had some bad luck with contractors."

"So I heard. My family's known Mitch and Libba for a long time, you know. From when they lived in Ardsley Park. Harris was two years behind me in school, and Holly must be in her mid-twenties by now. I'd lost track of them, after they sold the house in town and moved over there full-time."

"Have you been to Cabin Creek?"

"Not in years, since we were little kids. She said something about fixing up the old barn?"

"That's right. Their son's wedding is July sixth, and the hope is that we can have the after-party in the barn."

He wrinkled his nose. "A wedding? In a barn? In July?"

"They moved the horses to a new stable several years ago, and once they clear out all the junk that's accumulated there over the years, and you get the roof patched up, it'll be great," Cara said.

"Kinda hot." Jack fanned his face with his hand.

"We'll bring in air conditioners."

"Ryan and I are going over there tomorrow to check it out," he told her.

"Speaking of weddings." Her eyes twinkled with mischief. "Where were you last night?"

"Last night? I dunno. Home, I guess. We worked late, finishing up at Ryan's house. Why?"

"I did the flowers for a wedding—and you weren't there. I thought you went to every wedding in Savannah."

"Who got married?"

"Emily Braswell and Rob Mabry."

He shook his head. "Never heard of 'em. They must be new in town."

"As a matter of fact, her father was just transferred here last year by the Army Corps of Engineers. And the groom is from Macon."

"Then that explains it. Nice wedding?"

Cara leaned over and picked a dead frond from a fern, crumbling the browning leaf between her fingertips. "It was okay. Bert and I give them about a fifty-fifty chance."

"Of what?"

"Surviving." She shrugged, and one of the skinny straps of her tank top slipped off her shoulder. She left it there, and it distracted him for a moment, affording him a tantalizing glimpse of the pale skin of her upper breast.

He looked away, and then back, and by then, she'd adjusted it. Too bad. It was a nice view. Nicer even than all these cool green and white flowers. Now, what had he been about to say? Oh yeah.

"You rate their marriage chances? That seems pretty cynical."

"You see as many couples as I do, work with as many crazy brides and overbearing moms as me, you'd be cynical too," she said calmly. "I've only been in business for myself two and a half years here, and I can't tell you how many couples don't even make it to their first anniversary."

Poppy stirred, getting to her feet and staring intently at the brick wall running along the back of the courtyard. A squirrel paused there. Shaz saw the squirrel, too, and both the dogs went bounding toward their intended quarry. Instead of scampering away, though, the squirrel held its ground, chattering angrily at the two dogs four feet below, who were now balancing on their hind legs, whimpering and pawing ineffectively at the brick.

"Shaz!" Jack called. "Down!" The dog ignored him.

"Poppy! Leave that squirrel alone," Cara added. "I swear, it's the same squirrel. He does this every day, just to torment poor Poppy."

After a moment, the squirrel, bored with the contest, took off again, and the dogs, defeated, ambled over to the water bowl, where they took turns drinking, until the empty water bowl clanged loudly against the brick walkway.

"Just out of curiosity, why do you refer to the squirrel as a he? Did you see something I didn't see?"

"Oh, for Pete's sake," Cara said crossly. "Isn't it obvious? I'm a man-hater.

That's why I think all marriages will inevitably fail, and why all annoying squirrels must be male."

Jack laughed despite himself. "What was wrong with yesterday's couple? Why are they doomed?"

"For one thing, the groom was unbelievably domineering. He had to have a say in every detail. He even picked out Emily's gown."

"That's unusual?"

She stared at him as though he'd grown a third eye in the middle of his forehead.

"Are you kidding? Yes, it's unusual. There's an old superstition that says it's bad luck for a groom to see the bride's dress before the wedding."

"Or?"

"Or his testicles will turn black and fall off. I don't know, Jack. I just know this guy was controlling and domineering, and it doesn't bode well for the marriage."

"I see. Anything else? So, he's the only one at fault?"

"No, of course not. After all, Emily allows him to boss her around about all this stuff. When she gets fed up, she sulks and then cries. Buckets and buckets of tears."

"Oooh." Jack grimaced. "I hate a crier."

"Me too!" she exclaimed. "But it's an occupational hazard with my job. Now that I think of it, I've only done flowers for one wedding that that didn't involve at least one tearfest or temper tantrum."

"And that was?"

"Last Friday night's wedding, as a matter of fact. Maya and Jared."

He nodded. "I don't know Jared that well. He only worked for us a year or so. But Maya's always been pretty chill. So, how did you guys rate their chances?"

"Mmm. Bert and Maya have been best friends, forever. He gives them a hundred percent. Says he's positive they'll make it."

Jack studied her face. "But you're not so sure."

"Shit happens. People change. What seems like a sure bet, suddenly turns into a sucker bet."

"Is that what happened to you?"

Cara didn't answer. She got up, turned on the hose, and refilled the water bowl. On the way back to the table, she paused to right a flowerpot one of the dogs had upended.

"Cara?" He said it gently.

25

Her glass was nearly empty. She stared down into it, wondering if she should make an excuse, get up, offer a refill, hope he'd forget the topic while she was away. Somehow, she doubted it. She hadn't known Jack Finnerty long, but she could tell he was very focused when he wanted to be.

"Why do you want to know about my marriage?" she asked finally.

He stared, apparently taken aback. "Is it still painful to talk about?"

"It's not my favorite topic, no. But I'm over him, as I told you before."

"Yes. You did say that." He waited.

Cara sighed. "He cheated on me, okay? He had a little girlfriend, and they'd have their twosomes every other week, at a motel out by the airport, when he was supposed to be at a sales meeting in Atlanta. I was too dumb to realize what was going on. When I found out, I ended it. I moved out, stayed a while with Bert, then rented this apartment, upstairs over the shop."

"And that was it? No counseling, no attempt at a reconciliation?"

"Now you sound like Leo," she said. "Why would I want a reconciliation? Or need counseling? He was quite clearly in love with somebody else. No need to prolong the inevitable."

Did she sound bitter? she wondered. Maybe that was because she was bitter.

Jack had gotten quiet again. He sat back on the bench and took a sip of the iced coffee. All the ice had melted. She should really ask if he'd like another. But did she even want him to stay? What was the point of all this?

"The woman he cheated with. Are they still together?"

She felt her face go pink. "He says not. But then, he's a liar. And a liar will tell you whatever they think you want to hear."

"I'm not on his side, you know. I never even met the guy."

"His name is Leo," she said. "Leo Giardinella. He's in sales with Great South Office Products. He plays golf with an eight handicap, and he's an Auburn fan, even though he never went to Auburn, and you'd probably like him a lot. Everybody likes Leo a lot. You never met anybody who didn't like Leo. He could totally sell ice to Eskimos. My dad? The Colonel? He still thinks it's somehow my fault our marriage broke up."

"What about your mom? What did she think of him?"

Cara shrugged. "She died while I was a freshman in college. But knowing her, she would have loved Leo too."

She was suddenly close to tears now, and he'd just told her he hated a crier. So maybe now he'd leave, and she was pretty sure she didn't care if he did.

"For the record, I went to Georgia Tech," Jack said evenly. "I tried golf, but I don't have the patience to chase a little white ball around all day. I run, and sometimes I play tennis. And Leo? Your ex? He sounds like an asshole."

"He was," she said, sniffing.

Jack got up and came around the table and sat down on the bench beside her. With his little finger, he wiped away the huge tear that was welling up in her right eye. And then he leaned in, and he very gently kissed her.

"You wanna get some lunch?" he asked.

The Firefly Café was on Habersham Street near Troup Square. They leashed up the dogs and walked over, sitting at a café table outside. Cara ordered a crab salad and Jack had the patty melt and fries, and they sat in the sunshine, eating and talking about not much of anything.

Shaz and Poppy lolled in the shade under their table, strategically positioned for stray bits of food.

As usual, Jack seemed to know half the people who walked past, or were seated nearby.

Cara sat, a look of amusement on her face as he chatted with two elderly ladies still in their church clothes, at a table nearby.

"What?" he said, when he turned back to her. "They play bridge with my aunt Betty. Irene O'Conner, the one with the pink hair? Her daughter is Meghan's godmother."

"Do you ever go anyplace where you don't know somebody?"

"I've lived here all my life, and my parents and grandparents did too. Is that a crime? Don't you know a lot of people in—where'd you say you grew up? Akron?"

"Columbus. And I know some people, but nothing like you. Anyway, I only finished high school there. Went away to college, met Leo, and eventually we moved down here to Savannah."

"Why Savannah?"

"Leo had a job offer. It was a promotion and a pay raise, and it seemed like a good idea. I didn't have much of a career going in Columbus, so there was no reason for me not to move. Even though I didn't know a soul down here. "

"And no reason to move back up there after your divorce?"

"The Colonel, my father, wanted me to move back. But by then I had the shop, and I was determined to make it work."

"And just as determined not to let the Colonel boss you around?"

She helped herself to a French fry from the paper basket that held his sandwich. "Look. I love my dad. I really do. He's tried to be supportive, in his own way. After Norma, the former owner, moved away and left me the business, the Colonel loaned me the money to make the improvements to the building and buy my equipment. I'm the creative type, not a finance genius, but he sent me books about drawing up a business plan, and bookkeeping, and all that."

"I sense a but."

Cara looked away. "Sometimes I think he wants me to fail. Things haven't been going so great. I've had a lot of capital expenditures—car problems, computer problems, equipment problems. Everything costs more than it should, and it's all stuff I didn't anticipate. And it took a long time for the business to start coming in."

"I don't know anything about flowers, but I've seen a lot of yours at all these weddings lately, and they looked pretty damn impressive to me. And I do know Torie, and Lillian Fanning. They wouldn't have hired you for Torie's wedding if they thought you were no good."

"I *am* good at what I do," Cara said. "But I'm an outsider in Savannah. These girls here, it's like a closed society. If you didn't go to Country Day or Savannah Christian or St. Vincent's you might as well be from Mars."

"But you did Torie's wedding. And that bizarro wedding for the Winships. And Maya's. And it sounds like this clambake the Trapnells and Strayhorns are planning is pretty extreme."

That stopped her cold. She was whining. And God knows she hated a whiner, almost as much as she hated a crier.

"You're right," she said, straightening her shoulders. "You're absolutely right. It's just that it's taken so long, and I'm still not really in the black. And stuff keeps happening to me...."

She filled Jack in on the broken cooler and the spoiled flowers, and all the rest of her financial woes.

He listened calmly, nodding, not judging.

"My dad wants his money back," Cara said, taking a deep breath. "And I can't blame him. When I borrowed it, the deal was that I'd start making payments in February. But I haven't. I couldn't. Not while keeping the lights on in the shop."

"And you explained that to him?"

"I tried. But the Colonel is the Colonel. He hears what he wants. And what he wants to hear is that I give up. He wants me to admit defeat, move back home, and be a dutiful daughter."

Cara felt her fists clench and unclench. "But I can't. I just can't!"

"Then don't," he said lightly. "Look, I know starting a new business is hard. Especially in a new town, where, as you say, you don't really know anybody. Ryan and I have been here all our lives, and it's been an uphill battle for us."

"Really?" It was hard to imagine anything was difficult for this charming Irishman, who'd apparently never met a stranger.

"Hell yeah," Jack said. "For one thing, our timing sucked. I quit my job, put all my savings into buying tools, equipment, all of it, everything it takes to start a new business. Our plan was to do high-end historic-restoration projects. And it would have been a good plan, except the economy was still stalled. People who'd bought an old house in the historic district had paid top-of-the-market prices and now, planning to renovate, they find out they're already underwater on their mortgages. That hundred-thousand-dollar kitchen we were supposed to build for them? Forget about it. New master suite? Not in the master plan anymore. It wouldn't have been so bad, if it had just been me. But I'd talked Ryan into coming in with me. And we had guys. Masons, carpenters, electricians. We had to let everybody go. Everybody who was expecting a paycheck, counting on us, we had to let go."

She leaned closer across the table. "How'd you survive?"

"We lived lean. Took whatever crappy jobs we could get. Our family's friends felt sorry for us, so they'd hire us to hang some Sheetrock, build a garage, replace a deck. I sold my condo downtown and bought the place over on Macon Street. It was a foreclosure. Ryan, he's actually got a teaching degree. He did some substitute teaching, hired on as an after-school soccer coach at the Y. And we just kept at it."

"And you're okay now."

"Finally. People are feeling better about the economy. The people we did those little jobs for, they were happy with the work. They're calling us back for bigger projects. And they've told their friends."

"So, a happy ending. You've got a good business, friends, a house, a dog."

"But in the meantime, Zoey left me. She got tired of hanging around, waiting for me to come home from work, to make her my number-one priority."

"You've still got the dog," Cara said, looking away.

"And I've got high hopes for everything else," Jack said. "There's this girl I keep running into at weddings . . ." And then he did it. He actually winked at her.

"You make me actually feel like I'm not a hopeless cause," Cara said, sitting back in her chair, feeling herself actually relax.

"You're a work in progress, darlin'," Jack said. "Same as me."

26

It was nearly 10 a.m. when Bert finally walked through the front door at Bloom. He dropped the morning newspaper on the worktable and headed straight to the coffeepot, ignoring Cara's pointed stares.

When he sat down at the worktable, he sipped from his mug and began leafing through the morning's phone orders. His hair was mussed, his beard unshaven, and it looked as though he'd slept in his clothes—either that, or he'd been rolled by a mugger.

He caught her watching him. "What?"

"Late night last night?"

"Maybe," he said, running his hands through his hair, which only made it worse. He stared her down. "And no. I haven't been drinking. Because I know that's what you're thinking. But I haven't."

He had her there. She had wondered. He'd worked so hard for his sobriety. She knew too well how it was with an alcoholic, though. They were always just one drink away from a fall.

"Would have been nice if you'd called to let me know you'd be in late." She kept her voice deliberately mild. It was unlike Bert to be late, or to fail to let her know he'd be late.

"Sorry," he said, looking contrite. "It won't happen again."

He mopped his forehead with one of the pink message slips. "Jesus, it's hot in here. What's going on with the air-conditioning?"

"It's been out since Friday night. I had to sleep with all the windows open over the weekend. I've left half a dozen voicemails for the Bradleys, but they haven't bothered to return any of them. I'm thinking of running over to their house. In fact, I was waiting for you to get here so I could go."

"Oh," Bert said. "Oh, crap. I forget you don't get the paper. Um, there's actually a pretty good reason you haven't heard back from Bernice."

"Such as?"

Bert flipped the *Savannah Morning News* open to the obituary page, and trailed a bony finger down the listings until he came to a block of type.

"Oh damn," Cara said. "That's awful. I didn't even know she was sick."

Bradley, Bernice, 91, of Savannah. Joined the band of heavenly angels Friday, after a brief illness. Predeceased by husband Alvin P. Bradley. Survived by faithful daughter Sylvia Bradley, 73, of Savannah. Funeral services, Tuesday, at Fox & Weeks Hodgson funeral chapel.

"Now I feel just terrible. I've been cussing Bernice all weekend. The last message I left on their machine, I even threatened to buy a window unit and subtract it from next month's rent."

"You shouldn't feel bad about that," Bert said. "That old biddy was so cheap she squeaked when she walked. And her daughter's just as bad. There's a reason Sylvia's a dried-up old maid. She's just as mean and stingy as her mama. The two of them have been living in that big house on Forty-fourth Street in Ardsley Park for decades, and even though everybody knows they're rolling in the dough, the place looks like it's falling to pieces."

"Still, it's not nice to talk bad of the dead," Cara insisted. She was still reading Bernice Bradley's obituary, the details of her membership in the United Daughters of the Confederacy, the Eastern Star, her thirty-year employment with J. C. Penney's.

"Bernice was my landlady, not a friend. I mean, I don't even think she liked me," Cara mused. "So I think it would be bad taste to show up at the service. We'll send a nice arrangement instead. One of those old-timey ones on stands. Do we have any of those metal easel thingies left in the back, from Norma's?"

Bert got up to check the stockroom, but then Cara read the last line of the funeral notice. Out loud.

"'In lieu of flowers, memorials may be made to charity.'"

"Hold it," she said, grabbing Bert's shirtsleeve as he passed. "That nasty old bat! In lieu of flowers, my ass!"

"She's dead, and she's still managing to give you the finger," Bert laughed.

By late afternoon, Cara had Bloom's front and back doors propped open and a large box fan positioned in the doorway, both as a ventilation aid and to keep Poppy from making another escape.

She printed out a photo she'd taken of Brooke's wedding dress, and had it taped to the wall just above her computer, while she leafed through online catalogues and sketched out ideas for the bride's bouquet and the other arrangements for the wedding and reception.

"That's Brooke's dress?"

"Yes. Thank God she finally went to Atlanta and bought one before her mother and stepmother took matters into their own hands."

"Pretty plain," Bert said, a note of disdain in his voice.

The gown, of heavy duchesse ivory satin, *was* simple. Sleeveless, with a deep V-neck, it was fitted close to the body, flaring out into soft folds just below the knees. Cara pointed a finger at the detail at the waist. "This is antique lace, reembroidered with seed pearls. No other lace, no sequins or flounces, or any of that. Brooke's a natural beauty, with a great figure. She doesn't need anything more than this. No veil either. I'm just going to make a hair ornament with flowers, and she'll use that to pin her hair back behind one ear."

The shop phone rang; she glanced over at the caller ID, and made a face before answering.

"Hi, Patricia."

"Hi Cara. I just thought I'd touch base and make sure that you've got things well in hand for the wedding. Is the caterer a definite, because if not, I've got Carlos on notice to hold the date for me."

"Yes," Cara said. "Fete Accompli is a done deal. Layne's signed the contract, and I'll send it over to you and Gordon for your signature. And when that's done, you'll need to put down a deposit."

"I understand," Patricia said. "When can we schedule a tasting, for the menu for the reception? Cullen says he always suggests the bride's family have a tasting at least a month before the wedding, so they can tweak anything they don't like."

Cara found herself grinding her back molars. Patricia Trapnell was determined to micromanage this wedding, whether Brooke wanted her to or not.

"Cara?" Patricia's voice was sharp. "Are you still there?"

"I'll talk to Layne about that, and get a couple possible dates, and we'll set that up based on Brooke's availability."

"Brooke's availability. That might be never," Patricia huffed.

"I'll ask her mother to let her know it's a priority," Cara said, unable to resist getting in a dig.

Which apparently went right over Patricia's head.

"Libba Strayhorn tells me that they're thinking of having the old barn redone to have the after-party out there," Patricia said. "Is that a good idea? I mean, a barn? Where horses have been?"

"I toured the barn with Libba," Cara said. "The horses haven't been kept there in years. And Libba's going to have it completely cleaned out and restored. We've done flowers for parties in barns and all kinds of unique settings in the past couple years. It's actually not all that unusual an idea. And this will give Brooke and Harris an opportunity to relax and mingle with their friends in a much more casual atmosphere."

"Couldn't they just as well do that in the house? Where there's air-conditioning and running water?"

Now it was Patricia's turn to get in a dig. Which Cara, in turn, decided to ignore.

"Was there anything else, Patricia?"

"Hmm. Just going down my list. I assume you've gotten a firm commitment from the photographer? Cullen says she stays booked for months and months in advance. I know we'll want to give her a list of shots we want taken, before and after the wedding. And Gordon is hoping to have Brooke sit for a portrait in her wedding gown."

"Yes. Meredith has assured me she has us on her books for July sixth. I'll let her know about your request for a portrait, but that's something you'll need to take up with Brooke, since I'm assuming it needs to be done well before the actual wedding day."

"I'll do that," Patricia said. "Or rather, I'll have Gordon do it. Brooke somehow doesn't seem to receive any of my phone calls, emails, or texts."

Big surprise, Cara thought.

"All right then," Cara said briskly. "I'll just get back to my flowers. Thanks for calling, Patricia."

After she'd disconnected from the call, Cara looked at the phone with distaste. This, she thought, was what she was in for, over the next five weeks. Weekly, if not daily, contact with Patricia Trapnell. When all was said and done, Cara was sure, she would have more than earned her wedding-planning fee for this event.

Cara went back to her catalogue and her sketches for the Trapnell wedding, and Bert worked efficiently through the phone orders, putting together hospital and birthday arrangements, answering the phone, and then going through their flower stock, to see what needed reordering.

The room grew warmer and warmer. They drank what seemed like gallons of water, and Cara silently checked online, pricing room-sized window air conditioners—one for the shop, and one for her apartment.

When the phone rang around three in the afternoon, Bert glanced over, crossed his eyes, and ignored it.

"Lillian Fanning," he told Cara. "If she's paid her bills, I don't see why we have to talk to her again."

"Maybe she wants us to do flowers for another event," Cara said crisply, reaching for the phone. "Which is why I don't want us screening calls. You never know..."

"I know that woman, and with her, it's never pleasant," he shot back.

"Lillian," Cara said, her voice radiating warmth she didn't actually feel. "So good to hear from you again. Are you all rested up from the wedding excitement yet?"

"Mostly. Bill and I just got back from two weeks in Bermuda. The weather was nice, but the service! I can't think why anybody would go there a second time...."

"Have the wedding proofs come back yet?" Cara asked. She really wasn't in the mood to listen to one of Lillian's rants this afternoon. "Please be sure to let me know when I can see them. I'd love to use some of them on my website. That photo of you and Torie, together on the dock, just at sunset, has to be great."

"The proofs aren't back, which is just so annoying," Lillian started. "I can't even get into that right now. Listen, Cara, I'm calling about the silver."

"Silver?" Cara was hot and tired. And her mind was a blank.

"My silver. The things you used for the wedding. The candlesticks, the bud vases, the punch bowl, and the epergne. They were all supposed to be returned to me after the wedding."

Cara noted that Lillian referred to the silver as things "*you* used." They had, of course, used the Fanning family silver at the mother of the bride's insistence.

She closed her eyes and tried to think back, to the night of Torie's wedding, and the Sunday afterward. She remembered rounding up all the pieces and checking them off against the inventory she'd taken, as she always did, when they used a client's own pieces for an event. She'd done it the morning after the wedding.

And she even remembered loading them into a large plastic bin lined with towels, to keep the pieces from being scratched. She could see the bin in the back of the van. But what she could not remember was taking the bin back to the Fannings' home.

"Hang on a minute, Lillian, please," she said. "Let me just check something."

She put Lillian Fanning on hold and turned to Bert.

"I heard," he said. "Her silver."

"Did we return it?" Cara asked, her voice urgent. "I guess maybe I was a little buzzed that night. I remember packing it up and putting it in the van, but that's it. Please tell me we returned it all to her."

"I tried," Bert said, already defensive. "I've been over there three different times in the last month, while I was out on deliveries. But nobody was home, and I definitely wasn't gonna just leave it sitting on their doorstep."

"They were in Bermuda for two weeks.."

He was unmoved. "Tell Lillian to take a chill pill. The silver is all still out in the van."

"The van?" Cara cried. "Half a dozen cars on this block have been broken into over the past six months. Why wouldn't you bring it in here, where it would be safe?"

"Here, where?" He gestured around the tiny, cluttered workshop.

Without another word, she got up, hurrying toward the back of the shop, to where the van was parked. "Please let it be therepleasepleaseplease." She felt acid rising in her throat. She unlocked the wrought-iron courtyard gate and stepped into the lane. The van was in its parking slot, which was boldly marked PRIVATE PARKING FOR BLOOM FLORAL.

Her fingers were trembling so badly she had to hold the key with both hands to unlock the back tailgate. Finally, she flung the doors open, and with her heart in her mouth, shoved aside a packing blanket to uncover the plastic bin, filled with the Fanning family silver.

Cara sank down on the tailgate to catch her breath, then jumped up quickly, the heat from the bumper searing the exposed flesh on her thighs. She grabbed the heavy bin, relocked the van, and went back inside.

She picked up the phone. "Lillian?"

"What on earth!" The older woman's tone seared almost as much as that overheated bumper. "I was just about to hang up and call back."

"I am so, so sorry," Cara exclaimed. "The silver is all right here at the shop."

No need to tell Lillian that her priceless family heirlooms had been riding around in her van since the wedding.

"We did try to return it to you, after the wedding, but nobody was home, so we just decided to leave it here, for safekeeping, until we heard from you."

"You're hearing from me now," Lillian said pointedly.

"And I'll bring the silver back to you immediately. I'll deliver it myself. Is now a good time?"

"Now's fine," Lillian said.

27

I'll go." Bert jumped up from his seat at the worktable. He pointed at the finished flower arrangements in the cooler. "It's my fault Lillian's pissed at you."

"I'll do the drops at Candler and Memorial. There's a funeral arrangement to go to Gamble Funeral Home too. Then we've got a delivery on the south side. I'll head out to Isle of Hope after that, and personally deliver Lillian's treasure right to her door."

"No, that's okay. Just take care of the other deliveries. I'll use my own car and take the silver back. Ultimately, it's my responsibility."

"Please?" He gave her his winningest smile. "I want to. You were right. I should have at least brought that bin into the shop and let you decide what to do with it. It was pure laziness on my part."

"Well . . . if you really want to . . ."

The phone rang and they both reached for it. And stopped, when they saw Lillian Fanning's name on the caller ID screen again.

"Now what?" Cara murmured.

"Hi Lillian. We were just heading your way."

"Change of plans," Lillian said, skipping a greeting. "I'm meeting a friend for drinks at the club. But I'll leave a key to the back door. It'll be under the lid of the gas grill on the patio. Just put the silver in the kitchen and leave the key where you found it afterward."

"We can do that," Cara said, grateful that neither of them would have to experience their client's wrath face-to-face.

She quickly put together a small nosegay of pink roses to fit inside one of Lillian's silver bud vases. Then she helped load the flower arrangements into the built-in racks in the van while Bert put the bin of silver in the front seat.

"There's a key under the gas grill lid on the patio around the back of the Fannings' house," she told her assistant. "Put the little nosegay in the middle of the kitchen table, will you? Leave the rest of the silver in the bin, on the kitchen counter. And for God's sake, be sure you've locked up tight when you leave."

He nodded and hopped into the driver's seat. Then he stuck his head out the open window. "Okay if I keep the van and use it tonight, Mom?" He cocked his head to the side. "I promise to put gas in it. Pretty please?"

Cara laughed despite herself. She could never stay mad at Bert for long, and he damned well knew it. And it wasn't an unusual request. His own car was an unreliable seventeen-year-old Honda, which was why he mostly relied on his bike for transportation around town.

"Okay, but make sure all your homework's done first! And no riding around town picking up strange girls."

"No problemo," Bert said. He backed up the van and drove slowly down the lane.

28

Shaz was sprawled on the floor in front the air-conditioning vent in the living room. When Jack came out of the bedroom Sunday morning, dressed in running clothes and holding her leash, she regarded him with total disinterest.

"Up, Shaz," he said. She yawned and stayed put.

"Come on Shaz. Be a good girl. Let's go for a run before it gets too hot."

He clipped the leash to her collar and tugged gently. "It'll be fun," he lied.

It was nearly nine o'clock and the temperatures were already in the high eighties. But he'd worked long hours all week, returning home just at dark most nights, too worn out to do much more than take the puppy for a quick stroll around the block. A run, he decided, would be good for both of them.

Most days, he took Shaz with him over to South Carolina and Cabin Creek, where he and Ryan had started work on the old barn. After only a week, they'd already worked out a routine. He and Ryan would leave Savannah while it was still dark, and by dawn the two men would be up on the roof, ripping off the old tin, exposing multiple layers of brittle tar, and then finally the wooden subroof.

Shaz was happy to start the mornings romping around the pasture, sniffing the horses, but otherwise keeping a cautious distance. The rest of those hot days, she found a place in the cool dim of one of the old horse stalls, leaving only occasionally to drink from her bowl of water, or to investigate strange new smells and sights outside.

During the worst heat of the day, Jack and Ryan loaded up the truck with the Strayhorn family's decades of junk and hauled it off to the nearby dump. It was hot, exhausting work, but they had a deadline, so they kept up the pace, only taking a day off on Sunday—and then only at Torie's insistence.

Jack tugged again at Shaz's leash now, and she reluctantly stood up and allowed herself to be led outside.

They took their usual route, loping easily north down Habersham. The street was Sunday-morning quiet. They passed Broughton, Savannah's version of Main Street, and ran through Warren Square, where a homeless man napped on a bench, and on to Bay Street.

An early-morning breakfast crowd milled outside around the door at B. Matthew's, and Shaz stopped abruptly, sniffing the aroma of bacon when the restaurant door was opened.

"Later," Jack said, tugging again. They continued west on Bay Street, where tourists stood in groups on street corners, consulting their maps, or aiming cameras at the photo-ready moss-draped oaks on the far side of the street.

After only a mile, Shaz was panting, and Jack's shirt was drenched with sweat. He slowed to a walk, crossed Bay at Bull, and escorted Shaz to the shade under an oak, where he bought a bottle of water from a street vendor, uncapped it, and let Shaz refresh herself, laughing as she eagerly lapped the glugging water. He poured the last few drops of the water into his palms and splashed it onto his face, and they set off again.

Man and dog ran up Whitaker Street, past the chic boutiques and home-furnishing stores, until they got to Forsyth Park. It was shadier here, and the sidewalks were already crowded with other runners, walkers, and skateboarders. After two laps around the park, he stopped and bought another bottle of water to share with Shaz.

He set off north again on Whitaker, telling himself it would be natural for their route home to pass by the red-brick building on West Jones Street. And if Cara and her dog happened to be out for a Sunday walk, well, that would be just fine.

As it happened, Cara and Poppy weren't out for a walk. But they were sitting on the stoop in front of Bloom. Or rather, Cara was sitting on the stoop. Poppy was sitting at the base of a crepe myrtle tree located in a planting bed of ivy in the middle of the sidewalk. The goldendoodle was staring intently up at the tree branches, where a large gray squirrel chattered indignantly.

Cara had her hair tied up in a sloppy topknot, and she was wearing the least amount of clothing she could get away with in public, a short periwinkle-blue cotton sundress, and matching cheap blue flip-flops.

The shop door was propped open with a box window fan, which she'd turned on in an effort to cool herself. Pages of the Sunday *New York Times* fluttered in the listless warm breeze from the fan, held down with a tall plastic tumbler of iced tea.

She spotted the familiar figure of Jack Finnerty and his dog as soon as they turned onto her block, and she felt a little shiver of excitement, followed quickly by the dismaying fact of her appearance.

Unable to sleep in the suffocating heat of the apartment, she'd been up since six. She'd fed Poppy, forced herself to eat a container of Greek yogurt and some strawberries for breakfast, and walked over to the coffee shop and newsstand on Liberty Street, where she picked up the iced tea and the Sunday paper.

She'd tried reading out in the back garden, but swarms of gnats and mosquitoes forced her inside. The courtyard was cooler, but at least out here on the stoop she could use the window fan to keep the biting bugs at bay.

Despite the fan, her face was sheened with perspiration, and her arms were slicked with a combination of sweat and insect repellent. Her hair was a hot, damp mess, and of course, she wore no makeup.

"Hey!" Jack called. Poppy turned to see where the voice was coming from, and bounded over to greet her old friend and his dog.

"Poppy!" Cara called anxiously. But the dog was content to give Jack's out-stretched hand a lick of acknowledgment, falling quickly in step with the pair as they approached the stoop.

It was too late to run inside and try to clean up. Instead, she smiled up at him. "Good run?"

"Hot. Shaz wasn't really too much into it, so we just kind of took it easy this morning."

Cara leaned down and patted Shaz's head. "Let me get you guys some-thing cold to drink," she offered.

"That'd be great," Jack said. She moved aside the box fan to allow her guests to enter the shop.

"Sorry about the heat," she said, turning from the refrigerator in the shop's kitchenette. She held out a bottle of cold water, and went to the sink to run water into a bowl for Shaz.

"Trying to save money on the electric bill?" Jack asked. He'd been in the shop for less than five minutes, and sweat was already dripping from his face. He held the bottle of water to the back of his neck, wiped his brow with a paper towel Cara handed him.

She made a face. "The air conditioner's not working. Again."

"Geez," he said. "How long has it been like this?"

Cara set the bowl on the floor, and Shaz and Poppy both crowded around it, lapping water as fast as they could.

"More than a week," she said. "It's been hell."

"What does your landlord say?" he asked. "Didn't they send somebody over to fix it?"

"My landlady passed away week before last. I'd been calling even before that, and I've been trying to reach her daughter,, but so far, no call back. This is typical of them. Worst. Landlords. Ever."

"That's bullshit," Jack said angrily. "You can't live like this, with no air."

"Tell me about it. I've got two or three box fans, like the one I've got in the doorway, but all they really do is move the hot air around. Pretty miserable."

"Where's your thermostat?" Jack asked. "I'm no HVAC guy, but I can at least take a look."

She pointed down the hall, toward the staircase. "On the wall, there."

Cara followed Jack down the hall. He stood in front of the small metal box mounted on the plaster wall. He punched the Cool button, but did not hear the unit switch on.

"Okay," he shrugged. "Fuse box? It's an old house, I'm guessing maybe the electrical hasn't been updated in a while?"

"Probably not in at least thirty years," Cara agreed. "Sometimes if I'm using my hair dryer or iron, it shorts out a circuit. The fuse box is back there, near the back door to the courtyard."

He flipped open the fuse box and studied the row of breakers and fuses. "Doesn't look like any of the breakers have been flipped. Do you change the filters pretty often?" he asked.

She nodded. "Every month."

"Is the unit outside?" Jack asked, his hand on the doorknob.

"In the courtyard."

"Got a screwdriver?"

The unit, a rust-speckled gray cube, sat on a wooden platform in a corner of the courtyard garden. Jack unscrewed the back panel of the unit and peered at the exposed machinery.

"What are you looking for?" Cara asked, looking over his shoulder.

"Just anything that looks obviously wrong. I was hoping maybe it was something simple, like a slipped or broken blower belt. Or maybe that the condenser was iced over, but that doesn't seem to be the case."

He fetched the garden hose from a large terra-cotta pot where it was coiled nearby. Turning on the spigot, he sprayed it over the box, in a deliberate back and forth pattern.

"What's that for?" Cara asked, swatting at a mosquito on her neck.

"Rinsing off the coils," he explained. "They can get blocked with all the pollen and dust and leaves and crud, and then you don't get cooling."

She nodded, acting as though she understood.

"I turned the controls off before we came out. Would you go inside and flip it on and see if we get lucky and it starts up?"

Cara crossed her fingers, flipped the thermostat on, and prayed for the dull thump that signaled the unit coming to life. Nothing. She ran her hand in front of the air register. More nothing.

"Sorry," Jack said, meeting her at the back door. "I looked at the manufacturer's plate on the back of it—it was installed in '82. The average life span of a central-air unit is supposed to be ten or fifteen years. I think that thing is DOA."

"Crap." She leaned her forehead against the wall beside the thermostat. "I don't think I can go on like this."

"You shouldn't have to. Tomorrow, first thing, send the landlord a registered letter, telling her you plan to have the unit repaired or replaced, and that you'll deduct whatever costs you incur from your rent."

"And what do I do in the meantime?" she asked. "I looked at the weather report this morning. This heat wave isn't going to let up. We don't even have any rain in the forecast. And anyway, I don't have the money to buy a central-air-conditioning unit like that. It's probably at least three or four thousand dollars."

"Can you open some windows? At least get some air circulating? These old houses were built to catch cross currents."

"I've tried, believe me. They're all painted shut. I hacked at the window in my bedroom with a screwdriver and even a steak knife, but I couldn't get it to budge. Every window in this house is like that."

He glanced toward the stairs. "Want me to give it a try?"

"Be my guest."

The staircase opened into a hallway that was the twin to the one on the first floor. The second floor, as she'd warned, was stifling. What had probably originally been a bedroom was now a combination living/dining room, visible through an arched entryway that Jack estimated had been installed sometime around the turn of the 1900s.

A large bay window looked out on the courtyard garden, and there were double banks of windows on the side walls, overlooking the sliver of side garden that separated this building from the ones next door.

A faded Oriental rug in muted blues, greens, and roses covered the wood floors, and a pair of overstuffed white slipcovered sofas faced each other, separated by an old painted trunk that was used as a coffee table. Bookcases flanked the windows. In the dining area, a round oak table was surrounded by a set of four mismatched high-backed chairs painted a soft fern green. A matte-green vase in the center of the table held a bouquet of wilted daisies. A small side table held another box fan, humming ineffectively in the corner.

He'd seen some of the finest, most elegant parlors in the historic district, spaces filled with valuable antiques, priceless art, silver, first-edition books, and designer trappings. But none of them looked as welcoming as Cara Kryzik's living room.

This room looked to Jack like a room where you could sit and sip a glass of wine, read a book, or just be. There were paintings scattered about, on the walls and propped on the bookshelves, watercolors and oils, all of them either landscapes or still lifes with flowers. He was no art expert, but he thought these were probably the works of gifted amateurs—flea-market finds, most likely. There was also a laughably small flat-screen television nearly hidden on the bookshelves among the books.

He thought of the living room in his own cottage on Macon Street, cluttered with bins of his clothing, books, and detritus. At least when Zoey lived with him, the place was clean. There was a ratty leather sofa, now covered in dog hair, a lumpy brown leather recliner where he fell asleep more nights than he'd like to admit, this facing his prized sixty-four-inch high-definition surround-sound television propped on a pair of sawhorses. No pictures hung on his walls, no rugs softened his floors. It occurred to him that although he owned his own house, he had never taken the time to make it a home.

"Where's the kitchen?" he asked, turning toward her. Cara stepped into the hallway and pushed aside a flowered green and white curtain that concealed what he'd assumed was probably a closet or bathroom.

At one time, it had probably been another small bedroom. But now the space was fitted with a set of 1950s-era flesh-pink metal kitchen cabinets, a small two-burner stove, with a cherry-red teakettle on the back burner, a stained porcelain sink barely big enough to hold a medium-sized saucepan, and the skinniest refrigerator he'd ever seen. There was a single window over the sink, and it held a jelly jar with a cluster of faded pink flowers. A flowered mug in the sink held a teaspoon.

"You cook in here?" he asked.

"All the time," Cara said with a laugh. "It's tiny, but it does the job."

They continued down the hallway, and Cara pointed through the open door. "My boudoir."

Cara's bedroom was a large, high-ceilinged room, with wide coved crown molding at the ceiling, and high baseboard molding, all painted a yellowing white. The wallpaper was old and age-speckled, but the pattern of ivy and white roses against a pale aqua background made the room look like the inside of a garden.

The ceiling was painted a soft aqua, and there was a large Victorian brass gaslight that had been electrified, hanging from the middle of an ornate plaster medallion. The scarred heart-pine floors were bare, with the exception of some scattered braided rugs in muted colors. An elaborately carved and gingerbread-decked mantel on one wall held a small coal-burning fireplace.

Her bed, a white-painted four-poster, was unmade, its crocheted bedspread tossed aside, the pillows and sheets rumpled.

"You caught me," Cara said lightly. "I usually make my bed, but last night was so miserable, and it's so hot, I couldn't stand being up here one more second."

"I'm shocked," Jack said, with a laugh.

"Nice room," he said, looking around. "All original woodwork and plaster and wallpaper. Even the fireplace. I guess that's the upside of having a cheapskate landlord. They left everything alone. You'd be surprised how many downtown houses from this era I see that have been carved up or stripped of everything original."

"Oh, it's all original," Cara said ruefully. "Right down to the ancient plumbing, the leaky roof, and the crappy wiring."

He went over to the double set of windows facing the street, took the screwdriver she'd given him earlier, and ran it across the windowsill. Paint shavings fell onto the floor, but the window stayed shut.

He went around the room, examining the other windows, but they were all in the same condition, as Cara warned, painted shut with years and years' worth of layers.

"Okay," he said, turning to her. "I'm gonna run home, get my truck and some tools, and I'll be back in about half an hour."

"Really?" Her face lit up. "It's your day off, and I know you do this for a living and I hate to ask ... but if there's any way you can cool this place down—even a little—you would totally be my hero for life."

"No big thing," he said lightly, heading for the stairs.

"Just leave Shaz here with me and Poppy," Cara called. "They can stay out in the garden where it's a little cooler."

29

Half an hour later, Jack eased his pickup truck into the lane behind Cara's town house. Back at home he'd taken a quick shower, and grinned at himself in the bathroom mirror as he shaved for the first time that weekend. Wouldn't hurt to not look like like a Yeti, he decided. He changed into jeans, a T-shirt, and work boots, then went outside to load what he needed.

He went around to the bed of the truck, grabbed his tool belt, and fastened it around his waist.

Cara met him at the gate from the courtyard, unlocking it so he could enter. She eyed the tool belt, then looked over his shoulder at the truck. "Ladders?"

"Yup. I'm thinking I'll probably need to unseal the windows from the outside as well as the inside. No telling what all they did to paint those windows shut."

"I had no idea this was going to be such a production," Cara fretted.

Like those of many homes and shops in the historic district, Bloom's front windows were covered with decorative and functional wrought-iron burglar bars. Jack attacked these with his cordless screwdriver. Cara helped him lift off the bars, and set them aside, along with the flower boxes she'd planted with ferns and Nikko Blue hydrangeas.

He pulled a lethal-looking tool from his belt. It had a spade-shaped head with wicked serrated edges, and he ran it along the edge where the windowsill met the bottom of the lower window sash.

"What the heck is that thing?" Cara asked.

He held it up for her to examine. "It's called a window zipper. We have to use them on almost every historic restoration we do downtown."

"Gotta get me one of those," she nodded.

He performed the same operation on the top of the window sash, then ran the tool along the sides of the sash.

"Now we move inside," Jack told her.

He used the zipper on the interior of the front window, and then, with an X-Acto knife, removed globs of old paint from the sash lock before he could finally flip it open. Then he examined the window jambs. "If we're lucky, these babies will still have the sash cords and sash weights."

He took a small pry bar and worked it cautiously under the edge of the jamb, popping off the molding and exposing the channel, where he pointed at the cotton sash cord. "Good news."

He pushed hard on the bottom sash, but it didn't budge.

"Uh-oh," Cara said glumly.

"I'm not done yet." Now he took a slender putty knife, inserted it between the windowsill and the bottom sash, and lightly tapped it with a hammer, working the knife from side to side along the sash. He did the same thing on the top of the sash.

This time, when he pushed, the window slowly slid open.

Cara threw her arms around Jack. "My hero!"

He grinned. "And it only took what? About forty-five minutes?" He poked his head out the open window. "I'll put the burglar bars back up—but you're definitely gonna need some window screens, or you'll get eaten alive in here. Do you happen to know if there are any still around?"

"I think I remember seeing some screens in the toolshed," Cara said, with a shudder.

"What?"

"The last time I opened the shed, I saw a rat. I haven't been out there since."

"Does that mean you want *me* to rummage around in the shed?"

"Yes, please," she said meekly.

Twenty minutes later, he was back, with an armload of wood-framed window screens. His shirt and pants were streaked with dirt, and a bit of cobweb hung from his hair. She silently picked it off.

"See any rats?"

"Mmm. Not the rats. But evidence that they've been there. You might want to put some poison out there. I also found more sets of burglar bars, probably for the second-story windows. I'm thinking I'll need to put those up if we can get those windows open."

"Absolutely."

After he'd worked his way around to the back of the house, unsealing the windows, Jack got out the extension ladder and clambered up to work on the second-story windows.

Declaring herself his assistant, Cara did what she could to help, rinsing off the window screens with the hose, wielding the window zipper on the inside windows, breaking the painted seals with the putty knife and hammer the way he'd shown her, fetching tools from his truck, and even ferrying the newly cleaned window screens up the ladder.

Overhead, the sun blazed down. It was hot, sweaty work. But by six that evening, Cara had enough open windows—with screens and burglar bars in place—to admit what little hot breeze existed.

After loading the ladder and the last of his tools into the truck, Jack came into the town house.

"Up here," Cara called down. He found her in the kitchen alcove. She handed him a cold long-neck bottle of beer before uncapping her own.

"Just what the doctor ordered," he said. "Thanks." They clinked bottles and he drank thirstily.

"Are you kidding? You just spent your whole day—your day off—doing what you get paid thousands of dollars to do."

"Wait'll you get my bill."

Her face fell.

"Kidding. Really. I was happy to be able to help out. I just wish I could have resuscitated your air conditioner. Getting the windows open is only a temporary fix, you know. You're gonna have to make your landlady install a new air unit."

"I'm calling Sylvia first thing in the morning, and I'm going to keep on calling, and I'll send her a registered letter, like you suggested. But in the meantime, I am so, so grateful to you, Jack. Let me at least take you out to dinner, as partial payment. Okay?"

He gestured down at his grimy clothes. "Like this?"

"Okay. I'll cook here. What do you like?"

She opened the refrigerator, and stood in front of the door, letting the cold air wash over her. "Ahh."

Jack leaned against the doorjamb, appreciating the view.

"I like you," he said.

And he did. Her topknot had mostly come undone, and loose strands of her butterscotch hair fell over one eye and around her exposed collarbone. Her face was pink and sunburned, and her chest, arms, and legs were dirt-smudged. She was barefoot, and he noticed that her toenails were painted sort of a coral color. Her cotton sundress was thin and faded, and in the dim light of the kitchen he could see her body clearly silhouetted through the light from the refrigerator.

She had worked as hard as he had today, without complaint, eager to learn the skills he took for granted. Now she was as grimy as he, but she was totally unself-conscious and unapologetic about her appearance.

"Me?"

He put his hands around her waist and drew her to him. "You," he said, and kissed her deeply.

She kissed him back, without hesitation. They stood there like that, with the cool refrigerated air washing over them. His lips traveled to her earlobes, and then to the nape of her neck and her collarbone. Her skin tasted warm and sweat-salty, but she still smelled faintly sweet, like floral shampoo.

"I could make us a salad," she whispered, as she worked her hands up the back of his shirt.

"Mmm. Salad's good."

Her dress had skinny little straps that tied in a bow. He took the end of one of the stringlike things between his teeth and pulled, and it easily came undone. He kissed the bare spot, nibbling it just a little.

She inhaled sharply, but there was no protest, so he kissed his way, slowly, across her collarbone, pausing at the hollow just below her chin, where he felt her pulse quicken. Her head was thrown back, eyes closed, but her hands were busy on his back, massaging his shoulder blades, running down his back, then around, to his chest, her thumbs brushing his nipples. He detoured for a moment, burying his hands in her thick hair, and then he was kissing her again, their tongues darting in and out of each other's parted lips. Her hands roamed down to his hips, and then back to his chest again.

She was saying something, but he'd lost his concentration. "Hmm?"

"I said, what kind of dressing?"

But before he could answer, not that he had an answer, she'd gathered the hem of his T-shirt in her fists, and abruptly jerked it upward. Helpfully, he crossed his arms over his head, and allowed her to pull it all the way off.

She took a half step backward, and assessed him lazily, through lowered eyelashes. Jack felt the blast of cold air on his bare chest. Caught her chin in his hand. "Did you say dressing, or undressing?"

Cara had drunk exactly one-half of a beer. So why did she feel so dizzy, intoxicated, and totally unlike herself?

It was all Jack Finnerty's fault. She was not the kind of woman who noticed men's bodies, ogled the way their jeans fit, obsessed about their muscled physiques, or fantasized about their romantic prowess.

So why had that been not far from her mind? All. Damn. Day. Why had she paused at the foot of that ladder, gazing up at his butt with an unexpected heat that seemed centered somewhere south of decent? Why had she obsessed about that thin-cotton T-shirt, sweat-soaked, clinging to his chest and his belly, wishing he'd just rip it off? And when the weight of his tool belt dragged his jeans down, and she'd glimpsed his navel and a downward-pointing arrow of dark hair, why had she been forced to go inside and slap cold water on her neck and face? Why?

Maybe it was inevitable that they would end up like this. After all, the second time she locked eyes with Jack, he'd dropped his trousers in front of her with absolutely no hesitation.

Jack kissed her again, and worked his knee between her legs.

"I could grill us a steak," she whispered.

Dinner was the last thing on Jack's mind. "Hmm?" His lips were working their way toward her left shoulder. He took the other thin strip of fabric between his teeth, pulled, and performed the same cheap trick as before. The strap fell away, and he nuzzled her bare, salty shoulder. Like a pretzel. Only way better. With his thumbs, he leisurely worked the dress downward, until he found her breasts, and her nipples, lowering his head to kiss them each, in turn.

Another brief gasp.

For a moment, he debated about the proper way to do this. The top of her dress had some kind of elastic. Should he pull it over her head, as she'd done with his shirt, or downward? Such a delicious dilemma.

"Steak." She'd plunged her own hands into the waist of his jeans, her fingertips easing lower, digging into the flesh of his backside, at the same time, pressing her torso against his. He was already hard.

He nudged her backward, until she was pressed against the refrigerator shelves.

"I like steak."

Down was the way to go, Jack decided. While his lips concentrated on her breasts, he skimmed his hands over her hips, pausing there. He found the hem of the dress, and in one easy movement, tugged it downward, past her hips and then her knees. From there, the dress fell to the floor, puddling around her bare ankles. Cara stood on her tiptoes, and with her right foot, delicately swept the discarded dress to one side.

The one remaining, infinitesimal rational part of her brain not subsumed with crazed lust told Cara that this current situation was insane, indecent, and yet, weirdly intoxicating. She was naked, except for her panties, which weren't all that substantial, with her tushie pushed up against the cold metal shelves of her refrigerator. It was broad daylight outside. Her front door wasn't even locked. What was she thinking?

Right now, the contents of her fridge, not all that exciting—the past-expiration-date quart of milk, half-head of Romaine lettuce, containers of no-fat Greek yogurt and assorted Tupperware containers of leftover roast chicken, steamed broccoli and molding strawberries, not to mention the pickles, mustard and Paul Newman balsamic vinaigrette—were getting the show of their lives. What was she thinking?

She didn't care. And she definitely didn't want to think.

Cara smoothed her hands over Jack's flat belly, hooked her fingertips into the waistline of his jeans, pushed them down to his narrow hips, appreciating the hollow of his hipbones. She let the palm of her right hand drift leisurely down to his crotch, pausing there. Now it was his turn to gasp. She glanced down, and just the tiniest smile played across her lips as she saw his erection straining against the denim fabric. She grasped his waistband and nimbly unbuttoned his jeans.

She stopped then, and ran her hands back up his chest, feeling the rough texture of hair, of muscle and bone. And something else. She opened her eyes, frowned. Tiny black flecks of some hardened substance dotted his chest. With her fingernail, she scraped off a fleck and held it up for him to see.

"Roofing tar."

"Oh."

"From the barn at Cabin Creek. So it's all your fault."

"We'll have to work on that," Cara said. She lowered her head, and with her tongue and teeth, gently teased his nipples as her hands slowly inched downward, down toward the waistband of his jeans. With her thumbnail, she raked the metal tines of his fly. Down. Up. Down again. She cupped him with the same hand. He moaned into her hair. "You're killin' me here."

She was naked, except for that languorous smile and a tiny pair of panties.

Pink, with flowers. Naturally. He rolled them easily past her hips, her thighs and knees. And then gravity did the rest. She stepped daintily out of them and kicked them in the direction of the dress.

He kissed her and pulled away, finally able to feast on the sight of her— naked, just the way he'd imagined her since the first time he'd spotted her in that pink dress at his brother's wedding. Only much, much better.

Her hair tumbled down around her shoulders, and her chest was lightly freckled, her full breasts flushed pink. She had a narrow waist that belled out to full hips and a delicious, rounded butt.

Cara didn't have the taut, angular physique of Zoey, who spent most of her waking hours at the gym, and the rest of them obsessively weighing herself and measuring every morsel, every calorie of food she ingested.

This was a woman's body, the body of somebody with an appetite for the good things in life. This was a body he could spend a long time exploring.

Only now, her lips were slightly blue, and her skin was pebbled with goose bumps. And those shivers he'd felt, when he'd pressed himself urgently against her?

"Are you cold?"

"G-G-G-God y-e-s-s-s."

30

W hat about the dogs?" Cara asked, as he pulled her down the hallway, toward the bedroom. She was glad he had his back to her, convinced her frostbitten butt was probably permanently imprinted with the Frigidaire logo.

"They're on their own." Jack plopped down on the edge of her bed, unknotting the laces of his work boots, kicking one free, then the other. He pulled her down beside him.

Suddenly shy about her state of undress, she clutched for the quilt draped over the foot of the bed, pulling it across her exposed breasts. "Maybe we should check on them. They're awfully quiet out there. I hope Poppy isn't showing Shaz how to dig up my peonies."

He yanked the quilt off. "I'll buy you a carload of peonies. Later."

Cara crossed her arms across her exposed breasts. Was she actually going to go through with this? She hadn't been with a man since leaving Leo, had only slept with two other men before marrying Leo. And what about birth control?

Too late. Jack scooted backward onto the pile of pillows at the head of her bed, tugging at her hand. "C'mere."

She was stretched out beside him. He turned toward her, gave her a lazy smile. He ran his hands down her side, all the way down, and then back up. One hand slid between her thighs and paused there. Cara gripped his shoulders.

"Um, Jack?"

His tongue was making slow, excruciating circles around her nipple. Her body curled into his as he stroked and nipped and kissed, and she knew she could lose her mind—and self-control—any minute now.

"Hmm?"

He rolled away from her, just a few inches. "Don't worry. I've got something in my pocket."

Cara looked down. "So I see."

"Dirty girl." He flopped onto his back, waiting.

She hesitated only a moment. Propping herself up on one elbow, she pressed the flat of her hand lightly against the bulge of his jeans. "Here?"

He was touching her again, his gaze locked with hers.

Cara worked the metal zipper down half an inch at a time, stroking as she did so. "Here?" she whispered.

"You're getting warm."

Cara laughed. "You don't even know. . . ."

She had the zipper all the way down now, and could see the waistband of his gray knit briefs, the erection straining against it. She let her fingertips trail across him.

"Warmer."

Cara rolled onto her knees and grasped his jeans and the waistband of the briefs with both hands, sliding them lower. He stuck one leg between hers, so that she was directly over him. He ran his hands down her flank, and then around, and upward, suckling one breast, and then the other.

She nearly lost her concentration. The jeans were down around his hips now, and he thoughtfully thrust his hips upward, off the bed, so that she could tug them down, past his thighs. As her hands explored all the possible hiding spots for what she was seeking, as well as potential pleasure points, she felt the small square packet in his right front pocket.

She took her right foot, swung it over his leg and down, sliding the jeans all the way to his ankles.

Cara sat up with the jeans in hands, reached in, and extracted the foil-wrapped condom. "Got it," she exclaimed.

"You win," Jack said, reaching for her.

If she'd been cold standing in front of the Frigidaire, she was on fire now. At some point, Jack dragged a second box fan into the bedroom, placed it on a chair, and angled it toward the bed. The fan blades whirred ineffectively, but at least, she thought, remembering her open windows, they would have prevented anybody on the sidewalk below from hearing what was going on up here.

Their lovemaking started out slowly. She wanted him badly, but was too shy to tell him how badly. But Jack Finnerty seemed to know what she wanted, and what she needed. Eventually, whatever inhibitions she'd initially felt disappeared. She lost herself in the joy of pleasing him and letting him please her.

"You're beautiful, you know that?" He was lying on his side, facing her, their bodies slicked with sex and sweat.

"I'm a hot mess and we both know it," Cara retorted. "I can't believe I let you take me to bed as filthy as I was. And I really can't believe I let you into my bed as filthy as you were!"

"Who took who to bed? You were the one who asked me what I liked?"

"I was referring to dinner options," she said, trying in vain to sound prim.

"So now I know. You like your men dirty. And you like your sex dirty." Jack chuckled as he leaned forward and gave her a lingering kiss.

"No. Really. This was lovely. But now, I have *got* to have a shower." Cara sat up and swung her legs over the edge of the bed, reaching for the quilt to wrap around herself.

He sat up too, in time to grab the edge of the quilt and pull it away from her.

Cara crossed her arms over her bare chest, then shrugged. They'd spent the last hour and a half naked. He'd explored every inch of her body, and she his. It was too late to play shy.

"Wait up," he said, standing. "I could use a shower myself. No use in wasting water." He gave her a hopeful grin.

She opened her bathroom door and gestured inside. The room was tiled in pale pink, with a burgundy tile border. There was a pink toilet, a pink sink, and the smallest pink bathtub he'd ever seen—and he'd seen a lot of bathtubs in his job.

"Is that a Barbie dream tub?" he asked, pushing aside the flowered shower curtain to look down at it. It was barely big enough for one adult, let alone two.

Cara stepped around him, turned on the faucets, and stepped in. "Don't worry, I'll save you some hot water."

She emerged from the shower wrapped in a thick white terry bath sheet, with her damp hair wrapped in another towel. He was standing, bemused, and stitch-stark naked, leaning against the doorway outside the bathroom.

Jack Finnerty had to be the least inhibited man she'd ever met, Cara decided. She handed him a clean towel and a washcloth. "Your turn. Listen, while you're in the shower, I'm going to run to the store for a couple things."

"More condoms?" He waggled his eyebrows in a comic leer. "Whipped cream?"

"Steak," she said. "And a couple baking potatoes. Where are your clothes?"

He hooked a finger inside the edge of her towel and pulled her toward him. Good God, he was already aroused again.

"Why, you wanna hide 'em so you can keep me here as your love slave?"

"Dream on." She kissed his nose. "I'll throw 'em in the wash. Rapid cycle. You don't want to put on those grubby jeans again after a shower, right?"

"Not really. It would be great if you'd go ahead and wash 'em, but I always keep a spare pair of jeans and a shirt in the truck."

"Okay. I'll check on the dogs on my way out."

He'd seen her grill on his various trips in and out of the courtyard earlier. "I'll start the grill, if you tell me where you keep the charcoal."

"There's a big galvanized trash can just outside the back door. The charcoal's inside it and the lighter fluid should be sitting right beside it."

When he got out of the shower, Jack wrapped the towel around his waist and wandered into her living room. The room was like her, he decided, and he approved. Lots of books. Novels. She had eclectic taste, from classics to recent best-sellers, heavy on mystery with some girly-looking romance novels mixed in. There were three whole shelves of gardening and interior-design books. And one devoted to nonfiction. Some history, some pop culture.

He'd never seen Zoey read anything heavier than *Us* magazine.

There were also half a dozen self-help books with dreary, depressing-sounding titles on Cara's bookshelves. These, he decided, would be classified as "relationship books." *When Love Dies. Divorce: Getting Over It, Getting Through It.*

And then there was his favorite: *Putting Back the Pieces: Post-Divorce Recovery.*

He pulled it from the shelves and leafed through it, noting several pages that she'd dog-eared. The author photo of this little gem showed a grim-faced Slavic-looking woman, who, according to her bio, had a thriving marital therapy practice in New York. The author, a Dr. Jankovic, reminded him of Frau Blücher from *Young Frankenstein.*

For a moment, he felt a spasm of guilt, for invading Cara's privacy. But that didn't stop him from skimming down one of the pages, and when he saw a passage heavily underlined in ink, he read it aloud.

Over and over again in my thirty years of practice, I find a recurring pattern among patients whose marriages have failed. After careful examination, we discover that all too many of them have been attracted to a partner, in part because something in that spouse's family life supplies that which was lacking in a person's own life. Children of failed marriages often choose a partner from an intact home, in the mistaken belief that marital happiness can be genetically transferable.

What was that about? All Jack knew about Cara's parents was that her father was a strict, controlling military type and her mother was dead. And of the ex, Leo, he knew even less, except that the guy was a shit.

And he also knew that no matter what she said, the divorce had left Cara emotionally fragile.

He found the stacked washer-dryer unit in a closet just off the kitchen, and transferred his clothes into the dryer. Then he padded outside, with the towel wrapped loosely around his hips, to get the grill started.

As soon as he opened the back door, Poppy and Shaz bounded over to greet him, tails wagging. He winced when he saw the havoc they'd wrought in Cara's garden. Flowerpots were upended, plants matted down, and yes, it looked like one or both of the dogs had been digging up the beds. He'd have to make good on the peony IOU.

He dumped charcoal in the grill, added lighter fluid, and looked around for matches. Finding none, Jack went inside, found his truck keys on a small table in the hall, and went through the garden gate, into the lane where his truck was parked.

Stepping carefully to avoid broken glass and worse on the lane's crumbling asphalt paving, he unlocked the truck and reached under the front seat, pulling out the rolled-up jeans and clean T-shirt he kept there. He stretched across the seat, opened the glove box, and scrabbled around until he found a box of kitchen matches.

He was just locking the truck again when a shiny black Lexus rolled slowly down the lane. The car's windshield was tinted, so he couldn't see the driver, until he stopped right beside Jack and the electric window slid down.

The driver was a white guy, late thirties, with blond hair and a deeply tanned face. Despite the tinted windows, he wore a pair of Ray-Bans.

Jack didn't know the guy. He tucked the clean clothes under his arm and started back toward the gate.

"Hey man," the stranger called out.

Jack turned around, but said nothing.

"What's goin' on?"

Jack shrugged, and the towel settled lower on his hips. He retucked it. "Not much." He turned to go again.

"Some kinda party goin' on in there?" The blond jerked his chin in the direction of the courtyard and the town house beyond and smirked.

"Nope." Was the guy trying to proposition him? The historic district had a vibrant gay community, and it was well known that people sometimes trolled the quieter lanes and parks looking for a casual hookup. It wouldn't be the first time he'd been approached. And after all, Jack was standing in the lane, barefoot and dressed only in a towel.

"See ya," Jack said, and he motored back inside, being careful to lock and padlock the gate behind him. The Lexus rolled on down the lane, and he went inside to get dressed.

While he was grilling the steaks, Cara put the potatoes in the oven and threw together a salad, slicing fat, ripe red tomatoes she'd bought at the Saturday farmers' market in Forsyth Park, and crumbling locally made goat cheese into a vinaigrette dressing. She went out to the garden to snip some dill and chives from her herb patch, and handed Jack a cold Moon River.

He gave her an appreciative kiss, and wrapped his arms around her waist. "You smell nice," he murmured, nuzzling her hair.

"So do you. Hey—did you use my shampoo and conditioner?"

"Sure. If that's a problem, next time, I'll bring my own."

"What makes you think there's gonna be a next time?" She stifled a giggle.

He ran his hands up under her T-shirt. "There will be. You can't get enough of me, right? You're insatiable, right?"

Cara pushed him away lightly. "Don't burn my steak, wise guy."

The mosquitoes and gnats swarmed the garden right at dusk, so they ate at the dining-room table, moving the box fans from the bedroom into the living area.

Jack sipped the last of the wine she'd poured him, and pushed back from the table.

"That was great," he said. "I guess I could cook if I took the trouble, but living alone, hell, most of the time when I get home from work, I have a microwave burrito or something like that. Having a real steak, and salad, all of it, that's a treat." He turned and flipped a bit of steak to Shaz, who had spent the past hour crouched by his feet, hoping for a treat.

"The books say you shouldn't give dogs table scraps," Cara said. She looked down at Poppy, who'd also been hanging around, hoping for a handout.

"You always go by what the books say?"

"No. But Poppy's breeder said the same thing."

He grunted something noncommittal, then sighed. "I'll get these dishes cleaned up, then I better get on down the road. Early day out at Cabin Creek tomorrow."

She nodded, and helped carry their dishes into the kitchen. He ran soapy water in her sink, carefully washed and rinsed everything while she dried. When the kitchen was cleaned up, he whistled for Shaz.

"Let's go girl," he called. The dog stood slowly.

Cara followed them downstairs. "Oh. I almost forgot. Your clothes." She moved toward the washer-dryer, but Jack caught her by the hand. "Why don't I leave 'em here? You know, just in case?"

"You mean for next time? You're not very subtle, you know." She put her arms around his neck and kissed him.

"Subtle no. Smooth yes." He kissed her deeply and sighed.

"Hmm?" Cara inhaled his scent, and halfway wished he'd stay.

"Today was fun," Jack said. "I mean it. It wasn't like work at all. We make a good team, you know. And then dinner was awesome—the only time I get a real Sunday dinner is if I drop by my mom's house."

Cara raised one amused eyebrow. "And before dinner?"

"I was pretty amazing, wasn't I?"

She swatted his arm.

"Okay. You were amazing too."

She grinned. "Wait'll you get the bill."

31

Monday morning hadn't started well. It was hot. And sticky, and the box fans at Bloom did little more than circulate more hot, sticky air. At eight o'clock, Cara called Sylvia Bradley and left a message on her phone.

"Sylvia? This is Cara Kryzik calling again about the broken air-conditioning over here on Jones Street. I'm sorry about your mother, but I really, really need you to get somebody over here to see about replacing our unit. Please call me."

At nine, she called again.

"Sylvia? Cara. It is eighty-eight degrees in my shop. Eighty-eight degrees! Upstairs it's in the nineties. This is totally unacceptable. Please call and let me know when I can expect to have a new unit."

Slamming the phone down, Cara got up and walked over to the fan, pulling her damp tank top away from her chest. She had a million things to do today, but the heat had already drained her of energy.

She was in the kitchenette, fetching another bottle of cold water, when she heard the shop bell tinkle.

"Cara?"

Crap. She knew that voice. Why today, of all days?

Forcing a smile, she walked into the front room. "Lillian! So nice to see you. And what a beautiful tan from Bermuda!"

Lillian Fanning did not return her smile. Actually, her narrow, carefully made-up face was more pink than tan, and Cara had a feeling it wasn't just from the heat.

"What's going on?" Lillian demanded, pointing at the dueling window fans. "It feels like a third-world country in here."

"Our air-conditioning is broken. I've called our landlady but . . ."

"Appalling. Look, Cara," Lillian interrupted. "This isn't a social call. My epergne? Where is it?"

"Epergne?"

"Yes. My grandmother's silver epergne that you used at Brooke's reception."

"Isn't it with the rest of the silver? I mean, Bert delivered that silver to you Friday afternoon, didn't he?"

"The rest of the silver, yes. It was in the kitchen when I got home late Friday. But not the epergne. The most valuable piece I own. Is it still here, Cara?"

Cara felt a familiar knot of fear and panic in the pit of her stomach. She tried to think, tried to remember if she'd actually seen the epergne in with the rest of the Fannings' pieces.

"I . . . I don't know, Lillian. I put the bin of silver in the back of the van Friday afternoon, and I guess I just assumed it was in there. You're sure it's not at your house?"

"Of course I'm sure! Sunday morning, I unpacked all of it. I wanted to polish everything before putting the pieces back in the tarnish-proof bags I keep them in. But the epergne wasn't there."

Cara's mind raced. "Maybe it fell out of the bin. I can check in the back of the van."

"You do that." Lillian's voice was steely. She crossed her arms over her chest. "I'll wait right here."

"The thing is, I can't. Bert, my assistant, is driving the van. He's uh . . . out on a delivery."

The truth of the matter was, her assistant was MIA again this morning. Along with the van, which he'd had over the weekend.

"Can you call him? Ask him to check to see if it's there?"

"Of course." Cara gestured toward the chair closest to the window and the fan. "Please sit. I'll get you a bottle of water. . . ."

"I'm not thirsty." She lifted her hair from the nape of her neck and exhaled noisily. "How do you stand this?"

"Be right back," Cara said. She fled into the hallway with her cell phone and punched in Bert's cell-phone number, which immediately went to voicemail.

"Bert! Where the hell are you? Lillian Fanning is standing in the shop with smoke coming out of her ears. Her epergne was missing from that bin of silver you dropped off Friday. I need you to check in the van to see if it fell out. Call me immediately, either way. Like right now!"

Cara reluctantly retraced her sheps to the front of the shop.

"Well?" Lillian Fanning hadn't moved. "What did he say? Did he find it?"

Cara's throat was so dry she thought she might spit cotton. "Um, actually I couldn't reach him. He's probably out on Wilmington Island. There's a dead zone there, do you know the spot? Right on Johnny Mercer? My cell calls always get dropped there."

"Did you leave him a message? Does he understand how important this is?"

"I did, and we both understand how important this is. I promise, Lillian, as soon as he calls me, I'll call you. I feel sure the epergne probably just spilled out of the bin in the back of the van, and Bert didn't notice it."

"I hope that's the case," Lillian said huffily. "That epergne is a family heirloom. It was made by a Savannah silversmith in the eighteenth century, and of course, it's a museum-quality piece, which means it's irreplaceable."

All she could do was nod and walk Lillian to the door.

"I'll call," Cara promised, yet again.

After Lillian's departure, Cara called Torie's wedding photographer.

"Billy? It's Cara. Can you do me a huge favor? I know you haven't delivered the proof book from the Fanning wedding yet, but I've got a problem. Can you look through your shots of the reception and see if you've got one of the table for gifts and cards? I'm looking for a shot of this silver epergne we used to hold cards. It's gone missing, and if it doesn't turn up, I'm in a shitload of trouble."

"Damn, Cara," Billy Shook said. "Was it Lillian's?"

"Unfortunately."

"Damn. I don't ever want to deal with that woman again. I feel your pain, Cara. Pretty sure I've got at least one shot like that. I'll look right now and email you whatever I find."

Half an hour and two more panicky phone calls later, she heard the van pull into the lane in back of the shop. It was nearly ten o'clock.

Cara did a slow burn while she waited to confront her assistant.

He strolled in through the back door, whistling. His damp hair was slicked back from his forehead, still bearing comb marks. He carried two grande iced macchiatos, one of which he handed to Cara, with his most ingratiating smile.

"I know I'm a little late. Before you say anything, I'm sorry. Okay? Whew—it's hot in here. What's going on with Sylvia Bradley? Are they gonna fix the air, or what?"

"We'll get to that," Cara said. "First off, why haven't you returned any of my phone calls?"

His face went blank. "Calls?" He reached into the pocket of his black skinny jeans and pulled out his phone. "Oh man. My battery's dead. Sorry. I didn't even realize. I left my charger at home."

"Second—this is the second Monday in a row that you've been over an hour late. And not a word to give me a heads-up. I'm running a business here, Bert. We've got orders to fill, deliveries to get out, work to do. What's going on with you?"

He shrugged and stared down at the floor. "Nothing. Hey, I said I was sorry. . . ."

"And last week you said the same thing, and that it wouldn't happen again. This isn't like you, Bert. As your employer—and your friend—I think I deserve some kind of explanation."

"It's nothing. I went out of town for the weekend, and we were delayed getting back this morning, and like I said, I left my phone charger at home."

" 'We'? This is a new boyfriend?"

"Maybe," he said, his expression sullen. "Since when does my private life become any of your business?"

Cara felt her spine stiffen and her temples start to pound. "You make it my business when your private life interferes with your ability to do your job. Which is what's been happening the past two weeks. I wasn't going to say anything, because I was happy for you. But you leave me no choice. You disappear for hours at a time, slack off, ignore phone calls, come in late . . . and now this thing with Lillian's silver epergne . . ."

"What about the silver? C'mon, Cara. I told you I took the damned silver back to that bitch. . . ."

"There's a piece missing. Lillian Fanning showed up here this morning, loaded for bear, and I can't say I blame her. Which is what I was *trying* to call you about. I wanted you to check to see if maybe it had fallen out of the bin and was in the back of the van. But you couldn't be bothered to keep your phone charged. Or to come to work on time."

Bert shook his head obstinately. "*Why* are you making such a federal case out of this? I'll go look right now."

"Fine," Cara said. "Go look."

He hesitated. "What the fuck is an epergne anyway?"

She pulled out the photo of the Fanning epergne that Billy Shook had emailed, and that she'd printed out.

"It's a centerpiece thingy. Multiple arms that can hold little fruits or candies or flowers. We used it in the tent at the wedding, to hold gift cards. Lillian's is an eighteenth-century family heirloom. And she says it's irreplaceable."

They took the delivery van apart. Removed the racks for flower arrangements, lifted the bed liner, but there was no sign of the aforementioned epergne.

Cara dragged herself back into the shop and held her head under the faucet in the kitchenette, letting cold water sluice over her face and hair. The thought occurred to her that this would be a handy way to drown herself.

When she turned around, Bert stood in the doorway, shifting nervously from foot to foot. Beneath all the pouting and bravado, he obviously knew he'd messed up. "Now what?"

She sighed. "I've got a menu tasting with Brooke Trapnell and her fiancé at the caterers in exactly forty-five minutes. So I've got to get myself present-able for that. In the meantime, I need you to take the van, and retrace—exactly—the route you took last Friday out to Isle of Hope and the Fannings' house. Every stop—the hospital, any house you made a delivery to—every stop, Bert. You go in, and show them the photo of the epergne, and you ask if they've seen it."

He rolled his eyes dramatically. "Like that's gonna work."

"Just do it," she exploded. "And get yourself another charger for your phone. "

32

Delicious smells assaulted her nostrils as Cara pushed through the door at Fete Accompli. Layne Pelletier stood at attention just inside the door, hands clasped behind her back. She wore the traditional black and white checked slacks, clogs, and a white kerchief tied over her hair. Her white chef's smock was spotless, her name embroidered in script over her left breast.

Her face fell when she saw that Cara was alone. "The bride's not with you?"

"No. She and Harris called right before I left the shop and said they were running late. They're supposed to meet me here."

"You don't think they'll stand us up, right? I've spent a small fortune fixing all this food."

"No, no, they're coming," Cara assured the caterer. "Marie made Brooke swear she had it on her calendar."

Cara followed her nose into the shop's small dining area. A long wooden table held a starched white cloth and a small floral arrangement of lilies, roses, and hypericum berries she'd had Bert drop by earlier on his way to track down the missing epergne.

"I'm so hungry, I could faint," Cara confided. A small round of roast beef stood on a carving stand under a red heat lamp, a pool of juices \radiating out from it. Silver chafing dishes held a dozen other hot dishes. Shallow bowls filled with finely crushed ice held arrays of boiled shrimp, oysters, and stone-crab claws. A smoked salmon fillet was sprinkled with capers, finely diced hard-boiled eggs, and lemon slices.

Wordlessly, Layne handed Cara a napkin, and loaded it with boiled shrimp.

Cara walked down to the far end of the table. A silver tiered stand held half a dozen iced cupcakes. She turned to Layne. "Cupcakes? Cute, but that doesn't seem like something the Trapnells are going to think is impressive."

"We won't serve cupcakes. These are just all the different options for cake flavors and icings I can do. It's not cost-effective for me to bake six whole wedding cakes for just a menu tasting," Layne explained.

The shop door opened, and Marie Trapnell stepped in. "Hi. Sorry to be late."

Cara introduced Layne and Marie, and Marie looked at her watch and frowned. "I can't believe the kids aren't here yet. Brooke texted me they were leaving her office fifteen minutes ago." A faint chirp sounded from the direction of Marie's pocketbook. She dug it out, read the text message, smiled, and held it up for the other women to see.

On way. There in 5.

"Wow!" Marie walked over to the buffet table. "This looks wonderful. Are we really going to have all this?"

Layne glanced at Cara for an answer.

"Not necessarily all of it. When I talked to your husband . . ."

"Ex-husband, actually," Marie said quietly.

"Oh. Right. Sorry, of course. Anyway, Mr. Trapnell said he and his wife wanted to sample everything we offer, so they could get . . ."

Marie's face paled. "Are you saying that Gordon's coming today? And Patricia too?"

This was news to Cara. And not happy news.

"Um, well, I think that was the plan. Isn't that the plan?" Layne asked Cara.

Uh-oh, Cara thought. Once again, Patricia Trapnell had managed an end run around her.

"When I set up the tasting with Layne today, I was under the impression that it was just going to be the bride and groom and mother of the bride." Cara chose her words carefully.

The door opened again, and Brooke Trapnell rushed in, a tall strawberry-blond man right behind. "Hi everybody. Sorry to be late!"

Brooke Trapnell wore pearls, white running shoes, and a crisp seersucker power suit, straight out of a Brooks Brothers catalogue. Her fiancé was dressed more casually, in khakis and a blue button-down dress shirt.

Marie gave her daughter an exasperated hug. "I was afraid you weren't coming."

"I tried, Marie," Brooke's fiancé said ruefully. "I even fibbed and told her we were supposed to be here half an hour earlier...."

"Sweet boy!" Marie Trapnell beamed her approval, then kissed him on the cheek and turned to Cara.

"Cara Kryzik, this is my future son-in-law, Harris Strayhorn."

"Hey there." Harris's handshake was firm, his smile genuine. He looked a lot like his mother, with fair hair, blue eyes, and the same ruddy complexion. But he was half a head taller than Brooke, long-limbed and gangly, like a colt whose legs had outgrown the rest of his body.

Harris's eyes widened as he took in the food table. "Oh man, is that all for us? Awesome!" He turned to Brooke, tugging at her sleeve. "Honey, check out this spread!"

Brooke laughed. "He is always hungry. Always. You wouldn't believe he just came from a breakfast meeting, right?"

"I happen to enjoy good food," Harris said. "Is that a crime?"

"It's a good thing you know how to cook," Marie said. "Because if it's up to Brooke, you might starve to death."

"That's not true. I can fix oatmeal, and scrambled eggs, and grits, of course," Brooke protested.

"Do you ever eat any of that yourself?" Layne asked dubiously, taking in the bride's slender figure.

"No," Marie said, frowning now at the way Brooke's jacket hung loosely from her shoulders.

"I eat," Brooke said.

Harris raised one eyebrow. "What? What have you eaten today?"

"Well . . . nothing, but that's just because I knew we would be pigging out at this tasting, and I didn't want to spoil my appetite."

"She has no appetite," Marie said flatly. "Except for work."

"And me," Harris said, wrapping an arm around his fiancée's waist.

Obviously ready to change the subject, Brooke pointed at the food table. "Okay so can we get started? This all looks great, but I've got a two-o'clock meeting back at the office."

Layne gave Cara a questioning glance.

"Yes. Let's go ahead and start tasting and comparing notes," Cara said. "I gather we're expecting Gordon and Patricia to join us, but I don't want to hold you two up."

Brooke had picked up a slice of roast beef from the carving station, but she dropped the fork now, with a clatter.

"Mom?" She stared at Marie. "You didn't tell me Dad and Patricia were coming."

"I didn't know myself, until just now. It's fine though. Really. I can deal. Let's just go ahead and begin."

Harris stepped over to the table and began loading a plate with food. He popped a shrimp in his mouth and chewed, nodding his head in approval.

"Can we have the shrimp? What, are they cooked in beer or something?"

"Boiled in beer, actually," Layne volunteered.

Harris dropped one on Brooke's empty plate. "Try this. We gotta have this for the wedding."

But Brooke ignored the food. "I can't believe she just invited herself today. I *told* Daddy she keeps trying to run things. . . ."

Marie put her hand on Brooke's sleeve. "Let's just let it go for today, okay? Layne has fixed all this beautiful food for us to try. You can have another discussion with your dad later."

"It's so not okay," Brooke said, stony-faced.

"Honey?" Harris said, soothingly. "C'mon. Just eat something."

. . .

They worked their way around the table. For as skinny as he was, Harris Strayhorn's appetite and enthusiasm knew no bounds. He was every mother's dream, every caterer's dream. He loved it all.

For her part, Brooke merely picked at the offerings, despite her mother's urging.

Marie was busily taking notes and conferring with Layne. "I love the little new potatoes with the caviar and sour cream. Brooke?"

"I'm not really into fish eggs, but if you like them, that's fine," Brooke said.

They were ten minutes into the tasting when the shop door opened and Patricia Trapnell swept in.

"Shit," Brooke said under her breath. Marie shot her a warning look.

Patricia didn't offer a greeting, or an excuse for her lateness. "You've started already?" She glared accusingly at Cara.

"Yes. We did, Patricia. Harris and I have jobs. We can't wait around all day for you." Brooke glowered at her stepmother. "Where's Daddy?"

"Something came up." Patricia picked up a plate and started down the line, but frowned when she saw the roast beef.

"Layne? I thought we discussed tenderloin, not steamship round. It'll be so hot that day, and honestly, I think that presentation is so passé. It reminds people of being on a second-rate cruise ship."

"Well," Layne began.

"I asked for this cut," Brooke said. "It's Harris's favorite. His dad's too. And it's not passé, but even if it were, nobody but you would care."

"Fine." Patricia's lips pursed and she moved on to the next dish. She pointed with her fork at one of the chafing dishes.

"What's that supposed to be?"

Layne dabbed a bead of perspiration from her forehead. "That's the roast asparagus you requested."

"But it's wrapped in bacon," Patricia said, her nostrils quivering. "We're supposed to have prosciutto. Cold-smoked prosciutto. Don't think I don't know the difference."

"For the reception, we'll use prosciutto," Layne assured her. "But I have to special-order it from my supplier, and he only delivers on Tuesdays and Thursdays."

"We're going to want to taste the prosciutto before the wedding," Patricia warned. "It's an entirely different taste."

Brooke snorted, and this time, Patricia decided not to let it pass. She whirled around to confront the bride.

"You may not care about these things, Brooke Trapnell, but I can assure you your father and I do care. We're paying eighty dollars a plate for this reception. And that does not include the bar. So please excuse me if I happen to object when somebody expects me to pay for prosciutto when it's clearly only bacon. Is that too much to ask?"

Marie hesitated, then stepped between her daughter and Patricia.

"We all want a beautiful wedding, don't we, Brooke?"

Brooke rolled her eyes, then looked away.

"Hey, honey?" It was Harris's turn to referee now. He had a smear of chocolate icing on his upper lip, and a glob of coconut on his shirt collar. He grabbed her hand and towed her toward the opposite end of the table. "Come down here and check out the desserts. Cupcakes! I freakin' love 'em."

"Cupcakes?" Patricia's surgically stretched face registered her horror. She stalked down to the dessert offerings. "Are we having a 4-H picnic, Layne? Really?"

"No!" Layne hurried over. "These are just all the different cake types and frostings and fillings we do. I thought Brooke and Harris could taste everything and decide, and then, of course, we'll do a proper cake...."

"Forget it," Brooke said, her eyes blazing. "Just let Patricia decide. After all, she's the one running this show."

Brooke reached over and snatched the lemon-iced cupcake he'd just bitten into from Harris's hand. She set it down on the table.

"Aww, man..." he groaned.

"We've got to get back to work," Brooke announced. She turned and walked rapidly toward the door.

"Harris! I'm leaving."

Harris looked at Layne, then at Cara, then at Marie. He shrugged. "Sorry. Gotta go."

He was halfway to the door when he turned, returned to the table, picked up his cupcake, and hurried back to the side of his one true love.

Somehow, after Brooke had gone, the women managed to work out a menu that suited Patricia as well as Marie. When everybody was gone, Layne went to the door of Fete Accompli and locked the deadbolt. Wordlessly, she went to the big walk-in cooler in her catering kitchen. She took out a half-open bottle of chardonnay, tipped it to her lips, and swigged for at least a minute. Then she handed it to Cara. "Be my guest."

33

Bert met her at the door of the shop, and the look on his face telegraphed the bad news. "I've looked everywhere," Bert said, rubbing a hand wearily over his face. "Honest to God, Cara. Every single stop I made Friday, I retraced. I showed everybody the picture of the epergne. I even crawled around in the grass and the bushes at the Shutters. Since it was low tide, I even looked around that dock, thinking maybe somebody got drunk and chunked it in the water for a joke. But nothing. It ain't there."

"Oh God." Cara thumped her forehead on her desk. First Lillian Fanning, then Patricia Trapnell. Now this. What was wrong with her karma?

"What now? Will you call her and tell her?"

Cara popped three aspirin in her mouth and dry-swallowed them.

"I can't deal with Lillian right now. I think I might have heat stroke." She pulled her sticky shirt away from her chest.

"Did you call Sylvia Bradley again?" Bert asked.

"Yes, I called her. She doesn't pick up the phone, because she doesn't want to deal with me. I've sent her a registered letter, too." Cara reached into her desk drawer and got her pocketbook.

"Let's go," she told Bert.

"Where to?"

"To wherever they sell air conditioners. I can't spend one more hour living like this."

The salesman at Lowe's carefully explained the merits and options of all the room-size air conditioners the store carried.

"Which one is the next to cheapest?"

The salesman looked startled. "Next to cheapest?"

"My father taught me never to buy the cheapest model of anything. Or the most expensive," Cara explained. "I sure can't afford the next to most expensive, so I guess I'm buying the next to cheapest."

"Most affordable," the salesman said gently.

"Whatever. As long as you have it in stock and we can walk out of here with it in the next ten minutes."

She handed over her credit card and held her breath waiting to see if the transaction would go through. She'd maxed out most of her cards, but this one, a Visa that had come through the mail months ago, was one she'd activated but never used. She thought of it as her Plan B card. And she reflected, grimly, that there was no Plan C.

Cara had sent the Colonel a check for $15,000 the minute Gordon Trapnell had paid the deposit for his daughter's wedding. It meant letting her other past-due bills ripen a little longer, but at least, she thought, it would forestall her father for another few weeks.

But there would be no more stalling on purchasing an air conditioner. She couldn't have brides entering a shop that felt like a sauna. And she couldn't deal with all the crap life was throwing at her, working in those conditions after spending another sleepless night upstairs.

She and Bert carried the precious new air-conditioning unit into the shop and unboxed it immediately, fitting it into one of the front windows. Cara held out the thin plastic remote control, took a deep breath, and clicked the On button. The air conditioner's motor hummed to life, and a stream of chilled air wafted into the room.

"Sweet blessed baby Jesus," Cara murmured, standing in front of the unit. She ducked her head and let it blow her sweat-soaked hair, then turned around, lifted the back of her skirt, and let the cold air billow up it like a balloon.

"I should have done this ten days ago," she said finally.

"Yeah, you should have," Bert said. "Maybe you wouldn't be in such a pissy mood all the time if it wasn't so friggin' hot in here."

Cara clamped a hand on his shoulder. "Listen, my friend. My expecting you to be a prompt, reliable, responsible employee does not constitute pissini-ness."

"Gawwwwd," he exclaimed. "You act like it's my fault that damned epergne is missing. You're totally gonna throw me under the bus on this, aren't you?"

"I'm not blaming anything on you," she said, trying to keep her tone even. "I'm going to call Lillian right now, and let her know we couldn't find it. I own this business, and I'm taking responsibility for it."

"Great," he said.

"Bert?"

"Yeah?"

"In the meantime, you need to change your attitude and your performance. Or you can just find yourself another job."

He looked her in the eye. "Are we done? I've got the afternoon deliveries to get out."

"We're done. After you finish the deliveries, bring the van back here for the night, please."

He laughed unpleasantly. "So, what? You're grounding me? I'm twenty-nine years old, Cara."

"And you act like a fifteen-year-old. If I could lock you in time-out too, I'd do it."

After he'd gone, she closed the rest of the shop windows and sat at her desk for a moment, trying to enjoy the calm before the storm.

What, she wondered, was going on with Bert? He'd been working for her for two years. They'd never had a real argument, or even a disagreement. He had a real talent for floral arranging, and when he'd come to her, directly out of alcohol rehab, he'd been so grateful to have a job, he was like a puppy, desperate for love and attention.

But these past two weeks, he'd changed. He swore he wasn't drinking, but what else could she think, given his most recent disappearance?

Her halfhearted suggestion that she might fire him hadn't had the effect she'd hoped for. He'd merely stared her down. The thing was, she genuinely cared about Bert. He'd been a sounding board throughout her breakup with Leo, had even given her shelter on his sofa for the first week after she'd left Leo. He was funny, generous, and mostly even-keeled.

Cara didn't want to hire a new assistant. She wanted her old one back.

She was gazing out the shop window, trying to get up the nerve to call Lillian Fanning, when she saw a white Mercedes zoom up to the curb outside Bloom and park in the loading zone.

Her right eye twitched and she reached for the aspirin bottle again. Perfect. Speak of the devil.

Lillian was dressed in tennis whites, but not a hair on her immaculately coiffed head was mussed.

She pushed the shop door open and planted herself in front of the worktable where Cara sat. "Well?" She raised one eyebrow, expectantly.

"I'm so sorry, Lillian. Bert and I took the van apart. He retraced every stop he made last week, on his way out to Isle of Hope when he was returning the silver. It didn't turn up." Cara felt tears prick her eyes. She swallowed hard. "I don't know what to say. I feel terrible about this."

"Unbelievable!" Lillian exploded. "You feel terrible? You lose the single most valuable family heirloom I own, and that's the best you can do? Feel terrible? Is that supposed to mean something to me?"

"N-n-n-no," Cara squeaked.

"What do you intend to do about it?" Lillian demanded.

"What would you like me to do?"

"Have you called the police?"

"The police? Why would I call the police?"

"Because obviously, it's been stolen." Lillian looked around the shop. "Did you ask your assistant if he'd seen it?"

"Yes! He spent most of the afternoon looking for it."

"And you believe him?"

Cara felt her scalp prickle. "Yes. I believe him. Bert has worked for me for two years. Why would he lie about something like this?"

"Why wouldn't he? That epergne is worth thousands and thousands of dollars. What do you pay the man? Minimum wage?"

"I pay Bert a living wage," Cara said, struggling to keep her temper. "He's not a thief, Lillian. Or a liar. And neither am I. In fact, I resent your implying otherwise."

"What do you really know about him, Cara? Do you run a criminal-record check before you hire these people?"

"I know that Bert Rosen is a decent, honest, hardworking person."

"And how did you come to hire this decent, honest, hardworking person? Did he come to you with references?"

No, Cara thought. *He came to me right out of rehab. And I hired him because I believe he deserved a second chance. And he still does.*

Lillian took a step closer to Cara, and then another step. "I don't give a good goddamn what you resent. You and your assistant are responsible for the loss of that epergne. It didn't just get up and run away. It was stolen! And if you won't file a police report, I will."

"And then what?" Cara asked. She refused to take Lillian's bait. "Is the epergne insured?"

"I'll have to call our agent," Lillian said. "And our lawyer."

Cara felt first her right eye twitch, and then her left. Lawyer?

"Let me know what you find out," she said finally. "Of course, if the epergne isn't insured, I fully intend to pay for its replacement."

Lillian gave her a pitying look. "How sweet. And how do you plan to come up with that kind of money?"

Cara chewed the inside of her mouth. She felt bile rising in her throat. She searched for some clever, searing retort to Lillian's patronizing sneer. But she had nothing. Except that throbbing pain in her temple.

"Let me worry about that," she said finally.

34

Cara was creating her sixth new-baby arrangement of the morning. It wasn't a terribly creative endeavor—pink carnations, multicolored gerbera daisies, and white for mothers of baby girls, blue hydrangeas, daisies, and white carnations for those who'd delivered boys. Sometimes, she did dish gardens, with themed flowers tucked in. But she loved putting them together, loved the thought of new moms, smiling down at their own new creations, and then up at the candy stripers delivering their flowers.

She also loved the fact that few of the recipients of those arrangements had the time or energy to call up and bitch at her about misplaced epergnes or tacky-looking cupcakes.

True to her word, Lillian had reported the epergne as stolen to the police. On Tuesday, an apologetic Savannah police detective called to make an appointment to discuss the incident.

The missing epergne—combined with the hot sticky climate in her upstairs apartment—had kept her awake for two nights in a row. Finally, Wednesday night, Cara dragged a sofa cushion, pillow, and quilt downstairs and slept in the blissful cool of the workroom.

And Thursday morning, in the middle of all those happy baby flower arrangements, the detective arrived. She was a middle-aged black woman, who introduced herself as Zarah Peebles. "Zarah, like Sarah with a 'Z,'" she said, handing Cara her business card.

She showed Cara a photo of Lillian Fanning's missing family heirloom.

"Yes," Cara sighed. "That's the epergne. As I told Lillian, the last time I remember specifically seeing it was Sunday morning, when we went back to Isle of Hope to finish taking down everything used in the reception. It was placed in a bin in the back of my delivery van."

"If the wedding was held at the Fannings' home, why didn't you just take it back into the house?" Detective Peebles asked.

"It was the morning after their daughter's wedding, they'd had a late night, and I didn't want to disturb their rest. Anyway, I wanted to take everything back to the shop, and make sure it was cleaned up before I returned everything. The candlesticks still had wax on them, and some of the bowls had been used for flower arrangements."

"And did you bring everything back here and clean it up, as you'd planned?"

"No," Cara admitted. "We had an incredibly busy week, another huge wedding, and time . . . just got away from me. To tell you the truth, I'd forgotten we even still had the silver, until Lillian called on Friday to ask about it."

"So . . . where was this bin of silver during that next week?"

"In the van."

"And who had access to the van?"

"Just me. And Bert, my assistant."

Detective Peebles frowned. "Where is the van usually parked?"

"Sometimes, if there's a parking space out front, we park it on Jones. But usually we park in my dedicated slot in the lane."

"Lot of break-ins in this neighborhood," Detective Peebles observed. "Probably not the best idea to have a boxful of valuable silver in a van parked in a lane where any wandering crackhead could check it out."

Cara sighed. "No, it wasn't. I can't tell you how much I regret that. But the bin was at the very back of the van, and there are no windows there, so a thief wouldn't have known it was there. And the van was locked."

"All the time? You're sure about that?"

"Reasonably sure."

Detective Peebles was scribbling notes.

"Can I take a look at the van?"

"Right now, my assistant is out making deliveries. I can call him and ask him to head back here as soon as he's done. But I can tell you right now, the van hadn't been broken into. And all the rest of the Fannings' silver was there. Why would somebody take just that one piece, and not the rest of it?"

"Because it was the most valuable piece?"

"Was it?"

The detective flipped some pages in her notebook. "Mrs. Fanning says she had it appraised at the Telfair Museum a couple years ago, and it's valued at a hundred and thirty-five thousand dollars."

"What?" Cara felt her jaw drop. "Lillian never told me it was that valuable. I never would have used it at the reception. And I certainly wouldn't have just piled it in a bin with those other pieces. Or left it in the back of the van for a week."

"Hindsight," Detective Peebles said. "I looked at the picture she gave me of that epergne. Am I saying it right?"

"I think it's pronounced 'ay-purn,'" Cara said.

"Not my kind of thing at all. Kinda ugly if you ask me. But from what Mrs. Fanning says, that doohickey is worth more than my house and car put together."

"And mine."

"Okay," the detective said. "That's about all I needed to ask you. Oh yeah, your assistant's full name?"

"Bert Rosen. Hubert, actually." Cara hesitated. "Look, Detective. I know Lillian probably told you she thinks Bert stole the epergne. She said as much to me when she came in here Monday. But I know him. He's not a thief. He wouldn't do that."

"How long have you known him?"

"Two and a half years, and nothing like this has ever happened. Ever."

"What do you know about his background? How'd you come to hire this Bert Rosen?"

Cara bit her lip. "He was referred to me through an organization called the Step-Up Society. They work with men and women who've been through alcohol and drug rehab. Bert is a recovering alcoholic."

"You hired somebody right out of rehab? Kinda risky, don't you think?"

"His counselor at Step-Up is somebody I know. He vouched for Bert. I met him, we liked each other, so I hired him on a trial basis, and it worked out. It worked out great."

"Pretty generous of you," Detective Peebles said. She looked around the shop, taking it all in. "How about you? Have you gone through rehab? Is that why you're sympathetic to somebody like your assistant?"

"No. I've not been through rehab. I'm strictly a social drinker. But I grew up with an alcoholic. I know the struggles they face to keep sober."

"Your dad?" the detective asked.

"My mom," Cara said.

She was still brooding about her police interview when the shop phone rang. She picked up the receiver, not even checking the caller-ID screen. "Bloom Floral Design," she said, trying to sound perkier than she felt.

"Hello?"

Cara was so surprised, she nearly dropped the phone. The thready, high-pitched voice on the other end sounded just like her recently deceased landlady.

"Bernice?"

"Who the hell is this?" the voice on the other end demanded. "Is this some kind of joke?"

"Uh, no. I'm sorry. This is Cara Kryzik. Is this Sylvia?" Come to think of it, Cara had never actually spoken to Bernice Bradley's daughter. She'd always dealt with the older of the two women.

"Yes, it's Sylvia."

Sylvia Bradley sounded eerily like her mother.

"Um, well, Sylvia, I wanted to tell you how very sorry I am about your loss. Your mother was a remarkable woman." It was the nicest thing Cara could say on the spur of the moment. "I'm sure she'll be greatly missed."

"Thank you," Sylvia said curtly. "I see you've been calling to complain about the air conditioner on Jones Street? Again and again? Don't you think it's pretty indecent to be hounding me like this, with my mother not even dead a week?"

"Um, I'm sorry. Truly, very sorry," Cara heard herself stammering. And then she remembered what Bert had pointed out. The Bradleys were the worst kinds of landlords. She paid a premium price for the town house on Jones Street, and had never been even a day late with her rent. The least she should expect from her landlady was a livable building. And when temperatures were in the nineties, that was definitely not livable. Not for a home, or a business.

Cara was emboldened by that thought.

"The thing is, my air conditioner is broken again. It's the third time this spring. It's been broken for ten days, and you know how hot it's been. It's bad enough that I have to try to sleep with no air-conditioning. But it's embarrassing when I have clients, including brides, come into the shop, only to find it's like an oven. It's starting to affect my business, Sylvia. So I would really appreciate if you could get somebody over here to fix it. Today."

"That's not going to happen," Sylvia said flatly. "Even if I could get somebody on such short notice, which I can't. I have a lot of business to tend to, getting Mother's estate taken care of."

Cara's fuse snapped. "No disrespect, Sylvia, but that's not good enough. I've called you repeatedly, with no response, and I even sent a registered letter, so I know you've been notified. This week, I couldn't take the heat another minute. I bought a window unit and installed it downstairs in the shop. And unless you send somebody over here to replace the central unit, I'm going to buy a second unit to allow me to sleep upstairs."

"You do that," Sylvia said.

"And I'm going to attach the receipts and deduct them from my rent next month," Cara added.

There was a prolonged silence at the other end of the phone. *Gotcha*, Cara thought.

She heard paper rustling in the void. And another long pause.

"Maybe there won't be a next month," Sylvia said finally, with a dry, raspy chuckle.

"What's that supposed to mean?" Could she be hearing correctly? Was this shrew actually threatening her?

"Your lease expired in March," Sylvia pointed out.

"I know that," Cara said, trying to sound more confident than she felt. "But I had an agreement with Bernice. She was fine with me going month to month until June. Then she was going to have a new lease prepared. She'd talked about raising my rent, and I'd agreed, in theory, as long as she got the plumbing looked at and the air-conditioning problems resolved."

"Mother never said anything about that to me," Sylvia said. "Not that it really matters now. I was going to wait and notify you after the closing, but I reckon now's as good a time as any."

Cara felt her scalp prickle. "Closing?"

"I'm about sick and tired of dealing with whiny tenants and their piddly problems," Sylvia said. "Mama might have put up with that mess, but she's dead now. Jones Street is sold. As of June thirtieth. You got a problem, take it up with the new owner."

"Wait!'" Cara cried. "You sold my building? Without even telling me?"

"Sure did," Sylvia said.

"What if I wanted to buy the building? You didn't even give me right of first refusal."

"Didn't have to," Sylvia said. "Anyway, the way I hear it, you're just barely hanging on over there as it is. Where would you get the money to buy a valuable property like that?"

"What!" Cara exploded. "Where did you hear something like that? That's a lie! My business is solid, and growing. Who did you sell it to anyway? You owe me that much."

"I don't owe you one sorry thing," Sylvia Bradley said. "I reckon you'll be hearing from the new owner soon enough. Here's a word of advice to you though. Start packing. I think he's got plans for that building that don't include you."

. . .

After leaving half a dozen voicemail messages for her lawyer, Cara finally got a callback, shortly before five.

"Hi Cara," Melinda Ennis said cheerfully. "How's the flower business?"

Melinda had been another gift from Vicki Cooper, a smart, savvy young Emory Law School grad who wanted a champagne wedding on a beer budget. Cara had managed to pull it off, and in return, the grateful bride had handled Cara's divorce pro bono.

"It *was* picking up," Cara said. "But after today, I just don't know. It's like the universe is conspiring to grind its heel in my face."

"What's going on?"

Cara quickly filled the lawyer in on the conversation she'd had with Sylvia Bradley.

"She won't even tell me who the new owner is," Cara said, a note of desperation in her voice. "Can she do that—legally?"

"Well, morally and ethically, it sucks," Melinda said carefully. "But since you no longer have a lease in effect, legally, your landlord is correct. She's under no obligation to you whatsoever."

"But that's not right! I've been in this building for over two years, and I've never even been a day late with my rent. I've spent thousands of dollars of my own money fixing it up. And the Bradleys did nothing—nothing to keep up the property. The plumbing, the electrical, the wiring, even the roof, all need work."

"Maybe the new owner will be more responsive," Melinda said soothingly. "It sounds like you've been a model tenant. So hopefully, he'll want to work something out and keep you happy."

"I doubt it. Sylvia said the new owner has plans for my building that don't include me. She actually suggested I should start packing."

"What a hateful old bitch," Melinda said with a sigh. "I wish there was something I could do to help here, but I guess you'll just have to wait until you hear from the new landlord."

"Isn't there any way I can find out right now? Some kind of court records you could look up?"

"Once the property's closed and the deed is registered, it'll be public information," Melinda said. "But not until then. Sylvia actually told you the closing isn't till the end of the month?"

"The thirtieth," Cara confirmed. "Three weeks from now. What if this new owner really does kick me out? How am I gonna find a new place I can afford, pack up and move in the middle of my busiest time of the year?"

"We're just going to have to be proactive," Melinda said. "You know what Savannah's like. Everybody talks about everything. Especially real-estate transactions. Tell you what. I'll go over to the courthouse tomorrow, do some poking around. I'll get Andy to tap into his old-boy network too. We'll figure out who the owner is, come up with an offer you can afford, and approach him before he has time to shop around for new tenants."

"You really think that could work?" Cara asked. She had serious doubts.

"It's worth a try," Melinda said. "But Cara? I don't want to scare you or anything, but in the meantime, just in case, maybe you'd better start looking around for a new address."

Cara looked around her tiny shop, and thought of the comfortable aerie she'd fashioned for herself upstairs. Her budget was stretched to the max already. A new address?

She wondered what her brides would think of a florist who lived and worked out of a petal-pink van.

35

W hen the going got tough, Cara headed for the shower. She didn't know when she'd started treating the shower like a combination confessional and therapist's couch.

Maybe it had started when she'd first moved to Savannah. Leo was the kind of man who made friends effortlessly. Within a month of their move, he was having drinks after work with clients, weaseled his way into a golf foursome, was on a first-name basis with all their neighbors.

"Never met a stranger, that boy!" the Colonel liked to say of her ex.

It was harder for Cara. Every time she opened her mouth, people would stare at her and ask, "Where are you *from*?" And when she said Ohio they looked at her with pity. Nobody could pronounce her name—"Kryzike? Kris-shick? What kind of name is that?"

"Krizz-ick," she'd say patiently. "It's a Croatian name."

To which they'd look even more puzzled. "Croatia? That's a country?"

She had little in common with the neighbors in their subdivision, most of whom were young mothers, who already had their own friends—their own play groups, their own supper clubs, their own girlfriends. They never came right out and said it, but the situation was clear. Nobody was currently taking applications for new friends.

Once, that first fall after they moved in, out of desperation, she'd written out invitations to a soup supper and slipped them into the mailboxes of all eight houses on their end of the block.

She'd fixed a huge pot of Italian wedding soup, a salad, and an apple streusel pie, and set everything out on the dining room table, along with a gorgeous arrangement of fall flowers she'd placed in a hollowed-out pumpkin. Exactly one couple—Arnie and Sheila Jenkins, retirees who lived at the head of the street—came. They'd eaten their soup hurriedly, made lame excuses for why nobody else had come—"Georgia has a home game tomorrow"—and rushed off without even touching dessert. She would never forget the look of pity on their faces.

Cara had thrown the whole pie in the trash and retreated to the shower to weep and curse.

Friday nights during the spring were the worst. She'd come home from work, and see women standing in knots in the cul-de-sac, chatting, sipping from plastic wineglasses, while their children circled on bikes or scooters. She'd smell the charcoal drifting from backyard grills, see couples hurrying to each other's houses with covered casserole dishes, or coolers tucked under their arms.

Cara would retreat to the shower. She'd stand under the shower and cry while she washed her hair. She'd curse the snobby neighbors and call them crackers and ignorant rednecks while she shaved her legs. While she was rubbing conditioner into her scalp she'd tell herself it wasn't her—it was them. She'd had friends back home. Lots of friends.

When her marriage to Leo crumbled, Cara hid in the shower. She could still remember that night—that awful Valentine's Day night—when she'd figured out he was having a fling with the dental hygienist. She'd locked herself in the bathroom and stayed in the shower for two hours, only emerging after the hot water ran out. Then she'd packed her bags and run away from home. And cursed again, when she realized she'd left a nearly new bottle of expensive shampoo in her old shower. Would the dental hygienist use it?

Now, two years later, just when she'd thought maybe her luck was changing, just when she'd managed to feather a new nest for herself, the tiny pink bathtub in her downtown apartment—the one Jack referred to as the Barbie dream tub—became her solace once again. Her building sold? Where would she go? Where would she get the money to start over? Not from her father, she knew. She already had a missed call from the Colonel this morning. He always called on the shop phone, thank goodness.

The old lead pipes in the town house knocked and shuddered when she turned on the spigot, and normally the hot-water heater took a full fifteen minutes to heat up, and would run out before she'd finished crying—or rinsing her hair. But today she was taking a cool bath.

Somehow, this time, when she stepped onto the bath mat, she felt a little better. Maybe Sylvia Bradley was mistaken. Any landlord would be an improvement over the Bradleys. Maybe the new owner would finally fix up the building and allow her to stay. And if not? This was not the only house in the historic district. Nearly every block had at least one "for lease" sign in a front window. She'd call her real-estate agent and start looking. At least, she thought, she had the Trapnell wedding coming up. She'd have to postpone paying off her debt to the Colonel. She'd just have to make him understand. He was her father—he'd *have* to understand.

The one good thing about sleeping on the shop floor was that she was up early every morning. By eight o'clock, she'd already finished making the four bridesmaids' bouquets for Saturday's wedding. She'd pulled incoming orders off their internet server, and written up the phone orders so that Bert could get started on them when he got in at nine. She frowned, remembering the earlier confrontation with her assistant. He'd *better* get in at nine.

At 8:45, she was wheeling the vintage garden cart out to the sidewalk when she saw Jack's big black truck come down the block. She felt a little tug in her chest. It was pathetic and needy, but yes, she'd wondered if and when he'd call again.

He parked across the street and jumped out of the truck. He was dressed for work, blue jeans, clean white T-shirt, work boots. She found herself study-ing him, measuring him against Leo, Leo in his expensive sport coats and silk ties and spit-polished shoes. Leo with his salesman's smoothness. No. Make that slickness.

Jack Finnerty wasn't polished and he wasn't smooth, and his jeans were faded and ragged at the knee, and he looked so good right now she got a little weak in the knees as he crossed the street, bounded onto the curb, and grabbed her around the waist for a kiss.

"Some welcoming committee," he said, when he let her go.

"What are you doing in town?" Cara asked, smiling up at him. "I thought you were working out at Cabin Creek all week."

"Ryan's over there now, waiting on a lumber delivery," he said. "We found some old-growth heart pine that came out of a closed-up textile mill in Greenville, South Carolina, for the new floor for the barn." He hesitated, then frowned.

"You're not gonna like what I've got to tell you."

She sighed. "I guess you've heard. Probably Torie told Ryan and Ryan told you, right? Well, it's true. Somehow, I managed to lose Lillian Fanning's heir-loom silver epergne. She's called the police, and now it's a whole big thing."

"Epergne? No, I don't know anything about that," Jack said, running a hand through his hair. "But hell, that's bad enough. Lillian's not saying you stole it, right?"

"Not me. No. She's convinced Bert is a thief."

Jack rolled his eyes. "She probably misplaced it herself. It'll turn up."

"I hope you're right," Cara said. "Because the thing is worth like a hundred and twenty-five thousand dollars."

His eyes widened. "Holy crap."

"I know. So, what is it you have to tell me that I'm not gonna like? You're married? Carrying an STD? Come on, Jack, just spit it out and get it over with."

He picked a bloom from a potted gardenia on the garden cart and handed it to her. A consolation prize? "I'm here because your new landlord wants an estimate of what it's gonna cost to renovate your building."

"Well, at least you're not married, and you haven't given me a venereal disease," Cara said, making a weak joke.

"Did you have any idea your landlady was selling the place?" he asked.

"None. Sylvia finally returned my calls yesterday, and while I was in the middle of chewing her out about the air-conditioning, she dropped the bomb. Said it didn't matter because she'd sold the building. Without even telling me! And then she basically told me I should start packing, because the new landlord has plans that don't include me."

Jack nodded sympathetically. "It sucks. Big-time."

She grabbed the front of his T-shirt. "So who hired you? Who bought the building? Sylvia wouldn't even give me the satisfaction of telling me. I guess maybe she's afraid I'll call the guy and tell him everything that's wrong with the building before the sale closes."

"He hasn't hired us yet. But I get the feeling the guy already knows what all's wrong with the building. He's been in it a couple times, from what he told me."

"What?" Cara's fists clenched and unclenched. "She let somebody in the building when I wasn't home? She didn't even have the decency to call me? Who is it?"

"You know a guy named Cullen Kane? Another florist in town? He's the guy."

Cara's jaw dropped. She was well and truly flummoxed. "No. That can't be. Not him. Anybody but him."

"You know him?"

She nodded dumbly. "I think he wants to put me out of business. And this is step one in his Kill Cara Kryzik campaign."

They went inside the shop and he sat at the worktable while she recounted how she'd unwittingly managed to become Cullen Kane's business rival.

"It's not like I went after Brooke Trapnell to get her to hire me. But she did, and this wedding is too big a deal for me to pass up. It's the biggest budget I've ever worked with, and I'll make enough money from it to finally pay back my dad—maybe even get a decent delivery van."

Jack still wasn't convinced. "You really think Cullen Kane bought this building out of revenge? That's pretty far-fetched, Cara."

"I know," she admitted. "I'm really not normally this paranoid. But you didn't see the look on his face when I ran into him at the wholesale house. It's like I've taken his favorite toy and he'll do anything to get it back."

Jack drummed his fingertips on the table. "Okay. If that's his game, I don't have to work for him. I'm pretty sure he's getting bids from other contractors. I'll tell him I've got too much work on my plate right now. Which is actually kind of true."

"Thanks." Cara gave his hand a grateful squeeze.

"I'm not the only contractor in town though," he reminded her. "It won't be hard to find somebody who will give him an estimate, and do the work, when it comes right down to it."

"I know." She sighed. "Just out of curiosity, what did Kane say when he called you?"

"He told me his name, that he was in the process of buying a building on Jones Street. That it had retail space on the ground floor—currently occupied by a florist shop."

"Currently," Cara said bitterly. "But not for long."

"He said there was an apartment on the second floor, and that the top floor was currently not occupied."

"That's true," Cara said. "What else did he say? Did he tell you his plans for the building?"

"Not really. He said it looked like the previous owners had been pretty slack on maintenance. He'd seen the water stains on your apartment ceiling, so he wanted the roof and chimneys checked, and was concerned about the air-conditioning unit after seeing how hot it was on the second floor. I think he must have been up there in the past week, now that I think about it."

"Oh my God." Cara shuddered. "It gives me the creeps, knowing he was sneaking around, looking at my stuff, checking everything out, and I had no idea he was even here."

"Yeah. It sucks your landlady didn't even have the decency to let you know she'd let him in to check it out," Jack said.

"Did you tell him you know me?" Cara asked.

"I didn't see any reason to tell him, especially since I figured you'd be pretty upset about all this anyway."

"'Upset' is putting it mildly."

"Have you ever been up to the top floor?" Jack asked.

"No. There's stairway access through a door at the end of my hallway, but that door was locked when I rented the place. I just figured the Bradleys were too cheap to get it redone. And I was glad to have the building all to myself."

"Did you say the Bradleys were your landlords? Do you mean Bernice and Sylvia Bradley?"

"They're the ones. So, you know them?"

"They live a couple streets over from my parents. Couple of old tightwads," Jack said. He held up a key. "I got the impression Cullen Kane plans to open up the third floor and get it redone. We could take a look—if you're curious."

"I am curious. But I've got too much work to get done this morning. I'm already behind schedule—and we're not even officially open." She glanced up at the clock on the wall. "Bert's got five minutes to get here, and if he's late again today, I might have to start looking for a new assistant as well as a new address."

Jack stood up. "I'll leave you to it then. But if you don't mind, I think I'll run upstairs and take a look at that third floor."

"Suit yourself," Cara said.

He went down the hallway toward the stairs, then thought better of it.

"Hey. Whose wedding are you doing tomorrow? Not Lindsay Crawford and Will Becket by any chance?"

"No way," Cara said. "What? Are you the best man?"

He grinned. "Nah. Just an old friend from high school."

"Does that mean I'll see you there tomorrow night?"

"I wasn't gonna go," Jack said. "Ryan and I are working tomorrow. But now that you mention it . . . maybe I'll change my plans. Especially if you're gonna wear that pink dress of yours."

"Oh geez. That's right. You've seen me in that same dress now what? Three times? How embarrassing."

"I love that dress," Jack said enthusiastically, remembering how it swished about her knees when she danced, and the view of her cleavage. "You were wearing that dress the night we met."

"And I was wearing a dirty T-shirt and grubby shorts earlier that day when you stole my dog," she reminded him.

"Wear the pink dress, okay?" He waggled his eyebrows in that comic way of his. "For me."

36

At the stroke of nine, Bert walked in the back door. He held only one coffee cup in his hand, which he emphatically set down on the worktable before beginning to leaf through the day's phone orders.

"Hello," Cara said pointedly.

"Hey." He got up and went to the walk-in cooler, plucked an armful of roses, carnations, and ferns from the buckets, and slammed the cooler door. In another moment, he was whacking away at the flowers, stripping leaves, snipping stems in a flurry of barely contained violence.

She debated asking Bert why he was pissed—because his body language told her he was. And then she decided she didn't care why he was pissed. Some days it was better not to poke the bear. Was that an expression her father used, or was it one of her grandmother's?

After another fifteen minutes of silent sulking, Bert abruptly slammed down his clippers.

"That police detective? Did you know she showed up at my apartment? That bitch Lillian Fanning told her I stole that epergne!"

"I knew Detective Peebles wanted to talk to you," Cara said quietly.

"Yeah. She basically called me a thief. What the hell would I want with that hideous piece of crap?"

"Just calm down, okay?" Cara was startled to realize she sounded just like her father. "It turns out that hideous piece-of-crap epergne is worth about a hundred and twenty-five thousand dollars. And I told the detective you're not a thief."

Bert's eyes narrowed. "You also told her I was a drunk."

"She asked me what I knew about your background and how I came to hire you. I wasn't going to lie about it, Bert. So yes, I told her you'd been in rehab. I also told her you've been sober for two years and that I trust you completely."

"Except that you don't. Do you?"

Before she could ponder that question, the shop phone rang. Bert snatched up the receiver, listened for a moment, then handed her the phone, his face an expressionless mask.

"It's the Colonel."

Bert was really, really pissed at her.

"Hi Dad," Cara said cautiously. "I was just getting ready to call you. Did you get the check?"

"I got it," the Colonel said. "But it's not what I was expecting. Only half of what you owe?"

She crossed her eyes and glanced over at Bert, whose job it was to make her laugh during ordeals like this. Nothing. He stared studiously down at a handful of pink carnations as if they were the most fascinating things he'd ever seen.

"I know, Dad. But it's the best I can do right now." She took a deep breath. How to make her father understand the financial pressures she was under, without making it sound like she was broke and desperate—especially when she actually was broke and desperate?

"I have a huge wedding coming up July sixth, and in a couple weeks I'll get paid the balance of my fees, and then I'll try to send you the rest."

"Not good enough, young lady," her father said.

"Dad. If you'd just listen . . ."

He wouldn't, of course.

"I'm just glad your mother's not alive to see what's become of you," the Colonel said. "She'd be so disappointed."

Cara blinked. The Colonel invoked her late mother' name rarely, if at all. This was unfair, a sneak attack. What did her mother have to do with her failures at business?

As a child, Cara sensed there was something different about Barbara Kryzik. Her mother loved books and reading, and painting. Maybe that's where Cara had gotten her artistic talents.

Wherever the military sent them, Barbara Kryzik always managed to find an art studio, where she could work on her paintings, mostly dreamy abstract pastels, and a group of bored officers' wives who liked to play cards and day drink. Somehow, it had managed to escape Cara's notice that her mother had quietly become a lush.

In her freshman year of college, second semester, a neighbor had called Cara's dorm room, to register concern that Barbara seemed to have lost an alarming amount of weight. Cara had skipped class and driven home to see for herself. She'd been horrified at her mother's appearance. Her mother had always prided herself on her svelte figure, but now Barbara was gaunt, a withered human coat hanger. Her skin was pale and waxy, her once-lustrous dark hair so thinned that Cara could see patches of scalp.

She'd somehow managed to bundle her mother into the front seat of her car and driven her directly to the emergency room.

The young resident in the emergency room had run a battery of tests on Barbara, and then called Cara aside for a chat.

He was very young, that doctor, young enough and cute enough so that, to her enduring shame, the first thing that crossed Cara's mind was not what he would tell her about her mother, but whether or not he was married—or looking.

"Your mom tells me your dad is stationed overseas?" he'd said. The doctor had blue-green eyes. So light, they reminded her of the water at Panama City Beach, where she'd spent spring break just a few weeks earlier.

"Yes. Turkey right now. Air Force."

"When was the last time he saw your mother?"

Cara had to stop and think. "Maybe a year. A little more? Look. Is it cancer? Do I need to call him and get him home?"

"It's not cancer, and it's not life-threatening. Unless she ignores my advice and keeps on drinking."

Cara still remembered that sensation—that she'd been kicked in the stomach.

"Drinking?" she'd said stupidly. "My mom doesn't drink. I mean, not that much. Maybe some wine at dinner."

"Are you sure?" His voice was so gentle, almost a whisper. "Aren't you away at college?"

"Yes, but . . ."

"She's drunk right now," the doctor had said. "It's a good thing you drove, because her blood alcohol is sky high. Her liver function, everything, points to acute alcoholism. The weight loss—that's a side effect. She's malnourished. And dehydrated. We're giving her fluids, and we'll keep her overnight."

Cara was mesmerized by those sea-green eyes. "And then what?" she heard herself ask.

"That's up to you and your father," the doctor said. "But if it were my mom, I'd want her to go to rehab. Because if she doesn't stop drinking, she really will kill herself."

The colonel had come home from Turkey, and Barbara had cried and apologized and begged for forgiveness, and willingly gone to a very expensive private facility in Florida that her father insisted on calling "the hospital." He'd somehow managed a transfer, and gone right back to work at the base an hour from "the hospital."

Her mother had emerged from rehab proclaiming herself a new woman. And then she'd died six months later from liver failure.

Sometimes Cara wondered if, had her mother lived, she and the Colonel would have stayed married. She wondered whether her father's attitude toward his only child would have somehow softened. Sometimes, and these were the times she was most ashamed of, she wondered what life would have been like if her father had died and her mother were the survivor.

She'd returned to college after her mother's funeral, and at a roommate's insistence, had seen a therapist for grief counseling.

When Cara mentioned her father's career in the military, the therapist had frowned. "If you're looking for your father to fill the hole your mother's death has left in your life, you're going to be disappointed. To say that all career military men are distant and forbidding is a cliché, but from what you've told me about your father, in this case, the cliché fits."

Despite the therapist's warning, Cara had hoped her mother's death would bring her closer to her father. And just as predicted, she'd been disappointed. And her father, in turn, had been disappointed in her. Continually, it seemed, since the day Cara announced she'd left Leo.

Now, it appeared, the Colonel was out of patience with her, and her numerous failings.

"Here's the point that seems to be escaping you," he said irritably. "Your business is not a success. I'm sorry to be blunt, but since you refuse to face facts, I will. I know you've worked hard, but nevertheless, you've run up debts, and it's admirable that you want to pay them off, but there comes a time when it's foolish to sink good money into a bad idea. That's what I want you to realize. I don't intend to let you keep running away from the truth. I can't keep underwriting a doomed enterprise like this flower shop of yours. I think now would be a good time for you to face the truth."

"And come home," she said dully.

"Exactly," the Colonel said.

"Dad?" Cara's temples were throbbing. "My business is not a bad idea. I'll send you the rest of your money as soon as I have it."

She hung up and placed her phone facedown on the tabletop.

37

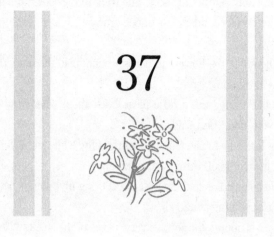

Bert swiveled around in his chair to face her. "The Colonel really wants his money, huh?"

"He wants me to throw in the towel and admit that I'm a failure," Cara said. She shook her head, as if by shaking it she could shake loose the image of her mother, and her real or imagined disappointments.

From a file folder on her desk Cara picked up her notes about tomorrow's bride, Lindsay Crawford.

She studied the photo of Lindsay's gown. It was the look of choice this season, strapless, of course, with a heavily beaded bodice, asymmetrical shirring at the waist, and a long fishtail train.

Cara held up the photo of the dress for Bert to see. "This dress? I know for a fact Lindsay paid six thousand dollars for it. Six thousand dollars! For a dress she'll wear for what? Four hours, tops? I've had at least five other brides this year with this dress. That's thirty thousand dollars. Do you know what I could do with that kind of money?"

"Tell me about it," Bert said. "And I don't even like their chances that much. She hates his mother, and the word on the street is that he's got a wandering eye. I'm thinking less than a fifty percent chance for those two."

"You're probably right," Cara said. She went to the cooler and gathered the flowers she needed for Lindsay's bouquet: orange tulips, red and yellow roses, and yellow stocks.

Cara gathered all the flowers in her left hand, held them up, then snipped all the stems to the same length.

"Sounds like things got a little tense back there when you were on the phone with your dad," Bert said.

Cara shot him a look. She found a length of the white satin ribbon Lindsay had chosen, measured off three yards, and cut it.

"Yeah. He as much as told me it's a good thing my mom is dead, since I'm such a big disappointment and all."

Cara began stripping the soft, velvety leaves of the stocks. "He never mentions my mom. Well, hardly ever. So today he brought out the big guilt guns. That's how the Colonel plays the game. Pile on the guilt. Your mother's dead, and I'm all alone. You're a failure. At marriage and at business. You're a bad daughter. And a lousy credit risk."

Cara picked up her scissors and carefully trimmed the bright orange stamens from the Stargazer lilies, sweeping them off the tabletop and into the trash can at her feet. She selected four stems of glossy green lemon leaves, arranging them around the perimeter of the bouquet, like a ruff.

Blinking back tears, she picked up the ribbon. Twirling the bouquet with her left hand, she began wrapping the ribbon around the flowers. She felt a sharp stab on her right thumb and looked down to see a single huge droplet of crimson blood drip down onto the flawless white satin of Lindsay Crawford's bouquet.

Cara tossed the ruined bouquet onto the worktable. She'd forgotten to trim the rose thorns. The Colonel was right. She was a hopeless fuckup.

Bert busied himself with the altar flowers, stuffing long stems of gladiolus, ferns, roses, and lilies into the trumpet-shaped vases provided by Lindsay's church.

He glanced over at Cara.

"What are you going to do about the damned epergne? I mean, Lillian can't prove anything. Maybe she lost it herself."

Cara shrugged. "The problem is, it was my responsibility. And I can't prove we didn't lose it."

"In other words, you're saying it's my fault."

Cara stood up from her chair. Her head was throbbing, her back hurt, and she was about sick of her assistant's attitude.

"For the last time, I do not think that you're a thief. Okay? But something is going on with you, and it's affecting your work. You won't tell me what it is, so what am I supposed to think?"

"It's just some personal stuff I'm dealing with."

"You've got personal stuff? Seriously? Look around you, Bert. This shop? I'm about to lose it. Literally. Yeah. Sylvia Bradley sold the building right out from under me. And the new owner is already breathing down my neck to get me out. So I don't give a hairy rat's ass about your personal stuff. Just do your job, okay?"

He got up, shaking his head. He put the altar arrangement on the bottom shelf of the cooler and slammed the door.

"I'm taking lunch. Back in an hour."

"You just got here."

"Dock my pay. I'm gone."

Cara watched through the front window as Bert strode quickly down the sidewalk. She wished she could run away, too. Instead, she picked up Lindsay's bouquet and began cutting away the blood-spattered ribbon.

38

Bert was giving her the silent treatment. And Cara was slinging it right back at him. Throughout the day the phone rang, customers walked in and out of Bloom, and they conducted business. But commerce was the only conversation that day. If she asked Bert a question he answered in clipped monosyllables.

Their normal easy work rhythm was out of sync, and as the day wore on, Cara's anxiety increased. Arrangments for delivery backed up, and without Bert's cooperation, she realized she'd have a long night of work ahead.

Even Poppy sensed the tension in the shop. The dog stayed directly beneath Cara's feet while she worked, moving only to follow her owner every time Cara moved.

At five on the dot, Bert stood up. "I'm gone." Cara glanced over at him, and then at the cooler, where only one of the six boutonnieres for the next day's wedding was completed. She had to bite her tongue to keep from suggesting that if he left for the day, he should stay gone.

"See you," she said.

. . .

At six, her cell phone rang, but she didn't bother to see who was calling. She still had Lindsay's bridesmaids' bouquets to make, the boutonnieres, and two large table arrangements for the buffet table at the reception. Poppy paced around the shop, but there was no time to take the dog for a walk.

Her phone rang three more times over the next two hours, and she let it roll over to voicemail, all the while cursing her absent assistant, and also cursing herself for letting him get away with slacking off.

She was so lost in her work the first soft knock at the shop door barely registered. At the second knock, she frowned. "We're closed!" she called out.

"Cara, it's Jack."

He had a huge brown paper bag with grease spots in one arm, and Shaz's leash looped around his wrist.

"What's this?" Cara asked, as he walked in and set the bag down on the worktable.

"Dinner. I've been calling and calling, but you didn't answer. I rode by an hour ago to see if you were here, and I could see you working through the window, so I figured the only way I was going to see you tonight was if I brought dinner to you."

She sniffed the bag. "Chinese?"

"I wasn't sure what you liked, so I kinda got a variety. Moo shu pork, shrimp with lobster sauce, chicken with snow peas, beef and broccolis, egg drop soup . . ."

Cara's stomach growled loudly, and she opened the bag and began parceling out the white boxes. "You are a lovely man, Jack Finnerty. I just now realized I haven't eaten anything today since a banana at seven this morning."

"Busy day?"

"Busy and horrible. I'd tell you about it, but it would just spoil your appetite. And I'm still not done. Will you hate me if we just eat down here?"

"I could never hate you," he said.

"Hang on and I'll go get some forks and paper plates."

"Plates? I thought that's what those little white boxes were for?"

"Only if you're a lonely old maid," Cara said, heading for the kitchenette. She glanced at the back door and saw a puddle.

"Oh, Poppy," she said with a sigh.

The dog hung her head. Cara felt flooded with guilt. She hadn't taken the dog for a walk, hadn't paid her the least attention all day.

"Not your fault, girl," she muttered, fetching paper towels and spray cleaner.

Cara had to force herself not to scarf down every morsel of fried rice and moo shu pork. He'd brought a six-pack of Tsingtao beer, and Jack sipped his beer and watched with obvious amusement as she made quick work of dinner.

Finally, she set her fork down with a sigh of happiness. "Thank you for that. I feel better already. But how was your day? How's it going out at the Strayhorns'?"

"Good. We got the roof finished. Galvalume standing-seam tin, and it looks awesome. Once we finished that, Libba decided she wanted some windows to lighten the place up. We've ordered those. And we got the ductwork installed for the HVAC. We power-washed all the walls inside and out and now we've also got the floors down. Wait till you see them. We were gonna re-mill them, because of all the gouges and stains from oil and machinery, but once we took a look, we decided to leave them as is. Even Libba loved the character. We just gave the floor a light sanding, and it brought out the most amazing color, a soft gray-brown. . . ."

"Mouse ear," Cara said.

"Huh?"

"Oh, it's a paint color I saw once. I think it's supposed to describe the color of the inside of a mouse's ear, but I like to think of it as that soft gray-brown you just described."

Jack leaned over and with the tip of his little finger removed a grain of rice from the corner of her mouth before kissing her lightly. "Mouse ear? As I remember, you're not too fond of rodents."

"No. Hate rats. And mice." She kissed him back. "But you? I kinda like you."

"Thanks. The feeling is mutual."

Jack followed her into the kitchenette and they cleaned up the dinner dishes together.

"How much more work do you have to do on the barn?" Cara asked.

"The new windows should get shipped this week, and we'll get them installed. And then Libba decided she wanted a powder room, and a kitchen, so we've stubbed in the plumbing for that. . . ."

"A kitchen and a powder room?" Cara frowned. "I had no idea they were doing that too. This is getting pretty expensive, huh?"

"Just materials, so far? We've spent around sixty thousand dollars, and that's not including our labor."

She shook her head. "All that money just for an after-party. Don't get me wrong, I'm glad it turned out to be a good job for you and Ryan, but it just seems like a crazy expense—and all for an after-party. Not even the reception. And why? Brooke Trapnell doesn't even really care about most of this stuff."

"Libba cares," Jack assured her. "She's really stoked about getting that old barn fixed up. She's got all kinds of plans for the place."

"I know. Grandkids. Libba is such a sweet lady. I hope she gets her wish."

"Why wouldn't she? What? You don't think Brooke and Harris want kids?"

"Honestly? I'm not sure Brooke knows what she wants."

"Harris seems like a decent guy. I guess I was expecting some snotty, stuck-up punk. The Strayhorns have more money than God. But he's okay. He came out to the farm yesterday and helped us unload some materials. He asked a lot of questions. He's really interested in the old building."

"He's nice," Cara agreed.

"What? You don't like their chances either?"

Cara shugged. "Doesn't matter. It's not like I'm an expert."

"You seem pretty down tonight."

"Just a little tired. Want to go upstairs?"

He grinned. "I thought you'd never ask."

Their lovemaking had a different edge this time, but neither of them could have said why.

Afterward, Cara lay with her chin on Jack's chest, and with his fingertip he traced slow circles on her bare back. "Want to talk about your day? I'm happy to listen. Are you still worried about your building being sold?"

"It's just been an all-around sucky day. And not just that. I haven't even really had time to think about calling my real-estate agent."

"Why don't you just go see this Cullen Kane? Put your cards on the table. Let him know you want to stay."

She hesitated. "The thing is—maybe I shouldn't stay."

"Hey!" He cupped his hand under her chin. "What's that mean?"

"The Colonel—my father, called this morning. He wants his money back, which is not new, but now he's taken things to an entirely new level of guilt inducement. He actually told me it was a good thing my mom was dead—so she can't see what a disappointment I've become."

She forced a brittle smile. "He never says he misses her. But I know he does, and I guess his pressuring me to come home is his screwed-up way of saying he misses me too."

Jack wrapped both arms around her. "Oh God, honey. I'm sorry. No wonder you're so on edge tonight. So . . . what? You're saying maybe you should close up the shop and go home to be with your dad? I get that. But if you're not sure?"

"No," Cara cut him off. "I don't want to go home. Ohio's his home, not mine. It's the last place I want to be right now. Which pretty much makes me the worst daughter ever. I'm a horrible person, you know."

She gave him a sad smile. "Run away, Jack Finnerty. You're much too nice for a selfish, rotten person like me."

"I'm not going anywhere," he said firmly. "If you don't want to go back to Ohio, you must have your reasons. And you're not a horrible person."

"Maybe not. But I'm pretty screwed up." She gave him a condensed version of her parents' toxic marriage. "I can't remember a time when either of them seemed happy together. When my dad was stationed overseas, my mom resented his being gone. I guess that's when the drinking started. But when he was home, it was even worse. When I was away at college, I used to look for any excuse not to go home to see them. Freshman year, I even went skiing with a friend in Tahoe, just so I wouldn't have to spend Christmas listening to them snipe at each other. I went away for spring break too, and as soon as I got back, that's when she got really sick. Six months later, she was dead."

"Why do you think they stayed together all that time?" Jack asked.

She gave a rueful laugh. "I've asked myself that same question a hundred times. I don't know. Maybe they were so used to miserable they didn't know there were any other possibilities."

Jack squeezed her shoulder.

"In a way, I think maybe that's why when Leo asked me to marry him, I said yes."

"Just so you could get away from home?"

"That was part of it. But a big part of it was Leo's family. They are absolutely the nicest, most normal people you ever met. His parents have been married forever. They ran a business together, and they're retired now, but they still do everything together. They hold hands in the grocery store, and his dad calls his mom his bride. And he has this sweet grandmother—everybody calls her Grannie Annie. Leo has two younger brothers and a sister, who was like my best friend, until the divorce. I think I convinced myself that if I married Leo, we would have the same kind of marriage his parents had."

"If he comes from such a great family, how come Leo turned out so bad?"

"I wish I knew. Sometimes, I wonder if things would have been different if we'd stayed up in Ohio, you know, around his family, instead of moving down here to Savannah."

"No," Jack said succinctly. "He would have had an affair with an Ohio secretary or an Ohio babysitter. Your ex sounds like a player, darlin', and a player is always gonna play."

Cara smiled up at him. "Did you just call me darlin'?"

"I dunno. Did I? Did you like that?"

"Say it again."

"Maybe later. Something I've been wondering. Why were things so bad here for you? Is it the town? Do you hate Savannah?"

"Not really. Well, at first maybe I did. It's just that—this is pathetic. I still sometimes feel like an alien down here. I guess part of it's that I sound like a Yankee."

"Not all the time."

"You're just saying that so you can get in my pants," Cara teased.

"It worked, didn't it?"

"Leo? As soon as we moved down here, he was in his element. He was here a week and he was already saying 'fixin' to,' and 'hey y'all' and 'bless your heart.' He just fit right in."

"Like a pig in slop," Jack said.

"Huh?"

"It's a Southern thing, darlin'. And you're saying you didn't fit in?"

"Not really. After I left Leo, I didn't even have a girlfriend I could call up to help me move. I only had Bert, who, come to think of it, is my only girlfriend in Savannah."

Cara sighed deeply. "That's why I'm so bugged by how he's been acting lately. He's apparently got some new boyfriend he won't talk about. Which is not like Bert at all. Usually, he wants to spill all the tawdry little details of his latest conquest. I don't know. Maybe I'm just jealous."

"It sounds like you've got good reason to be upset with him, if he's not doing his job," Jack pointed out.

"The thing is, if he keeps up this way, I won't have any other choice but to fire him. And I don't want that. I want to keep him, as my assistant, and my friend."

Jack kissed her shoulder and ran his hands down her back, lingering on her butt. "I'll be your friend." He pulled her closer and nudged a knee between her thighs. "I'm a really awesome friend."

"Mmm," Cara said slowly. "But can you fix flowers?"

39

In the morning, Cara sat up and marveled at the man in bed beside her. Sunlight splashed across his shoulders, so brown against her white sheets. His dark hair was tousled and his cheek was stubbled. His breathing was deep and even. She could have watched him like that all morning, he was that nice to wake up to.

It had rained hard overnight, and with the windows open, there was still somewhat of a cooling breeze.

They'd closed the bedroom door the night before, and now she heard a soft scratching at the door. Poppy? Or Shaz? She swung her legs over the side of the bed, but before she could move, a dark arm snaked around her waist.

She glanced over her shoulder. "Don't go," Jack mumbled.

"Gotta let the dogs out. Go back to sleep."

"Mmm. Come back to bed."

Cara pulled on a pair of drawstring cotton boxer shorts and a cami and slid her feet into flip-flops. The dogs raced each other down the stairs, and out into the courtyard garden.

She went into the kitchenette and started the coffeepot. Did she have any food in the house for breakfast? There was nothing in the kitchenette fridge, except a pint of half-and-half, some bottles of water, two cans of Red Bull, and a jar of pickles. And two cardboard cartons of leftover Chinese takeout. Shrimp with lobster sauce for breakfast? She shuddered.

When the coffee was ready, she fixed two mugs. Realized she didn't know how the man she'd just slept with took his coffee. She shrugged. She knew the most important things there were to know about Jack Finnerty. He was kind and thoughtful. He snored, but softly. Unlike other men she'd been with, he didn't fall asleep instantly after lovemaking. She smiled, thinking back to last night. He'd been the only good thing about Friday.

Upstairs, she brushed her teeth quickly and finger-combed her messy hair. She set a mug on the nightstand and stood looking down at Jack.

Without warning he reached out, grabbed her hand, and pulled her back onto the bed.

"Hey," she protested. "I thought you were sleeping."

He rolled over on his side to face her and ran his hands up under her camisole, brushing her nipples with his thumbs. He kissed her deeply, and she tasted toothpaste. "You weren't asleep at all!"

"It's called playin' possum," he chuckled.

Their coffee got cold. Eventually, she made another pot. Jack leashed up the dogs and walked them over to Parker's on Drayton Street, bringing back two sausage biscuits—for him—and a blueberry muffin—for her.

While he was gone, Cara showered and dressed quickly in shorts and a tank top. Not even nine o'clock yet, and it was already getting hot and sticky upstairs.

They took their coffee and breakfast out into the courtyard garden. Jack pointed out a suspicious mound of dirt beneath one of the crepe myrtles. "Looks like Shaz was trying to tunnel out of here this morning. Sorry about that."

"It could just as well have been Poppy," Cara said.

She'd propped open the back door to the shop so the dogs could come and go, and now they heard a loud knocking at the front door.

"Ignore that," Cara told Jack. "Probably some guy desperate to buy flowers for a forgotten anniversary."

The knocking continued.

"Sounds pretty desperate," Jack said. "Maybe you should take pity on the poor guy and bail him out."

Cara rolled her eyes, but she stood up and went to the front door, where the knocking continued.

"Hang on," she called. "I'm coming."

She pulled up the shade and stared out at her desperate customer. Only it was no customer. It was Leo. Her ex.

Her first instinct was to pull the shade back down and run the other way. But it was too late for that. He'd already seen her.

He was dressed for work: sport coat, tie, slacks, polished loafers. His Ray-Bans hung from a band around his neck. He looked good, like the kind of cute guy you'd flirt with if you stood next to him in line at Starbucks. Which, come to think of it, was how they'd met all those years ago. Incredibly, he held a huge bunch of lilacs in his right hand, and a box of cheap drugstore chocolates in the other.

She unlocked the door and opened it.

"Cara!" His eyes lit up. "I didn't, I mean, I wasn't sure you'd be here. Or, if you were, if you'd open the door."

"I'm here, Leo," she said, forcing herself to look stern. "What do you want?"

"Here." He thrust the flowers and chocolates toward her. His sandy blond hair flopped into his eyes. In another minute, if she wasn't careful, she'd push his hair back, straighten his tie. Old habits died hard. Instead, she kept her hands at her side, fists clenched tightly.

"What's this?" she asked.

"It's an anniversary present. Happy anniversary Cara."

Anniversary? She frowned. And then it dawned on her. Seven years ago today, she'd made the biggest mistake of her life.

"Leo, we're divorced. We don't have an anniversary anymore."

"Sure we do. Just because you signed a piece of paper, that doesn't change the fact that we got married." He leaned in and touched her cheek. "I've missed you, baby."

She batted his hand away.

"Really? You missed me? Why's that? Did your girlfriend find herself another married man to fool around with?"

He rocked back on his heels a bit, eyes wide in surprise. He wasn't used to this attitude. Not from her. She'd been sweet as pie most of her life. Fun-loving, easygoing, eager to please. It had been Leo's idea to move to Savannah, a year after their marriage. A great job opportunity, he said. Unlimited chance for advancement in his sales career.

So she'd smiled and nodded, then packed up her life in Columbus, Ohio. Waved good-bye to family and friends. She'd quit the job she loved, managing a vintage clothing store near the university. And she'd moved to the South—a place she'd never even visited, except for a couple of spring break trips to Florida—to Savannah, a place where she didn't know a single living soul.

That Cara was gone now, she told herself. Never to return.

Leo, a born salesman, never met a deal he couldn't close.

"Aww, Cara," he said, his voice low, mouth turned down. A textbook picture of contrition.

"That's all over with. It was over as soon as it began. I was such a jerk. I can't believe what I put you through. And for what? For nothing. Swear to God, you were always the only girl for me. The only girl I ever loved. My mom calls me every Sunday and wants to know when we're getting back together."

Her face hardened. "Tell her we're not getting back together. Tell her you cheated on me."

"Grannie Annie had a stroke last month. Did you know that? Dad fixed her up an apartment in the garage at our place. She still has our wedding picture on her dresser."

She sighed. "Don't do this to me, Leo. Please?" She had her hand on the door, was about to close it. But he was too quick for her. Always had been.

He lowered his head, put his lips next to her ears before she could jerk away. "Cara Mia, why?"

It was a line from the song, the stupid song her mother named her for. In another minute, if she let him, he'd be warbling "Must we say good-bye?"

"This won't work, Leo," she said, shaking her head sadly.

"Just let me take you out to dinner. No strings, just a nice dinner with a nice bottle of wine. Please? It's killing me, to think of you alone on our anniversary."

"I won't be alone," Cara said. "And as it happens, I already have plans tonight."

"Oh yeah. Right. Saturday, and it's wedding season so you're probably working. But what about after? A late dinner? I know the maître d' at the new place on Orleans Square...."

Just then, Poppy trotted over to see what her owner was doing. She nudged the back of Cara's knees with her head.

Leo looked stunned. "A dog? You got a dog?"

He knelt down and tugged at Poppy's collar, until she was halfway out the door. "Hey, fella," Leo crooned, scratching her nose, then her ears. "What a good fella. What a good dog!" He looked up at Cara. "I never saw a dog like this before. What kind is he?"

"*She* is a golden doodle—a cross between an English golden retriever and a standard poodle."

"Beautiful animal," Leo said. Poppy, the shameless little slut, fell hard for him, flopping onto the ground and rolling over so he could scratch her belly. If she'd had a telephone number, she would have given it to him.

"What's her name?"

"Poppy," Cara said.

"Figures. A flower name for a flower girl's dog." He stood up. "I always thought we'd get a dog. Pick one out together. Take it for a run in the park."

He gave her that crooked little grin that always used to work, back in the day. "Another thing to add to my list of regrets. You went and got a dog without me."

Enough, she thought.

"Look, Leo. I have to go. I actually do have a wedding tonight, and every second I stand here with you puts me that much further behind."

"I know, I know," he said. "Tick tock, right? You're quite the career girl these days, from what I hear." He leaned in again, and before she could stop him, he was kissing her, a lingering brush on the lips.

"Happy anniversary, Cara Mia mine. I'll call you."

She was just about to close the door.

"Cara?" Jack stood in the hallway entrance to the shop. He strode to her side and glared at Leo.

"What the hell?"

Leo glared right back, then pointed at Jack. "You. The guy in the towel. Last week."

"Yeah. That was me. And you were the guy in the truck, cruising down the lane."

Cara looked from Jack to Leo. "You two know each other?"

Leo shook his head. "What? You're sleeping with this guy?"

Jack put an arm across her shoulder. "*This* is your ex? The dude is stalking you, Cara. He drove down the lane twice last week while you were gone. Hell, the way he stared at me, I thought he was getting ready to proposition me."

"In your dreams, towel boy," Leo sneered.

"That's enough, kids," Cara said. She gave her ex-husband a not-so-gentle backward shove. Then she closed and locked the door. And pulled down the shade.

"What was that he called you?" Jack asked.

"Cara Mia. Mia is my middle name," Cara said. "What's your middle name?"

"Joseph. John Joseph. But back to you. So, your name is Cara Mia, like the song?"

"Yep. Jay and the Americans. My mom was a big fan."

"Mine too," Jack said. He jerked his head in the direction of the front door. "What did he want? Besides to suck face with you?"

"He seems to think it's our anniversary." She looked down and realized she was still holding the flowers and candy he'd thrust into her hands. Cara walked over to the trash can and dropped them in.

"He's a tool," Jack said. "And the next time I catch him driving by here, I'm gonna take my pry bar and put a big ol' dent in that pretty-boy Lexus of his."

"Ooh. Drama," Cara said. But she was smiling when she said it.

40

It had taken Cara two weeks of calling, emailing, and texting, but she'd finally gotten Brooke and Harris to agree to meet for lunch and go over wedding plans.

But when Brooke arrived in the lobby at Johnny Harris, the iconic barbecue restaurant on Victory Drive in midtown, she was alone. She was dressed in a black and white herringbone checked suit, with black pumps and a pink silk blouse, and to Cara's shock, the bride's long, lustrous dark hair had been chopped off at chin length.

"Harris's flight from New York didn't come in," Brooke said. "Anyway, he pretty much said he's fine with whatever we decide." She caught Cara staring at her hair, and she pushed a strand behind one ear.

"You don't like it, do you?"

"It's just . . . different," Cara said. "Usually my brides are trying to grow their hair out before the wedding."

Brooke shrugged. "It's been so hot. And long hair is such a pain. Blowing it dry and everything, I just don't have the time. . . ."

The bride looked pointedly down at her watch, and then at the vacant hostess stand. It was a Monday, and the restaurant was already crowded. "Should we have made a reservation? I only have an hour before I need to get back to the office."

"The hostess will be back in a minute. A party of twelve came in right before you did," Cara assured her. She couldn't get over Brooke's hair. It was not a flattering cut, emphasizing the sharp planes of her hollow cheeks.

"What does Harris think of it?"

"He says he loves it, but I'm not so sure. Mom would never say anything critical—at least to my face. And of course, Patricia and my dad are appalled. Which kind of makes it fun."

"Brooke? Brooke Trapnell?"

A tall slender man with sun-streaked shoulder-length brown hair broke away from the group of men with whom he'd just entered the lobby. He wore a forest-green golf shirt with an embroidered logo, khaki cargo shorts, and Topsider deck shoes.

Brooke turned to see who was addressing her. For a moment, she looked puzzled, but then her face lit up. "Petey!" She flung her arms around the newcomer's neck. They hugged tightly.

Brooke pulled back a little, beaming up at his face. "Oh my God, Pete. I can't believe it's really you. Where have you been? What are you doing here?"

"Well, you know, I've been out west, Montana and Colorado, working for the Park Service. And I've just transferred here a couple months ago."

"Here? You're back in Savannah? That's awesome."

"Actually, no. I'm working on Cumberland Island. I'm just up here today for some meetings with our regional director." He gestured toward the group of men who were drifting toward the dining room. "What about you? Are you still living here in town? I heard you graduated from law school, so what, you're a lady lawyer now?"

Brooke's laugh was almost giddy. "I don't know about the lady part, but yeah, I'm a second-year associate. I do mostly corporate law."

"Cool." He snapped his fingers. "Hey. Didn't your folks used to have a place down on Cumberland?"

"My mom's family does. Loblolly. I can't believe you remember that after all these years."

"Do you ever go down there?"

"Hey, Pete." One of the park-service men was standing at the hostess stand, gesturing toward him. "Our table's ready."

"Coming."

Pete turned back to Brooke. "Gotta go. But we need to catch up. Wait. Let me give you my card."

He dug in the pocket of his cargo shorts, but came out empty-handed. "Damn. Wouldn't you know? I didn't bring any with me."

Brooke reached into her pocketbook and brought out a sterling silver case. She withdrew a thick vellum square and handed it to him. "Here's mine."

"Pete!"

"Coming!"

When they were seated and the waitress had taken their orders, Cara brought out her iPad, and they got down to business.

"So. Here's the reception menu we came up with after you had to leave the other day. . . ."

"You mean after Patricia took over the whole thing?" Brooke scanned the screen, nodding. "Sure. This looks okay. But it seems like a lot of food to me."

"We're doing a seated dinner," Cara reminded her. With her fingertip, she scrolled over to the next page. "These are the appetizers that will be passed during cocktail hour. . . ."

Brooke wrinkled her nose. "Fried calamari? Gross. Let me guess. Patricia's idea?"

"Layne's version is really lightly battered. If you want, I can set it up for you and Harris to taste that, and the rest of the appetizers."

"Never mind." Brooke took a bite of her salad and looked around the big, dome-ceilinged dining room, her eyes lingering on the men taking up a table at the far end of the room.

"Pete? Was that his name? An old friend?" Cara asked.

"Hmm?" Brooke's face flushed. "Yeah. Pete Haynes. We uh, I guess we sort of had a thing, the summer before I left for college. But then I went away, to

University of Virginia, and he was already a sophomore at Georgia. You know how that goes."

"And this was the first time you've seen him since then?"

Brooke stabbed a piece of chicken with her fork. "Um. Not really." She looked away, then down at her plate, then leaned forward across the table. "My parents totally don't know anything about this. Okay? In fact, none of my friends know it."

Cara waited.

"Summer after I graduated from UVA, my dad got me this big-deal internship with our congressman. In Washington." Brooke rolled her eyes. "What a blowhard that guy was. Typical, right? Anyway, Pete was living there too that summer, he'd graduated with a degree in marine biology, and he'd gotten a desk job working for some government agency. Something to do with endangered species? And we kind of, you know. Got together."

"Dated?" Cara laughed. "Brooke, you're almost thirty. Why does that have to be a secret from your parents? Or your friends?"

Brooke's face colored. "Because at the time, Harris and I were unofficially engaged."

"Oh."

"Yeah. It's like that." She smiled sadly. "Technically, I was sleeping with two guys. Which is *not* who I am. In August, Pete had a job offer, with the Park Service, out in Montana. His dream job. And he wanted me to go with him." Brooke fiddled with a strand of her hair.

"But you said no."

"I was supposed to start law school at Emory. Harris was already there, starting on his MBA. He'd rented a house for us. And right around then, that's when the shit hit the fan with my parents. My dad moved out, and moved in with Patricia. My mom was a mess...."

"Bad timing," Cara said sympathetically.

"The worst." Brooke stared down at her half-eaten salad. She picked up a cellophane-wrapped package of saltines and crumbled it between her fingertips.

"It's probably a good thing Mom couldn't come today." Brooke looked around the dining room, its dark paneling and leatherette booths, at the domed blue-painted ceiling with twinkling lights. "This was their place. Hers and dad's. Back in the seventies, when they were dating, it was kind of a big deal to come to dinner here."

"Really?" To Cara, Johnny Harris was just a barbecue restaurant. She liked their barbecue sauce, but it was hard for her to imagine the place as a hot nightspot.

"Yeah. They'd get all dressed up. I remember we used to have a photo album, with a picture of them sitting at one of those booths over there." Brooke pointed to the opposite end of the room. "You can't really tell from here, but there were curtains you could draw, for privacy, and you could push a little button to summon your waiter. The buttons are still there. Anyway, if you can believe it, Dad had this bushy hair, and big ol' sideburns and a kind of handlebar mustache. He looked like a porn star! And Mom's hair was really long and straight, and she wore dangly earrings. And she's sitting right beside Dad, with his arm around her shoulders and he's totally looking right down her cleavage!"

Brooke got a sudden fit of giggles, which were over nearly as soon as they'd begun. "After they split up, I thought Mom probably burned all those old pictures. But the last time I was home, I was in her bedroom, and she'd told me I could borrow her pearls, for this stupid engagement party, and I found that picture in the bottom of her jewelry box."

"You think your mom's still not over him?"

"Not really. She tries to put on a good show around me, but I think she's still really sad. And hurt."

"Does she date?"

"My mom? No. I wish she would though."

Brooke's gaze had returned to the table where Pete Haynes was sitting.

"How about you?" Cara asked. "And your friend Pete? After your breakup, he was okay?"

"Yeah...." Brooke's voice trailed off. "Pete—he knew how my parents were. Well, my dad, anyway. Snobby, right? Pete wasn't from the wrong side of the tracks, not at all, but he went to public high school, that kind of thing."

"Did Pete know about you and Harris?"

Brooke's eyes widened. "Oh God, no. That summer, it was just such an odd thing for me. It was like the first time I realized I was an adult, and I didn't have to be under my dad's thumb for the rest of my life."

"A summer of rebellion," Cara said. "I get that. My dad was career military. He still expects everybody to stand at attention and salute."

"Rebellion. Exactly. But at some point, even a rebel has to figure out what to do with their life. And for me, law school and Emory made sense. I've always wanted to be a lawyer. And Harris made sense. He's sweet and loyal and smart."

"Harris is a good guy," Cara said.

Brooke twisted her engagement ring. "The absolute best. He loves me. I don't know why, or how I got this lucky, but Harris loves me. Pete was cool with whatever I wanted to do. He probably only asked me to move out there with him because he thought he *should* ask."

"And you didn't keep in touch after that? At all?"

Brooke colored again.

"Facebook?" Cara guessed.

"He doesn't know it's me," Brooke said. "I made up a name, said I was a friend of a friend of a friend of his who likes whitewater rafting."

"Did you know he'd moved back to Georgia?" Cara asked.

"No! Pete's hardly ever on Facebook. Occasionally he posts a picture of his puppy, or a sunset or something. Nothing personal."

Cara arched one eyebrow. She'd done enough Facebook stalking of her own to know how this worked.

"You're telling me you don't check his status?"

"Not in a relationship," Brooke said, her voice barely a whisper. "Anyway, what else do we need to discuss? About the wedding? Patricia texts me every day, asking for a status report. She's making me nuts."

"Right. Okay. Did you get a chance to look at the photographers' websites that I sent you? Any preferences?"

"Yeah, but I thought Patricia already hired some photographer."

"Meredith. She only does portraits. This photographer is for the actual wedding."

"Geez. Does everything have to be so complicated? Anyway, yeah, I liked them both. Mom really liked the woman—what's her name?"

"Rita McCall. I think Rita really has a nice way with candids and black-and-white. And she's so good at capturing the mood of the event."

"Fine. Then let's go with Rita McCall," Brooke said. "What else? I've only got a few more minutes."

"Hmm. We really need to discuss table markers and favors. I've some ideas. Since the Strayhorns are in shipping, I thought we could do these miniature shipping containers, stencil your name and Harris's on one side . . ."

"Great."

"I've got a great artisanal chocolatier in town, he'll come up with a signature chocolate filling for us—do you like milk chocolate or dark chocolate?"

"Dark, I guess. I don't actually eat a lot of sweets."

Not surprising, Cara thought, looking at the bride's picked-over salad.

"I thought we could do maybe six or eight pieces of chocolate in each container."

"Okay."

"Now," Cara said, taking a deep breath. "The seating chart. It's going to get complicated, it always is when there's been a divorce in the family. You've got the list of people who've already responded, so if you would, maybe give me your thoughts on who should be seated where."

"My thoughts?" Brooke shook her head impatiently. "I look at the list, and I don't know most of these people. Maybe Harris does, but I don't. Here's all I want, Cara. Just don't put Patricia anywhere near me. Or my mom. Or actually, if you could just not put her in the same room with us, that would be good."

"Be real, please Brooke," Cara said sharply. She scrolled back over to the seating chart she'd made up—circles and rectangles drawn to scale and arrayed around the ballroom at Cabin Creek. "Just take a look, please, this is important, if not to you, to your parents and the Strayhorns. . . ."

Brooke frowned, but bent her head and studied the chart. A shadow fell over the iPad and they both looked up. Pete Haynes cleared his throat, as though he were about to make a speech.

"Listen, Brooke. I've got to get on the road if I'm going to make the afternoon ferry from St. Marys over to Cumberland." He handed her a scrap of paper. "That's my email. Cell-phone service on the island is pretty crappy. And I don't get up to Savannah that much because of the project I'm working on. With the wild horses. But if you're coming down there anytime, I was thinking it'd be great to get together...."

Brooke looked at the slip of paper, then placed it on the tabletop. She looked over at Cara. "Pete, this is Cara Kryzik."

"Hi," he said, shaking Cara's hand politely. "I'm an old friend of Brooke's. Pete Haynes. Sorry to interrupt your lunch."

"Not at all," Cara murmured.

"The thing is, Pete, Cara's my wedding planner. I'm getting married next month."

"July the sixth," Cara said helpfully.

If he was stunned, he didn't show it. "You're engaged?"

Brooke held up her left hand, where Harris Strayhorn's diamond solitaire twinkled from her slender ring finger. "I am."

"Oh." He shifted from one foot to the other as the news sunk in. "That's great. Good for you. Congratulations."

"Thanks," Brooke said. She gave him a bright smile. "How about you? Is there a wife down there on Cumberland Island?"

"No," he said, pressing his lips together. "Nothing like that. Anyway, I gotta get going. It was nice to see you again, Brooke. And uh, good luck with the wedding and everything. I hope you'll, uh, be very happy."

"I'm sure we will be," Brooke said. Cara watched Brooke watching him weave his way through the crowded tables to the dining room exit. The waitress came over, and dropped the leatherette folder with the bill on the table, but Brooke picked it up before Cara could.

"My treat," Brooke said. She tucked some bills in the envelope. They both stood to leave.

"You'll go over the seating chart?" Cara prompted.

"I swear. Email it to me again, and I'll let you know," Brooke promised.

"Today?"

"Absolutely."

Cara stood and took her pocketbook from the back of the chair. She couldn't help but notice that the slip of paper with Pete Haynes's email address was right where Brooke had left it.

41

Cara was headed back to the shop when her cell phone rang.

"Hi Brooke. Did you have a chance to look at the seating chart this quickly?"

"Sorry, not yet. Cara?"

"Yes?"

"About what I said. Earlier, in the restaurant. About me and Pete. You probably think I'm awful. A total slut."

"I don't think that," Cara said. "Anyway, it was a long time ago. You said yourself, until today you hadn't seen the guy in years."

"It's been five years. I'm not trying to excuse what I did, but you have to understand. That summer? Before I moved to Atlanta and started law school, it was like I was in this little bubble, and the only reality was me and Pete. I still can't explain it. I loved Harris, and I knew we would get married eventually. But he was in Atlanta, and I was in DC. And Pete was right there. And we had so much fun together, it was like we were kids back in high school again."

"Brooke. Why are you telling me all this? I'm not judging you."

"I know," Brooke said, sighing. "Maybe I'm trying to explain it to myself. The thing is, at the time, it didn't seem wrong. As long as Harris didn't know about Pete, and Pete didn't know about Harris, I thought nobody could get hurt. And they didn't. It was just that one summer."

"Five years ago," Cara said.

"And it's over," Brooke said. "Okay. This was weird. Forget I called. Forget I told you any of it."

"Any of what?"

"Thanks, Cara," Brooke said.

42

The bride leaned across Cara's desk and stabbed a long pearly pink fingernail at page 72 of the March 2009 issue of *Martha Stewart Weddings*. The page was dog-eared, and the rest of the magazine bristled with pink Post-it notes.

"This one. This is the exact bouquet I want. I've saved this magazine since I was eighteen years old. I picked out my wedding dress because I knew it would go with this bouquet."

Cara groaned inwardly. How well she knew this particular wedding bouquet. She was sure it was the most-pinned item on every single bride's Pinterest page in the universe. She wanted to rip page 72 out of this magazine, ball it up, and burn it.

Instead, she did what she always did. She picked up a pencil and pointed it at each flower in the bouquet.

"Heather, these flowers here? They are Casablanca lilies. They wholesale at thirty dollars a stem. I count five stems in this bouquet—so that's a hundred and fifty dollars right there. These pretty ruffly flowers? Like overblown roses? These are premium peonies. This size bunch wholesales at about seventy-five dollars."

"What?" Heather drew back as though she'd been slapped. "Thirty dollars for one lily?"

"Yes. Although one stem will have multiple blossoms. They're imported." Cara pointed at the petite bell-shaped flowers edging the infamous Martha Stewart bouquet. "Now these—these are the budget killers."

"Yes. Lilies of the valley," Heather said eagerly. "Kate Middleton's whole bouquet was made of them."

"Yes," Cara said. "I'm aware." Which was the understatement of the year. Ever since the royal wedding of Prince William and Kate Middleton, she'd been besieged with brides insisting upon having lilies of the valley.

"Here's the thing, Heather. Lilies of the valley are so tiny, you need a lot of them to make any impact at all. One tiny bunch, which is ten skinny stems, is ninety dollars. I'd say there are at least six bunches in this bouquet. That's three hundred and sixty dollars."

Heather's mother had been sitting beside the bride, frowning. But now the MOB's eyes bugged out. "That must be a mistake. We didn't spend three hundred and sixty dollars for her older sister's whole flower budget."

Heather rolled her eyes. "Mama, Jessica got married eight years ago! She only had one bridesmaid, and we had the reception at your house."

"It was still a lovely wedding," the mother insisted. "And I can tell you right now, your daddy is not going to pay five hundred and forty dollars for some itty-bitty flowers just because some English princess had them."

"Also? Besides being expensive, Lilies of the valley are extremely fragile. Your wedding is in August. In summer months, our suppliers won't even guarantee what kind of condition they'll be in when they arrive here." Cara gave the MOB an apologetic shrug.

"No lilies," the mother shot back.

Cara reached over and gently closed the March 2009 issue of *Martha Stewart Weddings*. "Heather, the bouquet you're looking at costs roughly twelve hundred dollars."

"No way," Heather breathed.

"Way. And what did you say your flower budget was for this wedding? With, what? Six bridesmaids?"

Heather looked at her mother for guidance. "Two thousand. And not a penny more."

"Okay," Cara said. Heather looked like a sweet girl. And her mother, as far as MOBs went, seemed nice, too. But with their budget, they could not afford a full-scale Bloom wedding. And with Cara's current cash-flow situation, she couldn't afford to take them on pro bono.

"Let's do this. Let's think about a nice, simple bouquet for you, Heather. I can make you up something very pretty, with white hydrangeas, tea roses, and white hypericum berries, for around a hundred and fifty. It won't be anywhere as big or showy as the bouquet in your magazine, but it will still be lovely with your dress."

Heather's nose wrinkled. "Hydrangeas? Like my meemaw grows in her yard?"

"Yes. Hydrangeas." Cara shoved Heather's magazine aside and snapped open her iPad. She scrolled through the photos of weddings she'd done until she came to what she privately called "Bargain Basement Bouquet."

"We can get these in all white, in a pale green, shades of pinks, blues, creams, and purples," Cara said.

"That's beautiful." Heather's mother nodded emphatically.

"It is kind of pretty," the bride begrudgingly admitted. "What do we do about the bridesmaids' bouquets?"

"You go minimalist," Cara said. "One or two stems of hydrangeas, and you do a ruffle of hydrangea leaves to fill it out."

"Wait. Are you saying you want me to make the bridesmaids' bouquets?"

"If you do them, you can get away with spending around fifteen dollars apiece, and that includes a pretty white satin ribbon binding, which you can buy at Michael's. You can find lots of tutorials online that show you how to make a simple bouquet. If I do them, I have to charge markup and labor, and that's going to bring the price of each of those bouquets to sixty dollars," Cara explained.

"I never heard of such a thing," the MOB said. "Anyway, we still need flowers for the church and the reception. Who's going to do them?"

Heather's eyes were pleading. Her mother was glaring at both of them.

"All right," Cara relented. "I'll do your bouquet and the church flowers, for two thousand dollars. But the altar flowers will also have to be carried over to your church parlor for the reception. You'll need to deputize one of your bridesmaids or girlfriends to be in charge of that."

"I'll ask Jessica to do it," Heather said.

"Two thousand is a really tight budget," Cara warned. "I need you to understand that you won't have exotic or imported flowers. We can do a lot with hydrangeas and carnations and glads and spray roses and local foliage. Do you have any friends with pretty gardens? We can use hosta leaves and ivy and ferns for greenery and that will save you a lot of money."

"My sister is in a garden club," Heather's mom said. "She'll let us cut whatever we need."

"Wonderful," Cara said. She stood up, as a signal that their meeting was over. "One more thing? The way this works is, you pay me half today, and the other half is due two weeks before the wedding."

"A thousand dollars? Today?" The MOB clutched her pocketbook to her chest, as though Cara might make a lunge for it at any moment.

"Yes," Cara said firmly. Some things were not negotiable.

"Mama?" Heather put an arm around her mother's shoulders. "We agreed, right? Two thousand for flowers."

"But I thought we'd just look at pictures, and discuss," the mother said.

Cara felt her patience wearing thin. In reality, her patience was flat gone. She gave the two women a bright smile. "You're welcome to check around with other florists, but this is standard in our business. I really can't give you any more of a consultation without receiving a deposit check. Today."

Let them walk, Cara thought. *I can't afford this kind of charity. I might not even still be in business in August.*

"Mama?" Heather was opening her own pocketbook, taking out her checkbook. She wrote the check, ripped it from the book, and handed it to Cara.

"Thank you," Heather said fervently. "Thank you so much."

. . .

Bert had been sitting at his side of the worktable, putting together hospital bouquets, listening throughout the consultation. When mother and daughter were gone, he slapped his scissors on the table.

"Looorrrrd," he drawled. "When I looked out the window and saw those two pull up in that tired old Ford Fiesta I almost told them they'd come to the wrong place. What I don't get is why you didn't just tell them you can't do a Bloom wedding for two thousand dollars. Why didn't you just tell them to take their sad little selves out to Sam's Club? They can get a whole lot of wilted chrysanthemums and daisies and carnations for two thousand dollars over there."

"Cut it out, Bert," Cara said sharply. "I can't blame the girl for wanting something nice. Most girls dream about their wedding day their whole life. It's not Heather's fault all those magazines and websites love to feature fairytale weddings—but never explain what the price tags are."

"You're not doing her any favor indulging in her little fantasy world," Bert said. "She'll never find even a half-assed photographer or a caterer with the kind of piddly budget she's talking about. She should just get her sourpuss mama to give her the money she'd spend on a tacky wedding and then elope. Spend the money on a trip to South of the Border, or a down payment on a double-wide."

"Fun is fun, but now that's just mean," Cara said. "When did you get to be such a bitch?"

"And when did you get so high-minded and holier-than-thou?" he shot back. "Come on, Cara, lighten up, will you? We always used to have such fun around here, but lately, you're so serious. Everything is so dire. Frankly, it's depressing."

Bert's phone, which he'd placed on the worktable beside him, buzzed to signal an incoming text. He looked down, read it, then scrambled down off his high-backed stool. "I'm going to lunch."

"You just got back from a coffee run that took thirty minutes," Cara said. "And you came in thirty minutes late this morning. You've been pulling this same disappearing act all week. I warned you earlier, Bert. We've got Mary

Payne's ninetieth-birthday party tonight, and the bar association dinner at the Chatham Club tomorrow night, not to mention the phone orders we need to get done and delivered. I can't get it all done by myself. And I shouldn't have to."

"Are you telling me I can't take a lunch hour? That's probably against the law, you know."

"I'm telling you you've already taken a lunch hour," she shot back. "If you're really hungry, I'll go upstairs and fix you a sandwich, or we can get a pizza delivered. But we both know that's not the case. We both know that text you just got is a booty call from your new boyfriend."

"Screw you!" Bert said angrily. "Just because you've got no life and live like a nun, doesn't mean I have to." He picked up his phone and walked deliberately toward the door.

"I mean it, Bert," Cara said, clenching and unclenching her fists. "If you walk out that door now, you're done. Don't bother coming back."

He had his hand on the doorknob. He hesitated, then strode back toward the worktable.

Relief flooded Cara's body. She didn't want this. But he'd pushed her right to the edge.

Bert opened the drawer on his side of the worktable. He picked up the backpack he'd slung over his chair and tossed in a paperback book, his favorite scissors, and a coffee mug. Then he reached up to the shelf behind the table, took his iPod station and iPod, and threw them into the bag with the rest of his belongings.

"I'm not giving you a reference for another job," Cara called, just as he reached the shop door.

"I don't need one." He slammed the door. Hard.

43

Poppy stood at the front window, watching the squirrel in the tree outside, and waiting, Cara felt sure, for her friend Bert to change his mind and come back.

"He's gone," Cara said, getting up to scratch the dog's ears and toss her a conciliatory puppy treat. "Anyway, he's just a man. They come and they go, girl, and when one decides to leave, all you can do is get out of the way."

Poppy gave her a baleful look, then concentrated on chewing her treat. In the meantime, a battered white pickup truck pulled up to the curb outside, parking in the loading zone. A youngish man in paint-spattered overalls and a green John Deere tractor cap got out of the truck and stood on the sidewalk. He pulled a smart phone from the bib of his overalls, stepped backward and began taking photos. He trotted across the street and snapped more photos as Cara stood, watching.

The man recrossed and walked past the shop window and out of her line of sight. Cara opened the door and peered out, just in time to see him rounding the corner and turning south on Whitaker.

"Here, Poppy!" Cara locked the front door and headed for the rear of the shop and the door into the courtyard. Poppy bounded out into the garden and gave a short, surprised yelp as the stranger stepped into the garden through the door from the lane.

"Hey!" Cara called, her voice sharp. "What do you think you're doing?"

Poppy barked loudly, and lunged forward, but Cara caught her by her collar.

"Uh, the landlord sent me over." Seeing him up close, she could see he was probably in his mid-twenties, with brown hair sticking out from the back of his cap, and a string of tattoos on both forearms. He took a half step backward.

"Which landlord?"

He looked confused. "The one who owns this building, I guess. Wanted me to give him some estimates for doing all the work needs doing."

"Him? The last I heard, Sylvia Bradley still owns this building. Was she the one who called you?"

"Look, ma'am, I don't want any trouble. I'm just doing my job. The guy called me, gave me this address, said he was looking to restore an old building on West Jones Street."

Cara felt her face go hot with anger. "You're talking about Cullen Kane?"

"Yeah."

"Did he give you the key to get through that gate just now?"

"Sure."

"You can't just come in here like this. I live here. This is my business. My rent is paid up until the end of the month."

"Hey, all I know is, the guy said it's okay. He has keys to the place, he sent me over to look around. I'm not gonna bother you or nothin'. . . ."

He took a step toward Cara, and Poppy let out a deep-throated warning growl, the likes of which Cara had never heard before from the people-loving puppy. She grasped the collar tighter. Her unwanted visitor looked uneasily around, as though he might need a weapon to fend off this fluffy white killer guard dog.

"What's your name?" Cara asked.

"Ricky Ucinski."

"Ricky, no offense, but I'm not letting you in my house."

"Geez," he said. "What do I tell Mr. Kane?"

"Tell him the crazy woman who lives here set her dog on you when you unlocked the back gate. And tell him if he sends any more contractors over here again, I'll do the same thing to them."

Ricky Ucinski looked distinctly uncomfortable with this message. "You wouldn't really set that dog on me, would you?"

Poppy growled again, as if on cue.

Cara gave a grim smile. "I really don't think you want to find that out, Ricky."

Apprentice floral-designer needed. Owner-operated floral design studio in downtown historic area seeks assistant/apprentice with artistic flair, design skills, working knowledge of flowers helpful, but not mandatory. Ideal candidate must be responsible, reliable, self-starter. Duties also include some clerical work and flower delivery. Must have valid driver's license and immediate availability.

Cara looked down at the Craigslist help-wanted ad and thought for a moment before rapidly typing the most important addition to the ad:

Whiners, sulkers, and self-involved slackers need not apply.

She added her contact information and hit the Send button. It was nearly four o'clock. She'd loaded the van with the afternoon's deliveries, and taken Poppy on a brief walk. But she had one pressing piece of business to attend to before anything else.

Cullen Kane Floral Design Studio was located in a former Piggly Wiggly grocery store on Habersham Street in midtown Savannah. As far as Cara knew, nearly everything in Savannah was located in a building that used to be something else, and everybody knew what that something was. In her case, she only knew it because she'd spent ten minutes staring at Kane's website, which trumpeted that his studio was located "in a sensitively upcycled circa-1946 Piggly Wiggly."

The old red-brick building had been painted charcoal gray, and now sported crisp red-and-white-striped awnings over the plate-glass windows. Huge terra-cotta pots on either side of the front door had palm trees under-planted with white lobelia and asparagus ferns, and the front door itself was painted a gloss red, with wrought-iron inserts featuring the intertwined CK logo, which was also painted in four-foot-high letters on the side of the building.

She parked the van in the lot beside his shop, trying to ignore the stabbing envy in her gut. Kane had at least sixteen spaces in his own dedicated lot, where more palm trees were planted in oversized wooden tubs. A gleaming black Mercedes box truck emblazoned with the CK logo was parked near the door. If a truck could look chic, this one did.

Cara took a deep breath and pushed the door open. The air inside the shop was lightly perfumed and deliciously cooled. The ceiling was open to exposed wooden roof rafters, and dropped ceiling fans whirred soundlessly overhead. A reception area had been screened off from the rest of the building with a red latticework partition, and in front of it, at a black midcentury modern desk, sat a familiar figure—Bert Rosen, dressed in an unfamiliar tight-fitting black T-shirt with the scrolling CK logo.

He was talking on the phone and tapping notes into the laptop computer on the desk and didn't notice her at first, which allowed Cara time to feel the full extent of the rage and jealousy boiling up from her gut.

Suddenly, it all fell into place. The no-shows, the long weekends, the long lunch hours and mystery text messages. Her assistant's phantom boyfriend had finally been unmasked.

Bert clicked off the phone, but kept typing. Without looking up he parroted the greeting, which he'd already mastered. "Welcome to Cullen Kane Design. I'll be with you in a moment."

"I can wait."

That got his attention.

"Cara?" His pale face bloomed a bright shade of red that exactly matched the screen behind his desk.

"Bert." She gestured around the shop. "You seem to have had a pretty busy lunch hour."

"You fired me," he said. "What was I supposed to do? Go on welfare?"

"I fired you four hours ago. You seem to have had a remarkably fast recovery. Or were you already working here—and I'm the last to know?"

He shrugged. "Whatever."

"Where is he?"

"Who?"

"Your boss," Cara said. "I need to see him. Right now."

"I'll call back to the workroom and see if he's available. What's this in reference to?"

Cara reached over and grabbed the neckline of Bert's black T-shirt, in the process knocking over a heavy crystal vase holding an arrangement of bamboo leaves and spiky red bird-of-paradise blooms. "This is in reference to him sabotaging my life, buying my building out from under me, and seducing a formerly valuable employee."

"Owww." Bert slapped ineffectively at Cara's hand. "Cut it out."

She abruptly released the shirt and he snapped backward like a limp rubber band.

A stream of water flowed across the desk and into his lap. "Look what you did!"

"Never mind calling. I'll find him myself."

She charged around the screen. Directly behind it was an informal seating area, with a pair of low white leather tufted sofas facing each other across from a chunky Lucite coffee table.

Behind that Cara saw six workstations, occupied by designers clad in signature black CK Design T-shirts, who were busily assembling what looked like enough extravagant flower arrangements to fill Savannah's largest cathedral.

She kept going. At the back of the open space she spied a glass-enclosed office. Cullen Kane sat at another midcentury modern desk. He was on the phone, his back turned away from the workroom, so he never even saw her coming.

Cara yanked the door of his office open. He spun around in his chair. "I've got to go," he told his caller. "We'll talk later."

Kane hung up the phone. If he was surprised to see her, he didn't show it. "Hi there. To what do I owe the pleasure?"

"We need to talk," Cara hissed.

"Love to," Kane said. He gestured to the chair facing his desk. "Please sit. Can I get you something to drink? What would you like? Perrier, some champagne? I'll get Bert to bring us something."

Cara bristled. "Nothing. I want nothing from you. Except my life back."

"Oh, please." Kane gave an airy wave. "You're upset that I bought your building?"

"Bought it out from under me," Cara said. Her face felt stiff and unnatural, and the anger, fizzing just below the surface, felt like a fast-moving rash. "To put me out of business."

"Not at all," he said pleasantly. "This was a good investment. That's all. What? You think I've cooked up some grand conspiracy against you?"

"Haven't you? You spread nasty rumors around town about my finances. You buy my building and then start sending contractors over to look at it— while I'm still living there. You poison my employee's relationship toward me. . . ."

Kane leaned back in his chair and studied her thoughtfully. "How long have you been harboring these paranoid delusions of yours? Really, Cara. First of all, yes, I bought your building. Jones Street is the most beautiful street in the historic district, and your block is one of the most desirable. I would have been crazy to pass it up."

"You don't need another shop," Cara cried. "This place has four times the space Bloom has. You've obviously spent a fortune redoing this. You've got parking, location, everything."

He shrugged. "I happen to like your building. It's quaint. I like real estate, and it was a good buy."

"It's a dump and you know it. The Bradleys haven't spent one nickel on it in probably twenty years."

"I know. That's what makes it so delicious. The possibilities are endless."

Cara swallowed the bile rising up in her throat. Swallowed her pride. "I want to stay in my building. I want a new lease. So. How much?"

"No telling," he said lightly. "You've turned away the two contractors I sent over there to get estimates."

"You walked the building before you signed the contract with Sylvia. While

I was gone. You went through it, went through my apartment. And you didn't even have the decency to ask my permission."

"Your landlord isn't obligated to ask for your permission to show the property. You don't even have a lease."

"How much?" Cara persisted. "I want to stay in my building. I don't want to move."

"Sorry. That's impossible. I'm planning a total restoration. Down to the studs. New roof, all new electric, plumbing, HVAC. After I'm done, well, we both know you won't be able to afford to stay."

"Why don't you let me worry about that?" Cara could hear her own breaths, coming fast and shallow. Was she about to hyperventilate?

He leaned across the desk. She could see the bleached blond highlights in his hair, the ghost of five-o'clock shadow on his cheeks. The skin over his cheeks and forehead was pulled unnaturally taut. Maybe he and Patricia Trapnell shared the same surgeon. He wore some kind of gold medallion on a fine chain around his neck. This close, she could see that he wore blue-tinted contacts.

"You're not listening to me," he said, his voice low and deadly serious. "You have two weeks to vacate the premises. You and your dog and the rest of your stuff? I want all of it out of there. Two weeks. If you're not gone, I call the sheriff."

Cara rocked backward on her heels, singed by the intensity of his animosity toward her.

"Why?" she whispered. "Why are you doing this to me?"

Kane's phone rang. He picked it up immediately. "Cullen Kane," he said smoothly. He looked over at Cara—his glance telegraphing just what an insignificant nuisance he regarded her as.

"It's nothing personal." He swiveled his chair around so that she was facing his back.

She stalked back to the reception area, where Bert was wearing a telephone headset, typing away at the computer. He didn't look up, although she knew he'd seen her coming.

She reached down and yanked off the headset. That got his attention.

"What now?"

"Answer me one question," Cara said. Her voice quavered so much that she could barely trust herself to say more. "How did he know my building was on the market, when I didn't even know?"

"Huh?"

"Don't play dumb, Bert. I asked you how Cullen Kane knew that Sylvia Bradley might be interested in selling Jones Street. Did you tell him?"

"I don't . . . what are you saying? Are you saying Cullen is the one who bought your building?"

"You know he bought it," Cara said angrily. "And the only way he could have known it was available was from you. Pillow talk, huh?"

"No!" Bert protested. "I mean, he could have seen old Mrs. Bradley's obituary. It was in the paper. That's how we found out."

"Yeah, but we knew who my landlady was. There was nothing in the obituary about that. So how would Cullen Kane figure out? You told him, right?"

Bert's right eye twitched. "I told him the old bat died, and her daughter wouldn't fix the air-conditioning, and the place was like a furnace. Yes! Okay? Big deal. I had no idea he'd go out and buy the place. I swear, I didn't know he'd bought it until you just told me."

"Did you also tell Cullen I owed my father a lot of money, and that he was bugging me to repay him? Did you tell your new boyfriend I was in dire straits—until Brooke Trapnell decided to hire me to plan her wedding?"

"He already knew you were broke," Bert said. "He was at Breitmueller's the day they put a hold on your credit, remember?"

"But you told him the other stuff, didn't you?"

Bert looked down at his computer terminal, and then out the window, anywhere but at Cara. "I might have mentioned it. In passing."

Cara grasped the edge of his desk with both hands. "How could you? I trusted you, Bert. I thought you were my friend. It's bad enough that you snuck around behind my back, sleeping with somebody we both know wants to put me out of business. He's kicking me out of my building in two weeks. Did he tell you that? Then you go blabbing my personal financial information to him. I just . . . I just can't believe you'd betray me this way. And for what? A hookup? A job answering his phone? A free Cullen Kane T-shirt? That's all this is, Bert, I guarantee it. He's using you to destroy me. And when he's done, he'll toss you aside, the same way he mowed me down."

Bert's face hardened. "You don't know what you're talking about, Cara. Cullen and I . . . you don't know anything about him. Or us."

The front door opened then, and a young couple walked in, holding hands. "You need to go, Cara," Bert said. He looked over her head, dismissing her the same way his lover had earlier.

"Hello! Welcome to Cullen Kane Floral Design Studio. You must be Kimberly and Stephen. Can I get you a Perrier? Some champagne?"

44

—I *am very innerested in you job. I like flowers. Can start immediately. What is pay?*

Cara stared down at the flood of responses to her Craigslist ad. She'd placed it six hours ago, and her inbox was jammed.

Dear Sir: I am the person for this situation. I don't know much about flowers, but that's cool. I learn fast and at the job I'm at now, people say I am an all-around awesome worker. Your ad said something about a driver's license. The thing is, I should get mine back in three months. Is that cool?

She shook her head. Not cool.

Hello! I am currently working as a floral designer in Indiana, but am looking to relocate to your area. I have 28 years experience as a florist. Am seeking a top-notch opportunity with an industry leader. My salary requirements are as follows: $70K annual minimum salary with bonus incentives, and company vehicle. I would also expect to be reimbursed for moving expenses. When can I expect to hear from you?

"Never," Cara muttered, hitting the Delete button.

She scrolled down the other responses and felt her spirits sink. She counted seventy-four emails. Two-thirds of the respondents either couldn't spell or apparently did not actually speak English.

Hey my name is Tiki and I seen your ad on Craigslist and I am very interested in the job. I feel like I would be good at this job because I like to drive and talk on the phone. Please give me a call, okay?

Greetings! My name is Evangeline Brody! I am ready to become your new assistant! Everybody says I have a bubbly personality and I really like flowers! I know a lot about computers too, so you should definitely give me a call so we can talk about how I can be an asset to your company!

Cara felt exhausted just reading Evangeline's email. She deleted it, and the next three responses, too. But the next response? Hmm.

Good afternoon. I have been a stay-at-home mom for the past seven years, but prior to that I worked as an in-house floral designer at Publix in Atlanta. I have basic computer skills, but am willing to learn any programs you need. I have a valid driver's license, and although my work references are a little out of date, I can offer character references from my neighbors and my pastor. I hope to hear from you soon. Best wishes, Ginny Best.

Cara typed as fast as she could.

Hi Ginny. Would love to meet you for interview. Can you be here tomorrow morning at 9 a.m.? She added the shop's address and phone number.

45

Jack and Ryan Finnerty sat on the tailgate of Jack's truck, finishing off their lunch of convenience-store heat-'n'-eat burritos and iced tea. Jack kicked the dust from his work boots and loudly crunched the ice from his cup.

"Hey, bro, what's with you?" Ryan asked, balling up the paper burrito wrapper and tossing it into the back of the truck along with the rest of the day's trash.

"Nothin'. Why?"

"You're all, like, happy and stuff. Right now, you're sitting there with this shit-eating grin on your face. And I know it's not because of the excellent cuisine we just consumed."

"Probably just gas," Jack said, thumping his chest with his fist and summoning up a belch on command, a talent he'd possessed since kindergarten.

Ryan matched his belch.

"Mom would be so proud," Jack said.

"So, back to why you're in such a great mood lately. Like the best mood you've been in since, like, a long time."

"Since Zoey left you mean?"

"Well, yeah. You heard from her?"

"Nope."

"You seeing somebody new?" Ryan studied his brother with deepening suspicion. "Wait a minute. I know that look. You're not just seeing somebody. You're sleeping with somebody."

"I don't know what you're talking about," Jack said, tossing his burrito wrapper at the trash heap.

"Sure you do. You were moping around, moody and grouchy as hell, for weeks after Zoey took off. All during the wedding, you were a total sad bastard. But now, this past couple weeks, you're Mister Happy Face. Mister Happy Face who's getting laid on a regular basis. Even Torie's noticed you were acting different."

Jack hopped down off the tailgate. "Enough chitchat. Let's go finish sanding that floor so we can get the first layer of stain put down before we knock off tonight. I told Libba we'd put down the first coat of poly tomorrow morning. The wedding's less than three weeks away."

"I'll get back to work as soon as you tell me who the lucky lady is that you're getting lucky with." Ryan leaned back on his elbows and watched his older brother rebuckling his tool belt. "Is it somebody I know?"

Jack tried to look indignant. "I would never kiss and tell."

"Sure you would. Come on, gimme something here. Some vicarious enjoyment."

"What's that supposed to mean? You're the one who's still on his honeymoon."

"Tell that to my bride. When Torie's not barfing up her breakfast she's locked herself in the bedroom crying about how fat her ass is getting."

"Morning sickness? How long is that supposed to go on?"

"According to the stack of books on her bedside table, it's usually for the first trimester. But we're heading into week thirteen right now, and I don't mind telling you, it's been a long dry spell, if you know what I mean."

Jack nodded sympathetically. "I feel for you."

"Just gimme some details. It somehow makes my situation more bearable if I at least know my big brother is getting some."

"Anybody ever tell you you're a pig?"

"All the time. Who is she?"

"I haven't even said I'm seeing somebody."

"You don't have to. I know the signs when I see 'em. Anyway, good for you. I was almost on the verge of agreeing to let Torie fix you up with one of her girlfriends."

"Thanks, but no thanks."

At the end of the day the two brothers climbed into Jack's truck and steered it back across the Talmadge Memorial Bridge, home to Savannah. Their skin and clothes were coated with a thick dusting of sawdust, their clothes damp with sweat.

They listened to the radio and discussed the plan for the next day's work.

"Other than not too much going on in the bedroom, how's everything else going with you guys?" Jack asked.

"Good," Ryan said. "I promised Torie we could go pick out a crib for the nursery this weekend. Which reminds me, I'll drive myself tomorrow. I'm supposed to meet her at the doctor's office at three. We're going to see an ultrasound of the baby."

"Cool. So you'll know if it's a boy or a girl?"

"That's what they tell me."

"I got five bucks says it's a girl," Jack said.

"That's what Mom says too," Ryan said. "I don't care either way. Boy, girl, just so it's healthy—and looks like her but has my temperament."

"I heard that," Jack said. "Do you guys see much of Torie's folks?

"Not as much as they'd like. Torie talks to Lillian all the time. I try to keep my distance. Her old man's all right—but Lillian? What a mouth that woman has on her. Swear to God, she wakes up every day and has a beef with some-body."

"Like who?" Jack asked, trying to sound indifferent.

"Anybody. Everybody. The dry cleaner who melted a button on her favor-ite jacket, the neighbor whose cat keeps crapping in her garden. Oh yeah, her current obsession is with some silver piece she claims our wedding florist stole."

"For real?"

"Yeah. It's crazy. Remember Cara, from our wedding? Real cute gal. You danced with her at the reception."

"I think I remember her," Jack said vaguely.

"Anyway, after the reception was over, Torie's folks went to the Bahamas for a getaway. When she got back, Cara returned all the silver they used at the reception. Except this one antique doohickey went missing. Apparently it's pretty old, belonged to her grandmother or somebody. Lillian went ballistic. She went over there, accused Cara of stealing it, called the cops and everything."

"Wow. That's pretty radical."

"Torie told Lillian that Cara wouldn't do anything like that. You met Cara. She's no thief. But once Lillian gets something in her head, she's like a damn bulldog, keeps chewing and tussling, and nobody can call her off."

"So what happens now? After she called in the cops?"

Ryan shrugged and wiped the sweat from his dust-caked forehead. "Some detective came over to talk to Lillian, then went to see Cara. They've talked to the assistant too. And I guess they're checking pawn shops around town to see if it turns up."

"But the cops aren't gonna arrest the florist, right? I mean, they can't prove she stole the thing, like you said."

"For all we know, somebody took the damn thing home from the wedding with 'em. You were there, everybody was blitzed. In the meantime, Lillian is bad-mouthing poor Cara all over town."

"Seems like a shame," Jack said. "Can't Torie do anything to calm Lillian down?"

"She's tried. In fact, they had a big fight over it last weekend. Now Lillian's not talking to Torie, which is fine by me."

"In-laws."

Jack turned the truck onto East Forty-sixth Street and pulled alongside the curb in front of his brother's Craftsman bungalow. "Porch railing looks good," he said, nodding toward the house.

"Yeah, it worked out okay," Ryan said. He gathered his tools and stepped out of the truck. "See you in the morning. Remember, I don't need you to pick me up."

As soon as he'd dropped his brother off, Jack headed north, toward downtown. He found himself smiling, and whistling. Mister Happy Face, Ryan had called him. Maybe he was. Maybe he had something to smile about these days.

He found himself cruising slowly past Bloom, on West Jones Street. It was nearly seven, but Cara hadn't brought in the garden cart full of plants she kept outside the shop. He halfway considered stopping and offering to help her bring it in, then, glancing down at himself, thought better of it. Maybe he'd go home, shower, then call and ask her out to dinner. Between all the weddings she always had on weekends, and his amped-up timetable for the Strayhorn project, they still hadn't had what he considered a real date.

He picked up his cell phone and tapped her number. It rang three times, and then went to voicemail. Jack frowned. She must be working on something. He knew she had a wedding over the weekend, and that her assistant was slacking off.

"Hey, it's me," he said. "I just rolled past your place and it looks like you're working. How about I take you out to dinner tonight? I'm headed home to shower. Call me, okay?"

Jack thought about the matter that had put a smile on his face earlier in the afternoon. He'd almost confided in Ryan. He and his brother were close, best friends, if you got right down to it. But then he'd decided it wouldn't be fair to Cara.

He hesitated, then tapped her number.

"Me again," he said ruefully. "Listen, I've got a proposition for you. Maybe we can talk about it over dinner."

When he got to his block of Macon Street, he pounded the steering wheel in frustration. A pair of bright yellow sawhorses were pulled across the street, and city work crews were busily tearing up the pavement.

"What the hell?" he muttered, taking a left turn down the lane. He had a single narrow parking space in back of his cottage, but he preferred parking on the well-lit street out front, since he still hadn't taken the time to install a motion-activated light in the backyard as a deterrent to thieves.

Grumbling, he shoehorned the truck into his allotted space between two sets of garbage cans. He got out of the truck, locked it, then went around to fetch his heavy tool kit. No way he'd leave it in the truck for any passing thugs to steal.

He had to set the toolbox down while he sorted through the keys on his ring to find the small one that fit the back-gate padlock. Finding it, he unlocked the gate, stepped into his ill-kempt back garden, and locked it again, tugging hard on the padlock to make sure it was secure. He wasn't taking any chances on Shaz making any more great escapes.

Although, come to think of it, the last time she'd gotten out, things had worked out okay.

"Shaz!" He looked around the yard, expecting to see the big white furball come bounding full-speed at him. He wasn't the only one at this address whose mood had improved lately.

Since he'd started taking her on regular walks, and even out to the job site some days, Shaz was a different dog. She was lively, playful, energetic, what you expected from a puppy.

But where the hell was she? He'd put her out in the yard before leaving this morning, being careful to make sure she had fresh water in her bowl, food, and chew toys. He'd bought a dog door that would allow Shaz access to the kitchen when he was gone, but hadn't had time to install it yet.

He peered around the yard, checking to see if she was nestled in the shade beneath the garden's only tree, a large water oak that desperately needed limbing up. No Shaz.

"Shaz!" Jack was starting to worry. Had she somehow managed to get out some other way? He scanned the fence line, but there was no sign that she'd managed to burrow beneath it, and there was no way she could have jumped the six-foot-high stockade fence.

His pulse raced as he considered the alternatives. Could somebody have broken in and taken the dog? How? The gate had been locked. He hurried to the back porch and tried the door. Locked. He turned the key and stepped into the kitchen, hoping, against logic, that Shaz had magically figured out a way to get inside.

"Shaz!"

"Wowf!" The dog raced into the kitchen and planted her paws on his chest, her tail wagging a mile a minute.

"Damn, girl, you scared me. How the hell did you get in here?"

"Jack?"

For a moment, he could have sworn his heart nearly stopped from a combination of shock and fright.

A woman's voice. Faint, but distinct, and it was coming from the front of the house.

"Jack, is that you?"

46

She was curled up on the sofa, dressed only in a bra and panties, drinking one of his Dos Equis beers. Her blond hair was lank and she wore no makeup, and there were dark circles under her eyes. A pair of battered Mexican leather sandals sat on the floor, along with her oversized pocketbook.

"Surprise!"

Shaz jumped up on the sofa and laid across her mistress's lap. Reunited at last.

Jack just stared.

"Zoey? What are you doing here?"

She offered him a weak smile. "I came back."

"So I see. Why?"

Zoey put the beer down on the floor. "What do you mean, why? I came back because I missed you." She kissed the top of Shaz's head, and the adoring puppy rewarded her with a lavish lick on the chin.

"What about Jiminy Cricket? Won't you be missing him?"

Her lips were dried and cracked, but she still managed to form her signature Zoey Ackerman pout.

"Jesus H. Christ, Jack. For the millionth time, his name is Jamey. Jamey Buttons. And for your information, that's all over."

"I thought you were on a cruise ship. For like six weeks. What'd you do? Swim back to shore?"

"In case you haven't noticed, I happen to be pretty damn sick. Ever hear of a thing called norovirus?"

"What? That's the name of your boyfriend's new band?"

"Ha ha. Don't you ever watch the news? Norovirus is a highly contagious virus that's like, the scourge of cruise ships. We were just off Raritan on our last trip when people started getting sick. I was teaching a Pilates class on the sunset deck when all of a sudden, I just, well, I barely made it to the bathroom. And the next thing I know, everybody else in my class is barfing and . . . you know."

"Diarrhea?"

She shuddered. "I barely made it back to my cabin in time. Ten minutes later, here comes Jamey—and now he's sick!"

"Too bad," Jack said.

"Have you ever seen one of the bathrooms on those cruise ships? They're like the size of a telephone booth. And we had to share it!"

"Poor you."

She narrowed her eyes. "You think it's funny, don't you? I thought I was dying. For two whole days, I couldn't leave our cabin. And neither could he. It was beyond disgusting. And there was like, nobody to help us. Almost everybody on the whole ship was sick. I kept ringing for the steward, but he was sick too. Finally, somebody brought some Gatorade and some saltines, but I couldn't keep anything down. I lost six pounds in three days."

"But you lived," Jack said.

"No thanks to that jerk Jamey." She sighed dramatically. "We are so over, it's not even real. I guess you never really know somebody till you're locked up in a shoebox-sized room with them with raging diarrhea and nausea, huh?"

"Words of wisdom," Jack said. "Very sage. But you still haven't told me how you ended up back here."

"They had to turn the ship around and go back to port in Lauderdale two days early," Zoey said. "They gave all the passengers discount vouchers for another trip and stuff, and the cruise line wanted me to stay on, and work on another of their ships, because now they have to completely sanitize the one we were on, but I was like, no effin' way. I hope I never see another cruise ship as long as I live. Or Jamey. I got off the boat Wednesday, but I was too sick and weak to travel, so I got a room near the port. Then, this morning, I drove straight here."

"To my place."

It took a moment for that to sink in. "Our place. I live here, Jack."

He squatted on the floor beside the sofa so that he could be at eye level. "Zoey, you left me. You said you were in love with another guy, so you packed up your clothes, and you left."

Huge tears welled up in Zoey's blue eyes. "It was a mistake," she whispered. "I, I can't explain it. That thing they say about women, going for musicians? It's true! He had like a spell on me. But it wasn't real. I figured that out. The whole time I was sick, I just kept thinking, if I get off this boat alive, I'm going back to Jack, and I'll never leave him again."

She grabbed his hand and clutched it to her chest. "I missed you so much, Jackie."

His cell phone rang. He stood, awkwardly, and pulled it from his pocket, checking the caller ID. It was Cara.

"Jackie?" Zoey looked up at him expectantly.

"I gotta take this call," he said, his voice brusque. He turned and strode back into the kitchen.

"Hey, you," Cara said. "I just heard your message. I'd love some dinner, if it's not too late."

He paused and glanced back over his shoulder. Zoey now stood in the doorway from the living room, glaring at him. Her skin was deeply tanned, but she looked gaunt.

"Uh," he stammered. "I just got in myself, and I haven't even showered yet."

"I can wait," Cara said. "What, thirty minutes?"

"The thing is, there's been kind of an unexpected development here."

"Shaz didn't run off again, did she?"

"No, nothing like that," Jack said. "I've got some out-of-town company, is all. Sort of out of the blue."

Zoey frowned. "Since when am I company? Who are you talking to? Is that a woman?"

"Jack?" Cara said. "What kind of company?"

Shaz trotted into the kitchen and rubbed up against his legs. He looked helplessly from Zoey to the dog to the back door. If he left right now, he could make it over to Cara's house, explain everything in person. And maybe Zoey would dematerialize.

"Hey!" Zoey called loudly. "Whoever is on the phone? Jack can't talk right now. Because his girlfriend is back. And he needs to take care of her. So just hang up, okay?"

He covered the phone with his hand. "Shut the fuck up," he said hoarsely, slamming the kitchen door in Zoey's face.

"Cara?"

There was a long pause.

"Oh," Cara said. "Was that really Zoey?"

"Yeah," he said slowly. "When I got home from work a little while ago, she was here. That cruise ship she was on? Everybody got some kind of stomach virus. She said they got back to port yesterday, and she drove here today. Out of the clear blue."

"*Siren of the Seas*? I heard about that on the news. That's the ship she was on?"

"I don't know and I don't care," Jack said, wearily rubbing his hand across his face, staring at his own grubby reflection in the kitchen window. "You gotta believe me, Cara. I had no idea she was coming back. I don't want her here. We're through. I was just trying to tell her that when you called."

"What's she want from you? What happened to the Jimmy Buffett impersonator?"

"She says they broke up. I guess she thinks she can just show up here and I'll take her back. But she's dead wrong."

"What'll you do?"

"Tell her to leave," Jack said. "She sure as hell can't stay here with me."

"Is she still sick?"

"Zoey? She's fine! Okay, it looks like she lost a little weight. But she was well enough to drive seven hours straight from Fort Lauderdale, so as far as I'm concerned, she can just keep driving."

"That seems awfully mean," Cara said. "The people on that ship were really sick. Some of them are still in the hospital."

He snorted. "You don't know Zoey. She's like a cockroach. No matter how many times you stomp on her, she just gets up and keeps going. Look. Are we still on for dinner? Let me grab a shower and I'll be over there in fifteen."

"Are you sure?"

"Positive. What do you feel like for dinner?"

"Doesn't matter. After the day I've had, I'll just be happy to see a friendly face."

"I can do friendly," Jack said. "Very friendly."

He stalked back into the living room. Zoey was stretched out on the sofa, with Shaz perched at her feet. She gave Jack a playful wink. "Was that your new squeeze? Did you tell her about me?"

"None of your business," he said, looking around the room. "By the way, where the hell are your clothes?"

She wrinkled her nose. "Gross. The health department people who met us at the port told us we should make sure and like, sanitize everything. So we don't spread the virus. Or get it again. God forbid. As soon as I got here, I threw everything into the washing machine."

"Everything? What were you planning to wear in the meantime?"

She arched one eyebrow. "I wasn't planning to wear anything. Actually, you kind of spoiled my surprise, coming in the back door the way you did. I had this big welcome back to Jack all planned out."

"Yeah. I remember the last surprise you planned for me. I came home to an empty house, and a puppy who'd peed all over the floor. I'm pretty much over your surprises, Zoey."

She stood up, stretched, and reached her arms out toward him. "It's different this time, Jackie."

"Forget it," he said, deftly stepping sideways. "Not interested."

Zoey was not to be deterred. "I'm not contagious."

"No," Jack said, deadpan. "You're not. Whatever you've got, I'm finally immune to it. I'm gonna take a shower now, then I'm going out for a while. While I'm gone, I suggest you finish up your laundry, get dressed, and move along down the road."

"What? You're kicking me out? Just like that?"

"Just like that," he agreed. He headed for the shower. "Why don't you check the washing machine? I bet your stuff is clean by now."

He'd just stepped into the shower when he heard the bathroom doorknob turn. And then turn again. Jack chuckled and turned his face up to the nozzle, letting the water stream over his face.

Zoey pounded on the door. "You locked the door?" she hollered. "Asshole! What if I need to pee?"

"Take it outside," he called back. He reached for the soap and frowned when he saw the familiar silver and pink bottles of shampoo and conditioner on the window ledge. She'd already begun the process of moving in again. This time, though, the process would stop. Tonight.

When he'd toweled off and put on clean clothes, he walked out to the living room to find Zoey still reclining on the leather sofa. Thankfully, she'd gotten dressed, and was wearing an oversized blue-and-white-striped shirt and jeans. She'd combed her hair and twisted it back from her face and was looking semihuman again.

"Is that my shirt?" he asked.

She shrugged. "You never wear this shirt, so I didn't think you'd mind. My stuff's still in the dryer. I found a pair of my old jeans in the laundry room. You look nice. Where are you off to?"

"Out."

"Like, out to dinner? Not that you've asked, but I haven't had anything to eat. Not in hours and hours. And there's nothing in the fridge. I checked."

"Maybe you should go find yourself something then. Right after you pack up your stuff. I'm not taking you to dinner. And you can't stay here, Zoey."

"Where would you suggest I go? This was my home too, Jack. I can't believe you're being like this."

"Believe it," he said. "Call up one of your girlfriends. Or go to a motel."

She sat up then and crossed one long, lithe leg over the other. "The thing is, I'm sort of short of funds right at the minute. We only get paid every two weeks. I gave the cruise line this address, and they're supposed to forward my final check week after next."

Zoey gave him a sad little smile. "See? You just have to put up with me for two more weeks. Then I'll get out of your hair. If that's what you really want."

"Oh no." He shook his head emphatically. "Oh, hell, to the no. You're not pulling that broke and helpless crap on me again. You've been living on a cruise ship for what, three, four months? Your room and food was free, you had no living expenses. If you're broke, that's your problem. Not mine."

She turned on the tears again. "I can't believe you're being like this. I told you I was sorry."

"Actually, you never once said you were sorry," he pointed out. "Not that I care. Here's the deal, Zoey. I'm leaving now." He reached into his pocket, pulled out a money clip, and peeled off five twenty-dollar bills. "This is my parting gift to you. Buy yourself some dinner, get a room somewhere, whatever. Just make sure you're gone by the time I get back here tonight."

Zoey looked at the bills with obvious disbelief. "A hundred lousy bucks? That's it?"

"Yup." He grabbed the leash from the hook by the front door and whistled. "Shaz! Come."

The dog looked up at Zoey, and then at Jack.

"Shaz!"

She trotted over and Jack hooked the leash to her collar. "Let's go girl." He picked up his truck keys and headed for the back door.

"You can't take my dog," Zoey said, running after him. "I bought her. She's mine. You didn't even want a puppy."

Jack kept walking. "She grew on me. Anyway, possession is nine-tenths of the law."

"You can't keep her," Zoey called. "As soon as I get my check, I'm taking her with me."

Jack stopped dead in his tracks and turned around. "That reminds me." He held out his hand, palm side up.

"What?" she said sullenly.

"My house key. I'd like it back. You can just push the thumb lock when you leave."

She stalked out of the room and returned a minute later. She flipped the key, and he caught it in midair.

He was almost out the back door when, out of the corner of his eye, he saw a beer can go sailing past his head before banging against the wall. Beer dripped down the door casing. He needed to paint anyway.

"Asshole!" she screamed.

47

Cara stepped out the front door just as Jack was pressing the doorbell.

"I brought Shaz. I thought she and Poppy could hang out together," Jack said.

"Good idea." They took Shaz outside, where Poppy seemed ecstatic at the prospect of company, and made sure both dogs had water and toys before heading back out to the street.

"You look nice," Cara said, as Jack leaned in to kiss her. "And you smell nice too."

"You clean up pretty good yourself," he said, his lips lingering on hers. "And you smell way better than me."

"Girls are supposed to smell better than boys," she said, then gestured down at her own capris and sheer cotton flower-printed tunic. "Am I underdressed? Where are we going?"

"You're not underdressed at all. I thought we'd go to Guale, over on Drayton Street. Does that sound all right?"

"I've seen Guale written up in magazines, but I've never been. Isn't it pretty fancy?"

"Not really. The food's great, but I've gone in there wearing jeans before, and nobody even looks twice. Parking's a pain though. Is it too hot to walk over there?"

"Walking's good." She lifted her right foot to show off her Kelly-green sandals. "I've even got on flats."

It was dusk now, and the streetlights had come on, and the faintest damp breeze ruffled the fronds of a palm tree on the corner. As they were crossing Whitaker Street, Jack casually reached over and clasped Cara's hand. And he didn't let go when they'd reached the other side. She flashed him a smile and kept walking.

"What?" he asked.

"Nothing."

"Tell me."

"You'll think I'm being ridiculous."

"Probably. Tell me anyway?"

"I don't know. This just . . . it feels so nice. And normal. Walking down the street holding hands with a cute boy . . ."

"A boy? You make it sound like we're teenagers."

"All of a sudden, I feel like a teenager. I've truly had the most appalling day in a most appalling week, and then Jack Finnerty shows up at my door, wearing a starched dress shirt and polished loafers, and smelling like aftershave. And he's taking me to dinner . . . and for a few minutes there, it made me forget my troubles. It made me remember what it's like to have somebody to care about." She blushed. "I told you it was silly."

"C'mere," Jack said. He pulled her into the darkened lane between Charlton and Jones and pressed her back against the wall of a pink stucco town house. "I'll make you feel like a teenager." He ran his hands beneath her shirt and slipped his tongue in her mouth.

Cara gave a very small, very feeble squeak of protest. She kissed him back, twined her arms around his neck, pulled him closer. Emboldened, he worked his thumbs under the band of her bra, teasing her nipples until she gasped and gave him a gentle backward shove.

"I am *not* having sex with you in an alley," she said, smoothing down her rumpled tunic.

He chuckled and kissed her again. "We don't call them alleys in Savannah. We call them lanes. Anyway, you're the one who said you liked feeling like a teenager."

"I didn't say I liked being felt up like a teenager in public," Cara countered. "There's a time and a place for everything."

Jack sighed and straightened his own shirt. "Same old story I used to get in high school."

They'd just given the waiter their dinner order when Jack's cell phone buzzed. He took it from his pocket, read the text message, and gave a loud grunt of exasperation before putting it away again.

Cara raised a questioning eyebrow.

"Zoey. I'm not answering her because I don't want to encourage her."

"Just out of curiosity, what does she want?"

"She claims her car won't start. Wants me to come give her a jump. Okay, poor choice of words. Her battery is dead. Or so she claims. It's all a ruse."

Cara leaned forward. "Can I ask you something? What's Zoey like? How did the two of you end up together in the first place?"

"How does anybody end up together? Dumb luck. I was dumb, she was lucky. Or the other way around. How about we talk about something else? Anything else? You said you'd had a bad day? Tell me about that."

Cara looked around the dining room. She was glad they had come here tonight. This was good. A nice distraction. The tablecloth was pale yellow linen. There was a candle in a glass jar, and a small clear bud vase held a stem of pink alstroemeria that was a day past its prime. Perhaps she should talk to the owners about doing flowers for them. Her eyes rested on Jack. With a start she realized she might never get tired of looking at him. He had a tiny spatter of white paint on his left earlobe. His sunburnt nose was peeling. She looked at his big hands. His left hand was resting on the tabletop and he was clutching a glass of red wine in his right hand, and she noticed his thumbnail was blackened.

Her day?

"Where do I start? The Colonel continues to hound me about my bad debt and bad business decisions. Also, another contractor showed up at the shop this morning, all set to come in and look around on behalf of Cullen Kane."

"That guy," Jack said.

"And on top of everything else, I fired Bert."

"For real?"

"He left me no choice. He's been coming in late, leaving early, just generally slacking off. I figured he had some new boyfriend, but he kept pushing the limits. And this thing with Lillian Fanning's missing epergne, he kept acting as though I was the one accusing him of stealing it. I never accused him. Whatever else he might be, Bert is no thief. Finally, today, I'd had it. I told him if he left early he could stay gone. So he did."

"Nothing else you could do," Jack said.

"Not long after that the second contractor showed up. He had a key to my place. He let himself in the back gate. That was the final straw. I was so mad, Jack, I couldn't even see straight. Who the hell does this guy think he is?

"I drove over to his shop——I mean, excuse me, Cullen Kane Floral Design Studio. And you'll never guess who was working as Cullen's new receptionist. Bert. My Bert!"

"Kane hired him that quickly?"

"Cullen Kane is Bert's new boyfriend. That's who Bert's been sneaking around with all these weeks now. And that's how Cullen found out my landlady died. Bert 'just happened to mention' to Kane that Bernice Bradley had died, and that Sylvia Bradley was refusing to fix my air-conditioning."

"Bert was spying on you for Cullen Kane? I thought the guy was practically your best friend."

"I thought so too," Cara said sadly. "Bert was probably planning to quit and go to work for Cullen all along. And he didn't even have the decency to feel guilty about betraying me. He just sat at that stupid desk wearing that stupid Cullen Kane T-shirt, smirking at me. He even had the nerve to ask me if I wanted a bottle of Perrier, or some champagne!"

"Did you let him have it?"

"I did. And then I went barreling to the back room to let his boss have it too."

"I'd like to have heard that."

"No you wouldn't have. You would have been ashamed of me. I'm such a spineless jellyfish. I ended up groveling at his feet—begging him to give me a new lease and let me stay in my building."

"I'm guessing you weren't successful?"

Cara nodded. "Big mistake. Kane was actually enjoying himself, telling me all about his big plans to gut the place and put on a new roof and all new systems, and then raise the rent—which he said he knew I could never afford. Finally, I flat-out asked him why he was so determined to destroy me. And he just looked at me—like I was nothing. And he said what every megalomaniac says these days when they do something unconscionable. 'It's nothing personal. It's just business.'"

"Bastard," Jack said. "So, what now?"

It was noisy in the restaurant, the tables were close together, so close she could hear snatches of conversation from all directions. A woman, her voice slow and syrupy: *"I told Mama you have to be firm with these people. Otherwise they walk all over you, but you know Mama."* A man's deep voice: *"You can't get there direct from Savannah. We'll lay over in Atlanta and get into Kansas City after five on Monday."*

Cara heard her own voice, too. It sounded tinny and somehow disembodied. "I've got to leave my building. Two weeks. That's all the time I have before I have to get out. Two weeks. To pack up and find a new shop and a new apartment."

All day long, she'd managed to push *that* reality to the back of her mind. She'd busied herself with the tedium of what had to get done, ordering flowers and answering emails and feeding Poppy, and dozens of other little things. But the enormity of what she was facing was gaining strength and velocity. And as she thought about it now, it felt like a huge boulder, inescapable, careering down a mountain, threatening to crush her under its weight.

She hadn't realized she was crying until she felt the big sloppy tears sliding down her cheek. And then she was full-out sobbing, sitting in the middle of a crowded restaurant, bawling like a baby.

"Oh, God," she said, choking back the tears. The voices around her quieted, and she knew people were staring. She crushed the linen napkin to her face, wishing she could crawl under the table.

"Heeyyyy." Jack scooted his chair beside hers. He put his arm around her shoulder. Her chest heaved, and she couldn't catch her breath. He put a glass of water in her hand. "Drink this."

She managed a sip. "I'm . . . so . . . sorry. . . ." The words were wobbly.

The waiter came with their meals, crispy flounder for him, shrimp bisque for her. He stood—statuelike, unsure of the proper thing to do in such a situation.

"Could you box that up for us?" Jack said quietly. "And bring the check?" Of course Jack Finnerty would know exactly what to do.

Despite Cara's feeble protests, he called a cab, and five minutes later he'd unlocked the door to the shop, and they were upstairs, and he'd sat her down on the sofa. While he went out to the garden to check on Shaz and Poppy, she went into the bathroom to try to pull herself together.

She was a mess. Her face was blotchy, her nose was red and running, and there were mascara trails down both cheeks. She washed her face and combed her hair and put on some lip gloss.

Jack was waiting in the living room with a glass of wine. She took a sip, and then another.

"Better?" he asked.

She nodded, afraid if she tried to speak the tears would start anew. He sat down on the sofa beside her, and gathered her into his arms. She pressed her face into his starched shirtfront, he rested his chin on the top of her hair.

"It's gonna be okay," he said.

The phone in his pocket buzzed. He swore softly and ignored it, but five minutes later, it buzzed again.

Jack shifted onto his left hip, took out the phone, and looked at the text.

"Dammit, Zoey," he muttered.

Cara looked up. He held out the phone so he could read the message.

Battery dead. No way to get to motel. Found unlocked window. Bring me some pizza?

"I never leave windows unlocked over there. I'm sure she broke one so she could get back in the house," Jack said.

"You should go home and check on her," Cara said, hoping he wouldn't.

He was already typing, and held up the phone again, so she could read his response.

Call a cab. Get out of my house and get your own pizza.

"You sure have a way with the ladies," Cara said.

"Zoey ain't no lady."

After a while, Jack heated up their dinners, and was surprised to find she was actually hungry. They drank another glass of wine and rinsed out the dinner dishes.

"Will you stay here tonight?" Cara asked, drying the glasses and putting them back on the shelf where she'd so carefully arranged them on moving day two years ago.

"Do you want me to?"

Cara grasped his shirtfront, pulled him to her, and whispered in his ear. "There's a time and a place for everything, remember?"

"I'll bring in the dogs," Jack said.

"Better text Zoey and tell her not to wait up," Cara teased. She really was feeling a little better.

48

As soon as he pulled up to the house with the peeling pea-green paint on East Forty-Fourth Street Tuesday morning, Jack Finnerty felt the old familiar sensation of dread seep into his pores. He hadn't been to this house in more than twenty-five years, but not much had changed. The grass was still bone-dry, because the old lady was too cheap to turn on a sprinkler. The shrubbery near the house still needed trimming and the concrete sidewalk was still cracked and potholed. The one thing that surprised him was how small it looked now.

But then, the last time he'd been here he'd been what, ten years old? He'd pedal slowly over here every Wednesday after school let out at Charles Ellis School on nearby Washington Avenue, lean the bike against the kickstand, and reluctantly drag himself up this same sidewalk, with the white envelope and the five-dollar bill tucked in his pants pocket.

He rang the doorbell, and felt his stomach muscles suck in, out of some decades-old force of habit. If he'd had a shirttail he would have tucked it in, and removed his ball cap, too.

The heavy front door, still painted that same mud brown, was open, and as he looked through the screen door, he could have sworn he saw that same ghostly-gray moth-eaten Siamese cat of his childhood flit from beneath the marble-top console table in the entry hall.

A moment later, Sylvia Bradley was peering out at him through the screen. She wore a flowered print blouse and baggy blue polyester slacks, and her ever-present old-school Keds. Like the house, she looked smaller now, too. And he was startled to see that she walked with a cane.

"Jack Finnerty?" Her voice was fluty, and overly loud.

"Yes ma'am," he said.

"Well, come on in then," she said, unlatching the hook.

The house was stifling, but in his memory, it had always been stifling. She plied him with a Dixie cup of warm Hawaiian Punch, and he was certain it came from the same can she'd opened twenty-five years ago, and that it had been sitting on her kitchen counter all this time. Sylvia motioned for him to sit down in the parlor, on an excruciatingly stiff tufted red velvet sofa. He pointed at the upright piano on the opposite wall, with its books of sheet music propped above the keyboard, and the metronome sitting on top.

"Do you still give lessons?"

"Unfortunately no." She held up her right hand, its knobby joints red and swollen. "Arthritis."

"That's too bad," Jack said. "You must miss your students."

"Not really," Sylvia Bradley said. "Children today don't want to study piano. They want to play 'keyboard' and be in rock bands."

"I suppose so."

"You don't play piano anymore, do you?"

"Uh, no ma'am."

"Good. You were a terrible student. One of the worst I ever had. I never understood why your poor mother insisted you should try to learn."

Jack laughed. He thought it was probably the only time he had ever laughed in this house. "It was my dad's idea. He thought everybody should learn to appreciate music."

"Appreciate it, yes. Play it, no. What was your little brother's name?"

"Ryan."

She nodded. "That's right. He was a ginger, as I recall. Nice boy. Totally tone deaf, of course. And your baby sister. Maureen?"

"Meghan. I think by the time she came along, Dad gave up on piano. Meghan took ballet, instead." Jack cleared his throat. "I was sorry to hear about your mother."

"Thank you. You know, she was nearly ninety-one, and still cooked for both of us and did all the grocery shopping. I took her car keys away a year ago, but she was still sharp as a tack right up until that last stroke."

Sharp as a tack, Jack thought, and mean as a snake, that would describe Bernice Bradley. And her daughter.

"You said you had a business matter to discuss with me?" Sylvia said, re- garding him through glasses with lenses so thick and convex they gave her the look of a giant insect. "What type of business are you in these days, Jack?"

"I'm a contractor. Specializing in historic restoration. Ryan and I are busi- ness partners."

She looked at him with distaste. "I have contractors leaving flyers and business cards in my mailbox every week. As though I would hire some- body who has to resort to passing out flyers to get work."

"Um . . . that's not really why I wanted to talk to you. Actually, I came here today to ask you about a piece of property you own downtown."

Suddenly the room got very quiet, and the ticking from the grandfather clock in the corner seemed synchronized with his own pulse-beat.

"Mother and I own quite a few properties downtown. My father worked for the C&S Bank, you know, but he believed in buying real estate, not stocks and bonds."

"Smart man," Jack said. "I'm probably not anywhere near as smart as your father, or as successful, but I believe in buying real estate too. Especially in this last economic downturn, Ryan and I found that we were able to pick up some distressed properties for a pretty modest investment."

"I don't own any distressed properties," the old lady shot back.

"Oh, no, no ma'am. I didn't mean to insinuate that," he said quickly. "Not at all. The thing is, I've always admired that three-story building you own on

West Jones Street. I like the retail mix on the ground floor, with the residential above it. And of course, that's one of the most desirable streets in the historic district."

"How do you happen to know I own that building?" Sylvia asked. "Are you one of those scam artists who hang around the courthouse records room, looking to make a quick killing?"

"Not at all. I only know about it because I got a call from a man named Cullen Kane—a florist here in town. Somebody gave him my name, and he called me up and asked me to take a look at West Jones Street. To give him estimates to do some work on the building. And he mentioned that he was buying it from you."

"That's right," she said cautiously. "We close on the thirtieth. Mother and I always kept our properties up, but, well, tenants these days are so demanding, especially the young woman who's renting the space right now. She's another florist, you know, but every week she had a new complaint. Mr. Kane called me up out of the blue, asked me what I wanted for the building, and I thought, Mother is gone. Why not? I named a price, and he countered, then I countered, and we agreed to it."

"Just like that?" Jack asked.

"He sent me a beautiful orchid plant," Sylvia confided. "And he has lovely manners, for a homosexual, I mean."

Jack almost choked on his Hawaiian Punch. "Miss Sylvia, would it be nosy of me to ask how much he offered you for the building?"

She told him, and he nearly choked again. Sylvia Bradley might be old, but she'd managed to squeeze top dollar out of Cullen Kane.

He put his Dixie cup carefully down on the marble-top coffee table. "I wish I'd known you were going to sell that building, Miss Sylvia. Because I would have been able to offer you more than what Cullen Kane did."

"Is that so?"

"Yes, ma'am," Jack said.

"How much more?"

He did some quick, painful calculations and named his price.

She sighed loudly. "I wish I had known you were interested, Jack. It would have been nice to sell it to one of my former pupils. I think Mother would have liked that. She always used to say she liked those Finnerty boys."

This was news to Jack. As far as he knew, Bernice Bradley hated all little boys, especially if they were named Jack or Ryan Finnerty. He'd once made the mistake of leaving his bicycle lying down in the driveway during a piano lesson, and Bernice had run right over it in her dark blue Pontiac.

"I guess you have a legally binding contract with Kane? No way to get out of it?"

Sylvia pursed her lips. "I could tell him I'd changed my mind and decided not to sell."

"He might make trouble for you," Jack warned. "From what I hear, Cullen Kane is a pretty astute businessman. He usually gets what he sets out to buy."

"Maybe not this time," Sylvia said. "My father taught me more about buying and selling real estate than either of you two will ever know. You leave him to me."

Jack's face lit up. "So we have a deal? For the price I named?"

"All cash?" Sylvia asked. "It will make things simpler."

Now Jack understood that foreboding feeling he'd experienced coming up Sylvia Bradley's front steps. He'd been a lamb led to slaughter.

"All cash," he said. He held out his arm and helped her to her feet, and as she was showing him to the door, she stopped suddenly.

"There is one other thing," she said. "A little leak in the roof over my back mud porch. My laundry room. I'm sure a reputable contractor could take care of that in no time."

Half an hour later, he slid behind the steering wheel of his truck and looked down at the dark dress pants he'd worn especially for this meeting. They were covered with fine gray cat hair. As he pulled away from the curb, he saw Sylvia Bradley, silhouetted in the doorway. Cullen Kane had gotten off easy with a potted orchid. As for Jack, he and a helper would be returning that afternoon to tear down the termite-infested mud porch and rebuild it. Gratis.

Materials alone would probably cost a couple thousand, but all he could think about was the look on Cara's face tomorrow when he would tell her what he'd done.

49

"You did what?" Cara had been about to take a bite of her sandwich, but instead she put it down on her paper plate and picked up the sheaf of papers he'd just presented with a flourish.

The look on her face was not anything like what he'd pictured. Her jaw tightened and her eyes narrowed as she skimmed the sales contract for West Jones Street. Her face paled when she got to the page with the sales price.

"Is this some kind of joke?" she demanded. "Because if it is, I don't get the punch line."

"It's no joke. I bought it. Sylvia Bradley was my piano teacher when I was a kid. I went to see her yesterday morning, and I bought this building. For you."

Cara stabbed at the contract with her fingertip. "You paid twice what it's worth! Are you crazy? Where would you get that kind of money?"

Now Jack put down his own sandwich. He was confused. Where was the jumping up and down? Where were the screams of joy and wild kisses of gratitude he'd been anticipating for the past two days?

. . .

Earlier that day, Jack and a helper arrived at Forty-fourth Street at dawn. They carted Sylvia's ancient rusted Kenmore washer and dryer down the crumbling driveway and into the back of Jack's truck for the trip to the dump. It took only a couple hours to tear down Sylvia Bradley's mud porch. He was shocked that it hadn't just fallen off of its own accord.

Even with a cane, the old lady was pretty spry, and she stood in the weedy backyard, in her flower-print blouse and old-school Keds, and supervised as they tossed the rotted timbers into the Dumpster he'd rented.

Late Wednesday morning, after she could see the yellow pine skeleton of her new porch, Sylvia finally called him into the kitchen, offered him a paper cup of warm Hawaiian Punch and the sales contract for West Jones Street.

He reached into the pocket of his cargo shorts and brought out a white envelope with the cashier's check for the earnest money inside, just as he'd offered those five-dollar envelopes from his mother every Wednesday the year he was ten. As he handed this one over to Sylvia Bradley, he halfway expected her to ask him if he'd been practicing his finger exercises.

She ripped open the envelope and studied the check, running a swollen forefinger over the embossed bank logo.

"How did you leave things with Cullen Kane?" he asked, signing the contract with a flourish.

"Never you mind," Sylvia said. She opened a kitchen drawer and rummaged around among the rubber bands, balls of string, and nubs of pencils until she found a set of keys with a white plastic C&S Bank key fob. "Here are the keys. My father bought that building in 1953. He was always partial to West Jones Street."

Jack pocketed the keys. "I'm partial to it too. Thank you, Miss Sylvia."

At lunchtime, Jack picked up sandwiches and chips at a deli on Habersham Street, and he headed over to Bloom to share the good news with Cara, and bask in the warmth of her admiration.

"You must be insane," Cara said, shaking the contract, as though she might shake the numbers right off the paper. "This is a lot of money."

"It is a lot of money, but no, I'm not crazy," Jack said calmly. "The price is a little on the high side, but it's not terribly out of line with comparable prices in the district. I checked the tax records. It's a decent deal, Cara."

And it might have been considered a decent deal, if you didn't factor in the cost of rebuilding Sylva Bradley's mud porch, replacing her washer and dryer, and having his painters sand, prime, and repaint her house. But those were details he didn't feel the need to share with Cara at this time.

"Where did you get the money to buy this building?" Cara asked. "You told me that you and Ryan were struggling to keep your business afloat, just like me."

"That's right. It *was* a struggle. Still is. But my dad helped us out a little. In a business like ours, we're sometimes in the position to pick up a house or a building on the cheap. So that's what we did. We bought crappy houses and crappy buildings for pennies on the dollar, fixed them up, and resold for a good profit. Right now, I'm not doing a lot of flipping, so a property like West Jones, that's one I want to keep. I'm not saying we're rich, but we've done okay."

Cara tossed the papers back in his face. "I didn't ask you to do this. I didn't want you to do this."

He was dumbfounded. "I wanted to do it. For you. You were so upset the other night, about having to move and everything. And I'd been thinking about it, ever since I found out Sylvia Bradley owned your building. So I went to see her yesterday."

"Without even asking me. You just took it upon yourself to go behind my back and buy my building. Just like Cullen Kane did. And you expect me to be happy about that?"

"Hell yeah," he said. "I thought you'd be delirious. Don't you see? Now you don't have to move out. I'll start working on the building right away. Well, right after we finish up the Strayhorns' barn. We'll have to run new electrical first, and then I'll get my HVAC guy over here to see what kind of tonnage he recommends, especially if we open up the third floor."

"*We'll* run the electric. *We'll* open up the third floor? Who is this magical 'we'? You and your brother? When were you going to consult me? Or were you just going to show up here one day and start tearing down the walls?"

"Whoa, whoa, whoa." Jack held his hands up in surrender. "Don't go getting your panties all in a bunch. It's just a figure of speech. Of course I was going to consult you before I started any work. But we talked about this. The day I helped you put in that window unit, we talked about how much work this place needed."

"No. *You* talked about it. And *you* decided what would be best for me. Just like the Colonel. Just like my ex-husband. Poor, helpless Cara is too dumb to figure out life for herself, so we'll just step in and take charge and tell her how to run her life."

"It's not like that!" Jack exclaimed. "You're twisting everything all around. I thought we could fix this place up together."

"With you supplying all the money and most of the labor," Cara said. "Did it occur to you that after you make all these amazing improvements I won't be able to afford the rent here? Or were you planning to go looking for a new tenant and move me to another building in your vast array of real-estate ventures?"

"Cara, for Chrissake—I don't understand why you're getting so worked up about all this. You know I'm not going to raise your rent or kick you out. I care about you, not the money. That's the only reason I got into this."

She felt the rage bubbling up from her gut. "Men always say that, and they always lie. Because it's *always* about the money. Look at my father. He loans me money, and when I run into problems repaying it, he starts with the emotional blackmail. It's not about the money, he says. It's about financial responsibility. What he really means is, it's about control. And as long as I'm in his debt, I'm in his control. We've slept together what, Jack, five times? And you're just going to give me a building that you spent three-quarters of a million dollars to buy? How do you amortize that out? About a hundred and fifty thousand per fuck? I had no idea I was that good."

"Since you seem to be keeping track, we've slept together exactly three times," Jack said quietly. He pushed away from the table and gathered up the lunch wrappers, tossing them into the waste basket. "So it looks like you've undervalued yourself. And underestimated me, and my motives."

"Guess I'm just a typical flighty female. No head for numbers," Cara shot back. She took the sales contract, shoved it into the manila folder he'd brought it in, and held it out.

"Here. You can keep your building," she said. "I can be out of here in by the end of the month. I don't want any more gifts from any more men."

"Fine." He grabbed the envelope and headed for the shop door. "But you owe me six bucks for the lunch."

50

Ginny Best was sitting at the worktable when Cara, still bleary-eyed, got downstairs at eight o'clock. She'd made coffee, rolled the garden cart out to the street, and was already on the computer, scrolling through the day's emails.

The day was already looking up. Cara mentally congratulated herself for having the sense to offer this woman the job immediately after her interview the day before.

"Good morning." Ginny beamed. "I hope it's okay that I came in a little early. I wanted to get a jump on the hospital orders first thing."

Cara yawned. "Early is good. Early is amazing. Just make sure you write down your hours so I remember to pay you for the extra time. I'm glad you're here, because I've got a crazy day today. I'm gonna go look at a couple properties with my real-estate agent, then I've got to meet Harris and Brooke over at Cabin Creek to walk through plans for the reception and after-party. Think you can hold down the fort here by yourself?"

Ginny's serious brown eyes blinked rapidly behind the thick lens of her glasses. "How long will you be gone?"

"Better part of the day," Cara said.

Cara heard scratching coming from the back of the shop. "Back in a sec," she told her new assistant. She hurried down the hallway and opened the back door to let Poppy in from the garden.

"Good girl," Cara said, scratching the puppy's silken curls. "Come on, let's go get you a treat." The dog followed Cara back into the shop, and when she saw the newcomer standing at the flower cooler, barked happily and lunged for her.

"Ack!" Ginny stumbled backward, flailing her arms wildly. "Get off, get off!"

"Poppy, down!" Cara called. But Poppy was intent on greeting the newest member of the Bloom staff. She lunged again, planting her muddy front paws on Ginny's pale pink blouse.

"No! Bad dog, bad dog," Ginny shouted, shoving the dog violently away.

Cara grabbed for Poppy's collar. "Poppy! No." Poppy sank to the floor and looked embarrassed at her outburst.

"I'm so sorry," Cara said, standing up. "She gets excited when somebody new comes in. I know it's terrible manners, and I've got to take her back to obedience school, but really, she wouldn't hurt a fly."

Ginny looked warily at Poppy, who was now crouched under Cara's side of the worktable, gnawing on a chew toy. She glanced down at the front of her blouse, brushing at the mud stains. "I'm not really a dog person," she said, frowning. "She doesn't have to stay here all the time, does she?"

"Actually, she does. Not necessarily in the shop, all day, because I let her out into the garden to play, but yes, since I live here, or wherever we move to next, Poppy does too. Is that going to be a problem?"

Ginny bit her lip. "Don't your clients think it's kind of . . . I don't know, unprofessional—your having a pet in your place of business?"

"I've never had any complaints. In fact, most of my clients love having Poppy around."

"It's just that, when I interviewed, you didn't say anything about a dog." Ginny went to the kitchenette, wet a paper towel, and began dabbing at the front of her blouse.

"I'll be happy to pay to have that cleaned," Cara said.

"No need. It'll probably come out," Ginny said. She looked over at Poppy, who, misinterpreting the moment, lifted her head, tongue lolling, tail thumping enthusiastically. "Down," Ginny said sternly.

Cara tied a pale blue satin ribbon and wrapped it around a potted azalea in a rattan basket. "Okay," she said, standing and reaching for her purse. "I'm off. You can load everything in the van by yourself and make the deliveries, right? There are just six this morning, three for St. Joe's, two for Memorial, and one for the Rose of Sharon apartments."

Ginny nodded vigorously. "Right. That won't be any problem."

"I may be back late," Cara warned, her hand on the front door. "Alice, my real-estate agent, has several properties to show me, and I don't know how long I'll be in South Carolina. If I'm not back by five, just bring the garden cart in, and lock up, like I showed you."

"Wait," Ginny called. "What about the dog? Aren't you going to take her with you?"

"I can't," Cara said patiently. "She gets carsick unless I medicate her. Anyway, it's ninety-two degrees already. I can't leave her in a car while I look at buildings. Poppy's really no trouble, Ginny. She's house-trained, so you don't have to worry about letting her out while you run the deliveries. If you do let her into the garden, please make sure the back gate is closed and locked, and check her water bowl to make sure it's full. I'll see you in the morning."

Alice Murphy pulled her Cadillac alongside a stretch of curb on Waters Avenue. "Okay, Cara," she said, her New England accent making it sound more like "Carer." "This is the last one."

She gestured at the single-story brick building. It was boxy, with a vaguely 1960s reference, but over the years multiple owners had successfully erased any kind of architectural personality it might once have possessed. Now it was painted the color of brown mustard. The tattered remnants of a tan awning stretched over a pair of dusty plate-glass windows, which were still

painted with the name of the building's most recently departed tenants—
ACEY-DUECY AUTO DETAILING.

Cara eyed the building with disbelief. "Really? You think this is a good option?"

Alice sighed. "Oh, Cara, sweetheart. With your budget and the time frame we're working with, this is the best I can do."

She held up her hand, ticking off the building's many desirable qualities. "One, it's available immediately. You could move in today, if you wanted. Two, it's dirt cheap. The owner's desperate to get somebody in here. Three, it's big. Huge. You can have a big workspace up front, and make a nice-sized apartment in the back. And four, you've got plenty of parking."

"Wait. Back up, Alice. It doesn't already have a living space?"

"Well . . . the owner says the last tenants were sort of illegally squatting. He thinks there were at least three families staying there."

"Great. A combination flophouse and auto-detailing shop. I can't wait to see it."

Alice held out the keys and gave her an approving smile. "That's my gal."

Ten minutes later, the two women burst through the front door, alternately gagging and gasping for air.

"Oh my Lawd," Alice exclaimed, wiping at her watery eyes. "Oh my Lawd."

Cara slumped against the door of the Cadillac. "I wish I could unsee what we just saw."

"I had no idea," Alice said. "I should call that owner. I bet he doesn't know the roof caved in."

"Or that raccoons have taken up residence. Or that the last tenants left a year's worth of rotting garbage in the so-called kitchen," Cara added.

Alice shook her head. "We cross this one off the list. That just leaves us the dry cleaner's shop on Paulsen."

"Which is too small and has no yard for Poppy," Cara said.

"Or the duplex on Hall Street," Alice added. "It had parking, a courtyard garden for Poppy, and a nice apartment upstairs for you."

"And it's twice as much as I can afford, and I'm not crazy about that block. Other than that, it's perfect," Cara said.

Alice unlocked the Caddy, turned the air-conditioning on the polar-ice-cap setting, and rolled the windows down to allow the hot air to escape. "We rode by a dozen properties today, hon. You nixed everything except for Paulsen and Hall. What do you want to do?"

"I want to stay right where I'm at," Cara said stubbornly, dabbing at her damp forehead with a tissue. "But since that's no longer an option, I guess we should call the duplex owner. Do you think you can talk him down any on the rent?"

"I doubt it. She told me she had two other showings this week. If you think it's a possibility, we probably need to jump on it pretty quickly, or we risk losing it."

"I know, Alice. But I'm really scared. I've got a big check coming from my next wedding next week, and with that, I can just barely scrape up enough for first and last month's rent for Hall Street, plus moving expenses. But what if something goes wrong? I'm one wedding away from skid row."

Alice patted her arm sympathetically. "I admire you young single gals so much. Starting and running your own businesses, I never could have done anything like that when I was your age. I got married at nineteen, started having my babies. John was always the boss. Don't get me wrong. He's always been a wonderful provider, but I went from living in my father's house to being somebody's wife and mother. I never would have had the guts or the smarts to do the things you've done, Cara."

Cara smiled ruefully. "I'm not so smart, Alice. I've had a rotten marriage, my business could come crashing down around me at any minute, and in the meantime, I've been so busy trying to save the business, the one promising relationship I've had since my divorce just went up in flames.

"At least you have your kids, and your grandkids, and a solid marriage," Cara went on. "What have I got to show for the last ten years? A crappy van, a website, and a dog who's an obedience-school dropout. I don't even own my own house."

"You will," Alice said. "You're having a run of bad luck right now, but I know things are going to change for you. I'm Irish. We know these things."

"I hope you're right," Cara said. She sank back into the Cadillac's buttery leathery upholstery as Alice turned the car back toward the real-estate office.

"Sure I can't take you out to a late lunch?" Alice asked, as she pulled alongside Cara's own car. "My treat."

"Thanks, but I've got to get over to South Carolina. We're doing a walk-through and site visit with the bride and groom and their parents, and I need everything to be perfect," Cara said, reaching for the passenger-door handle.

"Cara?" Alice put a hand on her arm. "Are you sure you don't want me to call the new owner of your building? See if we can't come to an agreement that would allow you to stay put? It seems a shame to leave a place that's so perfect for your needs, just because of some misunderstanding."

"No misunderstanding at all, Alice," Cara said soberly. "Jack Finnerty deliberately misled me. Jones Street is just a shrewd real-estate investment as far as he's concerned. He's just as bad as Cullen Kane, just as bad as my former assistant. Just as bad as my ex-husband. I wouldn't trust him as far as I could throw him."

"Okay," Alice said slowly. "Shall I call about Hall Street? See if we can get moving on a lease?"

Cara's shoulders slumped. "Yes. Go ahead. But I can't write any checks until next Friday. Make sure they understand that."

51

Her car's air conditioner thrummed ineffectively against the glaring mid-day heat. Sweat stung her eyes, and her pale blue linen shift, which that morning she'd thought would look so cool and effortless, now stuck to the back of her legs and resembled a limp, slightly used Kleenex.

The Eugene Talmadge Memorial Bridge was a suspension bridge that separated Georgia from South Carolina. Cara glanced down, toward the brownish green water of the Savannah River below, and saw a huge container ship gliding toward the port. Her arms were rigid as she gripped the steering wheel with two damp hands.

Alice had just called with the news that she was drawing up the lease for the duplex on Hall Street. Cara honestly didn't know whether to laugh or cry.

She had ten days to pack up her apartment and shop—her life, in essence—and move out of Jones Street and over to Hall. And she had to do it by herself. This time around there would be no Bert, to make her laugh and help pack and unpack boxes, and moan and bitch about schlepping stuff up and down stairs.

He'd only been gone less than a week, but she missed her former assistant more than she'd ever admit. Ginny seemed pleasant and efficient, but Cara knew that she and Ginny would never sip from the same cup of snark sauce.

And there would be no Jack, either. The angry words they'd hurled at each other the night before had guaranteed that.

So, fine. She was too busy for idle gossip and casual sex anyway. Cara pushed a strand of hair out of her eyes. Time to concentrate on today's meeting.

She and Marie had finally managed to bully Brooke and Harris into agreeing to meet at Cabin Creek to walk through the plans for the reception and after-party. Libba Strayhorn was anxious to show them the progress on the old barn, and if all went well, they'd even be able to finalize placement of all the tables, chairs, and "lounge furniture" Cara had already rented from the tents and events house in Savannah. And, of course, Patricia Trapnell would be there, too.

Cara's stomach was already in knots. She wondered if Patricia was aware of the way her "dear friend" Cullen Kane had managed to so thoroughly torpedo her personal and professional life.

She relaxed her grip on the steering wheel just slightly after her car was finally speeding along the flat, featureless low country on the South Carolina side of the bridge. Glimpses of marsh flashed by, of elderly men with cane poles fishing on muddy creek banks, of elegant white egrets soaring over the green-gold grass, of rusted, aging mobile homes separated from the highway by little more than a weedy patch of dirt.

Thirty minutes later she slowed the car for the turn down the crushed-gravel drive to Cabin Creek. It was five till two, and she felt relief at the sight of Brooke's white Volvo sedan parked behind her mother's sedate gray Mercedes. There was always a fifty-fifty chance their harried bride might not show up.

Libba Strayhorn met her at the back door, dressed in a short, mint green cotton dress, pearls, and low-heeled sandals. Her blond hair curled just below her chin. Cara realized she'd never seen her client's hair, because Libba was never without her baseball cap.

"You're staring," Libba said, as she ushered her inside.

"It's just that I've never seen you so dressed up before," Cara admitted.

"Doesn't happen very often," Libba said cheerfully. "I had an altar guild meeting at church this morning, and I haven't had a minute to change. But I'm going to, right this minute."

She gestured toward the kitchen wing. "Everybody's out in the kitchen getting something cold to drink. Go on in, and I'll be right with you as soon as I get out of this rig and into something comfortable."

As soon as she walked into the kitchen, Cara sensed something was amiss. Marie sat at the kitchen table, her hands folded in her lap, glancing anxiously in the direction of the French doors that led to the patio. Patricia sat at the far end of the table, her head bent, furiously typing something into her Blackberry. But where were the bride and groom?

Ahh. Finally, she saw Brooke and Harris, outside on the patio. They stood close together, talking quietly, but Cara could tell from the angry set of Harris's usually placid face and the animated flashing of Brooke's hands that they were arguing.

Marie winced. "They've been out there for about ten minutes. Brooke is really wound up about something. I've never seen her like this before."

Patricia looked up from her typing. "I heard them when I walked up to the house, they were so involved, they didn't even notice me. It's all over this silly bachelor party tomorrow night. Brooke is being ridiculous."

"Why do you say that?" Marie said, her voice uncharacteristically sharp.

"She's making this big fuss about nothing. It's a bachelor's party, for God's sake. A bunch of guys hooting and hollering at a strip club. So what? It's harmless. A rite of passage. My son's friends all do it before their weddings."

Marie stared down at her iced-tea glass. "Brooke won't see it like that."

"Then she needs to get over herself," Patricia shot back. "Harris is a big boy. He can take care of himself."

Marie's eyes narrowed. But before she could respond, Libba bounced into the room. She wore faded blue jeans, a loose-fitting T-shirt, tennis shoes, and her ever-present Cabin Creek baseball cap again, and her dog was right on her heels.

"Thanks for your patience, ladies," Libba said. "I feel soooo much better. You know, every year I swear I'm not going to dress up for these darned altar-guild meetings, and every year, I bow to peer pressure, and put on the dress and heels and pantyhose. And every year, I want to kill myself. It's torture! And I'll tell you right now, I am *not* wearing hose at this wedding. My mother-of-the groom dress is floor length, so nobody but me and Jesus will be any the wiser."

"Ooh, good idea," Marie chimed in. "Mine is long too. And I despise panty-hose. Let's make a pact. We'll call it a hose-free zone." She looked over at Patricia. "What do you say? Are you in?"

Patricia stopped typing on her Blackberry and slipped it back into her Louis Vuitton tote. "Sorry, girls. My dress is cocktail length. And Gordon thinks sheer black hose are terrifically sexy."

"You're wearing black to the wedding?" Libba blurted. "Isn't that consid-ered bad luck, or taboo or something?"

"Not for stepmothers," Patricia purred.

Two pink spots bloomed high on Marie's cheeks. The awkward silence was broken when the French doors opened and the bride and groom stepped inside.

Brooke's eyes were red-rimmed, and Harris was stony-faced. He looked from his mother to Cara to Marie. "Can we just get through this, please? Brooke says she has a meeting back in town."

"Sure thing," Libba said. "Let's start in the ballroom."

The ballroom had been freshly painted and wallpapered, and Libba Strayhorn was tickled to be showing it off. She linked her arm through Marie's as they walked around the room.

"I don't know why we waited so long to freshen this room up," she said, pointing out the new window treatments, and the polished floors. She looked over her shoulder at Brooke, who hadn't uttered a single word since the tour had started.

"Thank you so much, Brooke, for agreeing to have the wedding over here. Even that old skinflint Mitchell is pleased with how things have turned out."

Brooke forced a smile. "You're welcome, Lib. It looks great."

Cara paced off the room and showed the women the floor plan she'd drawn up for the bandstand, dance floor, ten-top tables and chairs.

"Do we have the fabric samples for the tablecloths yet?" Patricia asked, studying the sketches.

Cara blinked. "I thought you'd seen them, Patricia. I sent them to Brooke two weeks ago. The seamstress called yesterday, she thinks she'll have them done early next week."

Patricia glared at Brooke, who blandly looked away. "Sorry, I guess I forgot. I think I still have the sample in my car, if you really care."

"Not at this late date, I don't."

"Okay, good," Brooke said, smirking.

"I just love paying for something I haven't even seen," Patricia said under her breath.

Marie glanced helplessly from Cara to her daughter to Libba. The tension in the room was nearly as thick and unpleasant as the June humidity.

"Let's go out and see the barn," Libba suggested brightly. "You're simply not going to believe how it looks."

Cara let out an inward sigh of relief when they approached the barn and Jack's pickup wasn't there.

But there were signs everywhere that he and Ryan had worked their magic. A wide new walkway of worn flagstones wound through the newly mown field toward the barn. Nearby, an old farm wagon had been planted with white geraniums, trailing Swedish ivy and swirls of blue plumbago.

"After the guys cleaned the barn they dragged that out, and I told them to just take it to the dump," Libba said. "The next time I walked over here, it looked like that."

"The flagstones were Jack's idea," she said. "He pointed out that walking through the field would ruin everybody's shoes, and particularly Brooke's wedding gown, if they had to trail in the grass. And God forbid there might be rain that night."

"It looks like it's always been here," Marie said approvingly. She glanced at Brooke, who trailed a few yards behind. "Isn't it lovely, Brooke?"

"Nice," Brooke said.

Cara stopped dead in her tracks as they got closer to the barn. It had been a month since she'd last been out to Cabin Creek, and the transformation in that time was dramatic.

The cracked and faded exterior barn boards had been pressure-washed and patched, with the new boards carefully stained to blend with the old. The standing-seam tin roof gleamed brightly in the glaring afternoon sun. Wide new windows had been cut into the walls, but the glass was old and wavy, with true divided lights picked out in a deep gray that contrasted with the original silvery exterior color.

Libba walked up to the newly painted glossy black barn doors. "This is one of my favorite things," she crowed. She touched a black iron latch, and both doors slid open on the wrought-iron sliders.

"Isn't that amazing? Those old doors, I could hardly yank them open anymore. Jack and Ryan found these doors and rigged some system of weights and counterweights, and I can open them with no problem."

Libba spread her arms wide, her face wreathed in smiles as she stepped inside the barn. "Ta-da!"

Brooke stood in the middle of the barn and burst into tears.

"Honey?" Harris gingerly wrapped his arms around his fiancée. "Don't you like it?" He rested his chin on Brooke's shining hair and looked to his mother for help.

Libba shook her head, speechless.

It was Patricia who finally broke the silence. "It's spectacular."

"It's . . . it's just so beautiful," Brooke said, her voice breaking. She turned and hugged Libba. "I can't believe you did all of this just for us."

"Well, to be honest, it was for me too," Libba said, rubbing Brooke's back. "Just call it a labor of love."

Their footsteps echoed in the high-ceilinged room. Cara craned her neck to see the exposed trusses and beams overhead. Sturdy industrial-looking galvanized light fixtures hung from thick ropes, illuminating the space below.

"Should we take off our shoes?" Patricia asked, already slipping out of her own Prada pumps.

"Not at all," Libba said. She leaned down and ran a hand lovingly over the burnished wood floors. "These boards came out of a closed-down textile mill in Spartanburg. They're old-growth pine. If you look carefully, you can see old grease stains and holes where machinery was bolted to the floor, and gouges and dents. I love them just the way they are, and Jack and Ryan agreed. The more beat up they get, the better they'll look."

"If you say so," Patricia said, her tone implying that she thought otherwise.

"It's a barn," Libba said, chuckling. "A really expensive barn, but I didn't want it too tarted up."

"Look up there, Brooke," Harris said, pointing to the gabled east end of the barn. "The old hayloft."

"Harris and his high-school band used to practice up there," Libba said. "Mitchell used to say the racket they made would make the neighbor's cows go dry. Brooke, I bet you didn't know you were marrying a musician."

"I didn't," Brooke said.

"That's because we sucked," Harris said. "Called ourselves the Chiggers. We were trying to be badass, but mostly we were just bad. And asses."

"I'll bet you weren't that awful."

"Actually, they were," Libba volunteered. She drew Marie aside and pointed again at the hayloft. "I had the guys reinforce the floors with steel beams, and that rail is reinforced too. Someday, my grandbabies will play up in that loft, just like Harris and Holly did, and their daddy before them."

For a split second, Cara saw a tiny pucker form on Brooke's smooth brow.

"Jack had a great idea," Harris said. "He said we should put the DJ booth up there for the after-party."

Brooke pointed at the sturdy ladder leading up to the loft. "But how would he get his equipment up that ladder?"

"If you open that door back there behind that partition, you'll see how," Libba said. "The guys put in a nice wide staircase. And underneath it, there's a new bathroom too."

Marie shook her head. "Libba, I'm just stunned at everything you've accomplished in such a short time."

Cara was already pacing off the room, admiring the honest grace and simplicity of the old structure's lines. She reached out and touched a silvery board and felt a deep twinge of regret. Jack Finnerty had rebuilt this barn, poured his sweat and passion into every detail and rediscovered its beauty. She wished she could tell him how moved she was by the artistry of his work.

But that ship had sailed.

Libba was still beaming as she led the group out of the barn. "I asked Jack for a fireplace back in the barn, but he talked me out of it. There just wasn't going to be time to build a suitable rock chimney before the wedding."

She pointed to a cleared area on the south side of the barn. "Instead, he's giving me a fire pit over there. He and Ryan will build some benches from wood left over from the barn."

"I've got an idea," Cara said. "If you don't mind, maybe we could move that old cart over near the fire pit. We can use it to set up the bar and the dessert buffet."

Cara turned to Marie. "Layne is baking homemade chocolate-dipped graham crackers and her own marshmallows for s'mores at midnight. And we're going to do a signature Cabin Creek cocktail. It's basically an old-fashioned, but we'll use this new bourbon from a distillery in Americus. And we'll serve them in pint Mason jars."

"Americus as in Georgia?" Patricia laughed. "No thanks. Give me a dry martini any day."

Cara couldn't resist the challenge. "You might be pleasantly surprised, Patricia. I've had this bourbon, and it's really quite good."

"I think this all sounds great," Marie said. She looked around to seek her daughter's agreement, but Brooke and Harris had drifted away from the others. They were standing under the shade of a pin-oak tree several yards away, deep in discussion, and from the looks of their expressions, things had gotten heated again.

"Brooke, Harris," Marie called, determined to draw them out of their argument. "Did you hear what Cara said about the Cabin Creek cocktail?"

Brooke shook her head, tears spilling down her cheeks, and stomped off.

"That sounds fine, Marie," Harris called. Then he hurried off in his fiancée's wake.

A few minutes later, they heard car doors slamming, then Brooke's Volvo, roaring up the road in a cloud of dust.

"Oh my," Libba said, shading her eyes with her hand as she watched Harris's car follow a moment later.

Marie sighed and shook her head. "I'm sorry, Libba. Brooke's just a bundle of nerves these days. It's this trial she's working on. I'll be so glad when it's over. This is classic Brooke. She's so intense and driven when it comes to her job. She was the same way when she was in school. She'd make herself sick worrying and studying before a big test. She'd convince herself she couldn't possibly pass, and of course, she always did. I don't remember her ever making anything lower than a B-plus."

"Brooke is so unlike Gordon in that way," Patricia piped up. "He's always so calm and confident. I think he actually thrives under pressure."

Marie gazed wordlessly at her ex-husband's new wife. She started to say something, but stopped herself.

"Never mind," Libba said soothingly. "Whatever is going on between the kids, they'll work it out."

"I hope so," Marie said.

52

Cara felt like a wrung-out dishrag by the time she finally parked her car on the street outside Bloom. It was nearly 5:30, but she was surprised to see that the garden cart was still on the sidewalk, and through the window she spotted Ginny Best, still seated at the worktable, poking daisies and zinnias into a round glass bowl.

"Oh hi," Ginny said. She held up the arrangement. "What do you think?"

"Mmm. Needs something else. Maybe some of those little miniature blue irises." Cara looked around the shop. "Where's Poppy?"

"Out back," Ginny said, going to the cooler for more flowers. "Some guy came by to see you earlier. I told him you'd be back late in the day."

"What guy?" Cara asked, grabbing a bottle of cold water from the fridge in the kitchenette. She left the fridge door open, uncapped the bottle, and swigged deeply as the cool air chilled her damp skin. She felt a tiny prickle of hope. Could it have been Jack? Was it possible that he hadn't totally written her of?

"He didn't tell me his name," Ginny said. "He was kind of a hottie, though. Blond hair, Ray-Bans. Your boyfriend?"

Cara choked, spewing water over her chest and chin. She grabbed a paper towel and mopped her face. "Not even," she said.

"Oh." Ginny nodded. "I think I get the picture."

"Thanks, Ginny. You can go on home now. I don't want you working a ten-hour day. I can finish that in the morning," Cara said.

"Okay," Ginny said, hopping down from her stool.

Cara fished a puppy treat from the jar on the counter and unlocked the back door, bracing herself for Poppy's typical rocket launch of unbridled puppy love.

At first glance, she thought the dog was sleeping. Poppy lay motionless on the sun-baked bricks.

"Here girl!" Cara called gaily. "Treat time!"

Poppy raised her muzzle and whined. That's when Cara saw the taut rope leading from the trunk of the crepe myrtle to the dog's neck. That's when she noticed the reddish trickle staining Poppy's platinum curls.

"Oh my God!" Cara cried. She dropped to the ground, her fingers shaking uncontrollably as she worked at the knot attached to her pet's collar. Poppy whined again, but she didn't squirm. All the fight had already gone out of her.

The bricks beneath Cara's knees scorched her skin as she fumbled helplessly with the tangled cord. "Oh my sweet girl. My poor sweet girl," Cara crooned. Finally, after what seemed like an hour, but was probably less than a minute, she tossed the rope aside. Cara unbuckled the dog's collar, flinching at the sight of the bloodstained fur.

She felt Poppy's nose. It was dry. She looked around for her water bowl and saw it, just out of reach, turned on its side.

Cara carefully gathered the forty-five-pound puppy in her arms. She found the hose bib, turned it on, and, placing a finger over the nozzle, gently sprayed the dog's face and the top of her head with it. Poppy's pink tongue worked furiously, lapping at the sun-warmed water. At some point, Cara searched for the thermometer attached to the courtyard wall. Ninety degrees, and it was now nearly six o'clock.

Somehow, she got to her feet, with Poppy still cradled in her arms. She jerked the back door open, sprinted toward the front of the shop.

Ginny Best was standing by the front door, her pocketbook over her shoulder, smiling into her cell phone. "Okay, if you're sure you've done your spelling words, we'll go out for ice cream when we get home." Her eyes widened when she saw her employer.

"I'll see you in a bit," Ginny said hastily, ending the call.

"Did you do this?" Cara demanded. "Did you tie my dog to a tree and leave her out there all day with no shade and no water?"

"She had water," Ginny protested.

"What kind of heartless, stupid bitch are you?" Cara felt her whole body shaking with barely contained fury. "It was nearly a hundred degrees out there today. You tie her up with four feet of rope, so she can't get to shade, can't get to water? And you leave her there? She could have died!"

"She was fine," Ginny said. "You weren't here. You don't know. She kept whining to go out, then whining to come back in, and the phone was ringing, and when I went to load the van, she tried to get out of the gate. She would have run away! So I tied her up. And I gave her water. I did. She had a whole bowl of it. I figured she'd be okay."

"How about this, Ginny? How about I take one of your kids and tie a rope around their neck and leave them out in the sun all day—with no water and no food? And dressed in a fur coat? Would that be okay?"

"She's a dog, for God's sake," Ginny said. "I'm sorry. It won't happen again."

"It certainly won't," Cara said. "You're fired. Now get out of my sight before I do something we'll both regret."

The vet tech at the after-hours animal clinic found Cara in the waiting room, sitting beside an elderly man whose dachshund had eaten a remote control.

"Ms. Kryzik? Poppy's fine. Why don't you come back and see her now?"

Poppy was sprawled out on her side on an examining table, damp towels draped over her head and body, a small fan pointed toward her face. It reminded Cara of a spa treatment she'd once had. When the dog saw Cara, her tail thumped against the vinyl tabletop.

"My girl," Cara whispered, kissing the towel on top of Poppy's head. "My sweet, sweet girl. You had me so worried."

"It's a good thing you found her when you did," the tech said, giving Poppy's rump a fond pat. "Her body temp was right at a hundred and two. She was one degree from stroking out. You did the right thing too, wetting her down like that and getting her over here immediately. You'd be surprised how many people try to put a dog in an ice bath. They mean well, but that's totally the wrong thing to do. It makes the surface blood vessels constrict, and that can kill a dog."

Cara realized she'd been holding her breath. She exhaled slowly now. "I guess I just reacted. I was so scared, and then so furious, I didn't really have time to stop and think."

"We gave her some Pedialyte and her urine checked out okay, and her heart's fine," the tech said. "So you can take her home now. Just try to keep her quiet tonight, and cool, of course. Let her have as much water as she wants, but don't try to force her to drink."

"I will. I mean, I won't. I mean, I'm still pretty freaked out. Can you write all that down for me?" Cara asked.

She dragged Poppy's dog bed downstairs and placed it in the workroom, near the air conditioner, which she turned on high. Screw the electric bill.

Poppy flopped down on her bed, but seemed restless, getting up every few minutes to stand in front of the front door, staring out at the now-dark sidewalk. Cara didn't know if the dog was watching for enemy squirrels, or even worse, Ginny Best.

Cara was restless as well. She opened her laptop and checked her emails. There were at least forty more responses to her Craigslist ad. She read a few, silently, her reaction to the contents ranging from hopeless to hilarious. Finally, Poppy gave up her sentry post and returned to her bed.

"Here's a good one," Cara said, turning toward the drowsy dog and reading aloud.

"'Hello sweet mommy. My name is Khalika and I am living in Gambia. I have read your requirements and am saying I am excellent candidate for professional job you are wanting. Please be immediate wiring two thousand dollars (American) for air travel expenses.' "

Poppy's bright pink tongue lolled from her mouth.

"Wonder if he's single?" Cara mused.

She was still reading when the laptop dinged, signaling the arrival of a new message in her inbox.

"I don't believe it," Cara said, staring at the message.

"Poppy, listen to this. It's an email from that stupid bitch Ginny. The one who tried to kill you earlier today? Here's what she says."

Poppy opened one eye, lifted one ear.

" 'Hi. I'll come by the shop tomorrow to pick up my paycheck for ten hours worked. I'm assuming you won't be taking out taxes or social security? Sincerely, Virginia Best.' "

Cara's fingertips flew over the keyboard.

Hi Ginny. The bill for the emergency after-hours vet clinic for treating Poppy for heat stroke and deyhydration came to four hundred and fifty dollars. How about we call it even and you never come near here again? Otherwise you won't have to worry about a dog attacking you. I'll bite you my ownself. Sincerely, Cara Kryzik.

She read it aloud for Poppy's approval. "What do you think, girl?"

The dog's eyes were half closed. Her tail switched, and emitted a short, noxious blast of gas.

"I'll take that as a yes." Cara hit the Send button.

53

Poppy seemed good as new by Friday morning. Cara took her out for a brief early-morning stroll at 7:30, taking a cautionary interest in her urine output, as the vet tech had suggested. All was well.

Except that she was running a one-woman show again. Reluctantly concluding that there was no way she could do it all, Cara referred phone and email orders to another downtown florist, and even paid the florist to deliver the few arrangements Ginny Best had finished before her Thursday banishment.

Cara was working on placing the Trapnell order with her California shipper when the office phone rang. She grabbed the receiver.

"Bloom. This is Cara."

"Hi Cara, it's Meredith. Have you talked to your bride today?"

"Which bride?"

"Brooke Trapnell. She was supposed to sit for her wedding portrait in my studio today. She's nearly an hour late."

Cara squeezed her eyes shut in frustration. "Have you tried to call her?"

"I don't have her number. I made the arrangements with you, remember?"

"Okay, okay. I'll call and suggest she get her tiny little heinie over there pronto. Sorry for the hassle."

She considered her best strategy for contacting Brooke Trapnell. Emails were a waste of time, and phone calls were iffy at best. A text just might get the girl's attention.

Brooke! Call me ASAP! Very important! Cara

Ten minutes later, when she'd still had no reply, she tried again.

Brooke! Don't make me call Patricia.

Her phone rang almost as soon as the text sent.

"Very funny," Brooke said, chuckling. "What's so important that you had to threaten to bring in the big guns?"

"Do you know what day it is?" Cara asked.

"It's Friday. Lunchtime. I only know that because everybody else in my office is eating lunch, while I'm still sitting at my desk buried in Georgia code."

"You're supposed to be at the photographer's," Cara said pointedly.

"Oh hell! I completely forgot. I had a deposition that ran long this morning, and my whole day has been screwed up."

"You were due there almost an hour ago."

"I can't get away now, that's for sure. Give me her number, and I'll call and rebook."

"Do both of us a favor and see that you do, okay? Otherwise your step-mother is going to hound me into an early grave. She wants that wedding portrait as a belated Father's Day gift for your dad."

"Why? Gordon's not her daddy. He's mine."

"Take it up with her, not me," Cara said. "Um, while I have you on the phone, did you and Harris kiss and make up yesterday? Your mom and Libba were pretty upset when you left the way you did."

"Geez," Brooke said. "I should have known blabbermouth Patricia would tell you we were fighting about the damned bachelor party. My girlfriends keep saying it's no biggie—just a bunch of overaged frat guys getting hammered and cruising strip clubs. And Harris insists it's harmless. They've rented a van and a driver to take them to Atlanta and back. 'Good dirty fun' he calls it."

"But you don't see it that way."

"No. When I was a first-year associate I had a pro-bono client—a girl who'd worked in one of those clubs. She was barely twenty-one and had a five-year-old son and a string of prostitution and solicitation arrests. And a raging meth habit. She told me what it was like working in a strip club. They treat those girls like . . . trash. They post rules telling them they're not allowed to fraternize with the customers, but the only way the girls make tips is by coming on to the guys, offering them, you know, hand jobs or whatever out in the parking lot. My client got busted for meth, and her little boy ended up in foster care. I've never forgotten her."

"Did you tell all that to Harris?"

"I told him I hated the idea, and he said he couldn't cancel, because all the guys would say he was pussy-whipped."

Cara could see both points of view. They were both right, but there would be no winner over an issue like this.

"It's just one night," she pointed out.

"You sound like my mom. I know, I'm a bitch. I'll get over it. I guess I'm just really, really tired. This sounds awful but I wish I didn't have my own bachelorette party tomorrow night."

"Aww, you don't want to miss your bachelorette party," Cara said. "What are you doing?"

"Holly won't tell me. It's supposed to be some big surprise. All I know is, there better not be any male strippers involved."

"I'm sure they'll have something fun planned for you. Look, Brooke. I know you have a lot on your plate right now with the trial and the wedding. And it probably doesn't do much good for people to tell you to relax and stop stressing, but I've done tons and tons of weddings, and I'm telling you, relax. Your wedding is supposed to be fun, you know?"

"Fun," Brooke said dully. "Got it."

"Magical."

"Right."

"Never mind," Cara said, finally. "Please, please, I beg you, call Meredith and get over there and have your wedding portrait taken. And while you're at it, you might practice smiling."

54

Because her real-estate agent knew how to make things happen—or maybe just because her new about-to-be landlord had a certain laissez-faire attitude about legal matters—Cara picked up the key to the Hall Street duplex Saturday afternoon.

Friday night must have been a happening scene on this block. Empty malt-liquor bottles, fast-food wrappers, cigarette butts, and even something she feared might be a condom littered the sidewalk out front of the building. Cara made a mental note to bring a hose, a bottle of Pine-Sol, and a scrub brush on her next trip back.

Poppy sat down on the sidewalk while Cara unlocked the front door. "Come on, girl," Cara said, stepping inside and flipping the light switch. "Let's see our new place."

The dog wouldn't budge. "Let's go," Cara urged, gesturing toward the doorway. "Check it out. I'll bet there's a whole bunch of squirrels out back."

Cara couldn't bear to tug at the dog's neck, with its fresh abrasions from Thursday. In the end, she simply picked Poppy up and plopped her down inside the building.

The inside of the shop wasn't much cheerier than the exterior. Alice Murphy said the last tenant had been a dry cleaner and alterationist. The faded linoleum floor was gritty underfoot; the wide plate-glass window was streaked with dust and what looked like remnants of masking tape.

· She forced herself to overlook the negative and focus on the positive. The walls were the original exposed brick, and there was a handsome fireplace with a carved Victorian mantelpiece and stained marble hearth. The walls would be charming once she pressure-washed them, and the fireplace, which was intended to burn coal, could perhaps be fitted with gas logs, which might be nice on what passed for a cold winter day in Savannah. The front room was much wider and deeper than the shop on Jones Street. Eventually, maybe she'd have a large showroom here, with a counter and display shelves, with the workroom separated by a partition or finished wall.

For now, though, with the huge bump in rent, she'd have to leave things as they were.

Before being turned into commercial space, Cara knew this floor of the building, like most of the others on the block, had been residential. There were still a small kitchen and a tiny, squalid bathroom here, and a back door that led out to a large fenced area.

She opened the thick fire door and frowned at the sight that met her eyes. Impossible to find anything to like here. The space couldn't even be called a yard, and it certainly wasn't a garden. It was overgrown with weeds, and a tall, narrow, sickly-looking magnolia tree blocked whatever sunlight might otherwise have shone there. She could see a couple of bashed-up Dumpsters next to the stockade fence, and next to them was an abandoned supermarket shopping cart, probably stolen from the Kroger a few blocks away. Cara shuddered, sure the area was probably teeming with rats, snakes, spiders, and God knew what else. She would have to have the yard cleared out and mowed before she'd dare let Poppy out there.

One more thing to add to her to-do list. She closed the door, locked and bolted it.

"Let's go upstairs," she told Poppy. The dog yawned and dropped to the floor. Only a puppy, and she was already a prima donna.

The staircase was narrow and steep, with worn risers and a handrail and balustrades thick with gummy layers of old paint.

At the top of the stairs she stood and took it all in. Her new home. The wallpaper was a dusty blue pattern of baby ducks and tulips, circa 1982, Cara thought. She knew there were probably wooden floors under the cheap commercial carpet, but she also knew she wouldn't be pulling that carpet up to find out anytime soon.

"It's a nice, big space," Alice Murphy had pointed out. Big, yes; nice, not so much.

Whoever had installed that fugly wallpaper back in the eighties had also seen fit to install a dropped ceiling of stained and yellowed acoustical tile. She was standing in the living room, which had a fireplace that roughly matched the one on the first floor. It was also much bigger than her apartment on Jones Street, but with not a scintilla of appeal. An arched doorway led from the living room to the dining room, which led to the kitchen.

The kitchen was about what you'd expect. Yellow vinyl floor, cheap orangish-stained pine cabinets, laminate countertops littered with cockroach corpses, rusting stove and fridge, no dishwasher, tiny sink. Depressing. A window over the sink overlooked the Dumpster graveyard.

Cara meant to head up to the third floor, where her bedroom would be, but suddenly found she lacked the energy.

Poppy was where she'd left her in the living room. "Come on, girl," she said, opening the door. "Let's go back home. While we still can."

She stripped down to shorts and a tank top in the Jones Street apartment, and halfheartedly began packing boxes of books. After an hour or so, she gave up, and plopped down on the sofa. She'd brought her laptop upstairs, and out of boredom, logged on to Facebook.

Cara had a business page for Bloom, and in the past, she'd made a regular practice of posting pictures of happy brides and beautiful bouquets. It was good marketing, and most of the "likers" on her page were former clients or other vendors in the wedding business.

She was scrolling down the page when a bubble popped up on her screen—a private message from Layne Pelletier.

OMG—have you seen this? There was a link, and Cara clicked it, the link taking her to Harris Strayhorn's Facebook page.

The OMG-inspired item Layne referred to was a timeline photo at the top of Harris's page. It was definitely a cell-phone picture, with bad lighting and fuzzy focus, but there was no mistaking the subject matter: Harris Strayhorn, leaning back in a chair, his eyes heavy-lidded, his mouth slack, with a very naked, voluptuous redhead straddling his lap. And just to make it clear who the subject of the photo was, the caption read HARRIS STRAYHORN TAKES IT LIKE A MAN.

There was a whole album of photos, and each one was worse than the one before—fifteen in all, fifteen photos of a bunch of overaged frat guys in a cheesy strip club, including five or six starring the bridegroom and man of the hour, Harris Strayhorn, receiving lap dances from two different naked women.

Cara felt a little sick. It was nearly four in the afternoon. The photos had been posted hours ago. Why hadn't Harris taken them down? Brooke had to have seen them by now. She glanced at the post again. There were forty-two comments and sixty-eight likes.

She closed the laptop, went to the refrigerator, and got a bottle of cold water. She felt like she also needed a cold shower, to rinse away the ugly images she'd just viewed.

Dinner was a slice of pizza at nine o'clock. She wasn't really hungry, but she needed to get out of the house, so she and Poppy strolled over to Mellow Mushroom on West Liberty Street.

Cara ordered a slice of the Philosopher's Pie and a glass of wine, and sat at a table outside, with Poppy crouched at her feet. This was a college hangout, and SCAD kids swarmed the sidewalk around her, laughing, talking, swearing, smoking. They rolled by on bikes and skateboards, and the atmosphere was noisy and electric. There were old-timers in Savannah who hated SCAD, with its artsy, avant-garde faculty and wacky, and some said entitled, student body, but Cara loved the energy they contributed to her neighborhood.

She took her time finishing her wine, enjoying eavesdropping on the swirl of conversations going on around her. Finally, when she could stand the hot sticky air no longer, she walked home, being vigilant about staying under streetlights and away from dark doorways.

They were only a few steps from her own door at Bloom when a tall, slender figure suddenly emerged from the shadows, stepping directly in front of her. Poppy gave a startled bark, and she had to choke back a half-formed scream.

"Cara? Sorry. I didn't mean to startle you."

It took a moment for her heart to stop racing and to gather her wits.

"Startle me? Jesus, Bert, you scared the living beejesus out of me." She held up the can of Mace she'd been clutching in her right hand. "Another second and you'd have gotten a faceful of this."

He laughed nervously. "Yeah. Rookie move. Can I talk to you for a minute?"

She fetched them both bottles of water, and they sat in her living room, with Poppy's head placed contentedly on Bert's lap.

He was dressed oddly, and acting strange, even for Bert. He wore his usual weekend attire of baggy shorts, flip-flops, and white "wife-beater" undershirt, but tonight, despite the stifling heat, he'd seen fit to throw a calf-length raincoat over the ensemble. His hair was cut shorter than she'd ever seen it, and he was obviously on edge.

Cara had no time for subterfuge. "Why are you here, Bert? Did Cullen send you?"

"Cullen? God, no." He kept running his fingers along Poppy's ears.

She raised one eyebrow, expectantly. "I'm waiting."

"I guess you were right. I guess this is where you get to say 'I told you so.'"

"About?"

"Cullen. Us. Everything. You were right about all of it. He doesn't give a damn about me. He was just using me to get to you. He's evil, Cara. Evil and twisted, and smart as hell. Scary smart."

"How did you figure it out?"

"I started putting things together almost as soon as I left here and went to work for him. I'm such a twit. I actually thought he cared about me. I bought everything he was selling—that he'd make me a designer, and I'd get to do my own events. But you saw where he had me at his studio—answering the phone. I never even touched a flower. My actual job was to pour champagne for clients and tweet photos of Cullen's fabulous creations. And empty his cat's litter box. When I moved in with him? I had to stay out in the carriage house. I was a glorified house boy. With fringe benefits."

Cara knew she should have felt vindicated—everything she'd predicted about Bert's experience with Cullen Kane had come true—but it felt like a hollow victory. He looked so sad and defeated.

"So you broke up with him?"

Bert snorted. "There was nothing to break up. It was like you said. I was just an easy lay for him. He's got half a dozen guys just like me between here and Charleston."

"I'm so sorry, Bert," she said gently. "Truly I am. I feel partly to blame, because he did use you to get to me."

"No." Bert shook his head vehemently. "This was all me, Cara. Me falling into my old bad habits."

"Are you drinking again?" She had to ask it.

"I wanted to," he admitted. "Cullen did everything he could to make it easy for me. But somehow, I didn't. Maybe that's how I had the nerve to walk away. I started going to meetings again Friday. And that helped."

"I'm glad," she said. "At least you've got your sobriety."

"Two years, three months, sixteen days," Bert said. "But that's not the reason I came here tonight."

"Tell me you came to ask for your old job back," Cara said.

His face lit up. "That'd be great, but that's not really it." Then he reached into the raincoat and brought out a medium-sized linen bag that he'd shoved into an inner pocket. "This is the real reason I came."

Cara took the bag and loosened the drawstring opening. An heirloom-quality eighteenth-century sterling-silver epergne slid out onto her lap.

"Lillian's?"

"Uh-huh."

"Where on earth did you find it?"

"In Cullen's gym bag. The bastard has had it all this time."

"But *how* did you find it?"

Bert laughed bitterly. "House boy take Mercedes to get detailed. House boy empty trunk, think maybe he wash boss man's stinky gym clothes, score extra points with boss. Instead, house boy find missing shiny silver doodad."

"Unbelievable," Cara said, holding up the epergne. "I can't even process it."

"I can," Bert said. "Cullen must have swiped it from the van that weekend after Torie's wedding." His face flushed and he looked away, embarrassed. "That's when I first met him. I'd gone to an after-hours club in midtown with a couple friends, and he was there, kinda window-shopping I guess you'd say. He sent a drink over to my table, but I told the waiter to take it back, because you know, I don't drink. A few minutes later, Cullen came over. He said he recognized me from Torie's wedding, talked about what a great job we'd done with all the flowers. He bought cocktails for the whole table, and we sort of hit it off, and after a while . . . I can't believe I'm telling you this shit . . ."

"You went out to the van?"

"Yeah," Bert whispered. "I think he was kinda into that."

"Remind me to have that thing steam-cleaned," Cara said.

"So . . . what now?" Bert asked, after he'd related the whole tawdry Cullen Kane affair.

Cara put the epergne back into the linen bag. "First thing tomorrow, we take this thing back to Lillian Fanning. You know she's been going around town trashing my reputation, right?"

"Cullen was loving that," Bert said. "He's got quite the network of ladies who lunch."

"I can't wait to see her face when she sees the epergne," Cara said.

"What will you tell her?"

"Just that we figured out who took it from the van, and we were able to recover it. Don't worry. I'll leave you out of it."

"And what about that Detective Peebles? Won't she be asking a lot of questions?"

"If she asks, we'll tell her the truth," Cara decided. "Let Cullen Kane deal with it. He's got a lot to answer for as far as I'm concerned."

"And he's still not done," Bert warned. "He's seriously obsessed with grinding his heel in your face. He went all batshit when he figured out that contractor friend of yours managed to buy this building out from under him."

Bert looked around the living room and for the first time noticed the packing boxes. "Hey, what's up with all this? I figured you wouldn't have to move now, since Cullen got outmaneuevered."

Cara shrugged. "Long, sad story. Things didn't work out with the new guy. I'll be out of here by the end of next week."

"Oh." Bert sank lower into the sofa cushions. "Well, shit."

"Yeah." Cara finished off the last of her water, wishing it were wine.

"Bert?"

"Yeah?"

"You didn't give up your apartment when you moved in with Cullen, did you?"

"Yup."

"So . . . you're basically homeless now?"

"Sorta."

She patted the sofa cushion, then stood up. "I'll get you a pillow and a sheet. And PS. You're hired. Again."

55

In the morning, Bert was gone. The sofa bed was folded up, the pillow and sheet neatly stacked on top of one of the boxes of books. The smell of brewing coffee wafted from the direction of the kitchen. Poppy was missing, too.

Cara poured herself a mug of coffee and took it out to the courtyard garden. Out of habit, she deadheaded a spent rose and pulled a weed from the side planting bed. The big bell from St. John the Baptist was booming eight as she sat down under the shade of the café umbrella.

She wondered if she'd be able to hear the church bells over on Hall Street. Geographically, the new place wasn't all that far away. Emotionally? That was a different story. She tried not to think about how much she was going to miss this little garden, miss all the work she'd put into it, and the enjoyment it had brought.

There was a big new yard over at Hall Street. It had seemed so hopeless yesterday, but things had shifted just a little last night. Bert was back. Bert had a strong back and he was a hard worker, when he wasn't whining.

The timing of Bert's return couldn't have been more fortuitous. There was no way she could get through the Trapnell wedding without help.

Thinking of the Trapnell wedding made her remember what had triggered the sense of uneasiness that had propelled her out of the apartment the night before. She went inside and fetched her laptop, clicking onto Facebook and Harris Strayhorn's page.

Thank God! The stripper photos had been deleted. Maybe, through some divine providence, Brooke hadn't seen them after all. Just out of curiosity, she clicked over to Brooke's page.

The bride-to-be wasn't what you'd call a Facebook fanatic. It looked like she posted irregularly, whenever the mood struck. There were photos of Brooke and Harris toasting on the beach at Tybee at sunset, of Brooke in running clothes finishing a marathon, of Brooke and Marie at Mother's Day brunch. The most recent item had been posted yesterday morning at 10 a.m. by Holly Strayhorn.

Bachelorette party tonight for my almost-sister BROOKE TRAPNELL! Woot, woot! #CosmoCraziness #Alertthemedia #Whosgotthebailmoney?

There were six responses to Holly's post, including Brooke's.

Can't wait!

Cara was just about to post something on her own Facebook page about the Trapnell wedding when the kitchen door opened and Poppy came bounding out to the garden, with Bert right behind. He was waving a large white paper sack.

"Guess who went to Back in the Day for bacon cheddar biscones for breakfast?"

She called ahead to make sure the Fannings would be home. Lillian's voice dripped ice. "We've got brunch plans at eleven. What's this about Cara?"

Cara ignored the question. "It won't take long. I can be there in twenty minutes."

It didn't get much better than Isle of Hope on a warm June morning. The live oaks lent cool shade, the sun sparkled off sailboats skittering over the river, and not a single blade of jade-green grass at the Shutters was anything less than perfection. It could have been a cover for *Southern Living* magazine.

Lillian Fanning sat stiffly on a wicker armchair on her porch and looked down at the epergne, which Cara had handed over without a word.

She picked it up, turned it over, and studied the hallmark. She held it up to the light, turning it this way and that, looking for dents or scratches, or any other clue to where the epergne might have been for these past weeks.

"It doesn't look any the worse for wear," Lillian admitted, her lips pursed. "And you won't tell me how you managed to find it?"

Cara had been rehearsing her response all morning. She delivered her lines as practiced.

"Somebody . . . who has a grudge against me took it. Not because it was so valuable or to sell it. To cause trouble for me, and ruin my reputation. A friend found where this person had hidden the epergne, and last night, he brought it back to me. And now, I'm returning it to you."

"I don't know what to say." Lillian's face was flushed. "Torie was right. I should have known better. All these weeks, I've thought, and I've said, really terrible things about you. To that police detective, to my friends." She shook her head. "I am deeply, deeply ashamed of myself right now, Cara. And I'm afraid an apology won't even begin to make things right with you."

"An apology is all that's needed," Cara said. "Thank you, Lillian. I'll let you get to your brunch now."

Lillian reached out and touched Cara's bare arm. Her fingertips were cool.

"You know, Cara, we Southerners pride ourselves on good manners. Torie says I'm a big snob about these kinds of things, and that's something else she's probably right about. You're from up North someplace . . . Michigan?"

"Ohio."

"I knew it was one of those places. Anyway, I just want to tell you that the way you handled this whole episode, with such dignity, and the way you just accepted my totally inadequate apology with such grace, says a lot to me about who you are and how you were raised."

Cara smiled. "My mother would have been happy to hear you say that."

"Where was your mother from?"

"Actually? Kentucky."

Lillian's eyes twinkled. "That explains everything. Seriously though, Cara.

I guess that's a lesson learned for me. You don't have to be Southern to have good manners. And you don't have to be a Yankee to make a total ass of yourself."

That got a laugh from Cara. She was halfway across the lawn when Lillian called out to her. "I'm going to make it up to you, Cara. You wait. Your phone is going to be ringing. There won't be a bride within a hundred miles of this town who won't be calling you."

"Man, I hate it when you have to act all classy and grown-up, instead of going *off* on a bitch," Bert complained, after Cara gave him the blow-by-blow of her encounter with Lillian Fanning.

They were upstairs in the apartment, and he was helping her finish packing books. "Grown-up is definitely not as fun," Cara agreed. "But I'd much rather have Lillian as an ally than an enemy. Now she owes me, or she thinks she does. And that's a good thing, considering the rent on Hall Street is double what I paid here."

Bert gave her a quizzical look. "What happened with Jack Finnerty? I got the impression you two were pretty hot and heavy."

"Where'd you hear that?"

"Cullen has spies everywhere," Bert explained. "After Jack took a pass on doing the work over here, he started asking around. I think Patricia Trapnell probably helped him put it together because of all the work Jack and his brother were doing over at the Strayhorns."

"I can't believe Cullen Kane was that interested in my personal life."

Cara's cell phone was sitting on the coffee table. It buzzed and Bert picked it up and handed it to her. "It's Marie Trapnell. You want to take it, or should I tell her it's your day off?"

"Give."

"Hi, Marie," Cara said cheerfully.

"Cara?" Marie Trapnell's voice crackled with agitation. "Have you heard from Brooke?"

"Nooo, we haven't spoken since Friday. Should I have? Is something wrong?"

"Brooke is gone."

Cara felt a cold whisper at the base of her neck. "When? Where?"

"We don't know how long she's been gone. Holly went to pick her up for the bachelorette party last night at eight, but she wasn't there. She tried calling and texting, but Brooke never answered."

"Has Harris talked to her?" Cara's mind flashed on the pictures from the strip club. "Did they have another fight?"

"No. Not that I know of. I just talked to Harris. He hasn't seen her since she left for work Friday morning. He and his friends went up to Atlanta Friday, and he didn't get back till nearly ten last night. He went straight to bed, and he wasn't really worried about her until just now, when Holly called to ask him why Brooke skipped out on the party."

"Oh no," Cara said.

"I'm trying to stay calm, but I'm afraid I'm not doing a very good job of it," Marie said shakily. "It's just that Brooke is so emotionally fragile right now. The trial and the wedding, it's all just too much for her."

"Have you called her friends? When I talked to her Friday, she mentioned that she was sort of dreading the bachelorette thing. Because she was so tired."

"All of her friends were with Holly last night. Brooke was the only one missing. And none of them talked to her on Friday or Saturday."

Cara's mind was racing with possibilities. "Is her car there?"

"Her car?"

"Brooke's Volvo. Was it at her house last night?"

"I don't know. I didn't even think to ask, when Harris called to see if Brooke was with me."

"You might want to check on that," Cara said gently.

"I will. I'll call Harris right now and ask."

"Marie? You might also ask him if Brooke saw the pictures on his Facebook page."

"What pictures?"

"Just ask Harris. He'll know which ones."

Ten minutes later, Cara's phone rang. This time it was Harris Strayhorn. No surprise there.

"Marie says you asked whether Brooke saw some Facebook pictures? What are you talking about?"

"I saw the pictures from the strip club yesterday, Harris, before you took them down. I saw all of them. And I wasn't the only one."

"Fuuuuck." His voice sounded distant. "I'm gonna kill Mike Bingham. He swiped my phone and posted them on my page. We were all pretty hammered. I didn't even know they were on there, until another buddy texted me to warn me to delete them. Which I did as soon as I saw them."

"Did Brooke see the pictures?"

"Christ, I hope not. Maybe not. She doesn't look at Facebook on a regular basis." He groaned. "But if she did see them . . ."

"Exactly."

"They look awful, I know. But I swear to God, it was just a lap dance. Okay, two. Maybe more. I can't remember. I got so drunk I passed out in the back of the van after the third or fourth club. That's why I didn't come home until last night. I didn't want Brooke to see me until I got sobered up."

"Do you have any idea where she might have gone?"

"I've called everybody we know. Nobody's seen or talked to her. Wherever she went, she took her car. Marie told me you were asking about that."

"Did she pack any bags? Take a lot of clothes?"

"I'm walking in the bedroom now to check." Cara heard footsteps, and the sound of a door opening.

"She's got this duffel bag she takes when we go over to my folks' house for the weekend. It's not in the closet."

"What about clothes?"

She heard the sound of hangers on a wooden rod, of drawers being opened and closed.

"It's hard to tell with her clothes. Wait. Yeah, her favorite jeans are gone. Maybe some shorts. Definitely her running shoes, although she sometimes leaves those in her car if she's working out at lunch."

There was a long silence at the other end of the phone. Had he hung up? "Harris? Are you still there?"

She could hear him breathing heavily. And then, a sort of muffled sob. "Harris?"

"I should never have gone. I knew she didn't want me to go. We had a fight about it. And we almost never fight. I never should have gone to those stinking clubs."

"Maybe it wasn't about that," Cara said. "Was there anything else worrying her, something she was upset about?"

"Not that she talked about," Harris said. "Brooke was ... moody sometimes. She needed her space. I tried to give it to her. I love her, you know?"

"I know," Cara said. "And she loves you. She told me so."

"Then why would she leave? Where would she go?"

"We'll find out," Cara said soothingly. "Brides ... sometimes it all becomes too much for them. Sometimes they just have these little meltdowns. That's probably all this is. Like you said, Brooke needs her space."

"You really think so?"

"I do," Cara lied.

56

"H oly shit," Bert said. "Brooke Trapnell is a runaway bride?"

"Looks like it. Harris hasn't seen her since she left for work Friday morning. They'd had a fight, because she hated the idea of his doing the strip-club stag-night thing with his buddies."

Before Cara could explain any more, Marie Trapnell called back.

"What did Harris tell you?" she asked urgently.

"Her car is gone, and she apparently packed an overnight bag. So we know she went of her own accord. She wasn't abducted or anything."

"Thank God for that," Marie said. "I can't tell you all the things running through my mind right now. This is just such a nightmare. Why would she do something like this? If she needed to get away, why not at least tell me? She knows how I worry."

"I talked to Brooke Friday, to remind her about her portrait sitting, and she did seem stressed." Cara said. "She even admitted she was dreading the bach-elorette party, but she never said she was thinking of skipping it. So it looks like she probably left sometime Saturday."

"Why did you want me to ask Harris about his Facebook page?" Marie asked. "He told me he didn't know what you were talking about, but I know he was lying."

Cara hesitated. She hated to rat Harris out, but on the other hand, Marie had a right to know what might have triggered her daughter's flight.

"One of Harris's buddies posted some pretty risqué pictures of him from the bachelor's party on Harris's Facebook page."

"Risqué, how?"

"There were pictures of him getting a lap dance from a stripper."

"That's revolting. It doesn't even sound like Harris."

"He said he was pretty drunk. I saw the pictures, and he looked like he was about to pass out. Which he apparently did later that night."

"And you think maybe Brooke saw those pictures, and that's why she left?"

"That could be part of it. Brooke told me she and Harris had a fight about it, because she didn't want him to go to those strip clubs. But maybe that's just part of it. I don't really know, Marie. I'm not a therapist. I'm only a florist-slash-wedding-planner."

"I'm just trying so hard to understand what was going through Brooke's mind. I don't dare say this to Harris or Gordon, but I'm terrified Brooke will hurt herself."

"Oh, yikes. I hadn't even thought about Gordon. How's he handling this?"

"In typically Gordon style. He's furious at Brooke for quote 'pulling a stunt like this.' It doesn't occur to him that perhaps his daughter is in some kind of emotional distress. All he can think about is how it affects him. How embarrassing it will be if the wedding doesn't come off as planned. He's already talking about hiring a private detective to track her down."

"Would he really do that?"

"Maybe. I don't know. Gordon's not somebody who just sits around waiting for things to happen. He's used to making them happen. Right now. Times like these, I have no idea how we ever ended up marrying or staying together for as long as we did."

"But you did, and the two of you raised an amazing daughter. I'm sure Brooke is okay, and she wouldn't hurt herself, Marie. Like I told Harris, she probably just needs some alone time."

"Have you ever had a bride do anything like this before?"

Cara had to think. "Just disappear? Without saying anything to anybody?"

"Exactly."

"No."

"Oh God." Marie was weeping. "I'm so sorry, Cara. I'm trying not to fall to pieces, but I can't stand not knowing where she is, or what she's going through."

"It's all right, Marie," Cara said. "I don't blame you for being upset. Let me think a moment. Does Brooke have any special 'happy place'—someplace she likes to retreat to? Maybe a friend's mountain cabin, or a beach cottage or something?"

"Gordon and Patricia have a condo down at St. Simon's, but I doubt she'd go there. I don't think she even has a key."

"You might ask Gordon to check on that. Where else?"

"She and Harris have rented cottages in Highlands, North Carolina. They usually go in the fall, with other couples."

"Maybe ask Harris to call the real-estate company they rent from, to see if they've heard from Brooke."

"That's a thought. You're making me feel better already, Cara."

"I'm just taking stabs in the dark here Marie. There's just as good a chance that she found a motel room on the interstate and she's lounging by the pool, drinking a Margarita."

"No. That doesn't sound like Brooke at all."

Cara threw her hands up in exasperation. "I'm sorry. I'm out of ideas."

"I am too," Marie said, her voice nearly a whisper. "But I've got to keep trying."

"If I think of anything, I'll let you know," Cara promised. "Try not to worry too much, Marie. Brooke's a smart, resourceful woman. She can take care of herself."

"I hope so."

Cara hung up the phone and turned to Bert. "I've got a really bad feeling in my gut about this."

Bert's eyes widened. "What? You really think she might be in some kind of physical danger? Like, maybe somebody really did abduct her?"

Cara shook her head. "No. It's not that. Her car's gone, she packed a suitcase. Brooke went of her own free will. And that's what's got me so worried. If she doesn't come back—if that wedding doesn't come off? I'm through. That's a twenty-five-thousand-dollar paycheck that doesn't get written. I absolutely promised the Colonel I'd get him the rest of his money by next week. And I've got all these bills coming due, first and last month's rent on the new place, plus the expenses of getting moved in over there."

She swallowed hard, trying to suppress the tide of fear and panic that had begun bubbling just below the surface as soon as she'd heard the news that Brooke Trapnell was missing.

"Technically? It's not really your problem, Cara. As of yesterday, per your contract, Gordon Trapnell owed you the balance of your fee, whether the wedding happens or not."

Cara sighed. "That's true. But if this wedding doesn't come off, there's no way, short of suing, that Patricia will write that check. Anyway, I really care about Brooke and Harris."

Bert rolled his eyes. "So what are you going to do?"

"I wish I knew. I honestly do think this is just a classic case of pre-wedding jitters. If I could find Brooke, and talk to her, I really believe I could help her see that this is totally normal. I've never done a wedding where the bride didn't freak out, in some way."

Bert nodded agreement. "What was that girl's name—the one who kicked her maid of honor out of the wedding party because she wouldn't grow her hair out long like the rest of the bridesmaids?"

"Cherish Scanlon," Cara said. "And don't forget about Vanessa Pettigrew. She literally plucked out all her eyebrows and eyelashes three days before the wedding."

"Poor girl looked like a Chihuahua," Bert said.

"When I worked for Norma we had a bride who was so nervous during the ceremony she literally passed out cold, right at the altar. When she fell, she somehow bit her own tongue, there was blood everywhere. . . ."

"Maybe Brooke knows something we don't," Bert said gently. "Even in bizarro bride world, running away is pretty radical, don't you think?"

"No. This is just how Brooke Trapnell operates. I've been working with this girl for weeks and weeks now. It's just stress, that's all. If I could just talk to her..."

"Give her a call," Bert suggested.

"Everybody has tried calling her. Her mom, Harris. I'm sure Gordon's tried to reach her too. This is typical Brooke behavior. She never returns phone calls. The only success I've ever had reaching her is with a text."

"So text her. What have you got to lose?"

Cara stared at Bert. She grabbed her phone and started typing, her fingers flying so quickly over the keyboard she had to start over three times. Finally, she got it right.

Brooke. Where are you?

She hit send and held her breath. A minute later, Cara's phone dinged.

Promise u won't tell?

Cara looked over at Bert. He nodded.

Promise.

She waited five long minutes before her phone dinged again.

Brooke had typed only one word.

Loblolly.

Bert had been reading over her shoulder. "Huh? Is that a typo? Was she trying to write LOL—you know, laughing out loud?"

"No," Cara said slowly. She smacked her forehead. "I can't believe I didn't think of it. Loblolly is the name of some house that used to belong to Brooke's mother's family. It's on Cumberland Island."

"Why would she go to Cumberland Island of all places?"

Cara thought back to her lunch at Johnny Harris, of the lanky park ranger who'd dropped by their table, and Brooke's confession about their secret romance. What was his name? Pete something?

"I've been to Cumberland Island. There's nothing over there," Bert was saying.

"Wrong," Cara said. "There's a house, someplace that used to be special to Brooke. And a man. He used to be special too. Maybe he still is."

"And how do you happen to know all this?"

"When I had lunch with Brooke at Johnny Harris last week, we ran into this guy—he was kind of geeky-looking, not at all somebody you'd picture Brooke Trapnell with. But she got all flustered after they spoke. It turns out he was this secret college flame she'd had. She actually told me she was sleeping with him the summer before she started law school—even though she was unofficially engaged to Harris."

"Oooh. Quel scandal!"

"Right. Anyway, he came by the table before leaving, and was sort of hinting that he wanted to get together with her. He works as some sort of park ranger or something, and he's temporarily posted on Cumberland Island. Cara told him straight up that she was getting married. She even introduced me as her wedding planner. But she gave him her business card."

"Which you don't do unless you want somebody to call you again," Bert pointed out.

"He asked her if they still went to the family place over there. Loblolly. And Brooke said no, not in years. Listen, where exactly is Cumberland Island? Is it somewhere around Savannah? Or Hilton Head?"

"It's about two hours south of here. Almost to the Florida line. The whole island used to belong to the Carnegie family—the steel magnates? They had a couple big spooky old mansions and a farm and a few other houses for their staff going all the way back to the late 1800s. But a few years ago they deeded or sold almost all of it over to the National Park Service. One of the mansions burned down years ago, you can still see the ruins, and some of the Carnegie heirs run a really expensive inn you can stay at, but other than that, it's all just wilderness.. I remember, we went camping out there when I was a Boy Scout. I was totally traumatized when I figured out there was no outlet for my hair dryer in the outhouse."

"You were a Boy Scout?"

"I liked the uniform," Bert said. "Are you sure this Loblolly place is on Cumberland? I thought the only people who still had houses over there were Carnegies. Is Marie Trapnell a Carnegie?"

"Who knows? It doesn't really matter anyway. What matters is, I need to go down there, and find Brooke Trapnell."

"Is that a good idea?" Bert asked. "Why don't you just leave that to her fiancé, or her parents?"

"Because I promised her I wouldn't tell. Anyway, if Brooke really is on that island, I think there's a chance she's with that old flame, the park ranger. What do you think Harris would do if he figured that out?"

"Call off the wedding, probably."

"Which is why I've got to go myself," Cara said. "I'm going to go down to Cumberland Island, and find Brooke Trapnell, and then I'm going to drag her back to Savannah and put on the most amazing wedding anybody in this town has ever seen."

"High five," Bert said.

57

Cara raced into her bedroom and unearthed her backpack from her closet while Bert sat on her bed and researched Cumberland Island on Google.

"There are only two ferry departures a day from the Park Service dock at St. Marys, at nine and eleven-forty-five a.m.," he reported. "You're supposed to call weekdays before five p.m. to make a reservation."

"What if you decide on Sunday afternoon that you want to go on Monday morning?"

"Mmm, looks like if you don't have a reservation it's first-come, first-serve. You're supposed to be there half an hour before departure time. Only two return trips a day, at ten-fifteen a.m. and four-forty-five p.m."

Cara started folding a T-shirt to put in her bag.

"Bad idea," Bert said. "Long sleeves are the way to go over there. The place is crawling with bugs. Make sure you throw in some insect repellent and some sunscreen too. Can I ask about your plan of attack?"

"You can ask, but I don't really have one. I guess I'll get over to Cumberland, track Brooke down, and then hope and pray she'll listen to good sense."

"About the tracking-down thing. You do realize the island is like twenty miles long, right? And most of it's either woods, swamp, or beaches. And only rangers or residents are allowed to have cars."

Cara threw in a pair of running shorts, a long-sleeved T-shirt, and a pair of blue jeans, then added hiking boots, socks, panties, and a toothbrush to her pack.

She frowned. "Check that website, see if you see a place called Loblolly on it."

Bert skimmed the website, and clicked around until he found a reference.

"'Loblolly is a circa-1912 hunting lodge built to house overflow guests from Plum Orchard, the Carnegies' opulent hundred-room Georgian Revival mansion. In 1930, Loblolly was deeded to Jasper O. Updegraff, a wealthy friend of George Carnegie, who reportedly won the property in a high-stakes poker game.'"

"Updegraff." Cara turned the name over in her mind. "Vicki Cooper told me that Marie Trapnell came from a family with even more money than Gordon's, but I can't remember if she told me the family name."

"One moment," Bert said, typing in a Google search. "Okay, here it is. Brooke's engagement announcement from the *Savannah Morning News*. Mary Brooke Trapnell, daughter of Gordon Vincent Trapnell of Vernonburg, and Marie Louise Eagleton Trapnell, of Savannah."

"Gotta love the Savannah newspaper for running those engagement announcements so everybody in polite society can keep a scorecard on who's marrying whom," Cara said.

"Cullen reads the engagement announcements in the Savannah and Charleston papers religiously, and if he sees an upper-crust name, he always sends flowers to the bride-to-be," Bert said. "You'd be amazed the amount of business it generates."

"Yes, he's quite the entrepreneur," Cara said. "I wonder if he makes it a habit to steal heirloom silver from any of those brides?"

"Updegraffs," Bert muttered. "Updegraff?"

"Keep looking," Cara said. "If the house belonged to Marie's mother's family, maybe that's the Updegraff connection."

"Okay . . . yeah. Here we go. There's a story about Brooke's debut from a few years ago. Daughter of Gordon and Marie, stepdaughter of Patricia, granddaughter of so and so Von Moneybags the Third, and great-granddaughter of the late Dr. and Mrs. Warner Updegraff of Sea Island, Georgia."

"Bingo." Cara found a bottle of bug spray and threw it into the bag. "So, the question is, how far is Loblolly from the ferry dock, and if there are no cars, how do I get there once I'm on the island?"

"Checking. This says Loblolly is five miles from the dock. That's a pretty good hike in June. But it does say you can rent a bike." Bert looked up at her. "Did I mention there are no motels? Just primitive tent camping. And the Greyfield Inn, where rooms without a private bath start at around five hundred dollars a night."

"I'm not planning to need a room," Cara said. She hoisted the backpack to her shoulder to test its weight. "If I do have to hike, this shouldn't be too heavy."

"Ugh," Bert grimaced. "I wouldn't mind hiking and camping, if it weren't for the fact that you have to do it outside, in nature. They have boo-koodles of nature over on Cumberland. All these bugs buzzing around, and random animals. I mean, in addition to your garden-variety raccoons and possums and deer they have herds of wild horses pooping everywhere, not to mention alligators." He glanced down at the Park Service website. "Just listen to this: 'Venomous snakes present on the island include diamondback rattlesnakes, timber rattlesnakes and cottonmouth moccasins.'"

"I'll be sure to watch where I walk," Cara promised. They went back out to the living room, and Cara gathered up her cell phone and charger.

"What needs doing in the shop while you're gone?" Bert asked. "What do we have coming up?"

"The usual baby shower, retirement, and hospital stuff," Cara said. "Check the inbox on my desk. We've also got the Loudermilk wedding next Saturday, but it's a second marriage for both of them, very small, simple ceremony in the best friend's town house on Charlton Street. The couple are very sweet, very low maintenance. We're doing a bouquet for BeBe, one for Weezie, her maid-of-honor, boutonnieres for Harry and the best man, and a couple of arrangements for the mantel and the buffet table. But that's not until Saturday, and hopefully, I'll be back here tomorrow afternoon."

"Hopefully," Bert said.

"You'll stay here and take care of Poppy?" she asked. Her face darkened at the memory of the last, temporary assistant she'd hired, with such disastrous results. "And walk her and make sure she gets plenty of water?"

"When have I not done those things?" Bert asked. "You know I'll take care of everything around here." He grabbed her hand. "Hey. You trust me, right? I mean, I know I messed up, with Cullen. But that's history. This is the new Bert. Reliable, responsible Bert."

"Okay. Yeah, that's the Bert I need," Cara said. She hugged him tightly. "That's the one I missed. I was really starting to panic about doing these next three weddings without you."

"Three? Who do we have besides the Loudermilk wedding, and then Brooke's?"

"The week before Brooke and Harris we've got the Schroeders."

"Ohh. Wait. Is that the beach wedding?"

"Afraid so."

"Who gets married at the beach on Tybee in late June?"

"Somebody who's never been there in June," Cara said. "She's from out of town. The whole wedding party is from out of town."

Cara was raiding the shop's petty-cash drawer when she heard the sound of a car door slamming on the street outside. She looked up in time to see Jack Finnerty heading toward the shop door. She considered running out the back door to evade yet another confrontation with him, but it was already too late. He'd spotted her, and Poppy had spotted Jack, and she was barking and pawing at the door, eager to see her old friend.

As soon as he stepped in the door, Poppy pounced, slapping her front paws on his chest, and slathering his neck with her big pink tongue.

"Hey, girl!" he said, ruffling the fur on Poppy's neck. "Have you missed me?" He looked up at Cara, and it was obvious he was addressing them both.

Jack had obviously come directly from the job site. His work boots were covered in mud and sawdust, and his T-shirt and jeans were grimy.

Cara felt her heart pounding in her chest. Damn Jack Finnerty. He was the only man she'd ever known who looked as good dirty as he did clean. Come to think of it, she couldn't remember another man who made her palms sweat and her pulse race the way Jack did. Too bad he'd turned out to be such a world-class jerk.

"I've started packing, if you've come to check up on your investment," she said coolly. "I move over to Hall Street next week." She gestured around the small room. "And just in case Sylvia Bradley didn't mention it, all the shelving and fixtures are mine. And I intend to take them with me."

Jack's face flushed under his sunburn. "You know that's not why I came here. Look. Maybe I didn't express myself too well the last time. I was pumped, you know? So let me be clear. I bought this building for you. Not to give to you, or hold over your head so I'd have demonical power over you. It's a great building, and I thought it deserved something better. And you deserve something better, too."

"I see."

"Okay, so yeah, maybe I also bought it because I'm a typical competitive male and I wanted to keep that creep Cullen Kane from getting his hands on it. So yeah, my execution was pretty clumsy. But don't I at least get credit for . . ."

"What? Having a pure heart?"

"Yeah, that," he said belligerently.

She felt her spine weaken a little. Damn, she really was such a jellyfish. But his face was so damn earnest, and yes, deep down inside, she did have a sneaking suspicion that his heart was pure.

"Why didn't you tell me you were thinking of buying the building, instead of all this sneaking around? What is it with you men? Why do you all have to be so . . ."

"Devious?"

"Exactly! I'm just so sick of all the plotting and power plays and the secrets and the subterfuge. Can't you just communicate?"

Jack stood with his hands on his hips. "Fine. This is me communicating. Even if you and I are through, I'd really rather not have to find a new tenant. If you feel so strongly about not taking any favors, we can talk about escalating your rent, eventually. What do you say?"

She had to stick to her guns. This was a matter of principle, not a matter of the heart.

"Thanks. I appreciate the offer, but I've signed a lease for Hall Street. It's a bigger space, and when I get it fixed up, Poppy will have more room. Plus, I've already started packing."

He shook his head, then shrugged. "Have it your own way, then." He was on his way out the door when he noticed her backpack. "What's up? You've taken up hiking?"

She debated whether or not to tell him the truth. But why not?

"I'll tell you where I'm going, but this is strictly on the low-down, okay? Brooke has disappeared."

"That explains a lot. Ryan and I were going to get some stuff done at Cabin Creek today, because we're starting to get down to the wire with the wedding, but Libba just waved us off, which was kind of weird. She's been out there every day we've been working, taking pictures and coming up with things she wants done. So, wow. Brooke—what? Just vanished?"

"She and Harris had a fight Friday, and then sometime Saturday, while he was still in Atlanta for his bachelor's party, she took off. Skipped her own bachelorette party."

He whistled softly. "That sucks for Harris. And Libba too, of course. Does this mean the wedding is off?"

"Not if I can help it," Cara said fiercely.

That took him by surprise. "What? You're going after her? Cara Kryzik, finder of lost brides?"

"As a matter of fact, yes. I'm the only one who knows where she's gone."

"Cool. Tell Harris. Let him deal with it."

"Negative. I promised Brooke I wouldn't tell. Anyway, I don't want to hurt Harris. He's a sweet guy. If he went after Brooke this whole wedding thing could blow up in our faces."

"And why is that?

"I don't think Brooke is by herself. I think maybe she's with another guy."

Jack shook his head. "Oh shit. Another guy. That's a deal-breaker. What do you hope to accomplish by going after her?"

"Brooke is emotionally overwrought right now. Lots of brides get like that. Most of them, in fact, freak out in some form or fashion. I'll explain that to her, calm her down, and bring her home to get married."

"And what about this other guy? The one you said she might be with?"

"He's just somebody from her past, an excuse she's probably clinging to for why she should run away."

Jack's eyes narrowed. "You don't know that. How could you?"

"I met him. By accident. He's totally wrong for Brooke. He's a park ranger. Can you imagine Brooke Trapnell living on some wilderness island somewhere?"

"Why are you so dead-set on meddling in this thing, Cara? Why don't you just let Harris and Brooke sort things out for themselves?"

Instead of answering, Cara picked up her backpack and her car keys. "I don't have time for this, Jack. I've got to go."

He followed her out to her car, and before she could stop him, he'd slid into the front passenger seat. "I get it. If this wedding gets canceled, you're out a crapload of money, right?"

Cara went perfectly still for a moment. If that's what he thought of her, why let him know otherwise?

"Yes!" she cried. "That's right. I finally figured out that the only way to win at this game is to play by the big boy's rules. I'm going to find Brooke Trapnell and bring her home and by God, this wedding is going to come off and I am going to finally be out from under my father's thumb. Okay? Happy now?"

"Yeah," he said, his mouth twisting downward. "I'm just great."

58

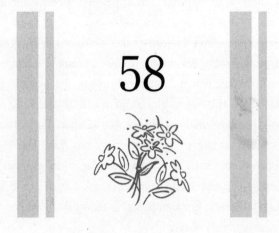

The motel room in St. Marys was tiny, but cheap. And most importantly, it had air-conditioning. Cara took a shower, brushed her teeth, and fell into bed. It was barely 9 p.m., but after the jarring encounter with Jack and the two-hour drive south from Savannah, she was exhausted.

In the morning, she had a convenience-store breakfast of coffee with a stale cheese Danish. As an extra precaution, she bought a bottle of water and two protein bars, which she tucked into her backpack.

By eight o'clock, she was in the ticket line at the ferry dock. A group of giggling Girl Scouts and their mothers were ahead of her in line, as were a pair of solidly built gray-haired ladies who were decked out for a day of bird-watching, with canvas rain hats, hiking boots, and cameras and binoculars strung around their necks.

After she bought her ticket for the early ferry, Cara took a brochure about the island from a display by the ticket window, found a seat in the shade, and watched with interest as cars and vans pulled up, disgorging campers and day-trippers loaded down with coolers, tents, beach chairs, and more.

It was an eclectic group, families with young children, gung ho hikers, and half a dozen college students, who stealthily swigged beer from brown paper sacks.

At 8:45, a voice came over the loudspeaker, and a couple of uniformed deckhands appeared, to direct them in loading onto the *Cumberland Queen* ferry.

With the sun beating down, Cara chose a seat on the lower deck and spent the forty-five-minute ride across the St. John's River watching as seabirds wheeled in the sky above, and dolphins chased along in the boat's wake.

She also studied the map in the Park Service brochure. The island's major sightseeing spots were clearly marked. On the far north end was something called the Settlement. She found Plum Orchard, something called Yankee Paradise, Stafford Beach, Sea Camp, and Dungeness. Nowhere on the map was there a spot marked Loblolly.

But according to the internet, Loblolly had been built as a guest house/ hunting lodge—adjacent to Plum Orchard. So. Find Plum Orchard, and Loblolly would be nearby. Wouldn't it?

In her mind, she rehearsed what she would say when she found Brooke Trapnell. Occasionally, doubt crept in. What if she couldn't find the bride-to-be? The brochure she clutched in her sweaty hands described Cumberland as nearly 17 miles long by 3.5 miles wide, with over 36,000 acres of beaches, marsh, mudflats, and wilderness areas.

And poisonous snakes, Cara thought, remembering Bert's description. And alligators. But this wouldn't matter. She wouldn't be hanging around Cumberland long enough to experience any reptile confrontations.

Planning a wedding or any event required organization, clear thinking, and flawless execution. By the time the *Cumberland Queen* was chugging toward the ferry dock on the island, Cara had worked out her game plan. Step 1. Get bike. Step 2. Find Loblolly. Step 3. Grab Brooke. Step 4. Take Brooke home. Step 5. Payday.

Bert had warned her about the primitive facilities on the island, so she hurried toward the ferry's bathroom, and spotting the snack bar, bought another bottle of water.

. . .

The middle-aged woman at the bike-rental concession smiled as Cara stepped up to the counter. "Day rate or overnight?"

"Day," Cara said firmly. She paid for the bike from her petty-cash stash, then held out the now-creased map of the island. "Could you please tell me where I can find Loblolly?"

"Loblolly? You mean, like the pine trees?"

Cara shrugged. "Loblolly, like the house. It's supposed to be near Plum Orchard, I think."

"Sorry, never heard of it. Just be sure you have the bike back here thirty minutes before the four-forty-five ferry this afternoon. Okay?" The woman looked over Cara's shoulder. "Next?"

She'd been relieved to find that her bike was a fat-tired beach cruiser. Cara wheeled it away from the concession area, and looked around. Campers were loading gear into large beach carts and headed down the crushed-shell pathway, bikers were wheeling away, and the hikers were setting off down the road on foot. But which way should she be going?

Spying a young woman in a khaki Park Service uniform addressing the group of Girl Scouts, Cara hurried over to her. She waited while the ranger explained the rules—no touching or approaching the wild horses, stay on the trails, leave no trash anywhere on the island.

When there was a pause in the drill, Cara touched the ranger's arm. "Excuse me, could you help me with some directions?"

"I'll try."

Cara showed her the map. "I'm trying to find a private home called Loblolly. I think it's near Plum Orchard, but I'm not really certain."

The woman shook her head. "This is a national park. There aren't any private homes here anymore."

"Right. Well, I mean, I know it's a park, but I read on the internet that there were still a handful of private homes on the island, right? Aren't there still some Carnegies and Candlers who still own homes here? And also, Loblolly is one of them. Owned by the Updegraffs?"

"Sorry. Yes, there are still a very few private homes whose owners have retained rights, but I don't know about one called Loblolly, and I don't know any Updegraffs. I can tell you that those homeowners are pretty vigilant about their homes being private property. And most of them are reached through privately maintained roads, which are not open to the public."

"Oh." Cara adjusted her backpack straps, which were already cutting into her shoulders. "Well, now I'm more confused than ever. I know this place is called Loblolly, and that my friend is staying there."

"Let me just go check with one of the other rangers," the young woman said. Five minutes later she was back.

"You were right," she said, handing Cara's map back to her. "There actually *was* a house called Loblolly. But it wasn't at Plum Orchard. It was actually on the south end near the Dungeness ruins."

"Was?" Cara felt her stomach lurch.

"Loblolly was torn down last year, because the former owner's life lease expired, and the Park Service didn't consider it historically significant," the ranger said. "That explains why I'd never heard of it. I've only been on Cumberland for about nine months."

Cara felt her jaw drop open. "Torn down?" she said stupidly. "But my friend's family owned it. She told me she was staying there."

"I don't know what to tell you," the ranger said. "Maybe she was mistaken?" She took the map and pointed at a red circle. "This is Dungeness, if you want to take a look at where your friend's house was. And this," she said, stabbing another point just north of Dungeness, "is where you are right now. Sea Camp. Good luck!"

"Good luck," Cara muttered, pedaling south. "Good luck, my ass."

Any other time, Cara would have been entranced by Cumberland's natural beauty. Grand Avenue wound beneath a canopy of live oaks whose heavy, curving limbs reached out from both sides of the hard-packed road. Lush green ferns grew up the trunks of the oaks, and the branches were festooned with thick, silvery Spanish moss. Beyond the oaks, Cara saw stands of pines, magnolias, palmetto, and palm trees whose names she'd not yet learned.

Far ahead of her on the road she could see a few specks of humanity, the

Girl Scouts, on foot, but if she looked behind, all she saw was the road and the trees.

Birds twittered from the treetops, and she saw an occasional winged flash, but the aloneness struck her. Maybe that was what Brooke had come here looking for. Solitude.

There had been a picture in the brochure of Dungeness Castle as it had looked when it was built by the Carnegies, before it had been torched, in the fifties, by a poacher. Now, looking at the brick and tabby remains of the once grand home, Cara could see the outlines of the great house, and the way nature had already begun to encroach and overrun the ruins. Vines crept up walls and chimneys, palm trees sprouted where rooms had been. Cara held her breath when she spotted a group of three horses, two adults, and a colt, grazing on grass just inside the stone entryway, oblivious of her presence.

She circled the outskirts of the mansion, looking for some sign of Loblolly. She found collapsed and charred outbuildings, wound with what looked like decades' worth of honeysuckle and kudzu vines, and even what looked like an old car graveyard, with the rusting hulks of the Carnegies' once-splendid touring cars.

Finally, on the west side of the ruins, on a rise overlooking the river, she spotted what looked like a recently cleared spot of land. Neat piles of old bricks and worn timbers had been stacked to one side, but the outlines of mature boxwood hedges, bushy camellia shrubs, and a pair of twin palms were the only remnants of what must have been the foundation plantings for a fairly large house.

Cara laid the bike on the ground and walked around the property. The Park Service had done an admirable job of dismantling whatever had been here. From the siting of the palm trees, she guessed where the home's porch would have been. She stood there now, wondering what her next move would be, kicking frustratedly at the pale sand with the toe of her sneaker.

"Ow." Her toe hit something solid. She kicked it again, then knelt down to get a better look. She dug at the damp sand, brushing it sideways, until she spied a glimpse of dark gray granite. Her backpack swung awkwardly to one side, so she took it off and resumed digging. Five minutes later, she'd dug away enough sand to reveal a block of tile mosaic lettering. L-O . . . She dug on, until she'd exhumed a three-foot patch of granite threshold with the word Loblolly spelled in tile.

Cara sat back on her heels. So. The ranger had been right. Loblolly was gone. But where was Brooke Trapnell?

She glanced down at her watch. It was nearly noon, and she was hungry and thirsty, and the back of her sweaty T-shirt clung to her skin. She looked around for a shady place to take a lunch break. Just a few yards away was another of Cumberland's enormous live oaks. And this one had a picnic bench beneath it. Perfect!

She sat in the shade, uncapped her water bottle, and devoured one of her protein bars while reading the dozens of names and dates that had been carved into the wooden bench, leaving barely an inch of ungraffitied space. The earliest one she found was from 1972, inside a crude heart with the names "John + Marsha." The most recent entry was from 2013.

Cara leaned back on her elbows and sighed. The first year they'd moved into their house in Savannah, Leo had carved a heart with their initials into the trunk of a tall, spindly pine tree in their front yard. Less than a month later, the tree came crashing to the ground during a violent lightning storm, leaving a huge dent on the hood of Cara's car, and an ugly uneven stump, which, as far as Cara knew, was still there. Had that been an omen of things to come?

She was contemplating omens and their meanings and staring at the Loblolly home site when the sun caught a gleam of metal nearly hidden in the canopy of another live oak close to the house site. She took another swallow of water and walked closer to take another look.

A tree house! It had been built on and around the tree's thick main trunk, and the glint of metal she'd seen was a bit of its tin roof. As a child, Cara had always longed for a tree house, but of course, they'd lived in base housing in those days, and the Air Force didn't consider playhouses for little girls as standard issue.

She was almost directly under the plank floor of the house when she noticed the foot ladder nailed to the oak's trunk. And at the base of the trunk, she spied a pair of expensive-looking Jack Rogers sandals. Cara had seen a pair of sandals like those not so many days ago. She tilted her head as far back as it could go.

"Brooke?"

There followed an almost imperceptible rustling of branches, but the tree's foliage was so dense, she could see little besides brown branches and green leaves. Cara pulled herself onto the first rung of the foot ladder, holding on to the step above it. She climbed another step, and then the next. Finally, when she was nearly six feet off the ground, she saw the hatch that had been cut into the floor. Two more steps and she poked her head through that hatch.

Brooke Trapnell sat in the corner of the wooden house, her legs folded beneath her Indian style.

"Olly-olly-oxen-free," Cara said.

59

Brooke smiled wanly. "I saw you come riding up on your bike. I was hoping you wouldn't see me. What were you digging for over there? Buried treasure?"

Cara hoisted herself up and onto the floor of the tree house. The floor platform was a little larger than a king-size bed. The side walls were actually three foot railings, and the roof was held up by four-by-four posts. This must be what a rich kid's tree house looked like.

"When I was kicking the sand I felt something solid under my shoe. I guess it was the old threshold for your family's house."

That perked her up. "The one that said Loblolly?"

"Yes."

"I can't believe you found that. It must be the one thing the fucking Park Service didn't destroy."

"You didn't know they'd torn the house down?"

"No! I had no idea. When I got down to St. Marys on Saturday, I'd already missed the ferry. I should have just gotten a motel room and come the next morning, but in the frame of mind I was in, all I could think of was getting over here to Loblolly. I went to the marina and took a charter boat to the Sea

Camp dock. By the time I'd hiked down here, it was almost sunset. For a minute there, I thought maybe I'd somehow gotten turned around and gone the wrong way. Which made no sense. I mean, Dungeness is right over there."

Her finger stabbed the still, humid air, in the direction of the brick-and-stucco ruins. "So where was our house? I mean, how could it have just disappeared? Then, I saw the pile of bricks, and of course, you can still sort of see the outline of where the house was. I kind of went a little crazy. Okay, I was already halfway there, but the house being gone, that pushed me over the edge."

"What did you do?" Cara asked.

"You mean after I cried and carried on and stood over there on the bluff and screamed so loud I scared the feral horses and nearly gave a hiker a heart attack because he thought I'd been bit by a rattlesnake?"

"Yes. What did you do after that?"

"I turned around and started to walk back to Sea Camp. But then I realized there wouldn't be a ferry back to the mainland until the next morning. I had my overnight bag, but no tent or sleeping bag—and it was getting dark. I didn't know what else to do, so I called Pete."

"Your ranger friend?"

She nodded. "That day after we ran into him at lunch and I gave him my business card? He texted me after I got back to the office. I texted back, just to say how glad I was to have seen him, and that was it. He asked me to meet him for a drink, even suggested I should bring Harris, but I said no. I never intended to see Pete again."

"Then why come over here to Cumberland?" Cara asked. "You knew he'd be here, right?"

"I knew Loblolly would be here." She laughed ruefully. "Anyway, that's what I told myself. But with Loblolly gone, what else was I going to do? I had Pete's number in my phone, so I called him and told him where I was, and he came and got me, no questions asked."

Cara looked around again at the tree house. "I'm guessing you didn't stay up here."

"God, no. Pete has one of the little ranger cabins, so I stayed with him. The mosquitoes would have carried me away up here. Anyway, I'd forgotten all about the tree house until I came back over here yesterday, to see if there was anything left of the house that I could salvage. You know, a doorknob, anything at all. The Park Service was very efficient about obliterating every trace of Loblolly."

"And you really didn't know the house was going to be torn down? When was the last time you were here?"

"Mmm, maybe my senior year of high school, so that's like, ten years ago."

"Nobody in your family mentioned that the house was gone?"

"No, but that's understandable. My mom was never really crazy about staying at Loblolly. It was too much like camping for her, but I adored being here. We used to come over a couple times a year for a week or two at a time with my uncle Les and his family, but Les has been dealing with his own family stuff for the past couple years. His wife has breast cancer, and my cousin was nearly killed in a car wreck last Christmas and is still in rehab. I don't even know if Mom knows Loblolly has been torn down."

Brooke propped her elbows on her knees and looked out toward the riverbank. Cara took the time to study her. Her short, uncharacteristically messy hair was held back from her face with a rolled-up red bandanna, and she wore a pair of too-big wrinkled khaki shorts and a lime-green tie-dye T-shirt. It looked like she'd gone shopping at the St. Marys Goodwill.

"Did my mom send you to get me?"

"No. I promised not to tell where you'd gone. The only other person who knows where we are is Bert, my assistant. It was his idea for me to text you."

"Then why are you here?"

Cara didn't answer at first.

"Shhh. Look." Cara nodded in the direction of Loblolly. A herd of horses had drifted up and they were nosing about the vegetation around the foundation. There were six of them, four mares and two colts. They were so close, she could hear them whinnying.

"They're so beautiful," Cara whispered. "Where did they come from?"

"Nobody really knows. When we were kids we used to pretend they were pirate horses. Some people think they came over with Spanish explorers in the 1500s, but there would have been horses on the early plantations too, plus the Carnegies had their own stables. The Park Service has tried to figure out ways to manage the size of the herd, because they say the horses eat the sea oats and beach grasses that are needed to control beach erosion, but a lot of people love those horses, so it's just another hot topic on the island."

"Did you ever try to ride one of those horses?" Cara asked.

"You still haven't answered my question."

"I came here to Cumberland to find you and make you understand what a big mistake you're making. Now you. What are you doing here, Brooke?"

Brooke hugged her knees to her chest. "I guess I'm looking for me too."

"Oh God," Cara groaned. "Spare me the existentialism."

"I just wanted things to slow down a little, okay? I've been working all these hours for this trial coming up, and then Friday, my boss came in and said the other side had decided to settle out of court! It was like this huge load had been lifted. But I still had all the wedding stuff to contend with, and my dad and Patricia, and yes, even my mom, although she means well, it was all too, too much."

Brooke studied Cara. "Haven't you ever wanted to run away?"

"Sure," Cara said. "All the time. Everybody wants to run away at some time or another."

"But not everybody does."

"True that." Cara paused, trying to remember the speech she'd rehearsed on the ferryboat. "Harris and your mom are worried sick about you, Brooke. Your mom knows the pressure you've been under, and she told me she's afraid you'll hurt yourself."

"Me?" Brooke looked shocked. "Mom thinks I'm suicidal?"

"She doesn't know what to think. And Harris—he really loves you, Brooke. He broke down in tears when I talked to him. He blames himself for your leaving."

"He did?" Brooke looked away.

"Why didn't you just let them know you were going to take a few days off?" Cara asked. "They would have understood."

Brooke was looking down at something on the floor. She lowered a fingertip to a plank, then lifted it up so Cara could see a tiny ladybug perched there.

"I didn't plan to leave. I'd been dreading the bachelorette party. I've never understood why a girl feels the need to get dressed up in some stupid 'I'm the Bride' tiara and beauty-pageant sash and go riding around town with her girlfriends in a limo, getting shit-faced on candy-colored cocktails."

"Then why have one?"

"Holly—she's my best friend. And Harris's sister. I couldn't hurt her feelings and tell her I didn't feel like going clubbing. It's not normal to not want a bachelorette party. Finally, I made myself put on my game face. I was almost ready when I got a text from a number I didn't recognize. There was no message, just a link."

"To Harris's Facebook page," Cara said. "And the stripper photos."

Brooke's head bent over the ladybug, who was beetling her way up her wrist.

"We had another fight about the bachelor party Friday morning, before I left for work. Harris offered not to go—said he'd stay home if it was going to make me that upset. Which made me even angrier. I knew all the guys would blame *me* if Harris didn't go, and they'd say he was pussy-whipped."

"Damned if you do, damned if you don't," Cara said.

"He sent me a beautiful bouquet of flowers at work Friday, with the sweetest note, apologizing again and telling me how much he loved me." Brooke's face softened.

"He sent you flowers from another florist?" Cara said indignantly.

"He's a guy. I'm sure he got his secretary to send the flowers," Brooke said. "Anyway, so then I was feeling guilty about making him feel guilty, but I was still dreading going out. And then that text came Saturday afternoon. And I saw those pictures of him—with that woman—riding him—with her boobs pushed up in his face. . . ."

"I saw the pictures too, Brooke. He was drunk. So drunk he passed out in the van afterward."

"Harris told you that? Is he the one who told you the pictures were on Facebook?" She buried her head in her arms. "Did everybody in Savannah see them?"

"Layne, your caterer, saw them, and she sent me the link. Harris deleted the pictures as soon as he found out his friend Mike Bingham had posted them. Brooke? Did you ever figure out who texted you with the Facebook link?"

"No." She looked up. "I deleted it afterward. Does it matter? Somebody would have told me sooner or later anyway."

Cara felt herself grinding her back molars. "I have a pretty good idea who wanted to make sure you saw them."

"Who?"

"I can't prove it, but I bet Cullen Kane was behind it."

"The florist? The one Patricia wanted to hire?"

"That's the one. He'll do anything he can to mess with me."

"I don't get it," Brooke said.

"It's a long story. But let's get back to you. That's why you left? Because of the photos?"

"Yes." She held her right hand up to her left and let the ladybug cross over the fingertip bridge. There was a faint band of pale skin where her engagement ring had been. "Honestly? No. That's the lie I told myself the whole drive down here. I thought I wanted to hurt Harris as much as he'd hurt me. I decided I'd come over here, stay a couple nights at Loblolly, and then go back and get married."

"You can still go back and get married. Harris won't care where you've been. He just wants you to come back."

Brooke shook her head. "It's too late for that now. I can't marry Harris. I won't marry him." She looked over at Cara. "And nothing you can say is going to change my mind."

She tilted her right hand slightly, and the ladybug nimbly transitioned into the palm of her hand. Brooke stood up and leaned over the wooden railing. She raised her palm to her lips and blew gently.

60

Brooke sat back down and looked at the thin gold watch on her wrist. "If you leave now, you can still make the afternoon ferry back to St. Marys."

Cara's mind was working frantically. Where was that rational, well-planned speech she'd rehearsed? All she could think of was—why? Why not marry sweet, lovely, loving, wealthy, wonderful Harris Strayhorn? Why not return to her loving family in Savannah? Why not beg forgiveness and get on with a wedding that might mean the difference between financial success or suicide for Cara Mia Kryzik?

Her mind went haywire. So she asked the burning question.

"Are you sleeping with Pete?"

Brooke looked up at her through lowered eyelashes. She had such long, luxurious dark lashes, Cara had major lash envy.

"Who wants to know?"

"I do. It might help me understand what's going through your head right now."

"I wanted to sleep with Pete. That first night in his cabin, I tried to seduce him. Does that shock you?"

"A little," Cara admitted. "What happened?"

"He turned me down. He was the perfect gentleman. Pretty depressing, huh? I mean, you're alone on an island. You're naked. Well, I was naked. He was dressed in some kind of ranger boxers. And then nothing. Zero. He wouldn't even kiss me. Just patted me on the head and suggested I might be more comfortable if he took the sofa."

Cara couldn't help herself. She just blurted it out. "Is he gay?"

"He says not." Brooke giggled. "And, um, from the looks of his boxers that night, I'd say he's not immune to feminine wiles."

"What did he say?"

"Oh, the usual. 'I care too much about you to let you do something you might regret in the morning.' And then there was 'I wouldn't feel right about sleeping with another man's fiancée.' And let's not forget the old 'I don't believe in rebound sex.'"

Brooke sighed dramatically. "What is it with me and nice guys? Harris is nice. Pete is nice. I've never dated a not-nice guy. Just once in my life, I'd really like to go to the dark side. You know, do it with some really smoking hot, gnarly semicriminal bad boy."

"Who *are* you?" Cara gave her a quizzical look. "What happened to the sedate, conservative, dark-suit-wearing debutante lady lawyer from Savannah? Did they give you some kind of mystic Indian Kool-Aid when you got off the ferryboat Saturday? Because this is totally not the Brooke Trapnell I know."

"That's sort of the root of my problem," Brooke said. "You asked me earlier why I left. I'm just beginning to figure that out. I do know it's not because Harris went to some titty show. It's not because I want to punish my dad and Patricia for pushing me into a giant wedding that I didn't really want. And it's not because I'm in love with Pete Haynes. Although yeah, I'll admit I'm attracted to him. Which in itself should be a reason not to get married to Harris, don't you think?"

"Do you love Harris? I mean, really love him?" Cara asked.

"I thought I did," Brooke said softly. "I knew I *should* love him. Harris is perfect for me, right? So why was I having panic attacks in the middle of the night? And throwing up every morning? Why did I deliberately miss those dress fittings and portrait sittings?"

Now, thought Cara. *Now is the time to tell her how normal it is to have doubts and fears and panic attacks. Tell her about the hairless Chihuahua bride, or the girl who lost so much weight her mother ended up force-feeding her Ensure every day for two weeks before the wedding. Tell her this is all perfectly normal, and then drag her butt back to Savannah and collect her daddy's check.*

"The wedding is still two weeks off," Cara pointed out. "Maybe if you come home, let Harris know that you're feeling confused and unsettled, or speak to a therapist, go to couple's counseling or something, you'll realize that this is all just a severe case of pre-wedding jitters."

"Is that what you'd do?" Brooke asked, regarding Cara carefully. "If you were me, knowing what you know about what I'm feeling and what I've done, would you go back to Savannah and go through with the wedding anyway?"

"Dammit, that is not a fair question," Cara said.

"Sure it is. You've been married. And divorced. You've seen what, a couple hundred weddings up close and personal? You're battle-scarred. So tell me, what would you do?"

"I guess . . . I guess maybe I'd try to find a graceful way out of this mess. There's no way to do this without hurting people you care about, but from what you've told me, I don't think you should marry Harris. Not now, anyway."

Brooke nodded and reached over and squeezed Cara's hands. "Thank you for being honest with me. And for not ratting me out to anybody."

"You have to talk to Harris right away," Cara said. "He's in agony. And so is your mom."

"I know. And my dad too." She winced. "What's Dad's reaction to all this drama?"

"He was getting ready to hire a private detective to track you down and bring you home, but your mother managed to talk him out of it," Cara said.

"That sounds like Warden Gordon, all right."

They both laughed, and then Brooke stood up and dusted off the seat of her shorts. She pulled Cara to her feet, too.

"Will you go back with me? And talk to Harris face-to-face?" Cara asked, as Brooke lowered herself onto the top rung of the foot ladder.

Brooke hesitated, then shook her head. "I can't. If I go back, Harris will probably succeed in talking me into going through with the wedding. And I just can't risk that. It's the coward's way out, I know."

Cara dropped her backpack to the ground, and then climbed down after Brooke.

"What will you do?" Cara asked. "Savannah's a pretty small town. It's going to cause quite a stir when word gets out that you jilted Harris."

"Ow," Brooke said. "Jilted. It sounds so cruel."

"I tell it like I see it," Cara replied. "Remember, it's not just Harris who's going to be devastated. You say his sister is your best friend, and his parents adore you . . . I'm not trying to guilt-trip you, Brooke, but you need to be aware of what the consequences will be. For everybody involved."

"I'm fully aware," Brooke said calmly. "I borrowed Pete's computer and emailed my boss this morning and resigned from the law firm. Cell-phone service here most days seems to depend on which way the wind is blowing. I guess maybe I'll catch the ferry back with you this afternoon and try to call Harris tonight, when he gets home from work. I need to get some more clean clothes from my car, anyway. I'll call Mom and Dad too."

"Attagirl," Cara said. "And then what?"

Brooke shrugged. "Who knows? I can't stay with Pete too much longer, that's for sure. Park Service regulations." She made a face. "I do love it down here, though. I'd like to see if I could rent one of the little caretaker's cottages on the north end for two or three months. Just hang out and chill. See if I can make my brain and body slow down long enough to enjoy life. I want to spend fall on the island. It's my favorite time to be on Cumberland. Mom knows people, so maybe she could get me the hookup."

"And after the fall?" Cara asked. They were walking in the direction of Loblolly, where Cara had left her bike. The horses were gone now, and the sky had started to cloud up.

Brooke wasn't listening. She was looking down at the spot Cara had excavated, and in the next moment, she was kneeling on the ground, brushing sand away from the Loblolly threshold. "Hmm?"

Cara walked her bike over. "I said, what will you do after the fall? How will you make a living?"

Brooke looked up. "I'll figure that out, right after I figure out me. Who knows? Maybe I'll hang up a shingle in St. Marys. There must be somebody over there who needs suing, right?"

"Right."

A wide, mischievous grin lit up Brooke's face. "I'll start with the Park Service."

61

Bert was seated on the living-room floor in what looked like the lotus position, his hands palm-up, resting lightly on his knees. He opened his eyes when he heard Cara come clomping up the steps from the shop.

"How did it go?" he asked. "Did you manage to lasso the runaway bride?"

"No." Cara dropped her backpack on the floor and collapsed onto the sofa. Poppy took that as the signal to rest her muzzle in Cara's lap, nudging Cara's hand until she obliged with a head scratch.

"The wedding is off. Brooke called Harris and her parents this afternoon to let them know where she is and to say that she's not coming back."

"Oh, wow. Major bummer."

Cara looked idly around the room. Bert had managed to pack up everything from her bookshelves, and now boxes lined the living-room wall. "What exactly are you doing?" she asked.

"Yoga. My AA sponsor says sober means sober, so no more drugs. He says the yoga will help with keeping me grounded and quitting the weed."

"Sounds good. How long have you been doing yoga?"

"Counting this morning, twice. It's very relaxing. You should try it."

"Maybe later," Cara said.

"Was Brooke shacked up with the geeky ranger like you figured?" he asked.

"She's staying with him, but not sleeping with him. And she swears that calling off the wedding is not about the strip club or the geeky ranger or even about torturing her father and stepmother. I think she basically wants to hit the reset button with her life."

"Hmm." Bert slid forward with his hands under his shoulders, straightening his legs, lowering his head, and pointing his butt toward the sky. He held the pose for only a few seconds before dropping back onto the floor. "Ugh! Now I remember why I hate the Downward Dog pose. It makes all the snot run out my eyeballs."

"Just out of curiosity, how are you learning yoga? Are you going to class?"

"Nah. Classes cost money, and I don't like the idea of being in the same room with a lot of stinky, sweaty women. I just watch YouTube videos."

"Makes sense. By the way, thanks for packing up all the stuff, Bert. I was dreading coming home to face that. But mostly I was dreading coming home without Brooke in tow."

"I really thought you would pull this one off, Cara. I was sure if you found Brooke you'd be able to talk her into going through with things."

"Me too. I even had a brilliant five-point plan worked out."

"What happened?"

"I was outgunned. So that's it. No humongous two-hundred-and-fifty-thousand-dollar wedding means no humongous check. Patricia called me to make that perfectly clear. I called most of our vendors during the drive back from St. Marys. Everybody's disappointed. Nobody more so than me. I'll have to talk to the Colonel in the morning to break the bad news. He's going to pop a vein when I tell him I can't send the rest of his money the way I promised."

"He called today, by the way."

"My dad?"

"Yup." Bert got up and handed her a stack of pink message slips from the console table. "He tried calling your cell phone too, but said the calls wouldn't go through."

"Thank God for crappy reception on that island. I don't think I could have dealt with talking with the Colonel today. Wait a minute. How'd he get my cell number?"

"Not from me," Bert said.

Cara shook her head, then held up the other message slips. "Who are all these people? I don't recognize the names."

"Ahhh. Well, it seems your former nemesis Lillian Fanning has transformed herself into your own personal patron saint. The top three slips are all from brides or mothers of the brides wanting an appointment to talk wedding flowers, and two of them said Lillian referred them. The third girl, Taylor Vickers, and her mom, you're seeing tomorrow at eleven because she just had a tragic breakup with her former florist, and the wedding is only three weeks away."

"What florist did she break up with?" Cara asked.

"Some old mean queen named Cullen Kane."

"What! Bert, I appreciate your trying to make things up to me, but I do not want to be poaching Cullen Kane's clients."

"It's not poaching," he assured her. "I met Taylor while I was um, seeing Cullen. You know he wines and dines all these brides when he's trying to get them to commit, but she just discovered he's doing another big wedding the same date and time as hers, at a church across town, and when you meet Taylor's mama, you'll understand that she is *not* having a florist double-book on her date. I ran into Taylor at Whole Foods this morning, and she remembered me and told me the whole sad story. I might have slipped her one of your business cards. Not an hour later, her mama called here."

"You are shameless," Cara said.

"You say that like it's a bad thing."

"I told the other two brides you'd call them in the morning. This one"—he plucked the top slip and waved it in front of her—"is from the general manager of that new boutique hotel that opens at the end of July in the old Kresge's store downtown on Broughton Street."

"The Ibis? Did he say what he wanted?"

"*She* would like to discuss your developing a signature floral look for the hotel. I told her Wednesday noon would be good for you."

"Here? She can't come here. The shop is going to be all torn up. We've got to be of here by Friday. And we've got to finish up all the stuff for that beach wedding Saturday. . . ."

"Relax," Bert said. "Deep, cleansing breaths. In, out. Release the tension. You're meeting her at their new lobby restaurant. She'd like you to bring along some concepts, which I told her you'd be pleased to do."

"Concepts? I can't just come up with a whole look out of thin air by Wednesday. I don't know anything . . ."

Bert grasped her by the shoulders. "I got this. Okay? I went online and looked at the chain's website. There are seventeen Ibis hotels, all over the country, mostly out West, in California, Oregon, Washington, and Colorado. This is their first property in the South. Each of the hotels has a different name and theme, keyed to the location. I printed out photos I found of their hotels in Portland, San Francisco, and Seattle. I think they go for a pretty eclectic, bohemian look."

"You did all that? Today? On top of packing up my stuff?"

"I also finished off one of the oyster-shell chandeliers for Saturday."

"How many do we have left to do?"

"Two."

Cara groaned. "Then I guess I better go fire up the glue gun, huh?"

62

Jack found Libba in the barn Wednesday morning. She'd left the big sliding doors open, and she was standing in front of one of the windows, staring out at the pasture, where a mare and her foal drank from a galvanized watering trough.

She turned at the sound of his footsteps. It seemed to him that Libba Strayhorn had aged ten years since he'd seen her last. Her gray-streaked hair was pushed behind her ears, and the sunlight revealed the network of fine lines and creases radiating out from her warm gray eyes and downturned mouth.

"The wedding is off, Jack."

"I heard."

"Already? Yeah, what am I saying? The gossip mill in Savannah must be working overtime."

"Ryan's mother-in-law, Lillian, is friends with Marie Trapnell," he said.

"I should call Marie," Libba murmured. "Let her know I don't blame her."

Libba thrust her hands in the back pocket of her jeans. "Right now, I feel like a big old fool putting all this time and money and work into this place. Libba's Folly, that's what the neighbors around here have been calling it, and they haven't even gotten the word yet that the wedding is off."

Jack set his toolbox down on the floor. "I don't know what to say, Libba. How is Harris dealing with all this?"

"About like you'd expect. He's crushed. Hurt." Her laugh was bitter. "Pissed off. He and Brooke lived together for six years. Six years! That girl was like family to all of us. Nobody understands it."

Jack nodded. "Uh, we don't have to finish the work here if you don't want to. We can leave off tiling the bathroom. The kitchen fixtures have been delivered, but I can probably send them back and just pay a shipping and restocking fee."

"No," Lillian said sharply. "Mitch and I talked about this last night. We want you to go ahead and finish everything, just as planned. Harris is going to get past this. We'll all get past it. He will find somebody who has her head on straight and eventually get married to a girl who can appreciate what she's found in him. Holly has a new boyfriend, and that's gotten pretty serious. They will get married, and eventually we will have a large time right here. And someday, my grandbabies are going to laugh and run and play in this barn."

With that, Libba Strayhorn burst into tears.

Not knowing what else to do, Jack awkwardly patted her back.

Libba took a crumpled tissue from her pocket and blew her nose. "Please forgive a crazy old fool. I know this must be embarrassing for you. Go on and do what you need to do. I'll get out of your way in a few minutes."

"It's okay," Jack said. He hesitated. "I don't know if this is any consolation, but earlier this year, my live-in girlfriend left me, too. It came out of nowhere. She met some other dude and blew town with him. At first, I was destroyed. I mean, what the hell? But then . . . the longer she was gone, the more I saw that things hadn't been going that great between us. We didn't have much in common. Zoey wanted me to be somebody I wasn't. This sounds mean, but when I look back on it now, I realize we were just a habit. She did me a favor by leaving. But it still hurts like hell when the other person does what she did."

"Don't I know it," Libba said, sniffing. "What happened to the girlfriend?"

Jack rolled his eyes. "She's back in town, pestering the hell out of me. I let her stay at my place one night, while I was away, and now she keeps turning up, claiming she's just visiting the dog. I'm gonna have to get the locks changed to keep her out."

"But I gather you were able to move on," Libba prompted.

"A couple months ago, I met somebody new." His face darkened. "Okay, I don't know where I was going with this, because that didn't have such a happy ending either."

"Cara?" Libba asked gently.

"Yeah."

"You two broke up? Already? I'm so sorry. She's a lovely girl. A joy to work with, and so creative."

"She's all of that," Jack admitted.

"Do you mind my asking what happened?"

He made a helpless gesture. "The thing is, I don't know what happened. One minute, things were going great. We had fun together, we like the same things. We even have the same kind of dog. Cara has had some bad luck and tough times, financially, and it seemed like everything was coming down on her at once. I wanted to help out. Her shop is in this cool old building downtown on West Jones Street, and some asshole was gonna buy it and put Cara out on the street, out of professional jealousy. It just happens that I used to take piano lessons from the old lady who owned the place. I went to see her and I guess I sort of sweet-talked her a little because I was able to outbid the other guy."

"That's so thoughtful," Libba said.

"I thought so," Jack said wryly. "But apparently I was mistaken. I kept it a secret because I wanted to surprise Cara. The building hadn't been maintained at all, and it needs a lot of work, but I thought we could work on it together, you know? Really transform the place."

Libba squeezed his arm. "You could make anything awesome. I still can't get over the miracle you worked with this old barn. That's the one good thing that came out of all this. I'm just telling myself I didn't lose a daughter-in-law, I gained a fabulous barn."

"Thanks, but that's not how Cara saw it. She was mad as hell. Furious. Accused me of going behind her back, and making some sinister power play to get control of her and her business. She actually thought I was going to jack up the rent on her after making the improvements, and when I insisted I wasn't, that pissed her off even more, because she said I was insinuating she couldn't pay her own way."

He shook his head again. "I just don't get it. I did this for her. Out of, you know..."

"Love?" Libba raised one eyebrow.

"I guess."

"Had you two talked about your feelings, or how serious things had gotten between you?"

"Not really. I didn't think we needed to. I mean, we were together, and it was going good...."

"And then you bought her building, out of love." Libba laughed. "Some guys would have settled for a nice piece of jewelry, Jack."

He looked confused. "Why would Cara want jewelry? She was going to lose her shop, and her apartment. Her father's breathing down her neck to re-pay him some money she owes him, and this seemed like a good solution."

"I'll tell you a little story, Jack. Back in the early eighties, Mitch and I had been married a couple of years, and we were renting a crummy garage apart-ment on Washington Avenue, when I got pregnant with Harris. One day, some friend told Mitch about a little fixer-upper in Kensington Park, so he went to see it on his lunch hour, then came home that night and proudly announced he'd bought us a house."

"And you weren't thrilled?"

"I was enraged! I had three years' worth of back issues of *Southern Living*, bookmarked with ideas for our first house. And this place was a dump. Two bedrooms, one tiny little bath that didn't even have a shower. No washer or dryer, and the kitchen was a nightmare. If Mitch had bothered to show me the place, I could have pointed that out. I could have pointed out the fire station across the street, and predicted that every time there was an alarm, those fire trucks would go racing out of there with sirens wailing, waking our sleeping baby. But most of all, I hated that my husband didn't understand me enough to know you don't make that kind of a decision without consulting your partner."

"Point taken," Jack said.

"I tell you, I stewed and fumed over that house every day, until when I got pregnant with Holly, I laid down the law, we sold that house, and we picked out another house together in Ardsley Park."

"And you lived happily ever after."

A smile crept across Libba's round, ruddy face. "We did, didn't we?"

"I don't see that kind of ending for us," he said. "Cara is determined to move into another building, over on East Hall. The guy who owns it is a bottom-feeder, had it on the market forever, and couldn't unload it. I took a look at it, just out of curiosity, and it's a real piece of crap. That block is no place for a florist's shop, and it's no place for her. But I've learned my lesson. I'm staying out of it."

"No chance of a reconciliation?" Libba asked.

Jack shook his head vehemently. "I tried. Now I'm done. A man can only crawl for so long."

63

Cara heard heavy footsteps on the stairs. She stuck her head around the kitchen doorway. "Bert? Is that you?"

A blond head came into view. "It's Leo." He topped the last stair and flashed her his trademark Southeastern Region Salesman of the Quarter smile. "The shop door was open and unlocked, but there was nobody around downstairs, so I thought I should come up here and check things out. You shouldn't leave your door unlocked in this neighborhood, Cara. Anybody could walk right in here, like I just did."

"Thanks for the helpful advice, Leo. What do you want?"

He glanced around the kitchen. "I saw all the boxes downstairs. You're moving?"

"Yes." She slammed the packing-tape dispenser on the top of a cardboard box of dishes and dragged it across the closed flaps, snapping off the tape at the end.

"How come? I thought you liked it here. It looked like a pretty sweet setup."

"The building has been sold." Cara moved over to the next box. Leo leaned over and plucked a mug from a nest of wadded-up newspaper.

"Hey, I remember these. They were a wedding present from my aunt, right?"

"Keep it," Cara said.

"That's okay," Leo said, handing the cup back. "I got plenty myself."

He leaned back against the counter, crossed one foot over the other, oblivious of the fact that he was in her way.

"Where are you moving to? Not out of town, right?"

She put the tape down on the countertop. "Is there a point to this drop-in, Leo? Because if there is, I wish you'd get to it. Bert will be back with the van any minute now, and I want to finish boxing up this kitchen."

He glanced around the kitchen. "What happened to your new boyfriend? How come he's not the one doing all the heavy lifting?"

Cara flushed. "None of your business."

"Sounds like he's out of the picture now. Just as well. The dude was not in your class, at all."

Leo reached in his pocket, brought out a Chap Stick, and ran it across his lips, smacking them noisily, and in the process reminding Cara of how much she'd loathed that particular nervous habit of his.

"Again. Why are you here?"

"Well yeah," Leo said. "The thing is, your dad called and asked me to look in on you."

"Why would the Colonel do that?"

"He's worried about you. He said he'd tried calling you several times, at the shop and on your cell phone. . . ."

"Who gave him my cell-phone number?" Cara demanded. "I didn't."

"Okay, I might have shared that with him. But only because he was really concerned about you. He called me because he said he hadn't heard from you, and he was even thinking of flying down here to see if you were okay."

"I knew I should have changed that number after we split up," Cara said. "He actually asked you to come over here and spy on me?"

"It's not spying. We were married for Pete's sake. I care about you." He ran an index finger down her cheek, and Cara flinched. "You dad cares about you. "

"The Colonel cares about the fact that I still owe him money,," Cara said. "Did he appoint you his new collection agency? Or are you his idea of a leg-breaker?"

"He never said a word to me about money. He said you're having some challenges, that's all. He thought maybe I could help. I would help, if you'd let me."

"'Challenges'?" Cara hooted. "I'm pretty sure my father never used that word in reference to me. He probably told you I'm a screwup and a failure. Did he tell you he wants me to close up the shop and move back home?"

"He mentioned that," Leo said cautiously. "Your mom is gone and you're his only kid. He's lonely. Why is that so hard for you to swallow?"

"Because I know the Colonel. If he's lonely, why has he never, not once, come to Savannah to visit me? And don't give me any bullshit about him hating to travel. He goes to Vegas two or three times a year. If he was so worried about how my business was doing, why didn't he come down here to see for himself? Since I moved here, I'm the one who has to fly or drive up to Ohio, to see him on his own terms."

"I can't answer why your dad does or doesn't come down here," Leo said. "Okay, he's set in his ways. That's the military, right? He's always been like that. The Colonel just wants what's best for you, Cara. I want it too. You say you're moving because this building was sold, maybe that's true. But I think you're moving because business stinks, and you can't make the rent here. It's no big crime to admit it, you know. So what? Walk away. I don't happen to agree with the Colonel about you moving up home again. There's nothing in Ohio for you. On the other hand, I think enough time has passed, we should take another shot at making things work between us."

Cara blinked. "You really think so?"

"Yeah." He nodded thoughtfully. "We've both changed a lot. Matured. Maybe we got married too young to be able to appreciate what we had. But now, I know where I'm going, and what I want." He leaned in so close Cara could smell his cologne. "I want you, Cara. That's all. Just you. What do you say we load all these boxes in my car and take them over to my place?"

She took a step backward, and then another step. She could actually feel the blood rushing to her face, her fingertips tingling—with what? He'd caught her off-guard, that was sure.

"Move in with you again? Is that what you're saying?"

"Yeah. Exactly."

"Close up the shop. But how do I pay off the Colonel?"

"I got money. I'm doing great. They just gave me the two biggest accounts in the territory. I've actually been thinking of selling the condo, buying a house again. Have you seen those houses out at Southridge? Four bedrooms on the golf course, swim and tennis club. You could decorate it like you like...."

"And then what?"

"Whatever you want. I don't know, you could maybe keep doing flowers if you wanted, work for somebody else, not as much pressure. And I was thinking, maybe next year, we could start a family."

"Have a baby?"

He nodded. "Yeah. My mom is crazy to have another grandchild...."

She felt a roaring sensation in her ears. "Are you crazy? I'm not moving in with you, Leo. I'm not closing up my business and moving to some country-club development. I am not taking money from you to pay off my dad, and I am most definitely not having your baby."

"We could wait on the baby like another year or so...."

"Leo!" Cara was shouting. "We are over. We've been over. I don't need your money, or your pity or your advice. Maybe you have matured, but I seriously doubt it if you were able to convince yourself that this fantasy of us remarrying and moving to the suburbs could ever become reality."

"You don't have to shout," he said, putting on that hurt look of his. "I was just trying to help out, okay? You want to talk about fantasy?" He gestured around the kitchen, with its chipped laminate countertops and faded linoleum.

"This right here is a fantasy. You can't even afford this place, and you think moving someplace else is going to fix things? Who are you kidding? The Colonel is right—you are a screwup. You're pathetic, Cara. Really. So you just keep on doing what you're doing. Stay right here in your dreamworld. Move on over to the next roach motel. You're all about doing everything for yourself, not accepting help from anybody. Maybe that's why the boyfriend left you.

Great. Keep it up. Be a ballbuster. You're going to end up the crazy dog lady of Savannah, broke and alone."

"Get out," she whispered. "Don't call me again."

"Not a problem," he snapped, heading for the stairs. She stood in the hallway, watching him go. She heard the front door open, and now Bert was heading back to start retrieving the moving boxes. "Some asshole parked a black Lexus in the loading zone out back," he called. "I had to park the van a block over."

Bert stood in the downstairs hallway, glowering when he spotted Cara's ex.

"I'm just leaving," Leo said curtly.

"Shitbird," Bert muttered.

Cara couldn't help it. She had to have the last word. She ran down the stairs after Leo. "Tell the Colonel he'll get his money. Tell him I have three weddings and a big fat contract to do all the flowers for a new hotel in town. Tell him . . ."

It was too late. She heard the back door slam.

64

It was nearly six by the time Jack got back to Savannah from Cabin Creek. He told himself he was only driving past the shop to see if Cara really meant what she said about moving out. He slowed the truck to a roll as he approached the shop, but when he saw the large, hand-lettered MOVED TO NEW LOCATION sign in the window, he pulled up and parked in the loading zone.

BLOOM HAS BEEN TRANSPLANTED TO EAST HALL STREET, the sign said in smaller letters. Trust Cara to make that seem like a good thing.

He fished the set of keys with the C&S Bank key fob out of his pocket and unlocked the front door. The first thing he noticed was that the little tinkling bell that announced visitors was gone.

The second thing he noticed was the smell of antiseptic. True to her word, Cara had stripped the walls of the reclaimed-pine shelves and the chippy wrought-iron trellis, the mirrors and the chandeliers. A slight indentation in the wood floor was the only sign that a flower cooler had once occupied this space. The shop was spotless. And empty.

He walked through to the back of the first floor, glancing into the kitchenette and noticing that this, too, had been cleaned out. The undercounter dorm-size refrigerator was gone, but he noticed that the coffeepot had been left behind.

Jack unlocked the door to the courtyard patio. To his surprise, the space looked the same as it had the last time he and Cara and the dogs had sat out here. He was relocking the door when he spotted a small yellow Post-it that must have fallen to the floor.

> *J—I won't be needing patio furniture in the new place until I get backyard cleared out. Hope it's ok to leave here for now.—C.*

He shrugged. This was her idea of a good-bye note. No "Dear Jack," no "Fondly, Cara."

The second floor had been as thoroughly cleaned out as the first floor. The walls bore the faded outlines of where Cara's pictures had hung, and there were depressions in the carpet left there by the now departed bookshelves.

Curtains still hung at her bedroom window, and when he brushed the thick linen panel aside to look out onto the street below, it released a scent he realized was Cara's. Her box fan was still wedged inside the window casing.

Jack slid down to the floor, his hands on his knees, his back against the wall. He inhaled and the faint floral bouquet of roses and some other flower— maybe honeysuckle—filled his nostrils. He thought about the night they'd danced at Ryan and Torie's wedding, the way she looked in that pink silk dress and how she felt in his arms.

Sweat trickled down his shoulders to the small of his back. It was unbearably hot up here. How had Cara stood it up here for these past few weeks? He stood slowly and started toward the stairs, but then he backtracked to the bedroom, where he unplugged the fan and tucked it under his arm.

As he was passing the kitchen, he spotted a lone coffee cup sitting on the kitchen counter. All the cabinets and shelves had been emptied. He wondered if Cara had meant to leave this one behind. He picked up the cup, and on the rim saw the faint pink remains of her lipstick. He told himself he would return the cup when he returned her fan. That's what he told himself.

. . .

The prospect of returning home alone to the cottage on Macon Street did not appeal. Anyway, there was a good chance he wouldn't really be alone. Zoey's check still hadn't arrived, so despite her sketchy description of a job offer in New Orleans, she was still hanging around, sleeping on the sofa at a friend's house, but "dropping by" Jack's place, ostensibly to be with Shaz.

Tonight he was in no mood for Zoey's laughably obvious attempts to seduce him. What he was in the mood for was a cold beer and some hot wings. He called Ryan.

"Hey bro," Ryan said. "What's shakin'? You finish up over at Cabin Creek? Pick up the rest of the tools and stuff?"

"Change of plans," Jack said. "Libba wants us to go ahead and finish everything. Including the kitchen."

"Even with the wedding off?"

"Yep. She wants it finished. How did you guys do today over at Sylvia Bradley's?"

"You don't want to know," Ryan said. "That old lady is driving me nuts. We put the new roof on that mud porch yesterday, and this morning when I got over there, she'd somehow managed to climb up on the ladder, and she proceeded to bitch me out about how the new shingles were a different color than the ones on the rest of the house!"

"Did you explain that those old shingles probably hadn't been manufactured since the Eisenhower administration?"

"I tried, but you don't explain nothin' to Sylvia Bradley. She wants you to call her. I think she's gonna try and talk you into giving her a new roof for the rest of the house."

"Not happening," Jack said succinctly. "Hey, I'm headed over to the Exchange to grab a bite. You wanna meet me?"

"Awww, man. Wish I could. We've got our first childbirth class at the hospital tonight."

"Okay, no problem. Listen, in the morning, I'm gonna get the HVAC guy to walk through Jones Street with me, to see when we can get started on that."

"Oh. So . . . Cara went ahead and moved out?"

"Yeah. Probably for the best. You know what a pain in the ass it is to rehab a building when somebody's living there. Anyway, good luck tonight. I hope you do better with childbirth class than you did with high-school algebra. Cuz I am *not* helping out with that homework."

"Smart-ass," Ryan growled.

Jack sat in a booth by the window. The tables around him were filled with groups, families with young kids, gray-haired couples there for the early-bird specials, and groups of office workers stopping in for happy hour after work.

He drank a beer and ate half a plate of wings before deciding he was tired of avoiding his own home. Zoey had managed to find his spare key. By God, he would go back to Macon Street right now, and if she was there, he would kick her ass to the street. And then he would go to Home Depot and buy a new lockset and install it himself.

65

I forgot the coffeepot," Cara said.

Bert dumped the last box of dishes on the dining-room table. Which was sitting in the middle of the large open space that would allegedly someday be Cara's living quarters.

"Forget about it," he said, collapsing onto one of the chairs. "We've still got to get your bed set up, and anyway, there's no telling where your dishes or pantry stuff are. I'll go over to Back in the Day in the morning and get us coffee and muffins."

"No more takeout coffee," Cara said stubbornly. "Our overhead here is going to be killer. We've got to start economizing. And that means no more five-dollar lattes. I'll just run over to Jones Street and get the coffeepot. I think the pantry stuff, with the coffee and the sugar, are in that box there." She pointed to a large carton on the floor. "If you'll start unpacking that, I'll take Poppy with me, and we'll bring back pizza for dinner.

"Come on, Poppy," Cara called. "Let's go, girl."

The dog came running and happily allowed herself to be loaded into the front seat of the pink Bloom van for the short ride back to their old home.

. . .

Cara let herself in the front door and felt the gloom descend on her, like a heavy wool blanket. She wouldn't allow herself to look at the barren walls, at the swept-clean floor. Get the coffeepot and get out, she told herself.

Poppy raced down the hall. She stopped in front of the back door, glancing back expectantly at Cara, and pawed at the door.

"Okay," Cara said with a sigh. "One more try. Maybe that squirrel will get careless, and you'll get lucky." She opened the door and Poppy was out like a shot.

She went back to the kitchenette and unplugged the coffeemaker.

"Hey!" a woman's voice called from the front of the shop. She banged on the glass window. "Hey, are you in there?"

Cara poked her head out of the kitchen nook. A willowy blonde stood on the sidewalk, peering in through the window.

She opened the door. "Can I help you?" Over the woman's shoulder she spied a yellow VW bug parked in the loading zone. A familiar fluffy white dog's head hung out the open passenger window.

"Rowlf!" Shaz barked a greeting.

Zoey was a stunner, even with her long blond hair pinned carelessly atop her head. She wore a tight-fitting turquoise tank top that showed off impressive cleavage and a span of flat, tanned abdomen above low-slung white denim shorts. She had dancer's legs, long and toned, if just the slightest bit bowlegged, and she stood at least four inches taller than Cara, making her feel like a dwarf. A dowdy, depressed dwarf.

Zoey was studying Cara, too, and not bothering to pretend otherwise. "So you're the new girlfriend," she said, her lips flickering amusement. "Sorry for the intrusion, but I just had to check you out for myself before I leave."

Cara was looking at the VW. The backseat was loaded with boxes, and there was a bike on a rack strapped to the rear bumper.

"You're leaving town?" she asked. Stupid question.

"Sure am. My severance check from the cruise line finally came today, so I am out—like the fat kid in dodgeball." Zoey laughed at her own little joke.

Shaz had managed to wriggle her whole upper body out of the toylike VW window.

"Does Jack know you're leaving?" Cara asked.

"He'll figure it out when he gets home and sees that Shaz is gone."

"Where are you moving?" In her mind's eye, Cara could picture Jack arriving back at Macon Street, opening the door, and waiting for the dog to nearly knock him down with her bad-mannered adoration.

"New Orleans," Zoey said brightly. "I'm going to teach at a new studio that just opened in the French Quarter. It's called Sweatbox. Cool, huh? And I've rented the cutest little furnished efficiency you've ever seen, on the third floor above it."

Cara frowned, thinking of Shaz cooped up in a third-floor studio all day. Jack's cottage might be small, but it had its own fenced backyard, and these days, she knew, more often than not, Jack took Shaz with him to his job sites.

She turned her attention back to Zoey. "Why are you telling me all this?"

Zoey's laugh was deep and throaty. She could have had a great career doing phone sex. "That's a very good question. First off, before I leave town, yeah, I wanted to check you out, see what the hot attraction was between you two. Honestly? I don't get it. But you know what? I have no regrets. You want Jack Finnerty? Honey, you can have him. Yeah, he's cute, and he's great in bed. But you already know that, right?"

Cara stared up at the blonde, wondering where this was going, and whether she should admit that she and Jack were no longer an item.

"But here's something you might not have realized yet. He might have a hot body, but deep down, Jack is cold. He's cold and he's emotionally unavailable. He walls himself off from you, and there's no breaking that down. And did I mention he's a tightwad? We lived together for over a year, and he never bought me the first piece of jewelry."

And yet, Cara thought. She and Jack had slept together exactly three times by his accounting, and then he'd gone out and bought her a building. A three-story $750,000 building. And to thank him, she'd thrown it right back in his face. Figuratively speaking.

Shaz barked, and Zoey looked over her shoulder and frowned. "Quiet, baby, we're leaving in just a minute."

Cara's mind was working. She kept picturing Jack, walking into that cottage and realizing just how empty it really was.

"It's a long ride to New Orleans," she said, trying to sound casual. "And it's so hot. You don't want her to get dehydrated. Why don't you let me take Shaz out back to my courtyard, where my dog is? I'll give her some water and she can have one more potty stop before you hit the road."

"Okay, yeah, whatever," Zoey said carelessly. She opened the VW's door and Shaz bounced out, like an overinflated helium balloon. Zoey pulled a cell phone from the pocket of her shorts and leaned back against the car. "I'll just wait here for her."

Cara opened the door to the courtyard, and on spotting Poppy, Shaz barked a happy greeting. Poppy dropped the headless rubber doll she'd been chewing on, and came over to sniff Shaz's muffle, and then her butt. A moment later, Shaz grabbed the toy Poppy had dropped, and lay down on the bricks to give it a chew.

"Come here, Poppy," Cara called softly, looking back over her shoulder to make sure she was unobserved. For once, the dog obeyed. Cara wrapped her arms around the dog's shoulders, inhaling the smell of her freshly shampooed fur. Poppy licked Cara's neck and chin, while, with trembling fingers, Cara unbuckled her pink plaid collar and slipped it from her neck.

"I'm so sorry to do this to you," she whispered in the dog's silky ear. "But you're just going to have to trust me. Okay? Do you trust me?"

Poppy's tail beat a happy tattoo on the bricks.

"Okay," Cara said, leading the dog out to the VW. "She's all set to go."

Zoey put her phone away, opened the car door and gestured. "Come on, Shaz. Let's go! Let's go for a nice ride."

The dog planted its butt on the curb and looked from Zoey to Cara.

"Damn it, Shaz," Zoey cried. She grabbed the dog's neon-green collar and tugged. "Come on!" The dog resisted, even backing away from the VW.

Cara held her breath. "Let's go, Shaz," she said cheerily, giving the dog's butt a gentle push. Finally, between the two of them, they managed to wedge her back into the VW's passenger seat.

"Jack spoiled her rotten while I was gone," Zoey griped, crossing around to the driver's side. "Which is hysterical, since he claimed he never wanted a puppy in the first place. Now, he treats her way better than he ever treated me." She gave Cara an appraising look. "You watch, he'll do the same with your dog, now that Shaz is gone."

"Maybe so," Cara said. She stood back from the curb, and when the VW lurched away, she gave a sad little wave as it drove off, with the dog's big fluffy head hanging out the window, looking backward.

Cara raced inside the shop and picked up her cell phone. She touched the icon with Jack's number, praying he would pick up.

Fifteen minutes later, he pulled the truck around to the lane in back of the shop. He used his key to unlock the courtyard door.

Cara sat at the table under the umbrella, clutching her phone in her hand, her face etched with worry.

"Are you nuts?" he exploded. Shaz jumped up and planted her paws on his chest. "Down!" he said sternly, but she was not to be deterred. Finally, he scratched her head and her ears. She dropped to the ground, rolled over, and allowed him to scratch her belly.

"What if this doesn't work?" he asked, glaring at Cara. "You don't know Zoey. She's a total flake. There's no telling what she'll do. She could drive straight through to New Orleans, and you'll never see Poppy again. And then what? You'll blame me, even though if you'd run this harebrained idea past me, I would have told you how crazy it was."

"Five more minutes," Cara said, glancing down at her watch. She reached her hand out for Jack's phone. "Let me see Zoey's number, so I can type it into my phone."

"She might not answer," Jack warned. "She won't know who's calling. Or maybe she won't even hear it. She plays the radio in that car at full volume."

"Just give me the phone, please," Cara said.

He handed it over and she tapped in the number.

"Why did Zoey even come over here?" he asked.

Cara was still staring down at her phone, but she looked up now. "She wanted to check out what she thought was the competition. And she clearly didn't see what you could have seen in me."

"That's textbook Zoey. She's about as deep as an Arizona mud puddle."

"She had a lot to say about you, Jack. And none of it was very flattering. She says you're cold and emotionally distant."

"Sounds about right."

"And cheap. She says you never gave her a single piece of jewelry."

His answering smile was grim. "Seems like I'll be buying her some now, whether I like it or not. I'd just walked in the door five minutes earlier when you called. She wasn't content to just take Shaz. She also cleaned out my sock drawer."

"Zoey stole your socks?"

"She left the socks, but she took my stash. Sometimes my subs want to be paid in cash. I figure she got about two thousand dollars."

Cara held up her phone so Jack could see it. "Okay, keep your fingers crossed. It's been thirty minutes. It usually only takes about twenty minutes for Poppy."

She tapped the Dial button on her phone. Zoey's phone rang once, twice, three times, before the voicemail recording came on.

"Hi, this is Zoey," the sultry recorded voice said. "You know what to do."

Cara shook her head and disconnected.

"See? I knew this would happen. She probably thinks you're a bill collector or something."

"Or maybe she's got her hands full right at the moment," Cara said, swallowing her fear.

She dialed again, and this time Zoey picked up. Cara could hear the rush of traffic in the background.

"Oh, Zoey," Cara cried with absolutely authentic relief. "Something awful has happened."

"You're telling me," Zoey said.

"I must have gotten the dogs mixed up. Poppy and Shaz were both running around in the backyard, and they look identical, and somehow, I must have given you my dog, Poppy, instead of Shaz."

"Thanks a lot," Zoey said. "This damn dog has been barfing for ten minutes. She barfed all over the car, herself, me, it's everywhere. It's disgusting."

"I am so, so sorry," Cara said. "I just realized my mistake."

"Yeah, ten minutes too late," Zoey said. "Okay, I'm turning around right now. I can't take much more of this."

Cara hung up and turned to Jack with a triumphant smile. "She's coming back."

"Thank God," he breathed. "But Zoey's not going to give up this easily. Once she hands over Poppy, she's gonna insist on taking Shaz with her, if only because she wants her revenge against me."

"I've got another idea," Cara said. "Do you trust me?"

Jack looked down at Shaz, who was curled up at his feet. Despite all the excitement, she was asleep, softly snoring. "Do I have a choice?"

Exactly twenty-seven minutes later, the VW zoomed up to the curb in front of Bloom. The motor was still running as Zoey jumped out, ran around, and opened the passenger door. "Out!" she screamed. Poppy's head hung limply over the edge of the seat. "Get out, dammit!" Zoey repeated.

Cara stepped up and gathered the reeking puppy into her arms. "Poor baby," she crooned. "My poor baby."

"*Your* poor baby," Zoey exploded. "Look at me! Look at my car! I can't go anywhere like this. I've gotta get out of these clothes, shower, get my car cleaned up. I was gagging the whole way back here. I mean, what the fuck?"

"I'm sorry," Cara said, setting Poppy carefully down on the sidewalk. "But

I'm surprised you haven't encountered this with Shaz when you go on car trips. The vet says it's something to do with the breed."

"I've never taken Shaz on a car trip before," Zoey replied. "What are you talking about?"

"Carsickness," Cara said. "The vet says it's hereditary with goldendoodles."

"The breeder never mentioned it to me," Zoey said. "And come to think of it, when I brought Shaz back from Atlanta, that was a four-hour car ride, and she was fine. She slept the whole way home."

"Exactly," Cara said. "My vet says it's something the breeders downplay. Like hip dysplasia in Great Danes. When they're really young, it doesn't affect them so much. But once they're seven or eight months old . . . bleaaahhhh." Cara pantomimed an Oscar-worthy rendition of canine carsickness. "Poppy's fine for a short ride, like to the vet or the grocery store, but if she's in the car for more than fifteen minutes . . . bleaahhh."

Zoey shuddered, then tapped her foot impatiently. "Jack never said anything about Shaz getting carsick."

"Like you said, he's totally selfish," Cara pointed out. "He was probably hoping you'd take Shaz with you so he doesn't have to deal with her himself." She gestured toward the shop door. "If you want to come inside and get cleaned up, I'll take Poppy out to the garden and hose her off, and then you can get Shaz. I've probably got some old towels you can take with you for the rest of the trip. Just in case, you know . . . bleahhh."

Zoey crossed and uncrossed her arms. It took less than thirty seconds to make up her mind.

"Yeah. Thanks but no thanks. I think I'm just gonna let Shaz be Jack's problem from now on."

"You sure?" Cara asked helpfully. "I've got plenty of towels."

"Positive," Zoey said. "I gotta get to a car wash before this mess soaks into my upholstery." She looked over at Poppy, and then at Cara. "Gross."

Cara stood perfectly still while Zoey slammed the VW into first gear and pulled away from the curb.

She held up her right hand and gave a soft finger wave. "Buh-byeeee."

66

The bells at St. John's were just tolling six. Cara led Poppy through the lane and into the courtyard garden. She fetched the galvanized tub and the bottle of dog shampoo from the toolshed, and filled it with water from the hose. Then she held a dog treat beneath Poppy's nose, and gently coaxed the puppy into the tub. Cara squeezed shampoo into her hand and worked it into the dog's fur, training the nozzle over Poppy's fur.

"Zoey's gone," she told Jack, who still held a tight hand on the pink collar around Shaz's neck. "And the coast is clear."

"I was inside, crouched down, watching through the front window," Jack said. "I figured, if Zoey tried to argue with you, I'd come out and try to buy her off. What did you say to get her to leave Shaz behind?"

Hearing her name mentioned, Shaz stood, her ears pricked up. Jack released his hold on her collar and she edged over to watch the proceedings.

"Does she like a bath as much as Poppy does?" Cara asked, looking over at Jack.

He looked chagrined. "Uh, I guess. I mean, when I take her to the groomers, she's okay with it."

Cara gave him a look of reproof. "She's half golden retriever. Most retrievers love the water.

"Come here, you," Cara said, and Shaz propped her front paws on the edge of the washtub. She looked over at Jack. "Put out your hand."

He did as he was told, and she squeezed a dollop of shampoo into his open palm. He gave a disdainful sniff. "Smells like flowers."

"Deal with it," Cara said. She trained the hose on Shaz's head and then body, deliberately splashing Jack's legs.

"Come on," he said, choosing to ignore the water. "What did you tell Zoey?"

Cara scrubbed at Poppy's coat with both hands, working up a thick lather of suds. "I told her my vet says all goldendoodles are subject to carsickness. Because it's hereditary."

"That's bullshit. Shaz has never gotten carsick. I've taken her over to South Carolina, to Cabin Creek, plenty of times. It's a forty-five-minute drive, one way. She loves riding in the truck."

"Mmm-hmm," Cara said. "I totally made it up. Luckily, Zoey was happy to buy my lies."

"Luckily," Jack said.

"In the end, she basically told me I was welcome to the guy, and the dog. I guess she decided you were both more trouble than you were worth."

He got up from the chair and gazed down at Cara, still bent over the tub, washing her dog. He'd never noticed the fine sprinkling of freckles across her shoulders and the back of her neck. Then he stood up, grabbed the hose, and trained it on her exposed neck and back.

She gave a yelp of surprise. He grabbed her hands and pulled her to her feet. "I don't know about the dog, but I do know that I'm definitely more trouble than I'm worth. I still can't believe what you just did for me out there. Thank you. Thank you so much, Cara. You let Zoey take Poppy, not really knowing if she'd bring her back, if your crazy scheme would work. You risked everything for me."

Cara sighed. "Sometimes, you just have to trust your gut."

He took her hands and placed them on his own hips, then wrapped his arms loosely around her shoulders and tilted his forehead until it was resting on hers.

"Sometimes you have to trust your heart, too. You give what you think the other person needs, and hope they know that you're doing it out of love."

Cara raised her chin and smiled. "It took me a while, I'll admit. I wasn't very gracious about accepting your gift. But I think maybe I'm ready now, for whatever you have to offer."

His lips found hers. He pulled her tighter, then whispered in her ear. "All of it. Everything. Darlin', everything I have is yours."

She felt her knees buckle, which forced her to clasp herself tighter against his chest. "I love it when you call me darlin'."

There was a chattering just then, from the top of the crape myrtle. Poppy scrambled out of the washtub, and dashed after the squirrel in mad pursuit, with Shaz hot on her heels. The two wet, soapy dogs crouched at the foot of the tree, snouts pointed upward, barking in perfect unison.

"We are not taking those dogs on our honeymoon," he muttered.

"Honeymoon?"

"Will you marry me, darlin'?" Jack asked.

She fluttered her eyelashes like a true Southern belle. "Since you put it like that, of course I will."

Epilogue

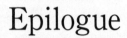

Afterward, Ellie Lewis, the wedding coordinator, would swear that this was the sweetest, most romantic wedding she'd ever witnessed. But in the middle of the melee, she merely swore.

When she arrived at Cabin Creek shortly after five that sunny day in early October, all was chaos. She found the bride in the barn, dressed in blue jeans and a faded T-shirt, putting the finishing touches on the tables for the reception, and the groom, also clad in jeans and a T-shirt, standing at the top of a ladder, fastening the last of the vintage-wagon-wheel chandeliers he'd made under Cara's tutelage.

A pair of nearly identical fluffy white dogs lounged in the vicinity of the kitchen, staring with hopeful black button eyes at the crew of caterers who were starting to chop the pork butts that had been on the smokers all afternoon.

Each of the fifteen handmade tables was draped in an artfully paint-spattered canvas dropcloth, and Cara was buzzing from table to table, fluffing the centerpieces of local wildflowers mixed with sunflowers, pink and coral dahlias, and lime-green bells of Ireland arranged in a variety of mismatched antique white ironstone vases, pitchers, and jugs.

"Cara!" Ellie was out of breath by the time she caught up with the bride. "What are you doing? Your guests start arriving in an hour. You've got to get dressed, get your hair and makeup done. . . ."

"Almost done here," Cara assured her, pinching a less-than-perfect petal from a stem of blue salvia. Cara stood back, hands on hips, and nodded in approval. "Okay, that's it. Now I can get dressed."

"And you!" Ellie stood at the bottom of the ladder, staring up at the groom. "Jack, you were supposed to finish those chandeliers last night. You promised, after the rehearsal dinner . . ."

"They're done now," Jack said, climbing down. "Anyway, it's Cara's fault. She decided at midnight last night that we had to wire vines and flowers and moss around those old wagon wheels. And by we, she meant me."

"Scoot!" Ellie made shooing motions toward the open barn doors. "And what about your brother? And your sister and Harris? And Torie? Are you telling me that not a single member of my wedding party is here yet?"

Jack grinned. "Torie's up at the house nursing baby Betsy." He glanced at his watch. "Ryan ought to be back any minute. He just made an emergency bourbon run. Meghan and Harris? Hell, I don't know." He jerked his chin skyward. "Check up there in the hayloft. Everytime I look for those two I seem to find them in some kind of compromising position."

His voice echoed in the high-ceilinged barn. Sure enough, a moment later, Harris Strayhorn poked his head over the loft railing, frantically buttoning his shirt. "Hey, I heard that! We were just, uh, checking the acoustics up here. For the bluegrass band."

"Since when does a sound check require the removal of clothing?" Jack demanded. "You better not be dishonoring my baby sister up there."

Meghan Finnerty peeked over Harris's shoulder. "Mind your own business, Jack Finnerty!" She deftly plucked a stalk of hay from Harris's hair. "And don't you say a *word* to Mama or Miss Libba, or I'll tell both of 'em what I caught you and Cara up to in that hay wagon after the rehearsal last night."

"I don't care what any of y'all have been up to," Ellie screeched. "I need everybody who is going to be in this wedding to get up to the house right this minute and get themselves cleaned up and dressed for this wedding."

Harris scrambled down from the loft, with Meghan following a moment later. He turned, caught her by the waist, and swung her to the ground, his hand lingering at her waist just a second longer than was absolutely necessary.

"Tell 'em, baby," he urged.

"Tell us what?" Jack asked.

Meghan gave a quick shake of her head. "Nothing." She grabbed Harris's hand. "Come on. Ellie's right. My mom will have a fit if I'm not dressed and ready for the photographer in fifteen minutes."

"Wait." Jack grabbed Meghan's left hand and held it up. A large diamond solitaire twinkled in the late afternoon sunlight. "What's this?"

Meghan gave Harris an exasperated look. "It was supposed to be a secret. Until after the wedding. I don't want anybody to think we're trying to upstage you and Cara. . . ."

Jack pounded Harris on the back. "You son of a bitch! Congratulations! That's great." He gathered his sister into a hug. "Do Dad and Frannie know?"

"I managed to get your dad alone to ask his permission after the dinner last night," Harris said.

"Daddy burst out crying!" Meghan said. "And when Mama walked over and saw Daddy crying, she started in. . . ."

Harris rolled his eyes. "Which will be nothing compared to the way my parents are gonna react when we tell them. . . ."

"You can tell everybody later," Ellie said. "After the wedding. Which starts in forty-five minutes." She fumbled in the pocket of her all-purpose light blue wedding-reception dress and pulled out a small bottle of pills. "I swear, I am never doing another wedding professional's wedding. Ever again." She popped a pill, swallowed, and mopped her face with a crumpled lace hankie.

Torie Fanning Finnerty tucked her slumbering infant into the bassinette, kissed her fingertip, and touched it to her daughter's velvety cheek. She turned and gave the bride an appraising look followed by a smiling thumbs-up.

"You are absolutely the only girl I know who can get away with wearing an antique pink wedding gown and still manage to look fabulous," she said.

"Thanks." Cara turned with her back to her almost sister-in-law. "Can you zip me up? My hands are sweating, I'm so nervous."

Torie grasped the metal zipper and slid it upward. "How old is this thing, do you think?"

Cara turned around and tugged at the dress's heavy satin bodice, revealing an additional inch of her cleavage. "Hmm. Well, portrait necklines and cap sleeves like these were all the rage in the fifties. And the full ballet-length skirt with the tulle petticoats were in back then too. So it's at least sixty years old."

"Do you think somebody dyed this wedding gown this shade of pink?" Torie asked.

"Oh no. This is the original color. And it was a cocktail dress," Cara said. "I bought it years ago, when I worked at a vintage-clothing shop in Columbus. It's a knockoff of a Pierre Balmain, who was a famous couturier back in the day."

She fluffed her skirts and stepped into her pink satin pumps. "And I'll tell you something I haven't shared with anybody else. I bought this dress thinking I would wear it to my first wedding. But Leo—and my dad, and Leo's mom—were *appalled* that I'd even consider not wearing white . . . or a brand-new bought special wedding gown."

Cara shrugged. "So I did what I always did back then. I gave in and bought this big, stupid expensive virginal white dress that made me look like an over-decorated lampshade."

Cara twirled in front of the three-paneled mirror in Libba Strayhorn's guest bedroom, and smiled when she caught her own reflection in the mirror.

"When Leo and I moved down to Savannah, I couldn't wait to donate my wedding dress to Goodwill. But I kept this one." She smoothed her hands over her hips. "It's been tucked away in pink tissue paper all these years. Just waiting for the right moment."

"And the right guy," Torie said. "And here you are." She reached for the velvet-lined box on the dressing table and carefully lifted a single strand of pearls from the satin lining and fastened it around Cara's throat. "Here's your something new. Jack's dad gave me a set of pearls just like this the day I married Ryan."

The bathroom door opened, and Meghan hurried into the room, dressed in bra and panties. "I'm late, I'm late, I'm late," she singsonged, grabbing her deep coral dress from a hanger and slipping it over her head. She turned her back to Torie. "Zip me?"

Torie picked a piece of hay from her sister-in-law's hair and held it up for Cara to see. "Can you guess where baby sister's been and what made her late?"

"I don't judge," Cara said, laughing. She gave Meghan a wink. "What goes on in the barn, stays in the barn, right?"

"Mmm-hmm." Meghan leaned into the mirror, a mascara wand poised in her right hand.

"Hey!" Cara said, grabbing Meghan's left hand. She held it up to Torie.

"Whaatttt?"

"You're engaged?" Cara asked. "Since when? I can't believe it!"

Meghan smiled and flashed a set of dimples. "Harris asked Daddy's permission last night, at the rehearsal dinner. But he didn't bother to ask *me*, until just now, in the, er, barn."

Torie held Meghan's hand and studied the ring with an experienced eye. She held her own left hand up to Meghan's. "Baby girl, that is a serious ring. Bigger than my diamond, for sure."

Cara held her left hand on top of the others. Her engagement ring was made up of a circlet of smaller stones, with a single raised one-carat cushion-cut diamond in a platinum band. "Mine too," she said carelessly.

"Way bigger than the ring Harris gave Brooke," Torie pointed out. "By at least a carat."

Meghan frowned for only a moment. "This was Harris's grandmother's engagement ring. She left it to him in her will, but he bought a new ring for Brooke, because he thought that's what she'd prefer."

Torie gave Meghan an apprehensive glance. "Has anybody heard anything from, uh, her?"

Meghan laughed. "It's okay. You can say Brooke's name in front of me."

Cara said, "We text. That's the only way you can communicate with Brooke. She's still down on Cumberland Island. I think the thing with Pete, the park ranger, is heating up, but she says she has no plans to marry anytime soon. She's working for the Georgia Conservancy, and is still feuding with the Park Service over any issue she can think of. I think Brooke is finally in a good place."

"I'm glad," Meghan said earnestly. "Because of her, Harris and I found each other. And that's the best place of all, for me."

"This ring is beautiful, Meghan, and it's totally you," Cara said. She hugged Jack's little sister. "I'm so happy for you. Have you set the date yet?"

"Nope," Meghan said. "And I made Harris promise that he will not go around talking about it today at your wedding. Although I can't promise he won't, because he is so excited."

"He should be excited," Torie drawled. "After everything he's been though these past few months. Have you told Libba and Mitch yet?"

"Libba caught me coming into the house from the barn just now. She admitted she knew something was up when Harris 'casually' asked her where his grandmother's ring was last week."

"I'll bet she's over the moon," Cara said. "And Mitch too."

"She was very, very happy," Meghan admitted. "She wants us to have the wedding here, too, of course, and I promised her we would. Oooh. I almost forgot."

She disappeared into the bathroom and came out with a small creamy satin drawstring bag, which she handed Cara. "Libba thought you might want to borrow these." Cara untied the string, and a pair of diamond-and-pearl earrings dropped into the palm of her hand.

"Gorgeous," Torie said, picking up one of the earrings. "And real, too."

"I don't know," Cara said. "I've got my little fake pearls I was going to wear. . . ."

"No way," Torie said, pushing her gently down onto the dressing stool. She handed the earrings back to Cara. "It's just a loaner. I'll be in charge of getting them back to Libba after the wedding."

The bedroom door opened, and Frannie Finnerty stepped inside. She was dressed in a short sage-green velvet cocktail dress that accentuated her hazel eyes.

"My girls!" she exclaimed, beaming. "My three, beautiful, amazing girls!"

Baby Betsy stirred in her bassinette, and Meghan scooped her up and handed her to her grandmother. "Four."

"That's right," Frannie murmured.

The door opened again and Ellie Lewis poked her head around the doorway. "Everybody dressed and ready? The photographer wants you all out in the foyer for a few pictures before the guests start stampeding."

Cara took a deep breath. "All ready."

"Oh, just one more thing," Frannie said. She picked her gold pocketbook off the bed, opened it, and handed Cara a frilly, beribboned garter. "Here's your something blue. It's probably not really your style, but my sister Betty made it especially for you. . . ."

"I love it," Cara assured her. She hiked up her dress and slid the garter above her knee.

"Good. Now, can we please get moving?" Ellie said, dabbing at her damp face with her hankie. The other women filed out of the bedroom, with Cara bringing up the rear.

"Wait," Ellie said. "Where's your bouquet? We can't take your picture without your bouquet."

"Bert was bringing it," Cara said. "He insisted on making it himself, as a surprise for me. Isn't he here yet? I swear, if he's late today, I'll . . ."

"You'll what?"

Bert stood in the hallway at the end of the guest wing. He wore a pair of dark green linen pleat-front trousers with dark red suspenders, a billowy cream-colored dress shirt, a vintage brown tweed three-button vest, and a brown felt fedora.

"You'll fire me? You can't fire me, now, I'm your business partner, remember?"

"Oh, never mind," Cara said, remembering her vow to stay calm. "Did you bring my flowers?"

Bert had been standing with one hand hidden behind his back.

"Ta-da!" he said, bowing deeply.

Cara had been holding her breath. But she exhaled slowly now, holding the bouquet in both hands, turning it slowly to take it all in.

"Oh, Bert," she breathed. "It's exquisite."

"Better than Martha Stewart March 2009?"

"Better than anything, ever," Cara said.

And this was no exaggeration. The bouquet was an explosion of creamy coral roses, light and deep pink dahlias, and hypericum berries. Tiny sprigs of white feverfew and celosia plumes were interspersed with the larger flowers. The flower stems were tightly wrapped with coral pink satin ribbon and fastened with a sparkly pink vintage starburst rhinestone brooch.

Cara inhaled sharply. "My mother's pin! This is just like her favorite pin. How did you . . ."

"You didn't think I'd skip our trademark Bloom touch now, did you?"

"But . . . where did it come from? My mother used to wear this when my parents had a fancy-dress party to go to. I used to call it her fairy-princess pin. I haven't seen it in years. . . ."

Cara hadn't seen any of her mother's belongings since before her funeral. She'd come home from college the day before to find that all her mother's possessions, her clothes, books, paintings, everything, had been removed from the house, overnight.

Valerie, her mother's best friend, confided in Cara that she'd done the packing at the Colonel's request. "It's too painful for him," Valerie said. "Seeing her clothes in the closet, her hairbrush on the dressing table, it was just too much. He thought it would be easier for you this way too."

"Easier," Cara had mumbled, her mind numb with the pain and confusion of her mother's sudden death. "Yeah, probably so."

But in the months and years that followed Barbara Kryzik's funeral, Cara would silently pine for anything that would be a tangible reminder of her mother.

"The pin was Jack's idea," Bert admitted. "He thought you might like to have something of your mom's. You know, for something old."

"I still don't understand how he found it," Cara continued, shaking her head.

"He called me and asked me if I'd mind bringing it down here."

Cara's head jerked up. The Colonel stood in the doorway to the hallway.

"You came," Cara breathed. "You're really here."

Bert took her by the elbow and steered her toward her father. He gave her a quick peck on the cheek and whispered in her ear before handing her off to her father. "He's nervous as hell. So go easy on the old guy, okay?"

Cara nodded, and then Bert was gone, and she and the Colonel were alone, in a small alcove just a few feet away from the entry hall.

With a start, she realized she hadn't seen her father in over two years. Since before her split with Leo. Was that possible? He'd let his military-issue brush cut grow out a centimeter, and now his once-dark hair was more salt than pepper. He stood erect in a proper charcoal suit with a burgundy tie, but Cara noticed that the collar of his starched white dress shirt gaped a bit. In her memory, the Colonel had always towered over her, but now they were almost at eye level.

"You're so beautiful," the Colonel said, his voice shaky. He took her bouquet and placed it on the gilded settee, then took both her hands in his. And true to Bert's warning, the Colonel's hands were shaking. As were Cara's.

He touched a lock of her caramel-colored hair, which she wore down, with a single coral rose pinned behind her right ear. "Your hair is longer," he said. "I like it that way."

"Yours too," Cara pointed out, and they both laughed awkwardly.

"When did you get in?" Cara asked. "I had no idea you were coming. You said you weren't sure. . . ."

"I got in just now. Jack's brother Ryan picked me up at the airport in Savannah and brought me straight here."

"They told me Ryan was making a bourbon run," Cara said.

"Oh, we stopped for the bourbon, all right," the Colonel said ruefully. "I was pretty nervous about seeing you again . . . after everything."

"I'm so glad you came," Cara said, her eyes misting up. "I've missed you, Dad."

"I've missed you too, Cara Mia," he said, squeezing her hands tightly.

"Ahem."

Ellie Lewis was beckoning them. "I'm sorry, Cara, but if we are going to start this wedding on time, you have to come have these photos taken with the wedding party right now! Jack and Ryan and Harris have already gone over. The barn is filling up, and we only have ten minutes till go time."

The Colonel shook his head. "Late again. Some things never change."

"We're coming," Cara said, tucking her hand through her father's elbow.

Cara peeked around the barn doors. She could see Jack and Ryan standing in front of the makeshift altar he'd built just for the occasion, from barn boards and leftover roofing tin. A violinist was playing softly up in the hayloft.

"Go!" Ellie Lewis said, sending Torie and Meghan on their slow march up the carpet runner Jack had tacked down earlier in the morning.

Cara twirled her bouquet in her hands again. "Dad?" she whispered. "Mom's pin. Where did you find it?"

"Right where it's been since she died," the Colonel said. "Valerie put together a box of her things for you. Some of her jewelry, her favorite blue sweater, her watch, that painting of pink flowers that she liked. It's been at the house, on the top closet shelf."

Cara raised an eyebrow. "All this time? I thought you got rid of everything."

"Not everything," the Colonel said. His piercing blue eyes met hers. "I have so many regrets. About her, about us. You. I thought if I wiped the slate clean, it would all go away. All the hurt. And the guilt. I wasn't there for her, or for you. And I regret that more than I can ever say."

"Doesn't matter anymore," Cara said, smiling. "You're here for me now, today."

"Thanks to this young man of yours," the Colonel said. "He called me, multiple times. I wasn't going to come down here, but he doesn't give up easily, does he?"

"No, thank God," Cara said fervently. "He wouldn't give up on me, either."

"I like him," her father said. "He suits you." He took a deep breath and took a step forward, then a quick step back. "Who are all those people in there?"

Cara looked again. Heads were turned in their direction. With a start she realized the barn was full. Full of familiar faces. Vicki Cooper sat on the end of one of the plank benches with her husband, and her son and her daughter-in-law Kristin, Cara's first bride. Other brides and their families were scattered around. Jack's extended family took up row after row, aunts, uncles, cousins, and second cousins. As an only child of only children, she continued to be amazed at how close and intertwined her new family was.

She felt a warm surge of happiness, at the surprising recognition that these were her people, and that finally, she belonged.

"I know Ryan tried to explain this, but tell me again how you're connected to the people who own this plantation?" the Colonel asked.

"Mitch and Libba Strayhorn are friends," Cara said, liking the way the word sounded. "And clients. Jack and Ryan totally rebuilt this barn," she added proudly. "And pretty soon, they'll be family. Their son Harris just got engaged to Jack's little sister Meghan. You'll meet everybody at the reception."

From inside the barn, they heard a piano softly playing, accompanying the violin. And the first strains of Mendelssohn's wedding march.

"Okay. Now!" Ellie whispered. The Colonel stiffened and froze.

"Now!" Ellie repeated, waving her hankie like a starter flag. "Go. Go. Go."

"Dad?" Cara squeezed the Colonel's arm. "Just this once, maybe I could be on time?"

Every head in the room was turned in their direction. Somebody, probably Ellie, had remembered to turn off the overhead lights and switch on the dozens of strings of café lights that crisscrossed from the barn beams. Their guests' faces were a blur of golden light.

She floated up the aisle on her father's arm, hurrying a little to match the Colonel's measured march steps. At one point, it occurred to her that she hadn't actually hired a piano player for the wedding. When she glanced toward the altar, she was shocked to see an elderly woman with a shock of white hair pounding the keys of an upright piano she'd never seen before.

Sylvia Bradley? Only Jack Finnerty could have managed such a feat.

Finally, they were at the altar. Jack and Ryan stood at ease, dressed in dark gray dress pants, open-collared white shirts, and mismatched vintage tweed vests. Cara had made their boutonnieres herself, from flowers she'd planted in the courtyard garden at Jones Street, sprigs of dusty miller, lavender, tiny white asters, and blue salvia wrapped with raffia, backed with a single quail feather.

The minister, one of Jack's high-school classmates, wore a dark suit, and a jaunty straw boater with a sprig of lavender tucked in the hatband.

The Colonel reached out and shook Ryan's hand vigorously, then shook Jack's, and after another moment, gave the bridegroom a hug.

He turned, kissed Cara on both cheeks, and stepped quickly away to a spot on the front bench next to Jack's mother and father and Bert.

Cara was dimly aware of all the faces watching theirs. She heard the minister's words, heard Jack's deep voice, firmly pledge to love, honor, and cherish her. She heard herself breathlessly promise to do the same.

"I now pronounce y'all husband and wife," the minister said. He grinned at Jack. "She's all yours, buddy." He nodded at Cara. "And he's yours."

Jack Finnerty swept Cara into his arms. She felt her legs buckle, gasped as he dipped her backward, low to the floor, felt his warm lips on hers. When he finally released her, she stood unsteadily.

"Okay?" he asked, his hazel eyes crinkling at the corners.

"Okay," she assured him, breaking into a smile that lit up the room.

Ellie Lewis, standing to one side of the altar, exhaled for the first time that day.

The Colonel stood and shook hands with Bert again, as the guests stood and began to make their way to the bar at the back of the room. "Nice wedding," the Colonel said, doing his version of polite conversation. "I think Cara finally got it right this time, don't you?"

"Absolutely," Bert said. "I'm kind of an expert on these things. They both got it one hundred percent right."

1. Cara Kryzik is a bit of a loner. What factors contributed to her cutting herself off a bit from others? How different would Cara's experience have been in recovering from her divorce and weathering the storms in her professional life if she had a couple of close girlfriends? Who do you envision as Cara's closest friends as the story draws to a close?

2. How do you think Cara's rootless upbringing (she went to six different schools between elementary and high school) affected her in adulthood? Why do you suppose she had such a tough time feeling at home in Savannah? Why and how do you envision that changing after the end of the book?

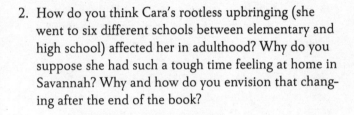
3. What did you think of the Colonel's relentless insistence at being reimbursed for the money he had loaned to Cara? Why do you think the Colonel could not make himself more emotionally available to his daughter? How would Cara's adult life have been different if her father was more supportive? By the end of the story, do you have hope that Cara's relationship with her father will change for the better?

4. Is Gordon Trapnell a supportive father to his daughter Brooke?

5. Does Patricia Trapnell have any redeeming qualities as a person, stepmother, wife, or friend? Why do you think she cares about Brooke and Harris's wedding so much? What are her motives in being so involved in the planning?

6. Why do you think Marie avoids confrontation with Patricia? With Gordon? If you were Marie, would you have stood up to Patricia and/or to Gordon?

St. Martin's
Griffin

7. Did you agree with Brooke's decision to call off her wedding to Harris? Why do you think Harris would have been content to marry Brooke? Do you think they could have lived happily as a married couple? What would their married life have been like?

8. Do you think Pete Haynes figured into Brooke's decision to call off her wedding? Were you surprised that Pete rebuffed Brooke's advances in the cabin on Cumberland Island? Do you think Pete continues to figure in Brooke's life after the story ends?

9. Why do you think Libba Strayhorn's relationship with her husband, Mitchell, has stood the test of time? To what do you attribute their contented marriage?

10. Leo makes several attempts to win Cara back after she divorces him. Do you think Leo genuinely loved Cara? What were his motives in trying to reconcile? Would you have been tempted to go back to him? How is Jack Finnerty different from Leo?

11. What do you think Jack saw in Zoey? Could he have been happy with her? Why did Zoey want Jack back?

12. The two dogs, Poppy and Shaz, figure prominently in the story in *Save the Date*. How did having a pet help Cara and Jack individually? How did the dogs help to bring Cara and Jack together?

13. Why do you think Bert falls for Cullen Kane? Does Bert redeem himself as an employee? As a friend?

14. What do you think Cullen's motives were in buying the building on West Jones Street that housed Bloom? Why is Cullen so intent on destroying Cara?

15. What did you think of Cara's reaction to Jack when he bought the West Jones Street building out from under Cullen?

16. In *Save the Date* we see many different types of weddings and affairs, from minimalist to unique themed affairs to high society extravaganzas. What did you learn about flowers and event planning from *Save the Date*? How did you approach choosing the flowers for your own wedding? Was it based on budget, color scheme, personal preferences? If you had it to do again, would you approach it differently?

17. What did you think of the unusual wedding that Cara planned for Maya and Jared at the Knights of Columbus hall? Would you have been comfortable as a guest at that wedding? Why or why not? Have you ever been to a wedding with a nontraditional theme or décor?

18. Cara and Bert make a game of guessing about the chances their married couple have of making it for the long haul. Have you ever had discussions like this surrounding a wedding you attended? Have you had gut feelings about couples making it and not? Discuss instances in which you've been proven right and wrong in your hunches.

Turn the page for a sneak peek at
Mary Kay Andrews's next novel

Beach Town

Available May 2015

Here is a sneak peek at Mary Kay Andrews's next novel, *Beach Town*! Greer Hennessy is a struggling movie location scout. Her last location shoot ended in disaster when a film crew destroyed property on an avocado grove. And Greer ended up with the blame. Now Greer has been given one more chance: a shot at finding the perfect undiscovered beach town for a big budget movie. So she zeroes in on a sleepy Florida panhandle town. . . .

Room 7 was stifling. Greer fiddled with the air conditioner's thermostat, turning it down from 78 to 72, but there was no appreciable drop in temperature. It was after eleven, and she was finally sleepy.

She removed her baseball cap, brushed her teeth, and released her hair from the confines of the ponytail. It cascaded around her shoulders, like some wild native shrub with a life of its own. Stripped down to nothing but a pair of panties, she climbed between the sheets, which were thankfully clean and smelled like bleach.

It was still hot. Her skin grew clammy with perspiration.

She got out of bed, turned the thermostat down to 68, fell back onto the mattress, closed her eyes and somehow, managed to doze off.

Two hours later, she awoke, drenched in sweat, to the metallic rattling of the air conditioner against the aluminum window frame. Condensation dripped down the wall and onto the pile of clothing Greer had discarded onto the floor.

"Shit," she muttered, stumbling into the bathroom. She turned on the shower and stood under the trickle of cold water for at least thirty minutes. Finally, when her skin was shriveled and her body temperature had dropped sufficiently, she stepped out, pulled an oversized T-shirt over her still-wet body, and dropped back onto the bed, covered only with a tissue-thin top sheet. She fell into a sleep that felt more like a coma.

The faintest rays of light shone through a bent slat in the metal blinds of Room 7. The air conditioner wheezed ineffectively. Greer was not even half-awake when she felt something brush against her cheek.

She swiped her right hand across her face, then opened her eyes and spied a huge black roach scuttling across her pillow.

Greer let out a scream worthy of a Hitchcock ingénue, but the roach took no notice. She screamed again, clenched her teeth and batted at it, at which point it took flight, winging its way across the room.

She stared at the bug, in open-mouthed horror, as it lighted atop the night-stand. A flying cockroach? When the roach flew onto the foot of her bed, she'd had enough.

She donned the T-shirt she'd left on the floor, ignoring the damp stains from the air conditioner, opened the door of her room, and groggily considered her next move.

Squinting into the blinding morning sunlight, she spied a male figure three doors down from her own, pushing a laundry cart mounded with linens.

He was wearing a sweat-stained T-shirt with cut-off sleeves, baggy shorts, and flip flops. His hair was as rumpled as the linens on his cart, and a pair of tortoise-shell glasses perched on the end of a nose that was sunburnt and peeling.

"Hey! Do you work here?"

He rolled the cart toward her. "Huh?"

She grabbed a handful of his T-shirt in her fist and dragged him toward her room. "Get in here and get it."

He poked his head in the doorway. The room was dimly lit. "Get what?" He didn't seem to understand the urgency of the situation.

"That!" Greer pointed at the roach, which was now hovering menacingly on her nightstand. "That thing. That roach. It flew. It flew directly at me."

"That? That's just a little ol' palmetto bug."

"It's a roach. But Jesus H. Christ on a crutch, I've never seen one that big. In my life."

"It's a palmetto bug." He took a broom from the cart and raised it over his head.

"Don't kill it!"

"Why not?" He took a swing with the broom, but the roach flew across the room again, landing on the rim of the lampshade.

"What the hell? Do you not understand? Just get it out of here. Take it outside and let it go. I didn't ask you to kill it."

The janitor stared at the crazed, half-naked stranger, and the gray eyes behind those glasses crinkled in amusement.

For the first time, Greer realized how she must look. She tugged at the hem of her T-shirt, which barely reached mid-thigh.

"Don't look at me! Just do what I say and get rid of that bug before I call the front office."

"You some kind of nature worshiper or something?"

"Insects are living creatures, for your information. I'm not some religious nut. I just think things have a right to coexist with us." She glanced uneasily at the roach. "Even really disgusting things."

He shrugged and turned for the door. "Go ahead and call. If you don't want to kill the palmetto bug, my work here is done."

She picked up the phone. "I'm reporting you."

He laughed. "Report away."

She was getting nowhere with this rube. She sighed, dug a twenty dollar bill from her pocketbook and flung it at him. Twenties were the international currency of efficiency. Even the dimmest bulb could get behind one. "Get rid of that bug, okay? But don't kill it. That's all I ask. Understand? Do. Not. Kill."

He nodded slowly. "Do not kill." He tucked the bill carefully into the pocket of his shorts, picked up a sheaf of papers from the dresser and advanced on the hapless insect.

"Not with that!" Greer screamed. "My film treatment. Oh my God. What the hell is wrong with you?" She snatched the treatment away from him, and replaced it with a spiral-bound booklet that comprised the town's telephone directory, which was half the thickness of Bryce Levy's film treatment.

"Here. And be quick. And then I'm gonna need you to fix that damned air conditioner, too. It's like a sauna in this place."

The janitor nodded thoughtfully. He took the phone directory and gently slid it under the roach, folding the ends envelope style. He walked over to Greer's open suitcase, shook the bug out and quickly zipped the suitcase shut.

For the first time in her life, Greer found herself stunned speechless. She stood there, wide-eyed, slack-jawed.

"Anything else?" He turned and headed for the door, but not before giving her a thorough up-and-down look, his gray eyes sparkling with mischief.

Greer narrowed her eyes. "Very funny. What? You're also the town comedian?"

"Nope." His hand was on the door.

"What about the air conditioner? It doesn't cool for worth a damn. And it's leaking all over the floor."

"Hmm." He walked over, squatted down beside it, ignoring the pool of water on the tile floor. He switched it off, then on again. The window rattling started up again. "Sounds okay to me. But I'm no mechanic."

"What the hell kind of piss-poor maintenance man are you, then?"

"Not much. I can do a little plumbing, unstop a sink, like that. You need any towels?" He nodded toward the cart in the open doorway. "I got plenty of towels."

"Just get out," Greer snapped.

"Okay." He gave her a quick salute. "One more thing, though."

"What?"

He pointed toward her suitcase. "Since you're so into bugs and coexisting with nature, you should know that that palmetto bug in your suitcase there is a female. And right about now she's probably laying eggs all over the place."

Greer shrieked. She ran to the suitcase, unzipped it and began flinging clothes onto the floor. When the cockroach scuttled away, she hesitated only a second, before slapping it flat with her rubber flip-flop.

She heard the door close noisily, and then, unmistakably, she heard him chuckle as he trundled the cart back down the corridor.

The bell on the office door buzzed to announce her arrival. Ginny Buckalew looked up from her paperback. "Morning. Everything okay with the room?"

"Now that you mention it . . ." Greer hesitated, not wanting to alienate the older woman. She was going to need an ally these next few weeks.

"What?"

"Well, the air conditioner doesn't seem to be working properly. It leaks, and makes a lot of commotion, but it doesn't really cool the room. My television only gets three channels, and they're pretty fuzzy. And there was a huge roach in my room this morning. It landed right on my pillow! And since you asked, I have to say, your maintenance guy is a rude jerk."

Ginny nodded as Greer enumerated her complaints. She got up and left the room. Two minutes later, she returned and plopped a 12-inch tall electric fan on the counter. Beside it, she placed a can of Black Flag.

"This is Florida," Ginny said. "The Silver Sands was built by my dad in 1946. It's hot. We got bugs. Deal with it."

Greer opened her mouth to protest, but thought better of it. With Bryce Levy and his entourage arriving in three days, she had other, more pressing concerns.

"Listen, Ginny, what can you tell me about that old closed-up casino at the end of the pier?"

"It's closed," Ginny said.

"Yes, I realize that. But what's the status on it? It would make an incredible location for the film I'm working on. Do you know who owns it?"

"Talk to Eb," Ginny said.

"Who's Eb?"

"The mayor."

"Does he own it?"

"You'll have to talk to Eb about that."

"How do I reach him?"

The older woman came out from around the desk. She opened the office door and pointed down toward the end of the corridor. For the first time, Greer noticed that a small wooden shingle was mounted outside one of the motel units, but she couldn't read the type from where she stood.

"That's his office," Ginny said.

The end unit wasn't like the other motel units. It had a plate glass door, but the interior of the office was obscured by a tightly drawn shade. The wooden shingle proclaimed this CEDAR KEY REALTY—EBEN THIBADEAUX, REALTOR-BROKER.

A hand-lettered sign taped to the door said GONE OUT. BACK LATER.

But a bulletin board mounted to the wall beside the door held thumbtacked flyers for various homes on the market.

Greer leaned in to get a look. She saw half a dozen advertisements for unpretentious-looking shacks labeled Cracker Cottages, none of them listed for more than $150,000. There were downtown commercial properties, a closed-up restaurant, a former art gallery, even the women's boutique Greer had photographed the day before.

She took special notice of three imposing-looking multiple-story waterfront houses located in a gated community called Bluewater Bay. No sales price was listed, but the flyers showed photos of swimming pools, huge state-of-the-art kitchens, and cathedral-ceilinged great rooms with spectacular waterfront views.

She plucked the flyers from the bulletin board and headed back to the office.

"Eb's not there," she reported.

"You could try the store," Ginny said, clearly not interested in Eben Thibadeaux's whereabouts.

"Which store?" She wondered if the old lady got a thrill from being deliberately cryptic and unhelpful.

"Island IGA," Ginny replied. "Three blocks up, turn right, you can't miss it."

. . .

"Hadn't seen him this morning," the cashier at the supermarket said. "Have you tried city hall?"

She hadn't, but she would.

The clerk at city hall smiled apologetically. "You just missed him." She turned to a young man with mutton-chop sideburns that made him look like a modern-day Abe Lincoln, who was busily tapping away on a computer keyboard. "Did Eb say where he was headed when he left here?"

"I think he was gonna show one of those condos over on the south end," Abe Lincoln said.

"Could you give me his cell number?" Greer asked politely. "I really need to speak to him."

The two clerks conferred quietly. "I guess that'd be okay," the woman said. "He usually likes to be accessible to constituents."

She found that if she stood on the top step outside city hall, her phone got exactly one bar.

And she was not surprised when the mayor's phone went directly to voice mail.

"Hi, Eben," she said brightly. "My name is Greer Hennessy. I'm a film location scout, and I'd love to talk to you about using Cedar Key for the film we're going to be shooting in this area very soon. It's a terrific opportunity for your beautiful little community to really shine for the whole world to see. But it's urgent that I meet with you today. I'm staying at the Silver Sands Motel, but you can reach me at this number, at any time. Looking forward to meeting you!"

She popped her head back into city hall. The clerk gave her an expectant look.

"I left the mayor a voice mail. Any other guesses as to where he might be?" Greer asked.

"Welllll . . . it's Friday, and it's lunchtime, so if I had to guess, I'd say he's either at The Deck or The Boathouse."

"Those are local restaurants?"

"The Deck is. It's on the bayside, right after you come across Kiss-Me-Quick."

Greer's face showed her confusion.

The girl smiled. "Kiss-Me-Quick is the last bridge after you come over the causeway from the mainland. The Deck is on the right side of the road. You'll see all the trucks out front. Today's Friday, so it's all-you-can-eat shrimp boil."

Greer nodded her understanding. "What about The Boathouse? What's the special there?"

"No special. It's just where Eb keeps his boat when it's not running, which it usually isn't. Keep going on the state route, after you've crossed Kiss-Me-Quick. The sign is so faded you can't hardly read it anymore, but I think it says 'Maring Marina.' That's on the right side of the road, before you cross the hump-backed bridge."

Greer found The Deck with little trouble, and just as the clerk had predicted, the sandy parking lot was crowded with pickup trucks and cars with local tags. The restaurant was a low, rambling affair, with a blocky faded driftwood building surrounded on two sides with decks that looked out on Blah-Blah Bay.

When she pushed open the heavy wooden door, she was greeted with the sharp scent of spicy seafood boil, fried fish, and beer. As she glanced around the crowded room, she realized she had no idea what Eben Thibadeaux looked like.

A hostess looked up from behind the cash register near the door. She was young and pretty, with short, pale blonde hair tucked behind one ear, and a tiny gold ring piercing her left nostril. "How many in your party?"

"Just one, but, uh, I'm actually looking for somebody. The mayor? Is he here?"

"Eb?" The girl's voice was sharp. She glanced looked over her shoulder, and then back at Greer. "Nah. He's not here."

Something about the girl's quick response seemed off.

"You sure?" Greer asked. "I see there are lots of people out on the decks."

The girl fiddled with one lock of hair, and then gave Greer a startlingly steely eyed gaze. "I'm positive. Eb's not here. Since you're by yourself, I can't give you a table, but I guess you could sit at the bar."

The girl gestured to a darkened alcove on her left, where a dozen men sat hunched over their beers and paper plates of boiled shrimp, staring at a baseball game on the television. Every barstool was occupied.

"Never mind."

She left another message on Eben Thibadeaux's voice mail, then drove three miles up the state route, following the city clerk's directions.

The Boathouse was right where it was supposed to be. Greer took out her phone and began snapping photos. Even if Eben Thibadeaux was still in the air, this would make a great location for the film.

The building was made of sun-bleached wood and salt-corroded galvanized tin. MARING MARINA—DRYDOCK, MACHINE SHOP, WELDING—the sign's wording was so faded it was barely visible. There were three vehicles parked in the lot—two pickup trucks and a tired-looking blue sedan with four flattened tires.

Four seagulls plucked dispiritedly at what looked like a piece of hamburger bun near the office door, but didn't budge as she walked past. The door creaked on its hinges. A high wooden counter faced the door, and behind it stood a desk—that was empty.

"Hello?" Greer walked around the counter and peeked into an inner office furnished with an old military surplus metal desk and a file cabinet of similar vintage. Papers and catalogs and cardboard boxes of engine parts littered the desktop, but there was no sign of its occupant.

She went back to the outer office and pushed through a swinging door that led her out into dank building, which smelled like dead fish and motor oil. It took a minute for her eyes to adjust to the dimness.

When they did, she saw that she was in a cavernous warehouse with rows and rows of boats suspended from harnesses three-high all the way up to the ceiling. A piece of heavy equipment that resembled a forklift was parked in the middle of a walkway that bisected the room.

"Hello?" Her voice echoed in the darkness. At the far end of the warehouse, a half-open roll-up door emitted a bright shaft of light.

She followed the light, walked out the door, and finally saw her first sign of life. A man stood just outside the door, bent over a pair of sawhorses that held a large black outboard motor. His back was to her, but he wore a white T-shirt and blue jeans, and a baseball cap.

"Hey there," Greer called. "I'm looking for Eben Thibadeaux?"

"Hang on a minute," the man muttered. He tinkered with the motor a little bit, dropped something on the pavement, and swore softly.

"Yes?" His face was sweaty and streaked with grease. He pushed the tortoise-shell glasses back from the bridge of his sunburnt nose, and when he saw his visitor, frowned.

"Christ. What now?"

It was the same surly maintenance man she'd encountered back at the Silver Sands Motel.

"You!" Greer squinted into the sunlight.

"Yes, me." He took a blue bandana from the back pocket of his jeans and wiped his hands before shoving it back into his pocket.

"You're Eben Thibadeaux? The maintenance man at the motel? You sell real estate? And you're the mayor?"

"You left out grocery store manager," Eb Thibadeaux said. He pointed at the outboard motor. "And failed boat mechanic. To what do I owe the pleasure of this visit?"